# MAURA'S DREAM

# MAURA'S DREAM

JOEL GROSS

Seaview Books

NEW YORK

*Manufactured in the United States of America*

FIRST EDITION

Library of Congress Cataloging in Publication Data

Gross, Joel.
     Maura's dream.
     I. Title.
PS3557.R58M3     813'.54     80-52416
ISBN 0-87223-654-4

*Designed by Tere LoPrete*

For each age is a dream that is dying,
Or one that is coming to birth.

*Arthur William Edgar O'Shaughnessy,*
*1844–81*

ALWAYS, FOR LINDA

# PART ONE

*County Kerry, Ireland,*
*1897*

# ❧ CHAPTER ❧
# ONE

Maura Dooley was seventeen, Irish, and Catholic. Yet she took no joy in her youth, hated every bit of her native soil, and had no spirits in her heart save banshees and demons.

She loved two people: her half-mad mother, and her sister Brendt. She loathed her old-maid sister Mary, her three ignorant brothers, her brutish father. She had one overwhelming desire, and that was to leave, to flee her family, her country, her life. Maura had as much reason to abandon those she loved as those she hated. Her mother was an image of Maura's future in Ireland: crazed. Her sister Brendt was a study in surviving the present: complacent, accepting. But Maura refused to accept the cottage of mud and stone, the slaps of her sister Mary, the drunken embraces of her own brothers. Maura refused to accept the beauty of mountains, breaking up the sunset over meadows and lakes and streams. She refused to accept anything about the state of her existence, good or bad; for as far as she was concerned, her life had not yet begun. Life began on the other side of the ocean, in America, and until she got there, she would not smile on account of her green eyes and auburn hair, she would not thank God for her daily bread, she would not fall in love, she would simply do nothing other than plan her escape.

She was peeling potatoes when her father entered the cottage in the early afternoon of a summer's day. Maura looked at his eyes, bloodshot from tending the turf fire of the whiskey still.

"It's an opening to the heart to see you looking so smart, girl," he said.

Maura said nothing out loud, but in her mind the familiar words ran: *Devil take him, devil take him, devil take him.* She looked away, staring into the fat potato in her hand, trying to conjure the picture of the American steamship in the great poster fixed to the church gate. No matter what tales of hardship were carried back to their village—stories of shipwreck and starvation, sickness and maltreatment on the voyage from Cork to New York—Maura had a perfect, unshakable vision of her future journey to America. Wrapped in a silken shawl, her back toward the view of the harbor, Maura would stand on the upper deck, eyes embracing the endless sea.

"Thanks be to God I have an idiot wife," said her father, and Maura looked up at him sharply. "And a daughter the spitting image of the mother. I said bring out the chair."

"What?" said Maura, not comprehending. But she put down her work and got to her feet. She was not afraid of her father, not even of his filthy fists, but there was no sense in asking for a beating.

"You silly scut. Tell me you're dreaming of fancy lords and ladies, of picking up gold in the middle of the street." Her father was smiling, but the smile was unkind, his lips twisting into happy contempt.

"What chair, father?"

"Och, the girl never listens, devil take her. Never listens except to what she wants to hear. Like your redheaded mother. Sure she's deaf as a post when I tell her to lie on her back. Sure she's quick as a fairy when I say the littlest, softest, sweetest complaint to her darling daughter."

"I'm sorry, father. I didn't hear you," she said. Maura picked up the heavy chair, the best of two in the smoke-stained cottage. Sighing, she took awkward little steps on bare feet, the worn wood floor planks creaking under the weight as she made her way to the low door. Behind her back she could hear her father stomp over to the pot simmering on the hearth fire, hear him grab the ancient ladle, hear him swallow down the warm meal mush. Maura put the chair down near the threshold, pausing to break the pain in her arms.

"Och, you lazy bitch," he said, speaking with his mouth full, his harsh northern accent mean to her southern ear. How could her mother have ever married this man? He had been nothing but a traveling laborer, and a bully, selling illegal whiskey from cabin to cottage to inn when he couldn't find work in the fields. What could her poor mother have wanted him for? Sure there were ships sailing for America twenty years ago. Even if they were not steamers, they were still capable of crossing the sea. Maura knew there were few enough marrying men in Ireland, and those who chose to stay in their native land had the chance of dowries in gold or land. Still, her mother must have been mad even then. No matter that she could read in an unlettered county, no matter that she was pretty and delicate and that her family numbered priests and nuns among its petty farmers, Maura knew that her mother could have escaped to America, as a lady's maid, if not as a governess; as a scullery maid, if not as a young farmer's wife. Maura knew that her mother had failed by marrying her father, and that this failure had slowly drained away her spirit.

"You blooming dough-face," said her father, chewing the mush and stomping toward her. "A fine lady's maid you're going to make. Sure in America it's the ladies who serve the servants milk and honey in bed."

"What is it that you're wanting from me, father?" said Maura, looking up at him sharply.

"Don't be a-getting all scared of your old dad," he said. The great ladle, black with age and running with mush, hung from his raised right hand.

"I'm not scared, father," said Maura. "And I know there's grain waiting to be turned. I won't turn the grain if you beat me."

Bill Dooley smiled. This was not the first time his daughter had countered a threat with one of her own. He needed her for the delicate task of turning the swollen grain in the malting process. The fate of Bill Dooley's whiskey-making rested in the almost mystical instinct possessed by his daughter: She knew when and how to turn the grain during the ten days before it was dried in the furnace. Any of his sons could dry the grain, or take the dried grain to the miller, or pour the boiling water into the malt-filled vat, or mind the barrels filled with malt and water and boiled hops and yeast while the mixture fermented to pot ale. But only Maura could turn the grain. "Sure you're your mother's daughter, you miserable scut," he said finally, his smile intact. In that same instant, he threw the ladle across the room onto the hearth, and took hold of the chair.

"I'll take it, father," said Maura, afraid she had gone too far.

"Take your blooming hands off of it, girl!" he said, but Maura had already picked it up, and her father let go his grip on it, and watched as she tried to get the chair through the low, tiny door. Clumsy with the great weight, Maura bruised the chair against the stone wall, and the back of her head banged into the door's lintel. "Och," said her father. "Sure you're good for nothing but a rich American husband. You're much too good for working and thinking and paying respect. I'm telling you to put it down, you stupid girl."

Maura turned, her hands still gripping the chair, her eyes reaching for the light outdoors and the roses planted by her mother all about the cottage. Suddenly her father clasped his hands about her forehead and pulled her back, away from the threshold. She let go of the chair and stumbled wildly across the room, falling to her knees in a corner where the wood planks had twisted up from the old mud floor.

Her father smiled at her now, letting her know what he thought of her threat. "You're a very big help with the heavy work, girl. Sure I don't know what we'd do without you around here." He picked up the chair with one hand and spoke quietly: "If I tell you to turn the grain, you'll turn the grain. If I tell you to marry a farmer, you'll marry a farmer. If I tell you you're not going to America, you're not going to America. Now get up, girl. There's company for you to meet, and for you to serve." And her father wheeled about and walked through the door, swinging the great chair before him as if the door were as large as a barn's, and the chair as light as a matchstick.

For a moment longer, Maura remained on her knees, her palms pressed to the floor. Company. Of course there was company, she should have known that at once, in the second he'd told her to bring out the best chair. They hadn't had company in years— not the sort of company too good to be received inside. The last time the best chair had been brought out of doors, into the rose garden on the south side of the cottage, it had been her mother's aunt, visiting from Galway. Even when the sunny day had turned soft, and a fine drizzle blew in from the South, Maura's parents had been reluctant to bring the best chair back into the cottage. There she'd sat, Maura's great-aunt, straight-backed in the chair, her booted feet firmly in the garden's grass, the drizzle settling in her bonnet, in the red roses all about her; even she, this visitor from Galway who'd brought them a gift of store-bought candlesticks and a packet of newspapers from as far away as Dublin, even she thought this was a perfectly proper way in which to be received. It was a mark of respect to be treated to the best of the house—the best chair—without having to suffer its dingy, stale interior.

Company, thought Maura, standing up slowly. Her great-aunt was dead. The men who bought her father's whiskey came directly to the still, or were led to the cave off the thundering salt-water inlet four miles from the cottage, where the Dooleys hid, and guarded, their barrels. They were not company. Maura walked to the door, her heart racing in expectation: Someone grand had come to their home; someone rich and respected enough to merit the best chair in the rose garden. Stooping, Maura left the cottage, turning to the left to skirt the vegetable garden and run to the rose garden behind their home.

"My son," Michael O'Connell was saying with a shake of his head, "is not much in the way of horseflesh either."

"No, sir!" said Bill Dooley, bobbing his head like a coward to his guest. "Patrick's a fine young man, with good shoulders on him."

"It's not his shoulders I'm thinking of, Billy Dooley," said O'Connell. Maura had stopped short, seeing him sitting in the chair. Why, this man wasn't *company*. He was a farmer, a man she had seen several times a year for most of her life. And there he was, sitting in the best chair, in the middle of the rose garden, smiling and making judgments like a king. "It's his head I'm thinking of," he said. "Paddy wants to run away to America."

Maura took a step back, away from the group gathered about the best chair. She was so wild in her backward motion that she scratched her bare left arm on the thorns of a rosebush and nearly tripped over her own feet.

Brendt was there, her beautiful sister, sitting on the grass like a peasant girl, so dear, so modest she never once lifted her eyes to the men who bartered her future back and forth between them. Maura's mother was there, not so still as Brendt, but just as quiet. She had planted twoscore rosebushes around the square where they all sat—the work of more than twenty years—and there were more roses besides. The front of the whitewashed cottage was surrounded by half a dozen rosebushes. In addition, Maura's mother had begun to plant honeysuckle between the bushes; when the sun came out, after a light summer's drizzle, the fragrance even penetrated the one-window, one-door cottage. Maura herself had helped her mother with the latest project—a rose border all about the garden of cabbage and onions. Even at this important moment—Michael O'Connell sitting in the best chair, Brendt averting her eyes as her father spoke of marriage, Michael O'Connell's son Patrick standing at the corner of the rose garden, leaning against a lone beech tree—Maura's mother was on her knees, picking at dead leaves, searching for weeds in the sunlight.

But no one paid Mrs. Dooley much notice. She was not so crazy that she had need of being locked away. She cooked, she sewed, she knitted, she kept up her appearance, she went to Mass. She was not so crazy that she couldn't tell fairy stories, or know when her husband bullied her girls. What was crazy about Mrs. Dooley was her inattention to everything that was harsh, ugly; and conversely, her pointed, half-mad absorption with anything beautiful. So if Bill Dooley raged, she shunted this rage aside, as if it didn't belong to her world. If a bird chanced by, its flight would grab her attention and she would follow its path past the horizon, staring into space for minutes, her mind at peace. Now, on her knees before her rosebushes, she was happy with the contemplation of a blossom, with the sight of a fat bee, with the delicious danger of endless thorns. Talk of her husband's debt to O'Connell, of her daughter Brendt's marital prospects in underpopulated southeast Kerry—Mrs. Dooley heard none of this.

"America?" said Mr. Dooley. "Sure the son of Michael O'Connell isn't a guzzling fool? You must be drinking Parliament whiskey, Paddy, if that's what you got in your head."

"No one's offered us whiskey of any kind, if it please Your Honor," said O'Connell. "Not Parliament, not Dooley's. And we're in a country where men can't talk with civil tongues without a bit of whiskey to take out the devil."

"Maura!" called out her father, without turning to look for her.

She stepped forward into the rose garden, eyes on her sister. Brendt was afraid to look up, and Maura was suddenly angry at her; three years away from the year 1900, her sister was still a slave.

"Bring up some doublings. From the first barrel," he ordered.

"And shall I bring some strawberries, father?"

"What?" he said, suddenly too angry to say more.

"Strawberries, father," said Maura. "For our company."

"What a pretty girl," said O'Connell, and Maura felt the O'Connell boy's eyes on her too. She chanced a glance at him, though she had seen him often enough before. He seemed to be wearing a new suit of clothes, and a dark ring of sweat stood out about his stiff shirt collar.

"Strawberries are selling five shillings a pound," said her father. "And what do strawberries have to do with doublings? If we're going to drink first-barrel doublings, you don't want to sweeten the whiskey taste." But now Mr. Dooley stopped talking, seeing that O'Connell was about to laugh.

"We don't grow them to sell, father," said Maura. "We grow them to eat."

"Your father's got a better crop, girl," said O'Connell. "Worth a lot more than five shillings a pound."

There was a barrel of doublings in the barn. The pot ale, or fermented liquor, prepared from brewing the malt and adding the boiled hops and yeast in a great barrel removed from contact with the air for three weeks, was distilled three times. Mr. Dooley's latest still cost twenty pounds, and he had been forced to borrow this money from O'Connell when the constables smashed up his last still eight years before. Only one of the Dooley boys had been present at the hidden cave, but even a half-dozen constables couldn't catch a terrified eleven-year-old boy in that wild area of caves and springs, cliffs and gorges, and boulders tumbling down to the sea. Maura had grown up hearing of this monumental debt, and about how O'Connell bled her father of his best whiskey, taking the liquor as interest on the unpaid loan.

Maura had been at the still most of the morning, working on the first distillation of some fresh pot ale. This first distillation produced a harsh, powerful liquor—singlings—best suited for rubbing into a sore body, or a cut. Only fools drank singlings; the liquor could prove poisonous. The second distillation was simply a conversion of singlings into doublings; the first few kegs out of this distillation had the finest taste. It was doublings that brought her father gold, though Dooley also made a good amount of money from "barn beer," the residue in the still that he sold as cattle food. But whatever gold her father made from selling illegal whiskey he kept to himself, sewing it into the lining of his old clothes, hiding it in a cave, in a corner of the barn whose location he revealed to no one. He could have long since paid back O'Connell, but Maura realized he would much prefer to forget the debt and sell his daughter in its place.

Maura entered the barn out of breath, more from anger than the little run from the rose garden. She threw the silly half-covering of hay off the big barrel and removed its lid, noting its low level with a frown: Her brothers were drinking up the work of her hands. Maura dipped a large jug into the barrel, letting the powerful liquor surge through its neck. Her sister Mary had sent her from the still to peel potatoes; she probably had known that Maura would be wanted to wait on the company. Everyone must have known about the O'Connells coming save Maura and Brendt. That's why the cottage had been deserted when she arrived from the distant still. Brendt and her mother must have been dragged by her father to meet the O'Connells at the foot of the hill. As Maura stoppered the full jug, she shuddered with distaste, imagining her father urging Brendt to smile as the O'Connells approached.

*Devil take him*, she thought as she left the barn and ran back to the house. *Devil take him*. She'd bring their distinguished company a pot full of strawberries, and let her father be damned if he didn't like it. If her father had told Brendt to smile, Maura was sure that she had smiled. If her father told Brendt to marry Patrick O'Connell, there would be no chance of rebellion, no question of refusal. No matter that Patrick was an awkward lunk of a boy, love-sick for Brendt since he was twelve. No matter that Brendt was afraid to take a coach ride to Cork, much less a steamer to America! Maura entered the dark cottage, loaded the freshly picked strawberries into a great pot, and escaped back into the sunshine, trying to catch her breath. If Brendt was afraid, she would show them that she was not. If Brendt would do whatever their father ordered, she would show them that she would do what she pleased.

Maura rounded the cottage, extending the whiskey jug and the pot of strawberries like twin talismans, protection against the wrath of her father.

"Praise the Lord!" laughed Michael O'Connell. "Praise the Lord for the devil's own brew!"

"And strawberries," said Maura. "I've gone and got you all strawberries, too!"

But something was wrong. O'Connell's face was no longer composed, kinglike. His smile was false, uncomfortable. Maura's father was on his feet, too distracted to be angry that she had brought the strawberries against his will. Michael O'Connell lurched to his feet, his hands reaching for the whiskey jug. His son Patrick was red-faced, abashed, looking into the fringe of rosebushes as if he wished to have them swallow him up.

"You're the good girl, aren't you?" said Michael O'Connell, bringing the jug to his lips. He took a great swallow of the whiskey and handed Maura back the jug. "You're the best girl, you're the very pulse of your daddy's heart." He reached out filthy, stubby fingers, gripped a half-dozen fat strawberries, and brought them to his whiskey-wet mouth.

It was at that moment, turning her eyes to avoid O'Connell's devouring stare, that she realized Brendt was gone.

Maura looked from the spot on the grass where she had last

seen Brendt, to the beech tree against which Patrick O'Connell slouched, to her father, frowning at her from five paces.

"Where's Brendt?" she said, her question addressed to the air.

"Give it here," said her father, standing in place, his great right hand open to receive the jug from his daughter.

Maura turned round, once, twice, looking in amazement from rosebush, to the best chair, to the green hills to the southwest, to the ancient ruined tower miles inland, where once a town had stood. "Where's mother?" she said, for Mrs. Dooley was nowhere to be seen either.

"Give it here," said her father again. His voice was free of menace, so soft and questioning that Maura felt as if she were standing on the uncertain ground of a bog. What did he want? Where was Brendt? Where was her mother? Her heart pounding, she let go the jug. Bill Dooley took an enormous swallow, pausing to cough and take in some air. Then he drank some more.

"Where's Brendt?" said Maura, speaking directly to her father. He was not a drinker, not without cause. "Where did she go? Why isn't she here?"

"She's not here, girl," said Michael O'Connell, taking the whiskey jug from her father with a smile, "because she loves a little schoolteacher."

"Oh, no," said Maura. The pot full of strawberries had somehow slipped from her hands. She dropped to her knees, aware of the intense fragrance of the rose garden, the dazzling red of the strawberries on the green grass. Good, modest, obedient Brendt. In love with a schoolteacher. There was only one schoolteacher. Grady Madigan. Skinny and tall and with a sparse blond beard. Maura returned the strawberries to the pot. Brendt had refused. Brendt had refused to obey their father.

"I'll take the blackguard and crack him in two," said Bill Dooley. "And Brendt hasn't refused Paddy, has she? She's a silly young girl and she won't know what's good for her unless I tell her. And I'll tell her, if it's all right with you and Paddy here."

"It's not all right," said Patrick O'Connell. "I won't have anything to do with her." The face was redder than before, and his words carried the sting of pain. "I didn't know. If I'd known, I never would have wanted this. No one's to harm her. This wasn't my idea. My brother's going to get the farm, and my father wanted to see me married before I go to America. This isn't the way things are done anymore. I won't marry someone who loves Grady Madigan."

"She doesn't!" said Maura, unable to contain herself. What did Brendt know about Grady? "Brendt doesn't love him!" Maura got to her feet, clutching the pot of strawberries. She was so angry that everyone she looked at seemed quiet and still, slow-moving compared to the force that ran through her. How could Brendt love Grady and not have ever said a word to her? They slept on the same straw pallet, just the two of them, in their own corner, away from the ears of their sister Mary. Brendt was only a year older than Maura, and the age difference had never mattered much, as the younger sister liked to lead, and the older one to follow. They had often talked through half the night, whispering in their corner, giggling into each other's hands. Why, Maura had even told Brendt that Grady had talked to her in town not ten days before—Grady with his sad look, with his dark eyes in the fair face. And Brendt had said nothing, not all through that night, or the next, when she had every opportunity to whisper whatever was in her heart. Maura had even gone so far as to tell Brendt that she found Grady interesting, for a man from Kerry. If she were not so dead set on leaving Ireland, a man like Grady— looking like Grady—was just the sort of man she might fancy. Even when Maura had admitted all this, Brendt had said nothing. She couldn't possibly love Grady Madigan. If she did, Maura would know.

"Where are you going, girl?" said her father.

"You can finish the whiskey without my help, father," she said. "I must go look for Brendt."

"Stay, girl," said her father. He seemed to be floating toward her, a big, coarse figure with his hands swinging at his sides.

Michael O'Connell took another swallow from the whiskey jug and offered it back to Dooley. "I've had enough drink," said Maura's father. He took hold of one of Maura's hands, so that the girl held the pot of strawberries in one arm, close to her belly.

"Let go of me, I want to find my sister," she said.

"What about this one?" said Bill Dooley, speaking to Patrick.

"Please. It's not done this way," said the boy.

"If he takes this one," said Bill Dooley to Michael O'Connell, "it's the same deal, right?"

"I don't think she wants my Paddy either," said O'Connell.

"I don't! Let go," said Maura, and she pulled and pulled, but couldn't free her hand from her father's grip.

"Let her alone, Mr. Dooley," said Patrick.

"What?" said Maura's father. "Sure you're not telling me how to mind my own daughter, Paddy."

"I'm not for sale! Let go of me!" said Maura, and she threw the pot of strawberries into her father's face. He let go his grip on her hand, and Maura ran.

Immediately, she was through the south line of rosebushes, tearing her arms and her cheeks on the thorns. She ran as fast as she could, sure that her father was chasing her on thick legs, ready to throw her to the ground and beat her with a stick. In the back of her mind, she heard Michael O'Connell laughing, laughing at the way she had gotten free. She heard, too, the enraged cry of her father, heard this with the laugh, and knew that these sounds were behind her, still in the garden. But there were other sounds—the crushing of dead branches, the snapping of twigs as she ran on bare feet through the marshy, wooded ground that led the long way around to the village road.

Maura ran blindly, her eyes filled with tears of exertion and pain. Try as she could, her legs would move no faster. The trunks of trees, the sharp, broad leaves of shrubs assaulted her limbs, twisted her about into deeper and deeper brush. She could not know if she was getting away. She couldn't distinguish between the sounds in the garden, the sounds of her own racing heart, the sounds of her feet slapping against mud, kicking through foliage. She tried to stretch her legs, to suck in air in an even, regular fashion, to ignore the pain starting up in her side, a pain that made her want to double up and collapse to the ground. But she could not be caught. Brendt must be found. She herself must be free. Maura had to find her sister and ask her if it was true that she loved Grady Madigan, if it was true that she had defied their father. Only then could she stop running. Only then could she stop running long enough to think.

"Maura!" she heard, a faint voice, unfamiliar and strained, coming from behind her. "Maura! Stop!" she heard, and the voice was stronger, closer.

Maura ran with renewed speed. There, through the shrubs and down the marshy hill, was the white stone fence that flanked the village road. She had only to snake through the tearing leaves, slip down the hill, and climb the fence, and then no one would catch her.

"Maura!" she heard, and she had an image of her father, his voice borrowed from a demon, chasing after her with super-human strength. She tripped going down the hill to the fence; and when she rolled to her feet, she heard her pursuer call out her name, so clearly that she thought he must be a hairbreadth away. More determined than terrified, she slapped her muddied hands onto the five-foot top of the stone wall, scratching at the turf placed there; even in this backward, poor county, daisies grew from the fencetops, lightening the gray colors of poverty.

"Come on with you," said the demon voice, and as Maura tried to follow her hands up the fence, two stronger hands took hold of her shoulders and pulled her back.

Maura fought, not uttering a sound, and, twisting out of the grip, she again tried to force herself over the wall. This time her pursuer didn't try to stop her, but it made no difference; she couldn't lift herself over the wall, not after that run, not after that chase.

"Do you want me to help you?" said the voice, and Maura, turning around in fury, prepared for the kick or the slap of her father, saw instead the red-faced boy Patrick O'Connell.

"If you want to get over so bad, sure I'll help you, Maura," he said.

"You," she said. "Get away from me."

Patrick looked at her, more embarrassed than ever. "I wanted to help you, that's all."

"Help me? You almost killed me."

"Sure I'm sorry if anything—I only wanted to—I have to explain something to you, if you'll stay still long enough to let me."

Maura slid down to the ground, resting her back on the stone wall, holding her drawn-up knees through her filthy skirt. "A hundred thousand welcomes," said Maura, opening her palms in a sarcastic gesture of greeting.

"You're beautiful," said Patrick O'Connell, looking at her with his pale blue eyes.

Maura stared at him as if he'd gone mad. "What the devil do you mean, Patrick O'Connell?" she said, with fury in her voice.

"Please, Maura," said the red-faced boy. "Don't be taking offense like that. I mean nothing. Sure I mean something, but nothing bad, is what I mean. Don't be looking at me like you hate me. I didn't do anything to make you hate me, I don't think. There are things I want to tell you, and that's all. Just words. You'll decide. But you have to listen."

Maura said nothing, just indicated her displeasure by drawing up her knees a bit closer to her belly and squinting sharply at him. Her anger subsided as her heart calmed down, leaving room for her vanity to batten on the compliment. And she was curious. "How dare you call me beautiful, when you came here to force Brendt to marry you?"

"No," he said, very softly, shaking his head from side to side. Patrick was tall and solid, an imposing figure of a man if only he would stand straight and not always be looking at the ground, declaring his defeat to the eyes of the world. "My father wanted it."

"If you didn't want Brendt, why did you come here today?"

"I want to go to America," he said, and he blushed, and he coughed, and he pulled at his nose. "I don't know Brendt, not really. I know you better."

"Me? How do you know me better than Brendt? Sure you're dreaming this, Patrick O'Connell." Her words were angry, but she allowed her eyes to widen, she relaxed the twisted frowning of her lips.

"You gave me whiskey, Maura," he said. "It was you always, not Brendt. Didn't I used to see you, six times a year?"

"I never counted."

"I did. Sure I did. I counted the days until I'd see you again." Here poor Patrick tripped up on his eloquence. He gulped back a rush of air, and almost choked in fright.

"Saving your presence, sir," said Maura with a little bow. "No guests in my home will be given to the fairies. You counted the days until you'd see me. You want to go to America. Yes. I'm listening, Patrick. Go on with you, please."

"My brother Seamus, he went to America last year. A year and a half ago, it was. He went the hard way. My father gave him nothing, and he had to find work in England. He was almost killed in Liverpool, but Seamus—you knew Seamus—he's strong, and he's afraid of nothing. My mother always used to say that he'd kill my father one day when he was drunk. Not a penny he gave him, my father. He didn't give Seamus a penny, and he made it to America anyway. From Liverpool. He worked like a slave for those damned English—I'm sorry—he worked on the docks in Liverpool, and after four months he had enough to cross over to America. He nearly died on the boat. He went to New York City. And then to Boston—there's a lot of Irish in Boston, you know. He got married in a month. A month after he got to Boston. We only just found out about it. Seamus married a Prod.

"My father hates him—he always hated him—but when he heard that Seamus married a Prod, he broke down and cried. My father cried like a baby. Because Seamus did that. That's when he told me. That if I married an Irish Catholic, I'd have my money. Money to buy a little land of my own, or money to get across to America.

"Please don't think me some kind of bad person. I'm not as strong as Seamus. I want to go to America. I never planned to marry Brendt unless she wanted me. I only wanted to meet her today. I didn't know they were going to talk about marriage like it was a horse trade. Please believe me. I only wanted to meet Brendt. She's the older of you two, after all, and what I thought about you I kept to myself, as it was the decent thing to do."

Suddenly, Maura reached out and touched Patrick's hand. She only held it there for a moment, but the contact thrilled him. "All right now, Patrick O'Connell," she said, "I understand."

He wanted to say something else then, to go on to explain that he had always longed for those trips to the still, longed for the moment when he took the whiskey jugs from her hands, trying to look past the indifference in her eyes.

But Maura wouldn't let him have his say. She held up her hands, smiled briefly, sadly. Here was the tragedy of Ireland, she knew, here in this love-sick boy. An overwhelming pity for Patrick O'Connell came over her: one of three sons of Michael O'Connell, in a poor time, in a poor county, in a poor nation. Only the eldest would get the gift of the farm—a gift that would sentence the heir to years of desperate scrabbling for survival. The less-fortunate sons had nowhere to go in their own country, unless they wanted to hire out for room and board and a few pennies for drink from some farmer too poor to pay a decent wage. No wonder half as many people lived in Ireland in 1897 as fifty years before. Poor Patrick wanted to leave his country as badly as she did, as badly as most of their generation. But he had no vision. He was not ambitious. Maura knew that he could see no further than his father's little purse, a good Catholic wife, and the steerage passage from Cork to New York. From the pathetic tales of the few villagers who'd returned to die in their native land, she knew what work awaited Patrick O'Connell in the New World. He would be a porter, a hod carrier, a stablehand, a stevedore. Maura didn't want him to make love to her, didn't want him to humiliate himself with further inarticulate dreaming. She knew enough about herself to know that she would never want to be the wife of such a weak man.

"You don't understand," he said finally. "It's the twenty pounds, you see. Your father owes mine twenty pounds, and if I marry Brendt, my father forgets the debt, and forgets any dowry. But I don't want to marry Brendt, not if she loves someone else. I know that you want to go to America. Sure that's what I want, too."

"No," she said. "Please don't say any more."

"We could get to know each other a little."

"It's no use, Patrick."

"Is it because you love someone else?"

"No," she said. "Of course not." This was true. It was not love she felt for Grady Madigan. It was not something that plagued her dreams, that had become the center of her life. Not at all. If she loved anything besides her mother and Brendt, it was the dream of freedom, of her future in New York, when she would be rich, and life would be long baths in steaming, perfumed water, dancing with tall, dark gentlemen in ballrooms lit by ten thousand candles.

"Listen," he said. "I know you don't know me. Sure I'm not the handsomest man in Kerry. Just please think about it. Think about maybe getting to know me. I want to go to America, too. It's easier to go together."

"Get it out of your mind once and for all," she said.

And then poor Patrick O'Connell surprised Maura once again. Awkwardly, not knowing whether to stand or to kneel, he bent low over where she sat, took hold of her chin in his sturdy farmer's hands, and kissed her cheek.

Maura pushed him away at once. "Now I'm telling you to be leaving me alone!" she said, with real anger.

"I'm sorry. I didn't know what I was doing."

"You knew what you were doing," said Maura, and now she got to her feet and pushed past him. But she didn't know where to go. What difference did it make whether she found Brendt on the village road or waited for her to show up at the cottage? Both of them were going to catch hell from their father, whenever they returned; and there was no choice but to return sometime that day.

"I just want you to know that I love you," he said.

"Get away from me," said Maura. "Get out of my sight. I don't want to hear you say boo to me. Just leave me be."

"Think about it, please," said Patrick, still red-faced, his eyes on the ground again, defeated. He shrugged his shoulders, he cleared his throat, he clapped his hands, and then he slowly turned round and shambled off, taking the path back toward the cottage, where his father and Maura's discussed the fate of their children.

When he had gone, Maura slowly touched her chin, touched the spot on her cheek where he had kissed her. It was the first time that she could remember having been kissed by a man. The sense of outrage vanished; in its place a wondering grew up, a glimmering awareness of power. Poor Patrick loved her, and her world had expanded in the wake of his love. She didn't love him, she didn't wish to marry him; but his kiss, his words, had created new possibilities of freedom and escape.

Maura turned back to the stone wall. With her strength renewed, she was easily able to climb over and jump down onto the hard-packed dirt road to the village. Maura smiled. For the first time, she believed in her own dream. For the first time, she believed that nothing could stop her from getting to America, and, once there, from becoming a princess, a queen.

# ❧ CHAPTER ❧
# TWO

Maura was sure she'd find Brendt before either of them could travel the four miles to the village. Her sister was by nature slow, methodical. Even her footsteps were straight and deliberate, placed with consideration. The simplest task took Brendt far longer than Maura; but Brendt's work with a needle, or with arranging their mother's flowers, was flawless. Only in the operation of the whiskey still did Maura proceed more cautiously than her sister. In everything else—eating, walking, talking— Maura was faster.

Nonetheless, Maura did not overtake Brendt. Along the hard dirt road, deeply rutted from the wheels of the donkey carts, Maura came upon half a dozen villagers she knew, but no one had seen her sister. Perhaps her sister's love for Grady Madigan was so strong that it gave her untold strength, thought Maura, resenting again that Brendt had never once told her of this love.

Following the sharp curve in the road a mile outside the village, she steeled herself for the sounds of drunken men. Bill Hurley's alehouse sold little ale, and was less a house than a hovel. Hurley was a friendly man who sold cheap whiskey on credit and never tried to force men to pay what they didn't have. He was also Bill Dooley's largest single customer, and fond of praising the illegal whiskey distiller to the skies. Even the occasional brave constable who ventured into Hurley's for a drink would praise the whiskey poured out of Hurley's "Parliament"— legal—casks, knowing full well that the casks were five years old and the whiskey pure Dooley.

The alehouse abutted the road at the heart of the curve. Maura kept her eyes to the ground and walked faster, taking care not to step in the refuse of nearby cottages, or the waste of animals. Without looking up for the church spire, she could always tell the advent of the village by the sudden muddying of the road, the gradual clogging of her path with garbage.

"Maura Dooley!" she heard suddenly; and against her will, she raised her eyes from the ground and slowed her pace. Bill Hurley was running to her, his paunch jumping up and down behind his ancient apron. The open door of the alehouse was just ahead, but no sounds of drunken revelry or riot reached her.

She had never seen jolly Hurley look so distraught. "What is it?" she said. "What's wrong?"

"Sure that's not for me to say, girl," he said, taking hold of both her arms as if he were afraid she'd run off, and motioning with sad eyes to the alehouse.

"But what do you want with me?" she said. "Billy, what is it? Billy, sure you're not crying? Och, Billy, tell me!"

Then Maura saw the neat blue uniform, the flat cap of a constable standing in the open doorway. She didn't bother to look at the constable's face, or to ask him to stand aside. Just the sight of that stiff uniform waiting for her approach drove her to a run, her heart pounding with terror. The constable got out of her way, and she ran into the alehouse, her bare feet slapping the hardwood floor.

Brendt was there, as Maura knew she would be, as she had known in the space of a moment, when, turning from Hurley's sad eyes, she'd seen the constable's uniform and a terrible fear had taken hold of her.

But Brendt was not dead.

Maura went to her at once, kicking aside a stool, a chair, an overturned table, and dropped to her knees where her sister huddled on the floor, against the wall, her eyes wide open, tearless.

"Brendt," she said. But the name didn't penetrate her sister's consciousness. She was staring into an underworld, a world of spirits, and it was outside Maura's ken. Brendt was on the floor, her pale eyes as lifeless as those as a fish out of water, of a corpse on a slap at the wake. All Maura could hear was a low tuneless humming twisting out of Brendt's open mouth.

"Brendt, darling," she said. "It's myself, it's Maura, it's your sweet baby sister. Don't you know me?" She could not understand why Brendt had drawn her knees up to her chest, why a thin spittle collected at the corners of her mouth. "Stop that," she said, very softly, wanting to shut up Brendt's humming, a rhythmless keening that seemed to echo in the back of Maura's brain. "Stop that," she said again, and she took hold of Brendt and shook her, but it was like shaking a man of straw, or a doll made out of rags.

Maura got to her feet so fast that the room seemed to be turning. She saw a young man's freckled face and down moustache, she saw poor, frightened Billy Hurley, and she shouted at both of them. "Get away with you!" she said. "Leave her be!" To Hurley, she added: "What is he doing here? What do we need with him?" The young man with the freckled face was the constable who had stood in the doorway before; and it was as natural to hate the constabulary as to breathe, particularly at a moment like this.

Since Hurley didn't answer, Maura turned her fury on the constable. "Get out of here! Go back to your landlords! Go find some other Irish to torment!"

"I'm as Irish as anyone," said the constable.

"Not in Kerry, you're not."

"I'm Irish from Wexford. What's wrong with Wexford, I ask you?"

"Get out of here, you murdering devil," said Maura. "Don't talk to me with my sister lying there out of her head."

"I picked her out of a lane full of garbage," said the young man. "I dried the blood off her nose. I carried her in my arms to this house. So don't go telling me I'm not an Irishman; I'm as good as any Irishman who wasn't born with a farm, or a ticket to America. Sure it's better to earn the queen's money, and help out such unfortunates as your sister at the same time. Don't tell me I'm not Irish, girl, or I'll crack you around this room, so help me Jesus, I will."

He was turning to go, very offended by the pretty girl's hatred of his uniform—a hatred that assaulted him from every side in his native country—but Maura stopped him. "I'm sorry," she said. "But what happened? Tell me what happened to her."

"I just found her, girl," said the constable. "There was blood gushing from her nose and she didn't seem to care. She was just like she is now, only out there it was worse, because of the blood, and the filth of it all. Sure I don't know what happened. If it had been a man who had hit her, I'd have brained him, that I can promise you. But she doesn't seem to have been hit. She's not bruised, she's not beaten up, is she?"

Maura turned to look at her sister, trying to fathom the source of her pain. Hurley had poured out a sloppy glass of whiskey, and now brought it clumsily to Brendt's open lips. "No, Billy," said Maura. "Let me do that." And she took the whiskey from his shaky hands and poured a few drops of it into her sister's mouth.

Brendt coughed, and twisted her head away so fast that she knocked it against the wall.

"Brendt, take a bit more," said Maura, trying to bring the whiskey to her lips again. Even in that instant, she could see the change in her sister's eyes. Brendt was not yet aware of Maura's presence, but her eyes were looking up from the netherworld, looking not at the luring face of death but at the real-life catastrophe that had taken place less than an hour before. "Brendt, what is it? It's Maura, who loves you best in all the world. Sure you're all right. Sure you're fine and flourishing mightily. Come on with you, Brendt, come on and out of it."

But Maura was terrified at the pain in Brendt's eyes. If Brendt was coming back from the spirit world, she was coming back against her will, coming back to memories that she would have preferred had killed her once and for all.

All of a sudden, Brendt remembered.

She remembered, and understood that she was alive, in some place of shelter, facing her sister Maura, who held a glass of whiskey close to her lips. Brendt ceased her horrible humming, her moaning from the house of the dead. But as her eyes widened to embrace her sister, as her strength returned to push back the glass, as every last one of Grady Madigan's words returned to her in full force, she suddenly let out a shriek.

It was the scream of a fiend, inhabiting Brendt's body. It seemed to Maura, to Hurley, to the young constable, that the banshee was in the room, delivering its curse, its promise of death. That famous creature of Irish legend, the banshee that the city-educated scoffed at, the specter whom Maura's father called the Lady of Death, and her mother called the White Angel of Sorrow, seemed to be announcing its presence in the unearthly shriek from Brendt's frail frame.

"Sure some one of us is dead," said Hurley.

"It can't be myself," said the constable. "All my banshees are west in Wexford."

It was only half a joke, the way the young man spoke it, but it was enough for Maura to return to her senses. There were no banshees, except in the tales of peasants. And Brendt's cry was no presage of death, no demon prophecy of someone's death agony — not unless it was Brendt's own.

"Brendt," said Maura. "Brendt, darling, it doesn't matter. Grady Madigan doesn't matter; sure he's nothing but a guzzling fool, nothing but another drunk who knows a little learning." She pulled Brendt closer, and the banshee's cry was done. Brendt had heard almost nothing of what Maura had said. She had only heard Grady's name, and she had felt the offer of her sister's love. Brendt looked at Maura, for the first time completely acknowledging her presence.

"Bejesus," Brendt said, startling Maura. Her sister had never uttered a strong word in her life. "That's what he said to me. Grady Madigan. Said to me. . . ." She was whispering, and Brendt suddenly turned on the men and waved her hand at them, imperiously, urgently. Hurley took the constable outside, and both guarded the open door.

"Bejesus," said Brendt again, laughing a bit through her tears. "That's what he said, and me loving him so much, so much that I would do anything. I never told you—" Brendt broke off abruptly, looking from Maura's rapt face into space.

Maura helped her up and Brendt fell into a chair, propping her elbows on a scarred old table like a whiskey-guzzling regular.

"I never told you because he said not to. Our secret, Grady told me. You would have told me not to."

"No," said Maura.

"Yes!" said Brendt, suddenly violent.

"If you love Grady," ventured Maura, "then I would never tell you to listen to father and marry that Patrick O'Connell."

Brendt looked at her closely, as if to better understand strange words. Then all of a sudden she understood, and laughed out loud, but before Maura could fully warm to this weird shift of temper, the laugh ceased abruptly. Perhaps, thought Maura, she's gone as mad as ma.

"Maura," said Brendt. "What happened?"

"What do you mean? I don't know what happened. You must tell me what happened. You were lying on the floor, curled up like a baby, with your eyes wide open, like a witch or a fairy gone into a state."

"I mean with father. Where is father?"

"I don't know. I ran after you, sure I did. Father can go to the devil."

"He's not in town, then? He's not coming after me?"

"Why should he? He'll be waiting for you. For you and me both. We'll have to go back sometime, won't we? Why should the blackguard chase us when he knows he'll soon enough find us home?"

That was twice, Maura noted, that Brendt hadn't jumped on her—for calling their father a devil and a blackguard. And even as Maura spoke, she could see Brendt's attention wander off to her own, far weightier concerns.

"Help me get to the village," Brendt said.

"The village? Why in the name of all the saints—" began Maura, but Brendt interrupted her.

"In the name of all the saints indeed. I must see Father Malachy," said Brendt.

"That fake," said Maura, without thinking. She knew very well how her sister admired the priest, how he had lent Brendt books and magazines, how he had encouraged her to write out the tales told by their mother.

"You're not to be calling him that," said Brendt. But she spoke without snapping, without any real show of anger. It seemed impossible to claim Brendt's full awareness, not with an insensitive remark, not with a caress. She still had one foot in the world where she'd been minutes before. "You must please help me get to the village," she said.

"It's getting late," said Maura. "The later we are getting back home, the worse it'll be on our backs."

"I'll go with or without you, sister," said Brendt. "But I'd be very much obliged for your help." She began to stand up, leaning heavily on the table, and Maura jumped to her feet to help. "Thanks be to God," said Brendt, "that my sister loves me."

The constable was glad to see the sisters leave together, and accepted Maura's thanks for his help with a very gracious nodding of his handsome head. Hurley offered a ride in his cart, but Maura thought it best to be alone with Brendt. As they walked, Brendt retreated to silence, but it seemed to Maura that her sister's color and strength improved with almost miraculous speed.

The town, in all its ugliness, continued to grow around their marching feet. Skinny lanes, twisting off the main path, led to clusters of mud huts, thatched with rotting straw. Even from fifty feet, the stench from the garbage-strewn lanes offended Maura. The hut dwellers sat in front of their open doors, listless and defeated, watching their children and their dogs play with sticks and ropes and rags, pulling and shouting in the mud. Spire and steeple of the church towered proudly over the misery of the village, but religion held no solace for Maura. To the northeast, beyond the church, stood the ruined tower of an earlier civilization, a tower that drew visitors from as far away as Dublin and Belfast. Maura felt a greater kinship to the men who'd built the tower than to the churchgoers of the village, looking up in awe at the immaculate house of God from their filth, from their ignorance. The tower spoke of strength, of life's glory; the church spoke only of deliverance from a life of degradation.

"Tell me," said Maura to Brendt, clutching her sister's hand. "What?"

"Tell me about Grady," said Maura. "Tell me what he said to you today." They were almost at the church gates. In the distance, Maura could see the splash of colors that would soon focus into the American steamship poster, its noble prow slicing through calm water, a thin wisp of white smoke rising from its painted smokestack to a clear blue sky. No wonder half the village dreamed of leaving it; leaving it for clear waters, for blue skies, for new lives.

"I have to see Father Malachy," Brendt said, but Maura stopped walking, and pulled on her sister's hand to turn her about. "Just wait for me a minute until I see Father Malachy," insisted Brendt. But Maura was surprised to note a change in Brendt's voice, a hesitation and a fear.

"Tell me," said Maura, and for a moment Brendt's beautiful eyes were full on her, loving her, wanting to let go of secrets, of shame.

"No," said Brendt.

"*Tell me*," insisted Maura, bringing her sister close to her, twisting her wrist. "I won't let you into the church unless you tell me."

"He doesn't love me," said Brendt, so suddenly that the words made no sense as they were first uttered. Brendt repeated them slowly: "He doesn't love me. He says I'm stupid, sure that's what he said—stupid."

"Grady Madigan said you were stupid," said Maura, letting go of Brendt's wrist. "Sure I'd like to know what you're stupid about. You're the smartest girl in the county. Does he know that you've got Shakespeare by heart? Pages of it."

"Stupid if I thought he'd ever marry me," she said, speaking without inflection. "Stupid if that's what I thought he could have meant by saying he loved me. Love has got nothing to do with it, that's what he told me. Nothing to do with it, with any of it. Love is pure and simple, and I curse the day I ever set eyes on him. I do, I swear I do, I swear on my life I do."

"No, don't go yet, darling," said Maura. "What can you tell a priest that you can't tell your own sister?" It was frightening to see how wild and desperate Brendt had become from the fact of love. She who had always been complacent, quiet, obedient, was suddenly swift, headstrong.

"I have to go," said Brendt, and she took half a dozen steps toward the gate before stopping and turning about. "I'm sorry," she said to Maura. "I should have told you. When it happened.

Only weeks ago, it was, at the fair. Sure I was a silly, lovestruck girl. Everyone knew the young schoolmaster, so thin and handsome and grand with the sound of his own talking. Oh, but it was awful when he spoke to me at the fair, talked to me about sonnets and castles and walking in the wet grass after a soft summer rain. Our secret, he said, always our secret that we knew each other, and that we read together, from his big book of English poems. I know his room, Maura, his room in the schoolhouse, and I know his eyes, and I know his lips, and I know his tongue."

Maura stood stock-still, trying to take in everything: the meeting at the fairgrounds, the lilting sound of Grady's voice, the talk of secrets, the touch of hands, the kiss. Maura herself had been kissed only hours before, but not overwhelmed in the way it had happened to Brendt.

"I told him about the marriage father wants to make," Brendt went on. "He said that I had my own mind to decide what to do. I looked at him like he had gone crazy, but he wasn't acting crazy at all. Sure he sat on the edge of the bed, swinging his long legs like a lazy man, without a care in the world. I thought you wanted to marry me, I told him. And that's when he called me stupid. I told you how he called me stupid, stupid because I thought he loved me and wanted me to be his wife."

Maura had taken Brendt's hands, and now she squeezed them gently. "We don't need the priest," said Maura. "There, you've told me, and isn't it better? Sure I love you more than Father Malachy ever could. And I'll give you better words of advice. Devil take Grady Madigan. Devil take Patrick O'Connell. Devil take father. All right? Sure, it's all right now. You don't marry Grady, you don't marry silly Paddy, you marry someone else. Someone you meet someday and fall in love with, just like in the legends. Just don't cry now, and try to imagine him. Someone big and strong, not a weak and skinny schoolmaster. Someone good and kind and handsome who would do anything in the world to make you his wife."

Brendt had shut her eyes against the force of Maura's words, but even so tears slipped out, even so her face whitened, even so her hands shook in dreadful spasms of sorrow.

"Stop it, Brendt," said Maura. "You'll be happy without Grady. Sure it'll be best when you love someone else."

"I'll never love anyone else."

"Yes, you will. You won't love Grady. It'll be like a bad cold in the head that just goes away, you'll see."

"I don't love Grady," said Brendt. "I *hate* Grady."

"Good," said Maura. "I hate him, too. We'll hate Grady together. Come, let's go then."

"No," said Brendt. "I've got to see Father Malachy."

"What do you mean? It's off your chest now, we can go home."

"You don't understand."

"I understand everything," said Maura. She took hold of Brendt's arm and tried to link it with her own. But Brendt pulled back, suddenly angry.

"You don't understand, I'm telling you."

"Stop it, Brendt," said Maura, speaking coldly to her sister for the first time. "I understand that you thought you loved Grady Madigan, that you kissed him, that you thought he'd marry you, that he called you stupid for thinking you'd ever be his wife. All right? You're not to see the silly priest, you're going to come home with me, and face father once and for all."

Brendt slowly turned her back to Maura and faced the great stone church. Without turning about, she said softly, so that Maura had to strain to hear the words: "I was his woman, Maura."

Maura heard, and took a step back from Brendt, trying to understand.

"You see," said Brendt, turning to face her sister. "I can't marry anyone else. I was Grady Madigan's woman, and I thought that meant something to him, but I was stupid, and now I have to go to Father Malachy. I have to go to Father Malachy and beg forgiveness."

"What do you mean you were his woman?" said Maura finally, speaking as softly, as painfully as her sister.

"It means that I was like a wife to him. In his bed, is what it means. Sure you know what it means to be a woman," said Brendt.

"What do you mean you were his woman?" repeated Maura,

but now her words were not soft but harsh and angry. "How could you be his woman? How could you do such a thing?" She had taken hold of Brendt and, without realizing it, was shaking her, holding on to her with all her strength. If she had let go, she would have used her hands to strike Brendt in the face.

"It's all right," said Brendt, acting the older sister for once in their lives. "It's all right, Maura," she said, and she let her sister shake her until all Maura's strength was spent, and then took her in her arms. "I'm better now, Maura, and I know what I have to do. If you will just wait for me, I'll see Father Malachy, and then I'll know if I can ever be forgiven for this terrible thing."

"Why did you let him?" said Maura. "What for? What if you've gotten with child? How could you let a man do that?"

But Brendt was no longer listening, and Maura was no longer wild. The older sister passed quickly through the church gates, leaving the younger to sink slowly to the ground, her back against the fence, looking past the little square to where the ugly schoolhouse stood on rocky ground.

How could Brendt have been so stupid? she thought, using the very word Grady had hurled at her. Both sisters had always known about the sexual act; it was something animals did in season, something humans did to bring children into the world. With enough drink in them, in the right season, humans could act like animals. Her brothers were like that, she was sure. And her father. Certainly her father had used her mother like the bull used the heifer, certainly he'd been drunk and demanding and violent. But what did that have to do with Grady Madigan? Grady had always seemed gentle, intelligent, above the common mass of men she and Brendt knew. A reader of poems, a teller of tales, a man of compliments and civility was Grady, not an animal. And yet just like the bull, just like her father, just like the filthy peasants, Grady Madigan had been wild, mad with lust, violent. He had forced her sister back on his bed, he had stripped away her clothes, he had forced himself on her, into her, possessing her as if she were a whore.

For an hour Maura sat against the fence, waiting for her sister to come back from the priest. The day was growing into evening, and Maura knew that if Brendt were much longer, they'd be walking the tree-lined dirt road in darkness. She trained her eyes on the distant schoolhouse, on the bedraggled day laborers returning from twelve hours of turf cutting, or fence mending, or barn cleaning for seven shillings a week. She wondered what the schoolhouses looked like in America, and how much American laborers were paid. Perhaps servants weren't paid in shillings there, but in pounds. How else could the Irish in America send their relatives so many dollars, enough to keep the family drinking their health in the alehouse every day for a month? Maybe now, for the first time, Brendt would agree with her. Sweet, modest, gentle Brendt would see the need to leave this place, to defy the wishes of their father and run off to America.

Maura stiffened suddenly, as if a cold wind had blown through her. She turned to see if Brendt was coming, but the churchyard was deserted. Perhaps the priest was browbeating her, shaming her past anything she had ever imagined. Disgrace, coupled with the anger of their father, would lend power to Maura's arguments about the American dream. They could beg enough money from their mother for the voyage, then hire out as servants in America until they'd earned enough for their mother's passage, so that she could join them in the promised land.

"Maura," said Brendt, speaking behind her. The voice was so flat and hopeless that Maura felt as if she'd been doused with cold water. She turned to see her sister's face, very pale and determined in the soft light.

"We'd best be hurrying," said Maura, getting to her feet.

"I don't want to go home," said Brendt.

"We have to go home," insisted Maura, smiling brightly at Brendt, as if she were encouraging a recalcitrant little girl.

"I'm going to sleep at the still," said Brendt.

"What?" said Maura. She had heard what her sister had said, of course, but it made no sense to her. Why go miles past their home, walking down the twisting, rocky paths toward the sea, climbing up the hidden narrow trails to the cave, high in the face of a great cliff, looking down over hundreds of feet of jagged rock outcroppings to the wild Atlantic below? Why creep past one of their brothers, sleeping at the lookout point a hundred yards below the cave entrance, and risk getting shot at by him in the dark? Why skin their knees crawling in the dark about the sand traps and tar pits, covered by thin turf in the last bit of pathway to the still? Why, above all else, delay the wrath of their father? If they would sleep peacefully at the still tonight, their beating tomorrow would be worse than the one they'd receive coming home to the cottage tonight.

"I'll walk you home," said Brendt. "And then I'll say good-bye and continue on myself."

"No, you won't."

"I don't want you to come with me."

"I won't have you go alone."

Brendt turned to look at her, as if weighing the strength of her sister's will. "It's dangerous to go to the still at night," said Brendt.

"I know that better than yourself," said Maura. "I spend more time than you there. I know every trap put in the road by father. But if you must go, I won't have you go alone."

"I must go," said Brendt.

"Is it because you're afraid of father?"

"I must go, and that's all I'll say on it," said Brendt.

"We'd better walk fast while there's still some light," said Maura.

They set off at once along the road that had taken them to the village. It was a moonless night, and cloudy. What stars rose in the sky were no match for the mist blowing in from the sea, chilling the ground so that the cold rose through their bare soles into their hearts. By the time they'd passed Hurley's alehouse it was too dark even to see the mist blowing in their faces; only the blacker outlines of the trees lining their path could be seen, and these, too, vanished in the mist from time to time.

They walked on, colliding with wayward branches and thick tree trunks, tripping in the deep ruts. Three times they passed single men who loomed up at them out of the dark. Two of the men were drunks, singing at the top of their lungs, so that their white faces came as no more of a surprise than the gray-white bark of the birch trees catching a flicker of starlight when the clouds and the mist shifted in the wind. One man was silent, a tired worker trudging home to his hovel with a stick over his shoulder. This man's approach was so silent on the dirt road, coming out of blackness without a song, without a word, that both sisters jumped back, howling in fright. The peasant was too tired to laugh, or to worry that they might be fairies, up to no good. He just continued on toward the village, his goal a dish of soft potatoes, milk and cheese, and a straw mat to wait out the dawn.

"This reminds me of ma's tales of the Pookah," said Maura in a loud, frightened voice.

"Don't speak of tales," said Brendt. "It's dark enough without you making me jump out of my skin."

"It's better to talk, isn't it?" said Maura. "Sure it tells the world we're here."

"What Pookah?" said Brendt.

"Pookah was the horse demon," said Maura. "You remember. Sure it could talk as good as a man, and it could ride for nights and days up the sides of mountains. It terrorized Ireland until King Brian Boru tamed him."

"Quiet, there's something ahead," said Brendt. A moment later they both heard the distinct slow gait of a walking horse. "Sure it's not old ma's Pookah."

It was a horsecart, with a single lantern swinging from above the driver's seat. Maura grabbed Brendt and pulled her violently into the bushes off the road. "What are you—" Brendt started to say, but Maura put her hand over her sister's mouth and held it there until the cart had passed them on its way to the village.

"That was Patrick O'Connell," said Maura.

"What was the need to strangle me over him?" said Brendt, getting to her feet.

"He was looking for us."

"What if he was? We don't have to go with him when he finds us."

"I don't want him to find us, not him," said Maura.

"I'm not going to marry him," said Brendt. "There's nothing to fear on that account." She got to her feet. "I'm not going to marry anyone."

"Oh, stop talking like that," said Maura. "There'll be time enough to change your mind when we get to America."

"I'm not going to America," said Brendt, as she had a hundred times before. They began to walk again, and their longer strides matched their sudden vehemence.

"Don't say that," said Maura.

"If you're fool enough to think that a godless place like Boston or New York is going to be the answer to a poor girl's prayers, for once in your life leave me out of it," said Brendt. "I am not going anywhere, least of all to America."

"In America you can start your life again."

"Why? What are you talking about? America isn't heaven, and it's not hell either. It's the same world that's here, not the one to come. God knows what I've done here. I can't start anything over. What's done is done, and that's all there is to it."

"What did the priest tell you?" said Maura.

"It's got nothing to do with your America. It's between me and himself."

"Did Father Malachy forgive you?" said Maura.

"It's not for him to forgive," said Brendt. "Sure he's not our Lord Jesus, he's only a man with a collar."

"Devil take him if he didn't forgive you," said Maura.

Suddenly, Brendt whirled about on the dark road and hit her across the face. "Don't you dare say that," said Brendt in a high-pitched, desperate voice. "Father Malachy is a good man. If the devil takes anyone, it will be myself." She took hold of Maura now and held her against her chest. "I don't want you to ever curse the church on my account, do you hear me?"

"Yes," said Maura.

"Never. Sure it's not Father Malachy's doing if I go off with Grady Madigan like a common prostitute."

"Don't say that."

"I'll say what's true, and you're to remember what I say. Not just for tonight, but for always. Listen to me, Maura. If you ever loved me, listen to me. The church is good, and the church is holy—the church is all we have. You must never blame the church on my account, never. Say it. Go on. Say that you'll never blame the church on my account."

"All right. I won't," said Maura. But the words tasted vile

coming through her teeth. Even then she hated Father Malachy, though he was a nice mild man with gentle eyes and soft, clean hands, like a gentleman's. She wondered what the priest had told Brendt, what terrible things he'd uttered.

Brendt let go of her. "You must remember that you promised," she said. "No matter if you leave Ireland and never see me again. You must not blame the church for your sister."

They walked on in silence for a long while. Though their eyes grew accustomed to the blackness, they still could see no further than a few feet ahead of them; and they grew no less fearful. For miles they walked, taking the fork toward the sea, bypassing the longer route that took them first to the cottage. This road was shorter, but lonelier. No farmers' dogs barked, pretending to be fierce; no workers came their way from a late supper of scraps from their employers' tables. The mist grew denser, and they could taste the salt in the air. No one came here save the Dooley family, en route to their whiskey still; no one had any other reason to be here, and certainly not at night.

The descent to the sea had given way to a slow and steady climb as the sisters followed the twisting path up the cliffside from memory. Maura didn't feel any fatigue. It was as if her body were fueled by the revelations of the day, from Paddy's declaration of love to Brendt's admission of disgrace; a fire of confusion and promise kept her alive to all sensations, kept her awake and aware. She knew where her father had placed his traps for the constables, or any other wanderers, and while she helped steer Brendt about these in the dark, she planned the arguments she would pump her sister with during the night. It seemed impossible to Maura that she could not convince her sister to run off to America with her. Surely it was only a matter of hours, of the proper words and caresses, and Brendt would agree to run off to Cork with her in the morning.

"The mist is lifting," said Brendt. Her voice was as soft and eerie as the thin light on the white cliffs about them. Below, they could hear the sea, alternately licking at the coast, then dashing at the rocks in sudden fury.

"Quiet, there'll be a guard," said Maura, pointing to an almost invisible outcropping of rock above them, where the pathway led. One of her brothers would be there, asleep, with a rifle in his lap, ready to wake at the sound of a falling rock, or the scream of a man falling into a trap. "We can go around," she said; and pushing off the path, she held out a hand for her sister to take, to follow her up a different incline.

"We're very high up," said Brendt, breathing heavily, her hand very cold in Maura's grip.

"Quiet," said Maura, and Brendt had to let go of her hand, to get on her knees and crawl the last fifty feet, pulling herself up and around a series of boulders.

Finally, they were higher than their brother; even in the dark they could recognize Jimmy, their youngest brother, sleeping just as Maura had pictured him. They walked faster now, both girls familiar with the last bit of pathway to the cave.

"We'll have to be up and out before first light," said Maura.

"Yes," said Brendt, turning her eyes from the mouth of the cave to the precipice a dozen yards away. There, at the edge of the path leading up to the cave, one had a view of the distant sea, and of the endless inlets all along the southwestern coast of County Kerry.

"Better not get too close to the edge," said Maura.

"It's a beautiful view, isn't it?"

"Sure you're joking. What's there to see now in the dark? Let's get in and find the mat and some blankets."

"Thanks for coming with me, Maura," said Brendt.

"You're crazy for doing it, but I love you anyway. Father's going to beat us bloody. Unless I can talk you into running off with me."

"No," said Brendt, looking away from the precipice and into Maura's green eyes. "I'm not running anywhere."

"It's yourself who's always telling *me* to be the sensible one," said Maura pleasantly, taking hold of her sister's wrist. "It's late, I know, and maybe you're tired, but I'm ready to be sensible and talk sensible and act sensible with you all through the night."

Brendt slowly released her wrist from Maura's grasp. "I love you very much," she said.

"Are you listening to me?" said Maura. "I love you, too, but I'll not be having you ignoring me when I'm talking sensible.

America is the subject, isn't it? Sensibly? Here we are, ready to go to sleep in the cave, having to sneak out before first light and run on down to the cottage for the beating of our lives. Or else we can be sensible. We can hide out from father, and find ma—sure we could find herself before father finds us—and she's got some money saved, and off we can go, with her blessing, off to Cork and to New York City."

"Stop, please," said Brendt, taking Maura's hands in her own. Maura felt that she had never seen her sister look so gentle, so open, so beautiful as at that moment. "I am not going to America."

"Why can't we just have a sensible talk about it?" said Maura, still not understanding that her sister was thinking of another life, another future.

"I love Grady Madigan," said Brendt.

"But that's not right," said Maura.

"It's not right, no," said Brendt. "But I love Grady Madigan, and I submitted to his caresses. I loved him, and I loved his caresses. I was his woman, and it wasn't awful, Maura. It was not awful, it was not awful to me."

"Sure it's better not to talk about."

"And Father Malachy says that I have no true repentance in my heart, and he is right. I do not have true repentance in my heart, and of course the church cannot forgive me."

A cold blast of air flew past the mouth of the cave, letting loose a whistle that chilled Maura more than the cold. "Let's go in and get under the blankets," she said.

"The church cannot forgive me," said Brendt, holding on to her sister. "I have no one to blame for that but myself, for what I myself have in my heart for Grady. Grady will not have me, neither will the church."

Maura didn't know what to answer. She had no love like Brendt had for Grady, and had no feeling for the church at all. But she loved Brendt, and understood that she was in pain, and wanted to offer her love for strength, for support. "Let's go inside," said Maura.

"No," said Brendt. "You don't understand."

"I do understand. But it's cold, and we need a little sleep. Sure everything will seem rosier in the daylight."

"Thank you for coming here with me," said Brendt. She pulled her sister close to her and hugged her. "Thank you, Maura," she said, and she kissed her cool forehead, and her soft cheeks, and she smoothed her auburn hair, and looked into her eyes as if she were about to take a long journey. "It's so good for me to know that you love me," she said. "I have nothing else, except for ma, and ma's crazy."

"Don't say that," said Maura. But already Brendt was letting go of her, and smiling, and standing squarely in the wind.

"I'm sorry, Maura," said Brendt, still smiling brightly. She took a step backward, toward the precipice, so swiftly that it froze Maura to the ground.

"Brendt, careful!" she said, her words emerging in astonished whispers.

"I'm sorry," said Brendt. And this time Maura didn't whisper, and she didn't remain frozen to the ground. She let out a howl, a shriek that was a plea, a cry that was her sister's name, an eruption of violent sound that was a frail attempt to stop Brendt's physical presence from stepping off the precipice into black space.

But nothing stopped Brendt.

She had said she was sorry, and then it was only a second, less than a second, Brendt had stepped off the side of the cliff, and Maura screamed and cried, and knelt at the edge, and she could see nothing, she could not even see her sister die on the rocks at the verge of the sea hundreds of feet below. Maura could see nothing but blackness, she could hear nothing but the relentless pounding of the surf, the timeless indifference of the natural world.

# ❧ CHAPTER ❧
# THREE

It took Maura the rest of the night to reach the sea.

There was no path, only a wild mass of rocks and stones, dark shadows reaching downward, poised to crack and to crumble, eager to collapse into the oblivion below.

*Brendt was dead.*

Everything reminded her of Brendt: the pounding of the surf, the heavy air, the false dawn, the tumbling rocks beneath Maura's bruised feet. *Brendt was dead*, battered by the sea, twisting wildly through the currents as the sky lit up, then darkened, then slowly took on a somber glow, a dull promise of a new day. Before the dawn, Maura sat on the rocky edge of the sea, letting the cold water lap at her feet, the harsh mossy boulder at her back digging into her skin. Idly, she wondered if she'd be sick from the damp and the cold. Brendt had nursed her through a terrible winter, when the rain never stopped for more than a few hours and the water had oozed up from under the rotting floorboards in their corner of the cottage. Maura had caught a fever, a cold in her chest, and her ears had rung with sounds that weren't there, and she had seen demons and devils and more than one banshee calling out her name. And always Brendt had been there, shooing away the bad visions, putting cold cloths on her steaming forehead.

Maura waited for the dawn, positive that Brendt could have been happy. Not on their straw mat in the corner of the cottage, but in her own room in the great house Maura dreamed of own-

ing in New York, in the New World. Not as Grady's abandoned
woman, but as the wife of a rich and powerful man in America.
Brendt could have been happy if she had listened to Maura, and
not to some confused god of despair and defeat. She could have
been happy, thought Maura, anger rising through the stuff of
her sadness, even as the sun rose over the water. Brendt was
dead, dead in the ocean that Maura would cross to leave this
place.

Brendt was dead, she said to herself, and the anger was gone,
and in the full light of day Maura slept, her back against the
boulder, the water warming about her legs as exhaustion obliterated sadness, memory, pain. When she woke, barely two hours
had passed, but the death of her sister had been accepted, if not
understood. And with this acceptance, she could stand up, she
could wash her face in the salt water, she could feel the chill in
her bones, the hunger in her belly. Brendt was dead, and must be
remembered, must be avenged in some fashion. But first of all,
Maura knew that she must survive.

There was no going back up the mountain. Her brother Jimmy
might be awake at his watch post, and anyone at all could have
joined him by now: father, sister, brothers, even friends in search
of the Dooley girls. She didn't know how she would get to
America, but she knew she must avoid being found by her father.
With Brendt gone, no story she could tell, true or false, would
save her from his wrath. She was afraid his anger would go
beyond a simple beating this time. And she could not afford to be
a prisoner, not with Brendt dead, and the ocean taunting her to
cross its endless surface.

Maura stepped into the water and began to follow the rocky
beach. There were stretches of fine sand that she had seen for
years, when looking from the heights of the still; and coming
from those beaches were thin brown lines, leading inland, crossed
by the sloppy blue lines and splashes of saltwater inlets and,
further inland, the fresh blue of creeks and streams and lakes,
feeding the green meadows and the checkerboard farmland of
coastal Kerry, each farm marked by its stone walls.

But for the moment, for the hour, there was no sand beach, no
road from the sea, no fresh water to drink. There was only the

deserted coast, stacks of giant boulders covered with slimy green vegetation, only the screaming of the gulls and the crash of the waves. Maura found no place to climb up out of the shallow water easily, and forced herself to go on, convinced that the easier beach, the level roads to civilization, to fresh water and food, would appear shortly.

She walked till the sun had risen to its highest point in the sky. She walked in water that rose to her ankles, to her knees, to her thighs. She walked along a narrow shelf of rock, ripping her palms on the overhanging cliff. A beach appeared, six feet long and five feet wide, and there she collapsed, sleeping face-down in the sand.

When she woke, she shivered violently, clutching her shoulders, her neck, blinking in the fading light of the afternoon. She was no longer hungry, but her thirst had become so powerful that she had to turn her eyes from the wild surf, with its false promise of slaking. There was little strength in her legs, but fear pushed her faster; she knew that she could not spend another night without food and drink and shelter, and she wanted intensely to live.

The little beach on which she'd rested was adjacent to another narrow rocky shelf, and when Maura wearily made her way along this, she found herself at the end of a tiny peninsula, looking out at the wild water. Turning from the sea, she saw that the peninsula led inland to much higher ground, an immense promontory high above the waves. She knew that she would never be able to climb that far; that the first step she took in that direction would be an acceptance of defeat, a way of self-destruction as sure as Brendt's.

But there was another direction.

Flanking the peninsula was a beach, part of the mainland, reachable by climbing the great promontory and descending through treacherous wet rocky ground—or by simply swimming two hundred yards.

Maura sat down on the rock, squinting through a light haze, trying to see past the beach, to see if anything was there beyond more impenetrable rock. She could swim, but she had never tried to swim in water as rough as what separated her from the beach, and she was so weak. She longed for some vision, some reason to give her the strength to cross the water; if she were merely swimming to a bit of sand, and not to an inlet to civilization, she would never make it to shore.

Suddenly, across the water, a rock moved. I'm dreaming, thought Maura, for the rock had twisted itself into the fat shape of a good Kerry cow. Maura got to her feet, a trifle stronger. Cows stood out clearly now, as exhaustion fell away from her, sharpening her senses: The sea was louder, and she tasted the salt on her swollen tongue, and surely those were cows—not fairies, not wandering rocks, but cows, aimless and stupid cows on the beach near their farm.

Maura stripped off her outer layer of clothing, looking across to the beach as if she were already there. She stepped off the rock into the water, not shocked by the cold; her feet had been in the water most of the day, and it seemed her clothes, her hair, her chest had been damp forever. She took a second step, and the rocky bottom gave way to sand, and the sand didn't hold her weight. Seawater swirled about her calves, about her knees, and suddenly, sinking further, the water was at her thighs.

Maura slapped her hands at the water, trying to steady herself. She was not yet ready to swim. The water was suddenly much colder, and the waves were whipping into her chest, into her face. She tried to shake off her fear, but couldn't; it was rising in her bowels, like a sickness outside her control. She couldn't see the cows through the waves, and for a moment she was certain that there were no cows, that she had only wished to see them, and that she was risking drowning now to reach a deserted cove, inhabited by rocks.

I must swim, she thought; but she remained where she was, buffeted by the waves, sinking into the sand, her mouth open with fear and amazement at what was taking place. She wanted to live, and yet she was going to die. Brendt was dead, and soon she would be, too, and there was nothing that could be done about it. She tasted the water striking into her face, and all at once a wall of water dropped on her, and another one hit her from the side, and she was swallowing water and spitting it up, and the stinging stuff was passing through her nose and the back of her throat, and a great red pain seemed to be pulsing from behind her wide-open eyes.

Then, in one awful moment, the sand beneath finally slipped away and Maura was on her back, down beneath the waves in the shallow water. The current gripped her and dragged her down deeper, so that her back scratched along the bottom, and her neck nearly broke as a crosscurrent twisted her body under the surface, away from the shore.

Finally, there was no more thinking. Maura wanted only one thing: to breathe. And there was only one place to breathe, and that was out of the water. No despair, no thirst, no hopelessness mattered now. She was a body beneath the waves, and the body struggled to the surface with every bit of its power.

But the surface was wild. Light and desperate and strong with purpose, Maura treaded water and breathed air and water in equal amounts. She was almost a fourth of the way to the beach, but she didn't know that. She couldn't imagine the speed with which the undertow had moved her, or the power with which competing currents were battling for the prize of her body. She only wanted to get out of the water, to stay on top of it, to live.

And so, after a fashion, she swam. She ducked her chin, she thrashed her arms, she kicked her legs. She was alternately horizontal, vertical, diagonal. Sucking in air, spitting out water, trying always, always, to keep her head above the raging water, she made a wild progress to the far shore, a progress that was none of her own doing. The currents swept her down, but they also propelled her across. If she had given up, she'd have arrived upon the beach at the same moment anyway; but she'd have arrived facedown, her lungs filled with water, dead. But Maura did not give up; she had a will to live. A fury kept her alive. A rage against the world for putting her in this whirlpool—for killing her sister and now trying to murder her. If only she could stay on top of the water, if only she could live, if only she could get to America . . .

There were cows indeed on the beach. A dozen cows of County Kerry. When the half-naked girl swept up on shore, one of them turned its head, slightly interested, but soon returned to its own lazy perusal of the sand.

The cows' keeper was far more fascinated. When he woke

up from a light nap under the oak tree not a hundred yards inland of the little beach, he thought she must be a sea fairy, come to taunt him to his death. But when he ran to her, he saw her blue face, her vomit, her shaking limbs—not the usual sort of fairy enticements to mortal men. He pulled her out of the surf, his eyes astonished at her white skin, her frail female form. He had never been rich enough to have a wife, and at thirty he had only once fornicated—with a prostitute; but she had removed only her petticoat, and he had been too terrified to look at what little part of her person she'd revealed.

"Hello," he shouted. "Hello, girl, are you alive or are you dead?"

But Maura heard none of it. She was lost in contentment, no longer struggling, air being sweet and plentiful all about her, and the real world a distant dream. She was unconscious, and her dreams were not stories but simply a succession of sensations: a flushing warmth, a cool trickle of water down her throat, a sudden swaddling in dry, thick clothes.

Maura was no more than a score of miles from her home, as the crow flies. But neither she nor her father were crows, and the tiny beach upon which she had landed, and the farm to which she was carried in the strong arms of the awestruck cow keeper, might as well have been fifty or a hundred miles from the Dooleys' cottage for all anyone here knew of a search for two runaway girls, or the fury of their father.

The farmer's wife to whom she was delivered for care and sustenance was a romantic. She saw in the auburn-haired Maura a princess, a fugitive from an unhappy marriage, a lover from a storybook; and she saw in her rescue a task that ennobled her own drab life. She bathed Maura, she fed her broth, she wrapped her in flannels, she held her hand and tried to calm the incoherent cries that were the product of Maura's delirium.

It took three days for Maura's fever to pass. She began, while still quite ill, to remember things: Brendt's stepping off into black space, the terrible swim through raging water, the cows on the beach. Later, a sense of purpose began to rise through the fever: She had to eat, she must think, she insisted on thanking this woman who ministered to her like an angel of mercy.

"What is your name, darling?"

"Thank you for the broth," said Maura. She knew her own name, of course, but she closed her eyes slowly on the question. Perhaps her father waited outside the door of this cottage, waited with a horsewhip in hand.

"Sure you needn't be thanking myself," said the farmer's wife, dabbing at Maura's forehead and clucking her tongue. "And it's best for me to be letting you quiet, I see that, plain as day. Quiet, there, no need to speak."

Maura felt the covers pulled up close to her chin, felt the cloth at her forehead, along her lips and cheeks and eyes, and heard the farmer's wife sigh. No, she would not mention her name. She would only stay long enough to grow strong, and then she would leave before her father could find her. Soon I will leave this place for America, she thought, and once again she retreated to sleep.

The next time she woke, the farmer's wife was ready with hot stirabout, poised on the edge of her bed with a bowl and a spoon. For the first time, Maura took a good look at her surroundings: a large one-room cottage, with chests and beds pushed against far walls, and all the household utensils hanging from pegs. Everything, from the hearth to the floorboards to the quilts to the framed family photograph on the largest chest of drawers, suggested clean, homely prosperity.

"You must eat some," said the farmer's wife when Maura shook her head at the sight of the breakfast mush. "You need your strength. Someone's here to take a look at you."

"Who's here?"

"Hush, don't be afraid," said the farmer's wife, smiling at Maura's alarm. "He's the gentlest soul in the county. And a neighbor. And a handsome young man."

"Who is he? What are you talking about? No one knows I'm here. You don't even know my name."

"I know it's Dooley, that's sure," said the farmer's wife with a smile. "Whether it's Brendt or Maura remains to be seen. Now, you'd better be eating some of this, or Patrick O'Connell isn't going to be happy at all with your color."

"I never told you my name was Dooley. I don't even know *your* name."

"You've been talking in your sleep for three days, child. And even in this part of the county we get news from the constables, we get the post, and we get the papers."

"Please," said Maura. Deliberately, she lowered her eyes, humbled her tone. "You've been so good to me. I'm afraid, and I have reason for my fear. I just want to know, why is Patrick here?"

"Patrick O'Connell lives not three miles from our walls. On a great farm that will be his brother's one day. If I see him once a week, it's a slow week. Sometimes I see him twice in one day. The big brute is half out of his mind with worry for the Dooley girls. For the Dooley girls on the other side of the mountain. Sure I didn't run to the alehouse with news of you, half dead and drowned, but my husband did. Proud as a peacock because our man found you on the beach, and myself brought you back to life, and pretty as a picture besides. So Patrick O'Connell hears of this wonder, and no sooner than the news is out, he comes running. He's outside, Paddy is. He wants to see if you're really one of the Dooley girls, and, from all you've said, I guess you are."

Maura had little time to collect her thoughts, to come to a decision. In a moment, the cottage door opened on the other side of the large room and Paddy walked in, his head bent to get under the low lintel. When he raised his eyes he saw her at once, and the shock of recognition reddened his boyish face.

"Thanks be to God you're all right," he said, hurrying to her side as quickly as his awkward frame and intense embarrassment would allow.

"Please, Patrick," said Maura. "Don't talk."

"Don't be crowding the girl," said the farmer's wife. "She's been at death's door and she needs the air, can't you see that, Paddy?"

"Could you please leave us?" said Maura, and with a great effort she raised her head from the pillow and tried to sit up.

"Now what do you think you're doing?" said the farmer's wife. "Get down with you, girl. You're not well."

"I'm better," said Maura, and she drew on all her strength and sat up in the bed, twisting her body so that she could lean against the wall. "Please," she said. "I must be alone with Patrick."

"Sure you know that can't be done—that's not decent, girl," said the farmer's wife. "And yourself in your bedclothes, and poor Paddy all blushing and panting like a bull."

"Please," said Maura. "Five minutes is all I'm asking. There's not a thing improper in five minutes."

"Who is she, Paddy? Brendt or Maura?"

"Maura Dooley, herself."

"And is it you, too, that wants me to leave?" said the farmer's wife, looking at the red-faced boy with severity.

"If it pleases you, ma'am," said Patrick.

"God save you if you're the cause of any of this girl's misfortune, Paddy O'Connell," said the farmer's wife. She got off the edge of the bed and stood next to Patrick's tall frame. "God save you if it was you who made her near to drowning. The poor sweet thing," she said, and she clutched Maura's hands and patted her cheek. "Five minutes, Paddy. And mind you be respectful of this house, and this young lady, as pretty as an angel."

The farmer's wife left them, leaving Patrick too stunned to ask Maura any of the questions that had been worrying him for days. But Maura, leaning against the wall, her mind very clear, very eager, began to speak at once.

"Patrick," she said, "Brendt is dead."

"Brendt," he said, tongue-tied. He was not stupid, but he looked at her stupidly.

"Do you understand what I'm telling you, Patrick?" said Maura. "Brendt is dead and gone."

Patrick's awkwardness at being in her presence broke. He was a spontaneous boy, given to wild enthusiasms, but everything he had ever learned about women had forced him to keep his emotions in check. Had Maura ever seen his joy at riding a horse, or winning an arm wrestle, or dunking his brother in a pond, she would have been amazed at his agility, his strength, his sense of purpose. But she had always seen him at his worst—clumsy with love, his passion twisting into silent blushes, dull eyes.

"Look at me," she was saying. "I need your help. My sister is dead. *Dead.*"

But he had already begun to react. He looked straight at her, his blush vanishing, tears filling his eyes. There was nothing awkward about the way he got to one knee before the bed, nothing clumsy about the way he took her hand, nothing stupid about the cries that broke the surface of his words. "Oh, my God— oh, merciful God," he said, and the tears ran down his cheeks.

Maura was struck by a sincerity, a good-heartedness, that had before been masked by his love. "I need your help," she said.

"Anything," said Patrick, letting the tears come, feeling the awful loss as if Brendt had been his sister, or his wife. "Please, Maura. My God. May God rest her soul. Poor Maura, poor Brendt."

"I'm all right," said Maura. "I've had all this time to understand."

"Let me help you," said Patrick. "I can't stand to see you looking so pale. Are you hungry? Are you warm enough?"

"Did you tell my father that you've found me?"

"No, I've only just found out myself. He's looking for you. For you both." Patrick picked up the bowl of stirabout left by the farmer's wife. "But you must eat something. I don't like how you look. Sure it does no one any good to have yourself starving."

"What is happening, Patrick?" said Maura, pushing away the stirabout. "Listen, we must hurry. What is happening? How is my mother? What does father say?"

"How could Brendt be dead?" said Patrick. "Tell me that, and I'll tell you everything. Where is she? How did she die?"

"It is enough to know that she is dead, I should be thinking," said Maura. "Sure the place of her body means nothing compared to the place of her soul."

"Brendt is at rest in heaven, with all the saints about her."

"If there's a heaven, she's there," said Maura. She was feeling strong now, and had to control all the sharp sensations and thoughts trying to grab her attention: If there was a heaven, Brendt could not go there, because she had broken's God's law by taking her own life. . . . Patrick had a lovely, clear look to his eyes, not at all like her brothers' squinty glances, the product of their dark, smoky cottage. . . . She had been in this place for at least three days, and surely she must leave at once if she ever wanted to get away from her father, from her home. "I will only miss mother," she said.

"What?" said Patrick, so that Maura realized she was thinking aloud, and steeled herself to be calm and clear.

"How is my mother?" she said.

"Your poor dear mother," said Patrick. "I saw her not two days ago and she gave me all the money she had in the world."

"What money?"

"And how can she live when she hears of Brendt? How can anyone tell her such a thing to her face?"

"Patrick O'Connell, *tell* me, what did my mother say? Why did she give you money?"

"It's my own fault, it is, for not finding you that night. It's my own fault that she's dead. Sure it's as if I put a knife into her heart, coming to your home and asking for her hand the way it was. She's dead, and sure I killed her, unless you tell me different. Please, Maura. How did she die?"

"Off a cliff."

"What?"

"Climbing," said Maura, and now she had a hint of what their relationship could be. He was not strong enough to know that Brendt had taken her own life; Maura was. She chose to spare him further pain, pain that could hamper his powers. She had need of Patrick whole and sane and full of right spirit. "We were in hiding up in the mountain, near the sea, and she fell. Sure it had nothing to do with you, Patrick. Brendt wasn't running from you at all, but only from our father. Know that, because it's true. She knew you were her friend, as I know you are mine."

"I am your friend, yes," said Patrick. "I will do anything for you."

Even in his guilt, in his sadness, she could see that he was admiring her, that his lips had the same tentative set that they'd had in the moment before he'd kissed her days before. But she could not imagine how far this admiration ran. She could not dream that Patrick worshiped her pale skin, her red-gold hair, her steady, fearless green eyes.

For Patrick, this beauty was but a shadow, a dim representation of her soul's worth. He could not help but idealize the girl, imagine her pure and perfect and capable of wonders of love, for this was how he himself dreamed of a wife. But now he could offer her nothing but friendship, unless she herself indicated a desire for something more. He could not bear to take advantage of his opportunity to carry her off, free her from trouble at home, if she did not love him. And with the terrible weight of Brendt's loss, he could hardly express his own needs. It was all he could do to speak out his offer of help, when what he really wished was to crush her lips to his and take her away in his arms to some fairy kingdom, somewhere beyond pain and sickness and death, somewhere beyond Ireland.

"What did my mother say to you?" said Maura, trying to keep the urgency from her voice.

"She knows that you can't go home—meaning you and Brendt both. She doesn't know about Brendt. How could she? Sure it will kill her, Maura. Who can tell a mother that her own daughter has gone?"

"Listen, Patrick. We only have a few minutes. No matter what you tell or don't tell others, the farmer's wife will have gotten the news about. It can't be long before my brothers come after me with their sticks and their guns. And how can I answer to my father for Brendt? You must help me. I must know what to do."

"I will help you with anything."

"The money." Maura took his hand and tried to hammer down his attention to her words. "My mother gave you money, you said. What for? How much? What does it have to do with you?"

"It's to run off," he said, his eyes wide with fear.

"She gave you money to run off?"

"Money for you and Brendt. To leave Ireland."

"Why did she give it to you?"

"I told her, Maura. I'm sorry, but I told her I'd marry you if you'd have me. It was only because of your father, himself getting crazy drunk and swearing to kill you, kill the both of you. Your mother said not to come home, never to come home; that she'd saved this money without your father knowing, and that it was for you to get out, to leave. She knew what you wanted, and she said that it was time, and I told her that I loved you, and she said that I must find you and take the money and take you and

Brendt to America." Without thinking, he'd gotten up from his half-kneeling position and sat down on the edge of the bed.

"You told mother that you wanted to marry me?"

"Yes."

"And did she give you her blessing?"

"She said to find you. Sure that's a blessing, a blessing that's with us."

"Can you write?"

"Of course I can write."

"Can you write a letter to my mother?"

"I can write anything, from my name to a book of the Bible."

"Listen, Patrick. I'm too tired, and I wouldn't know what to say. Tell her—write to her, I mean, and tell her that Brendt and I are going to America."

"What do you mean?"

"You heard me, Patrick. She must never know about Brendt. Her body has most likely washed out to sea. My mother must think that she's gone off to America. All three of us, do you understand? With my mother's money, we—all three of us—are going. Please write that in a letter, and then bring it back for me to see."

Still confused, Patrick was shocked to his feet by the sudden, thunderous voice of the farmer's wife. "Paddy O'Connell, how dare you!" she said. "How dare you sit on the young lady's bed!"

"I'm sorry," said Patrick, turning from the farmer's wife to Maura, and back again, his face reddening with speed.

"It's all right," said Maura to the farmer's wife.

"Not at all, not at all," she said. "It was my fault to allow him in here by himself, and yourself too weak to lift a finger."

"You don't understand," said Maura to the farmer's wife. And now she looked from her to Patrick. "Patrick and I are to be married."

"What?" said the woman, too astonished to notice the look of wonder and joy that broke across Patrick O'Connell's face. "You're to marry this no-good Paddy?" But she was laughing now, and clapping the tall boy on the back, and she kissed Maura's cheek.

"Maura is tired," said Patrick to the farmer's wife. He spoke gravely, gingerly, as if afraid to puncture the ethereal nature of the scene. It was the first time Maura had said she would marry him, and it was his way to believe that Maura had spoken spontaneously, from the heart. It would not have occurred to him for a moment that she had simply spoken to get rid of the farmer's wife. "If it pleases you, ma'am, we need a few minutes more together," said Patrick. He stood between Maura and the woman now, and he showed every intention of marching her out of her own room, her own house.

"But you must let her rest," she said.

"Of course," said Patrick. "Five minutes." And then they were alone, and he looked at Maura with wide, grateful eyes.

"Will you still have me?" said Maura.

"I love you," said Patrick.

"I want to be your wife," she said. "I want to be your wife, and I want you to take me to America."

"Yes," said Patrick. "That's what I want." And he was so sure of his love finding its way to her heart that he took hold of her hands and he kissed them, and he sat down on the edge of the bed and told her again that he loved her.

Maura leaned closer, seeing that he was about to grab her, and wanting to participate in the ritual. He kissed her lips for the first time, and she felt giddy, enjoying the sudden sensation of lightness in her head, of reckless freedom such as she had never before known. There was a possibility and a promise in that kiss, a promise that titillated more than it frightened. If she did not love him, she loved no other young man better. When she clutched Patrick to her, it was with all her force, all her will; there was nothing feigned about a passion urgent with discovery.

"You really must rest, Maura," he said. "Dear Maura—dear, sweet girl—oh, I'm so happy, I'm so happy." Only the sudden thought of Brendt, an unhappy specter passing through the back of his mind, cut short his ardor. He would have their whole lives to make love to her. Carefully, he kissed her cheek, helped her lower her head to the pillow.

"We must leave tonight," she said.

"Oh, no, you're too weak."

"If we don't leave tonight, my father will find me. You must write the letter to my mother. You must tell her that Brendt and I are both well and going with you to America. Tonight you will come back for me in your horsecart, and we will start at once for Cork."

"Maura, you don't know what you're saying," he said. But she scared him by her violent rising up from the pillow, by the anger flashing in her green eyes.

"If you love me, you'll do as I say. If you don't, we will never be married."

"I love you," he said in a small voice, wondering how she could possibly ever doubt him.

"Then come back for me tonight," said Maura.


Of course, he came back for her.

It was dark, and the farmer's wife screamed at her husband, and the husband spoke calmly to Patrick, asking him if he knew precisely what it was he was doing. But Maura had already dressed in the farmer's wife's clothing while Patrick continued to hold a shotgun in his hands, so nobody would run for the two hired men sleeping in the barn. Patrick left a guinea on the table, as much in thanks for the clothing that Maura took, and the food and care she'd been given, as for the promise of silence after their departure.

"I'm going straight to the priest," said the farmer's wife.

"Sure there's nothing I can do with the woman," said the farmer. "Not when she's like this."

But once they were in the horsecart, they cared little for what the farmer's wife could tell the priest. Patrick had not told his father a thing; he had simply taken the passage money from the lining of his father's ancient coat—the money due him for marrying an Irish Catholic—leaving in its place a letter of explanation and farewell. The letter to Maura's mother he had saved to show her, planning to post it from Cork.

"How much money do we have?" asked Maura. And when Patrick told her, the sum seemed vast, it seemed grand, it seemed the first step to a life of comfort and ease in the New World.

"It's not much, I know," said Patrick as they drove off in total darkness, letting the horse find his own way on the moonless night. "But it'll do for two steerage passages, and enough cash to keep us eating till I can get a job in New York. I'll do anything, sure I will, anything for my Maura."

But Maura, wrapped in blankets, was not thinking about steerage passages, nor was she imagining her Paddy sweeping streets. Drifting off to sleep, she dreamed of silks and satins, about buildings higher than mountains, about horseless carriages parading her about the grand boulevards of New York.


Nothing could break the back of her dreaming.

They drove for two weeks across Kerry and Cork, sleeping above the barns of friendly farmers. Patrick was careful not to touch her, fearful of further inflaming his passion. A priest outside Macroom married them, and then proceeded to lecture them on the evils of sexual desire. The union sanctified by the church, the couple continued on to the city of Cork, and rented a drab room at the top of a four-story house.

But none of this was grim, nor desperate, nor sad. Both of them could smell the sea from their room near the port. If their mattress ran with bugs, Patrick's lust blinded him to their presence. If her husband was covered with the dust and dirt of their voyage from the church outside Macroom, Maura's senses ignored this, drawing only on the closeness of the harbor, on the fact that ships waited at anchor, eager for passengers to the New World.

He didn't know how to be tender with her, though his love was sure, and kind. Clumsily, he pulled away her clothing. He pushed and probed at her breasts, into her belly, saying nothing, so in a hurry was he to consummate his wild desire. The sight of his penis, swollen and dribbling with semen, frightened her less than it was to hurt her moments later. When she cried out in pain, he laughed: He knew little, but he knew that it was the custom that virgins cried, that men exulted where women endured.

But Maura exulted, too. They were married. She had fulfilled her wifely duties. They were going to sleep that night in the port city of Cork. She had only to shut her eyes and she was transported: She saw herself on the upper deck of a great steamship, its prow cutting through the waves, her face framed in a silk shawl, Ireland receding behind her into the past forever.

The next day they saw the ship that was to carry them across the ocean. Even from a distance, its dull hulk looked filthy, ominously decrepit against a brilliant blue sky.

"We'll be all right," said Patrick. "'I swear to you it will be all right."

Maura blinked at him in the strong sunlight, and took a smile from her imaginary pose on the nonexistent upper deck and turned it on her loving husband. "Of course it will be all right," she said. "We're going to America."

# PART TWO

## Cork to New York, 1897

# ❀ CHAPTER ❀ FOUR

There was no glamourous mystery, no shimmering sea, no magic in those first tentative steps toward a distant horizon.

Maura and Patrick O'Connell followed the line of Irish peasants down the steep, narrow stairwell to the steerage compartment of the steamship *Knickerbocker*. The contemptuous Yankee sailors herding them below warned that no one was allowed topside the first day, and that anyone who tried to come up on deck would be tossed into the sea. No one listened very well to these empty threats. They had all paid twenty-nine dear dollars for one-way tickets to the land of promise; any harshness, any unpleasantness, were but motes added to the greater weight of suffering they had all endured in their homeland. Soon the ship would be under way, and any discomfort they experienced on board would vanish in the light of America. Most had heard that the voyage could take no longer than fourteen days, and was often accomplished in ten. What was such a short period of time?

"I love you," Patrick said as they took possession of a lower berth.

"Yes," said Maura. "Soon we'll be there."

"And it'll be grand," said Patrick, and he kissed her then, in full view of the growing crowd. But Maura didn't mind. Her husband was not the only one to be offering endearments in this squalid hole; there were many young couples, and much hand-holding and frenzied words of cheer to hold up against the fact of departure. And even before they had a chance to grow fully aware of their surroundings, most had to come to grips with their fear of the sea.

First there was the swaying of the ship as it pulled vainly at the dock and its anchors. The hatches were all open, bringing in the gray light and the scent of the endless water. Though born to an island, these men and women were people of the soil, and afraid to leave the shore. Even as they chattered, each listened for the sudden start of an engine, for the blast of a whistle, for the first great wave to batter the hull. They were sure they'd be seasick, though none could say with any assurance just how bad this would be. Bottles of poteen were passed from father to son; and one young newlywed, a Mr. Maloney from Dublin, sat on a low berth and slowly drank an entire jug of poteen he'd bought dockside, at Cork, convinced that it would prevent him from becoming seasick at all.

But after a half-hour in steerage, Maura had turned her thoughts from fear of the ocean to disgust at the prisonlike squalor being forced upon her. "Sure they don't mean to put any more down here," she said to Patrick.

"It will be all right," he assured her. No matter how many times he told himself that she was his wife, that he had made love to her, that he possessed her according to the laws of the church and the laws of man, he could not help but marvel at his fortune, could not help but revel in the sight of her beauty. Patrick touched her face gently, his eyes alive with passion.

"They're penning us in like sheep," said Maura, turning her face from his touch.

Patrick took her hand, to turn her about. Why, only last night he had lain with her; he had pushed her back on the narrow bed and insisted that she remove her clothes—all of them. And she had complied, of course, even if a bit reluctantly. It was a woman's way to be reluctant, even if only at first. Somehow he felt she must enjoy what thrilled him to the point of madness. They were both God's creatures, and, no matter what men said, he felt sure that women must derive some pleasure from the sexual act.

"Don't touch me now," said Maura sharply. "Sure there's all of Dublin here, and Cork and Belfast as well. Patrick, I mean it. Not here, with people about."

Patrick smiled. That was her way, but it was all right. She had married him, and that in itself was a statement of love. And no matter how strong her will, or how quick her temper, she was still his wife, still the beautiful woman with whom he slept in the black night.

Maura's concern with the steady stream of peasants filling the poorly ventilated space between the ship's hold and the deck began to be shared by other women and men in the steerage. Cries of wonder, shouts of rage, the indignant noises of people who had begun to understand their exploitation, drowned out the tramping of booted feet down the steel staircase.

The steerage compartment was almost completely filled with wooden bunks, arranged in three tiers, one on top of the other. Unless one was quite short, it was impossible to sit on any of the bunks without striking one's head on the bunk above it, or the bulkhead above the top bunk. Maura and Patrick had taken a lower bunk as soon as they'd entered, and as the passengers continued to crowd the compartment, every tier had been moved into by at least a pair of passengers.

"Four to a bunk, move it, move it, four to a bunk," said a tall Yankee sailor with a fierce black beard. He held up the line of passengers waiting to take possession of their sleeping quarters while he glared about the steerage with contempt. "Four to a bunk, move in there, this ain't first class. You there, sit down, move in with you, step lively, four to a bunk."

An old woman dared to voice her complaint as a young couple tried to share her bunk on a middle tier. It wasn't decent, she said, to allow the sexes to sleep in the same bed.

"Shut yer trap, Brigid!" said the sailor, slapping a cudgel into the palm of his hand. "No one's going to be interested in sex once we get a move on. Not you Irishers. You'll be too busy puking your guts out to think about anything."

"Sure it's not the words of justice and liberty I expected from an American!" said a kindly older man. "Sure we're all paying passengers, and decent people, and no one should talk to us like that."

"I said to shut it, Paddy! I'll break your bones in a second," said the sailor. "I'll throw you in the drink. You want to eat, you want to stay alive this trip, you keep your trap shut when

I tell you, and you open it for fleas if that's what I want. You
understand me, you dumb mick? This is our ship, and you're
going to our country, so don't give me no Irish lip."

Mr. Maloney, still drinking from his great jug, seemed about
to get up and make a comment. Patrick O'Connell, who was
bigger and stronger than most men on board, restrained him.
Even then Maura had a sense of her husband's poor qualifications for succeeding in this miserable new place. He was a good
man, one willing to follow orders, to respect authority, to obey.
Maloney and his young wife, Fiona, soon found themselves
pushing onto the O'Connells' lower berth, and Patrick not only
made no protest but welcomed them cheerfully. The berths were
six feet long and six feet wide; each person would have only
eighteen inches for the width of his body, crowded together like
convicts on the old transports to Australia. There were no chairs
belowdecks, and there was no room for them in any case. If one
stood, it would be to stand sideways between the bunks. If one
sat, it would be in the same filthy space where one slept. The
steamship company provided no blankets, no pillows, no mattresses; it had been their experience that such frills only led to
further infestation by a variety of vermin.

"I think that's the end of it," said Patrick with a smile.

Every bunk was filled. They lay there, exhausted, looking up
at the underside of the bunk above them, waiting for movement.
Fiona Maloney lay between Maura and Mr. Maloney, with Patrick on Maura's other side.

"Mr. Maloney is a very brave man," said Fiona, who was no
more than twenty but spoke to Maura as if from a height of
maturity and experience. "He's only drinking because of his
dad. His dad said the whiskey would numb his stomach; and if
the stomach's numb, you can't get seasick. Otherwise Mr. Maloney wouldn't be drinking. Otherwise he's a complete gentleman. If it wasn't that he was so cautious with his money, he says
to me, we would go second class. But it's all right, except for
the washrooms. The washrooms are bad. But they get seasick in
second class, too."

The black-bearded sailor slammed his cudgel against an overhead steel pipe to claim his captives' attention. He announced

himself as their steward, responsible for doling out their meals, apportioning their fresh water, listening to their complaints. "And if anything's really bothering Your Highnesses, I'll be happy to point you in the direction of home."

The steward laughed at his own joke, and then drew himself up seriously. "You get water once a day, unless we think the trip's going to take too long, and then we cut back. The water's for drinking, not washing. You got a whole ocean full of water for washing if you don't mind the salt. When you puke up, clean up after yerselves, because no one else is going to do it, you hear me? Now, I know you Irishers like to fight over who's taking up how much of the bunk, and didn't you steal my mother's best shawl while I was asleep, but I'm telling you all, once and for the last time, you try any fighting and I break yer bones and put you in irons in the hold. Do all you gentlefolk understand my English?"

At that moment, the enormous screws beneath the steerage began to stir. For a split second, there was total silence among the passengers. Then there was a shout of fear, followed by a hundred exclamations of surprise, wonder, and uncertainty. Were they moving? What was that noise? Couldn't the water get in through the open hatches? Oh, couldn't they feel the rocking? They must be moving—everything was shaking, everything was turning round and round!

"Shut yer bloody traps!" screamed the steward. He slammed his cudgel against a pipe, against a bulkhead, against the side of a bunk. "Nobody move! Stay in yer bunks, you chicken-hearted sodbusters! We haven't even started to go, and listen to you! Shut yer traps—nobody move or I'll break all yer bones!"

All at once a whistle sounded, loud and imperious. It blew again, and then three times in rapid succession. "Yer all going to be sick—you always are, damn you," said the steward contemptuously.

Maura found herself gripping Patrick's hand.

"Hey, sure it's going to be fine, dear girl," he said. "Close your eyes and we'll be fine and dandy in the United States of America, walking with our heads up high."

A pale wisp of black smoke blew past a hatchway. Mighty engines grew louder. For the first time that day, Maura was happy to be in Patrick's presence, to be his wife. He was weak, he wasn't the cleverest of men, but he was good. If he didn't know enough to struggle, she would show him how. If he didn't know enough to be aggressive, she would be aggressive enough for the both of them—and he would be always there to defend her.

"What's that sound, Patrick?"

"Only the motor. Sure it's good to hear. It means we're that much closer, darling."

"Of course," said Maura. "We'll be out of this soon, won't we?"

They were moving, everyone said so, and Maura felt Fiona Maloney clutch her wrist in terror. Someone on a high bunk began to sing in Irish, a lilting, happy song of the shepherd's life. But the man's fright could not be covered by the brave lyrics; as the ship took a slight turn, as the screws beneath the steerage let out a mightier groan the man's voice ran up the scale. A fiddler tried to take over for him when he had given up singing, but a jig was a very poor weapon against the black smoke, the sudden flash of western sun as they steamed out of the harbor. A hatch slammed shut of its own accord, a man's boot fell off his bunk, a woman complained about an elbow in her face; but in that first long hour of the sea voyage, what mattered more than the sudden fits and starts of the engine, the inexplicable whining of the ship's supports, the isolated crying of a baby, was the overwhelming sense that it was not so bad.

It was not pleasant to lie four in a bunk, the smell of the sea overpowered by the smell of the passengers' sweat—but it was not at all what they had feared. Soon, men were standing between the bunks, some climbing up the tiers to be able to look out a hatchway at the sea. The fiddler began to play again, and this time his tune was not so urgent, not so wild to cover up fear. Women began to air out their families' clothing, choosing the shawl that would line their part of the bunk, the pants that would be their blanket for the duration of the voyage. Mr. Maloney continued to drink from his great jug, but the liquor made him very content and quiet, and his wife let go her grasp on Maura's arm.

"I think I'm going to wash up," said Maura. She got off the bunk, narrowly missing a man's swinging foot as he began to jump off the bunk above her. When she stood up, she was very pleased. There was a sensation of motion, but there was no rocking or swaying, no terrible sense of imbalance. She walked sideways between the bunks, where an arrow pointed to the washroom for "Females."

Everyone seemed to be getting up from their bunks now, but the sudden overcrowding in the aisles created no arguments. People were too happy about the smoothness, the easiness of the voyage to do anything but smile and be gracious to each other. Maura got in line behind four other women waiting to get into the washroom, and she felt as patient, as good-natured, as any of them. This would be her last time sailing steerage anywhere, she told herself. Once in America, her life would soon become first-class, of that she was certain. What did it matter that she had to share this filthy compartment with hundreds of peasants? They were not hurting her, and the voyage did not make her sick. That was all that mattered at the moment.

The washroom was only a foot wider than her bunk, and about three feet longer. Ten faucets—five on each long side of the room—dribbled cold seawater into ten ancient basins. When it was Maura's turn to go in, she found a woman or girl at every faucet but one. This was hers for the moment; she filled her basin, and then splashed the cold salt water into her face, about her wrists, around her neck. The woman next to her had long white hair, and she had unaccountably let loose the hair from its bun and begun to lather saltwater suds into it. Another woman brushed her teeth with salt, rinsing with seawater and spitting into her basin.

Most of the women in the washroom simply did as Maura did, washing quickly, without benefit of soap, wanting only to refresh themselves and not take too much time. But there were women who would use their basins, once they had charge of them, for hours, fiercely guarding their space in the washroom. They would shampoo their hair, brush their teeth, wash out

their tin cups, and do their laundry, no matter how long it took
or how many people waited. It was their way of escaping from
the endless noise, the ceaseless motion of hundreds of crammed-
together bodies.

A woman came out from the other end of the washroom,
where six toilets were jammed together in an iron square. She
was red-faced and there were tears at the corners of her eyes:
"A disgraceful, ungodly ship this is," she said—and at that
moment, the ship hit the first great swells of the ocean voyage.

Maura felt the floor beneath her rise up and down, slowly,
gently. She swallowed, trying to force back the panic rising up
in her gorge. What could this possibly mean? There was no
storm outside the hatchways. Everything had been so easy, so
calm. Maura, like everyone else in the tiny room, held on to a
faucet, afraid to take a step. She felt swindled, as if the ship,
which had been so surprisingly pleasant at first, had betrayed
a promise.

Moment by moment the swells lifted the ship higher. And
as the floor moved up and down with the even rhythm of the
waves, a bar of soap fell off a ledge, a basin slid across the tiny
aisle between the ten women. There was a scream from the main
compartment, and then another, and another still. Maura wasn't
sure what she should do: whether she should simply walk out
of the little washroom and, holding on to the tiers of bunks,
make her way slowly back to Patrick; or remain where she was,
holding the faucet so tightly that it threatened to come off the
wall, until the ship returned to its earlier state.

"Are you all right?" said the old white-haired woman, who
had continued to wash her hair. "You look like you want to
chuck over, darling. It's only the waves, isn't it now? Just water,
you pretty thing." The old woman shrugged and went on rinsing
out her hair. "You'd better get used to it. This is the way it's
going to be for the next ten days."

Maura later learned that the woman had been married to a
fisherman, and now that she'd become a widow, she was following her children to America. She had sailed on countless fishing
boats from the small island where she'd grown up off the coast
of Clifden, in Galway. She knew that the endless rocking of the

ship was gentle, a reminder that the water was in motion, that they were steady and easy on their distant course. But Maura didn't know this, or, if she did, she didn't quite believe it. Her stomach was nearly empty, but a bubble of fear rose from there to the back of her throat; she could sense the vile odors within her body, she could feel the frailty of her flesh.

And Maura was not alone. Though most of the women in the washroom tried to be brave, their faces were as grim as Maura's. Each waited for the next blow of fate: a bolt of lightning, a collision with a monstrous creature of the sea. Still, when it didn't become worse, when the gentle rocking became a constant, an awful fact that wouldn't go away, but at least did not worsen, women went back to their washing, their feet solidly planted on the wet, swaying floor.

"Watch it, out of my way!" said a young woman, rushing into the crowded room, looking for an empty basin. There was none, however, and as she looked wildly about the room, her lips opened and she ejected a thin gruel through clenched teeth. Then she could hold back no longer. The sight and smell of this disgorged fluid of her stomach so weakened her that it was all she could do to sink to her knees and clutch at Maura's basin without smashing her head into the rusty iron wall. Immediately she threw up, vomiting the contents of her stomach in terrible spasms. Everyone clustered around her while she continued to vomit, her head shaking against the basin until the old white-haired woman knelt beside her and held her shaking head in large, work-worn hands.

Maura backed away from them. She knew she was about to be sick, and she didn't want it to be here, on her knees in front of the others. She stepped down the two iron steps to the toilet area, and was greeted by a fecal smell and the sight of another woman on her knees, violently sick.

*No*, thought Maura to herself, biting her tongue till the pain beat back her nausea. The ship tilted slowly up, and slowly back down. Maura looked away from the sick woman to the opposite row of toilets, determined to be stronger, determined to be well. Black bugs the size of her index finger ran across the floor and up the iron wall against which she leaned. She forced herself to think of the end of the voyage: New York with its buildings scraping the sky, with ladies in sable coats and men in silk top hats; and every rich man in the country was once poor, once an immigrant, fighting back nausea in a filthy hole like this one.

The toilets were no more than low trenches in an iron floor, fronted by a rusty iron step, backed by an iron wall that slanted slightly, reflecting not an accommodation for a woman's back but the shape of the ship's sides. Maura tried to back away from the stench, from the black bugs looking for food in the fecal waste, from the sick woman clutching the iron step while the ship continued to roll. But even as she escaped the tiny area of toilets, she backed into the washroom, and was overcome at once by the smell of half a dozen women, all vomiting into the basins where a moment before she and the others had been washing their hands, their hair, their teeth. It seemed as if every woman on the ship were trying to gain entry to the tiny space, and all for the same purpose. Maura felt herself gagging at the stench, and at the sense of being unable to escape fast enough. If only she could push away from the screaming bodies; if only she could be alone with her strength, under a slant of light, a shaft of air. But Maura could not budge.

All at once a sharp pain twisted into new life in the pit of her belly. She opened her mouth, and for a full moment of horror realized that she was about to lose control of her physical being. She was about to throw up, like these weaker women, and there was nothing she could do to prevent it. Incensed, humiliated, Maura struck out at the woman nearest her, determined to at least make a place for herself to vomit out her miserable insides. But she struck without strength, and the woman in her way was succumbing to the mass revulsion and hysteria and was herself sinking to her knees. Maura joined her on the floor, joined her and a dozen others, two dozen perhaps, throwing up into basins, onto the floor, no longer caring what she looked like, whom she failed, wanting only to rid herself of the roiling contents of her stomach.

It was over quickly, and she was able to stand without aid. But as she staggered backward into the wall of women, she became aware of the screaming from inside the steerage's main section. Maura was afraid to enter there, but she was more afraid to stay in the miserable washroom, sick with the smell of weakness and disease. Wiping the sweat off her forehead, out of her eyes, she followed the white-haired older woman, whose hair was still flecked with soapsuds, past the seasick women who were trying to enter the washroom.

"You'll be all right now, darling," said the white-haired woman to Maura. "It's not so bad when you've got it up and out of you, is it now?"

"I'm all right," said Maura. The two of them were looking at the pandemonium among the steerage passengers, and each wanted to dissociate herself from the general weakness. Most everyone had gone back to his or her narrow portion of bunk, where they lay looking up in wonder or sat with head bowed, groaning. Everyone who had left the tight tiers of berths seemed headed for the washrooms, or simply for a space in the aisle, to throw up.

The Yankee steward stood near the staircase leading to the deck. "Filthy weak-kneed micks," he said as Maura and the older woman walked past.

"Sure it's brave of you to be boasting of your iron stomach," said the widow. "I'd like to see you off the coast of Galway in a net full of dead fish, with the waters raging. These people have never been to sea."

"They're making their own sea here, a sea of puke, ain't they now, you old bag of bones," he said, massaging the length of his cudgel.

"The devil take you, you rotten bastard," said Maura.

The steward only smiled at this. He had seen the auburn-haired beauty when she'd first crossed the gangplank. Well, in a few days more she'd be less beautiful, and much less proud. "I ain't no Roman, honey," he said with a leer. "I don't worry about no devils. And if you don't neither, you ought to be a little nicer to me, or you're going to be one hungry little Brigid when you crawl off this boat."

The older woman dragged Maura off before mutual insults could grow into a vendetta. Anger had driven blood back to her face, and Maura walked the swaying floor of the steerage without trepidation. She felt weak, empty, and her head throbbed; but unlike so many others, whose seasickness had only begun with vomiting, Maura felt better, and was no longer afraid of the nausea that lingered about the corners of her throat, the restless pit of her voided belly.

She joined Patrick on the low bunk, and though he didn't complain, she could feel his fear, could sense his sickness. Mr. Maloney had stopped drinking, and his poor wife watched his sweaty, ashen face as if he were on his deathbed.

As the hours passed into darkness, and no light or food was brought belowdecks, the exhausted emigrants resolved to come to an understanding with their environment. The ship rocked back and forth, gently, inexorably, and would not stop this until they reached New York harbor. Smells of rotten fruit, garlic, fecal waste, whiskey, and medicine would not lessen; they would only intensify with each passing day. Babies would not cease their cries; neither would some men and women ever get used to the nausea, the dizziness, the terrible disorientation that constituted seasickness. Even those less sick, or not affected at all by the rhythm of the waves, had to come to terms with the pounding of ancient engines, the constant grinding of the giant screws beneath them, the inescapable sense of being assaulted by noise, and odors, and darkness, and close quarters; by the ineffable taste of poverty and death in the air.

In the middle of that first night, Maura felt her husband calling her, as if from a distance, his words obscured by the sound of the engines, by the whispered groaning of the passengers, trying to find solace in dreams. She woke to the light of a single candle, held before Patrick's bloodshot eyes.

"What?" she said. "You're not sick, are you?"

"Maloney," said Patrick. "Careful of your head," he added, for she was about to sit up too smartly, and would have knocked her head on the bunk above.

Maura turned to her dark side, groping for Fiona Maloney, and blinking and straining her eyes. Patrick got off the bunk and brought the candle around to the Maloneys' side. Maura saw that Fiona was on the floor, kneeling over the dark body of her husband.

"Help me," said Fiona. "Sure it's only air he's needing, but he's needing it bad."

Patrick handed the candle to Maura, and she could see that he was in no condition to drag anyone up the stairs to the deck and the night air. But she made no protest. Fiona was trying to help, her eyes filled with tears, showering her husband with incoherent Gaelic endearments. Maura slowly got off the bunk, very conscious of the hundreds of tired bodies sleeping in the dark.

"I can help," she whispered to Patrick as she put down the candle in its dish on the edge of the berth.

"Just hold the candle, and that's all the help Paddy O'Connell is needing, thank you," he said.

Like a scene from a miracle, Maura's husband lifted the still body of Mr. Maloney from the floor to his shoulders in a single movement. Maura picked up the candle and sidled off first, her bare feet on the worn wood floor between the endless bunks. Patrick followed with his great burden, and behind him Fiona, reaching up to Maloney's dangling hands.

If anyone woke, no one stirred from a bunk. After hours of nausea and weakness, this procession through the huddled masses could excite nothing but a distant curiosity, like figures in a swiftly passing dream.

"I'll get the steward," said Maura in a whisper when they had neared the staircase. She was certain that her husband could never make it all the way up to the deck with Maloney's inert weight on his back.

Patrick came up so close to her that she could see the veins standing out in his taut forehead. He spoke so softly that she could barely make out his words: "No steward," he said. "Go up."

Maura did as she was told. She had no idea where the steward was in any case, and he was hardly her friend. Slowly, she climbed the steel staircase, her feet cold on the damp stairs. As the night air drifted down to her, she woke up more fully. There was a breeze, and the smell of the sea overpowered the cabin smells in a delicious rush. Somewhere a bell sounded, then it sounded four more times, in rapid succession. Maura shielded the candle flame against the breeze and stepped out onto the deck, looking out in wonder at the black waters, lit by a full moon and an endless vista of stars. Without thinking, forgetting why she was there, she stumbled forward to the rail.

Here, on the deck, all the confused sounds of the steerage made perfect sense. There was less a sensation of swaying, more a feeling of forward motion, of swift churning through the waves. The screws were no longer directly beneath her feet, nor were the engines pounding next to her sleeping head. Here, their muffled sounds were delicious, comforting, a fit accompaniment to the sound of rushing water, the cries of the men on a higher deck, the clear, invigorating night air. Once again, Maura felt anything was possible. They would be free, they would be well, they would be wealthy and at ease with the world.

"Maura!" she heard, at a little distance, and she turned from the rail and walked slowly, with a smile on her face, to where Patrick and Fiona knelt over Maloney's supine body.

"Get her away from here," said Patrick to his wife. Fiona was quiet, her eyes wide with wonder.

"What?" said Maura, not understanding. She wanted to be alone at the rail, looking out to sea.

"Take her down," said Patrick.

"No," said Maura. "It's good up here. Sure it's what we came up for."

"Please, darling," said Patrick in a thin, weary voice. "His wife doesn't understand. You have to take her down, because she doesn't understand what's happened."

Two sailors, one with a lantern swinging from a short chain, approached the little steerage group. Bringing the lantern close to Maloney's face, one of the sailors said: "I'll get a blanket. If there's a priest, you'd better get him fast. The captain don't allow stiffs on deck for very long."

Maura felt a harsh stab of pain in the back of her throat. "He can't be dead," she said, her voice catching. "He was only drinking poteen."

"*Take his woman,*" said Patrick.

Maura looked stupidly from Patrick to Fiona. Of course he could be dead from poteen, she thought. Bad poteen could kill in a half-hour. Cheap poteen, drunk in quantity, on an empty stomach, could release a slow-acting poison, twisting from a man's belly into his brain. It used to be her father's best advertisement when someone in a neighboring county killed himself drinking badly distilled whiskey. Bill Dooley's whiskey was expensive, but it never killed anyone, and it tasted better than the Parliament liquor they brought in by the wagonload from the city of Cork.

"Fiona," said Maura, touching the older girl's wrist.

The twenty-year-old Mrs. Maloney turned to look at the seventeen-year-old Mrs. O'Connell, and Maura could see that the wonder in her eyes was not at the fact of death, not at the brutal sense of loss, not at the ineluctable state of widowhood. Fiona Maloney was filled with the wonder of a child. She had assimilated nothing of more impact than that her husband didn't move, he didn't speak, he didn't breathe. She would not be helped by being led to understanding. Maura allowed her the minutes of noncomprehension. She would not be the one to explain that her husband, who had simply been drinking whiskey so as not to be seasick, was dead. Instead, she took Fiona's hand and walked her away from the body, and the sailors, and Patrick, and took her to the rail at the edge of the lower deck.

"Look, Fiona," said Maura. "Look how clear it is tonight."

"Sure it's a beautiful night," said Fiona.

"The sky seems wider here than in Kerry," said Maura.

"It's the same sky," said Fiona. "Don't be getting silly now." And she took hold of Maura's hand with sudden, urgent power. "He was only drinking," she said. "Only because of what his dad said. Only so as not to be sick. He doesn't want to be sick when we get to America."

Fiona started to turn round, and Maura could see that the wonder was turning to horror. A short man in dark clothes came at a fast walk from the upper deck, carrying a bundle on his shoulder.

"No, Fiona," said Maura. "Come this way."

"What is that man carrying?" said Fiona.

"I don't know."

"He was only drinking!"

"Fiona, it's all right."

"What is that man carrying? What are they doing there?" Fiona would not go where Maura wanted, and the older girl was too strong in her sudden understanding to be held back. The short man threw down the blanket he was carrying at the side of Maloney's body, as Fiona and Maura rejoined the group.

"She shouldn't be here," said Patrick. "It's not decent."

"What are you doing?" said Fiona. "He was only drinking! Damn you, leave him alone, it's only the liquor that's made him like this!"

She threw herself on Maloney's corpse as the sailors began to wrap him in the blanket, and one of the sailors pushed her violently away. In a moment, Maloney was wrapped completely around. Only his bare feet showed, glowing in the yellow light of the lantern.

Fiona no longer tried to throw herself on the body. The blanket had removed him from the world of men; his still, naked feet were already walking in the world of the dead. She retreated slowly from the group about the body and huddled on her knees at the top of the steerage staircase. Fiona cried, she moaned, but quietly, releasing no great keen until the men had lifted the blanketed corpse and swung it over the lower deck's rail and into the sea.

Then the widow's cry broke out, wordless, powerful, reaching back a thousand generations, and blowing away in moments to nothing.

# ❧ CHAPTER ❧
# FIVE

On the fourth day at sea, Maura noticed bloodstains on the back of Patrick's trousers. It was midday, an hour before the black-bearded steward would appear with half a dozen sailors, each manning an enormous kettle of lukewarm food: probably a stew, with flecks of rancid beef swimming in a watery mess of potatoes and greens.

"Where are you going?"

"Sure it's no secret now," said Patrick, grinning broadly, though his face was as white as if he hadn't seen the sun in a hundred days.

"Darling, it's not good to go too much," she said, reaching out for his hand as he got off the bunk and stood before her in the narrow aisle.

"It's not me then, is it, who tells me when I go and when I don't?" he said with a smile. "The Lord works in mysterious ways—now that's a fact for you."

Irreverence for the Lord was so out of keeping with Patrick's nature that Maura started, even though in her heart of hearts she wouldn't have cared if the whole steerage got up and cursed the name of the Holy Church in unison.

"Sure I don't mean anything disrespectful," said Patrick, afraid he'd gone too far. "It's just that it's no better, and there's nothing I can do. I wish I could be stronger is all."

"You're strong," said Maura.

"No," said Patrick. "I'm one of the weakest on board, and

that's something I have to live with and I'll always be sorry for."

"Don't you have to go?" said Maura, seeing that he was about to sit down again.

"I think it passed," he said. "Thank God, I think it passed."

But before Patrick could reclaim his space on the lower berth, the pain in his bowels returned with sudden force, and he let out a little cry, shutting his eyes and reaching blindly for something to support his body. Maura took hold of him, getting to her feet and wrapping her arm about his waist.

"I'm all right," he said.

"I'll walk you."

"No. I'm fine, sure I am."

But Maura refused to listen to his pride. He tried not to lean on her; but every so often, as they made the laborious trek to the men's toilet area, the pain would clutch at him, and he in turn would pull at his wife with a force outside his control.

"Leave me, please," he said, when they were within a couple of paces of the washroom.

"I'll try and get you some more water."

"I'm not thirsty."

"If I get the water, sure you'll drink it," said Maura. "Now go on. And please be careful not to hurt yourself."

Even with the door shut and the toilets separated from the cabin by the length of the men's washroom, the stench was unbearable. In four days, no one had cleaned any of the washrooms or toilets in steerage with anything but a cursory splash of disinfectant, as if one vile smell tossed over another would make things livable.

With a strength that was unique among the women of the steerage, Maura ran up the staircase to the lower deck. Here, in an alcove not five feet from where Mr. Maloney's corpse had been wrapped in a gray blanket, the steward dispensed hot and cold drinking water.

"You've had your ration, Brigid," he said to Maura, before she could make her demand to his arrogant face.

Quickly, she caught her breath and stared at him with hate in her eyes.

"Well, it's water you want," he said, "and I'm saving your

breath so you don't have to bother asking for it. I'm doing you a favor, and that's all the thanks I get? Just that ugly face of yours?"

"There's plenty of water," said Maura finally. "I only need a little."

"Are you thirsty then?"

"My husband is sick, and you know it well."

"It's not good to marry a sickly man. Not good stuff for the life he's going to be leading in America."

"What do you know of it, you rotten blackguard?"

"You look pretty with a little color in your face. If you want, I'll give you a drink. You can have it right here."

"I want some boiling water for my husband," said Maura.

"I didn't think you Irish went in for tea."

"Hot water and brandy for his stomach," said Maura wearily. "He needs water because of his being sick."

"Because he's got the Irish shits you mean," said the steward.

Maura didn't strike him, because the black-bearded man began to look to his pot of boiling water. Perhaps he would give her an extra ration after all.

"Please," said Maura. "I would like some hot water."

"Well then, since you've said it so nice," said the steward. He turned to the great tub of cold water and, dropping a filthy bowl into it, drew out a pint of the precious stuff and splashed it into his face and beard.

Maura held back once again. She would have liked to tell him precisely why she hated him: For purposely letting half the portion drip back into the pot when he doled hot food into the battered tin plates. For ignoring the weaker element of the steerage, those unable to make their way past the stronger emigrants huddling about the giant kettles and demanding extra rations. For refusing blankets to those who were cold, medicine to the sick, water to the thirsty. For deliberately baiting strong men into fights with sailors, who outnumbered them and enjoyed bashing the Irish emigrants as a shipboard sport. For allowing the toilets to become cesspools of filth and degradation. For serving food that made dysentery rampant among the steerage passengers. And, even more than any of these things, she hated him for the way he looked at her. His eyes seemed to say that he knew her better than she knew herself, and that this knowledge was an understanding of her weakness—she would do anything to survive.

"I would like some hot water, please," Maura said again.

"D'ye mind if I wipe my face first?" he said. "Even if it ain't the custom where you come from, in America we wipe our faces." And the steward picked up a filthy black rag and dragged it across his brazen face. Then, finally, he took the tin cup she extended to him and dipped it into the kettle of boiling water. "I'm only doing this because you're pretty enough."

Maura took hold of the tin cup, but with his other hand he grasped her thin wrist. "Don't you say thank you when you get a compliment, Mrs. O'Connell?"

"Thank you," she said.

The steward still held her wrist, and he looked at her with a smile of possession. The gift of the hot water was something for which he was even now being paid. "I can get you some meat if you want. Good meat from second class. The whole second class is practically empty. It wouldn't be hard."

"Let go of my wrist," said Maura.

"Would you like some meat?" said the steward. "You don't want to lose your figure eating this steerage crap."

"I'd like some meat."

"Maybe I can get you some."

"Maybe you can," said Maura; but then her body revolted at his touch, and she let go of the cup of hot water and wrenched her wrist so violently away from him that the precious ration spilled onto the steward's lap.

"What the hell, you bitch!" he said, and he was out of his seat, slapping at his legs as if they were on fire.

"Don't touch me," said Maura, and she picked up the tin cup from where it had dropped onto the deck, and slowly dipped it into the kettle of hot water.

"You've had your ration," said the steward.

"Well, I'm taking another, you bastard," said Maura, and she took the full cup and walked off. If he had followed her down the staircase, she would have splashed the hot stuff into his face, she would have tripped him on the steel steps, she would have torn out his eyes.

Fiona Maloney was by herself on the lower bunk when Maura returned with the water. "Patrick's not back yet?" said Maura, though Fiona hardly heard.

"There's sharks there," said Fiona. "Sure they've eaten him up long since."

"Fiona, stop it," said Maura. Turning her back to the young widow, she found the little flask of brandy in the pocket of Patrick's worn greatcoat. She poured in a few drops of the rich liquid, and then added a spoonful of sugar from their single small can.

"It's all because my dowry was no more than my face and a couple of pins. What does it matter if I wanted to stay in Ireland? What does that have to do with anything? I'm just an ignoramus, and so was my dead dad, dead in a workhouse like a common laborer. My father, and his father, all were educated, but sure that doesn't mean a thing to the fine Maloneys. They have relatives in Pittsburgh, America, so they are big, smart people, all of them. He'd be alive if I had my way."

"Fiona, listen," said Maura. "He is in a better place. It's not your part to question the Lord in these things."

"Sure you're the religious one! Haven't I heard you cursing Jesus every night of this trip?"

"Never," said Maura.

"No? If it wasn't you, it was me then. And I've got the right to curse him, too. I'm twenty, and I'm as good as dead. They sent Mr. Maloney off to hell without a priest, without a bit of earth, without a service or a headstone. Just the sharks. And in the lining of his clothes he had American greenbacks, dollar bills that were in piles just before we left. Piles and piles, enough to give us a start."

Maura had heard this, too, many times. She put down the hot cup and took hold of Fiona's shoulders. "Don't make yourself sick, Fiona. If the man is gone, he's gone. If the money's gone, that's the end of it. You've still got your health, you're young and pretty, and America is still where we're all going. Don't forget that I'm your friend. And Patrick, too."

"I hope we all sink," said Fiona. "It would be only fair if we all went down like Mr. Maloney."

"Stop that talk!" said Maura, suddenly afraid that the wish might come true.

"I'm not going to do it," said Fiona. "I'm not going to spend the rest of my days on my hands and knees, cleaning up some great lady's floor. I'm not a slave, even if Mr. Maloney died like one. If I'd stayed in Ireland, I could've been something. My mother thought I'd be a schoolteacher. Now what have I got to teach? I'm nothing, and I've got no one, and I'm off to be a slave in a foreign country where everyone hates us."

"You have Mr. Maloney's relations in Pittsburgh. Sure you remember them," said Maura.

"I don't. I don't know their names, I don't have their address. Everything's gone with Mr. Maloney, and there's no one in the world who cares a damn about me."

"There's Patrick and myself—"

"Patrick and yourself," mimicked Fiona. "That's very grand. With him half dead, and you younger, poorer, and more ignorant even than me, that's a grand consolation you're offering, Maura O'Connell. A grand consolation."

When Patrick returned to the bunk, he held a weak smile on his face, but he was so debilitated from the dysentery that two men had taken hold of him at the elbows and supported him all the way to Maura. She administered the brandy and water, and Patrick took a few drops of it to show that he appreciated her care; but he was too tired to swallow more, too weak to think of eating any of the midday meal. Maura woke him in the early evening, insisting that he eat an orange—all the emigrants were laden with this fruit, mysteriously supposed to prevent scurvy and a hundred other ailments—and Patrick looked at her wonderingly in the soft, swaying lamplight, his eyes bright with an unending fatigue.

"I don't want an orange," he whispered. "I want you."

"Stop being foolish," said Maura trying to omit the distaste from her voice. On her left, Fiona lay in a fetal position, knees drawn up, chin tucked down against her chest, her thumb jammed into the corner of her mouth. Though the ship's engines pounded and the ocean swells were, if anything, a shade rougher than usual, most of the steerage passengers were quiet, lying flat in their bunks, trying to force the passage of time. Soon the dark evening faded into night, the few lamps were extinguished, and all tried to sleep in the shut-up, noxious air. There was more space in their bunk since Maloney's corpse had been tossed overboard, but with Fiona's awkward writhing, and Patrick's incessant desire to touch his wife, Maura had no more room than before. She waited for him to wake.

"Maura," said Patrick, his voice so dry and weak it terrified her.

"Please have a little drink," she said.

But he wasn't listening. Slowly, he turned his body to face hers. Opening his mouth as if to speak, he pushed his head forward and gently touched his lips to her eyes, to her forehead, to her cheek.

"Please have something to eat, Paddy," she said. "If you love me."

There was no doubt that he loved her. How else explain the madness that drove him? Too weak to eat, he was not too weak to think of making love. Maura returned his kisses, slowly, with a warmth that was part nursemaid, part maternal. She felt no desire for her husband, and wondered only at his lust for her in the midst of sickness, in the midst of this filthy hole. With her eyes shut, she could hear the animal grunts of other men expressing their passion. Above her, perhaps on the third tier, the handsome young man from Tyrone might be responsible for the muted sounds of wifely pain; the sudden exclamation of male satisfaction; the quiet, nearly inaudible sharp breaths, mingled with muffled sobs. Across from her there were more sounds—even an occasional indecent laugh. The steerage was filled with newlyweds, and, although in bed with another sleeping couple, some of them had no shame.

Soon Maura's kisses soothed her husband. Patrick rested his head on her breast and slept, and Maura allowed this for a long time. The giant screws stirred beneath her, the foghorn broke through the rhythm of the engines, and Patrick's breath came shallow and swift, but steady. Her eyes open in the dark, she

imagined the bunks above her swaying downward; she imagined
a black bug hurtling through the air; she imagined a great whale,
a sea monster, rushing through waters too deep to chart and
rising up with speed beneath their miserable ship, sending everyone crashing through the ravaged hull into the black, raging
waters.

Maura grew suddenly angry at her own vision. Did she want
to die, like Fiona, like her own sister Brendt? she thought. Was
she that weak, that afraid?

"Wake up, Patrick O'Connell," she said in a quiet, but determined, voice. "Come on, Paddy," she said and she touched
his cheek.

Patrick didn't move.

She was suddenly too tired and frightened to think rationally.
It would have been simple to turn his head, to feel if the breath
of life was running through him. But in the dark, in the filthy
space crammed with a hundred nightmares, a thousand dreams
coming and going throughout the night, it was easy to panic. In
a moment she decided that he was dead, and her worst fears
about her own character were realized: She shed no tear for
Patrick, only for herself.

What would she do, now that she was alone?

With his head still on her breast, the hungry, fanciful bride
of seventeen found herself enumerating her troubles rather than
crying for her groom. She imagined herself alone, leaving the
ship in New York without a penny, without knowing a soul. She
was strong, hale enough to take on domestic work, but the
thought that she had endured so much only to work as a poorly
paid servant made her seethe. Her mother hadn't given up her
last penny, Maura hadn't married Patrick, for her to end up as
just another servile, clumsy scullery maid, open to the abuse of
fat American matrons.

Convinced that Patrick was dead, logic left her completely.
Brendt's suicide became a part of the waves beneath the ship;
her mother's miserable existence in Kerry was linked to the
rancid food doled out by the steward; everything and everyone
in her past and present was against her. Even Patrick had
turned out to be an enemy, making her his wife, then leaving her
a widow. Without thinking, Maura began to cry.

Patrick's head moved on her heaving chest. "I love you so much," he said.

"Patrick," she said, and she was at once sorry that she was so bad, so full of evil that she had nothing in her heart for anyone but herself. For the first time since she'd thrown up days before, she felt her body rebel against her. She wondered if she'd been dreaming, or if she was simply dreaming now. Was Patrick alive or dead? "I love you, too," she said. And all of a sudden it was light in the cabin, and Fiona was swimming over her head as the ship rolled up and down.

"Are you all right?" said Fiona.

"Where's Patrick?"

"He had to go again, poor devil," said Fiona. "But, Maura, look at yourself. Sure you're burning."

"What's happening to the ship?"

"Nothing," said Fiona, but Maura sat up suddenly, remembering to bow her head so as not to bang into the overhead berth.

"It's rough, the water's rough," said Maura accusingly; only yesterday Fiona had been hoping for a cataclysm to take away everyone on board, just as poor Mr. Maloney had been taken away.

"I'm sorry about what I said yesterday," said Fiona. "About Patrick, I mean. With God's help, he'll be all right."

Maura looked at Fiona closely, trying to fathom her change of heart. "I thought Patrick was dead last night," said Maura.

"Don't even say that."

"Where is he?"

"I've told you where he is," said Fiona.

"Is Patrick dead? Is that it, then? Is that why you're acting so queer? Tell me, Fiona, tell me, or I'll kill you!"

The shouting attracted several of their fellow passengers, but no one approached them. It was not so unusual for someone in the steerage to begin shouting uncontrollably. Everything was pressing in on all of them—space, filth, air. It was natural that rage was allowed out now and again, even if it robbed more strength from fatigued bodies.

"It's not Patrick," said Fiona. "But last night there were three men who died, and one woman."

"What? Who? Died from what?"

"And what did my man die from then?" said Fiona, suddenly reverting to her own sense of loss. "What is it that anyone dies from on this boat?"

"Mr. Maloney died from bad poteen," said Maura.

"He died from this air, he died from this noise, he died from a hundred things, just like any of us can. Mr. Maloney was strong, Maura, you don't know how strong he was."

"Who died?"

"Men, I told you. Three men and one woman—what's the difference who? All stinking emigrant Irish, just like us. All without pennies to leave behind to their stinking Irish widows. All wrapped in gray blankets and thrown to the fish, just like my Mr. Maloney. Jesus, you'd better drink something, you look like you're going to burn up."

"I'm all right," said Maura. But she could feel the fever raging behind her eyes; and when she got out of the bunk, there was so little strength in her legs that the swaying of the ship was too much for her and she dropped back down to the hard surface of the berth.

Fiona fed her a quarter of an orange and woke her up with a bit of brandy. But all at once Maura felt her insides revolt at the food. She stood up, chancing the trip to the toilets on her weak legs. In moments, Fiona was forgotten, Patrick was forgotten. All she cared for was to find her way to the washroom, stumble down the steps to the toilets, and relieve herself.

It was the fifth day out, and the washroom was vile with dirt, its floor wet with seawater, with the sour-smelling mess of half-digested food. Maura fell against a woman washing her clothes in a sudsy basin, and recoiled when the woman shouted at her in Gaelic, cursing her for a weak and indolent whore. Groping along the wall of faucets, she found the steps to the toilets and stumbled down to this least-human level of the ship.

Weak as she was, she held her breath. She was afraid to throw up when there was so little in her stomach. Quickly she selected the trench least covered with human waste. She crouched in pain, and slowly opened her mouth to inhale. At once, she began to gag, and her bowels, a moment before so eager to expel their waste, contracted, driving a red wedge of suffering through her lower body. The torment was so acute that the moment seemed to stretch on forever. She couldn't summon the strength to get out of her crouch, and yet the force of keeping herself from collapsing into the trench was so debilitating that she began to experience shooting pains along her spine. *Oh, my God,* she said silently, not praying for anything other than an end to the moment.

She tried again to breathe. She tried to relax, so her body would be able to free itself of convulsions, of shudderings that seemed about to split her in two. Once again she gagged and her throat constricted, and against her will she took a great draft of noxious air through her nostrils. The stench broke through every other hold her muscles had on her body; in a second she was on her knees beside the trench, retching.

Soon, her own foul odor overpowered any other smell. Maura had never been more wretched in her life. She remained on her knees in a stupor, content to try and spit up something from the back of her throat, to vomit out whatever was not fully digested in her stomach every minute, or ten minutes. Other women came and went, ignoring her in their own separate discomforts or miseries. One woman had collapsed over the trench opposite where Maura now knelt; as Maura gradually came out of her lethargy, she began to grow increasingly afraid for the still, huddled shape, crumpled in her own mess, not three feet away.

"Are you all right?" said Maura, so low that it was no wonder that no answer was received. Maura tried to get to her feet, but she couldn't summon the strength. For a moment she thought she had to throw up again. A second later she found herself crouching over her trench, emptying her bowels in a swift, sensation-numbing burst of pain.

Maura couldn't see, she couldn't smell the vile odors about her. The intensity of the pain had so astonished her system that she remained crouching, her mind clear of anything other than the twisting grays and blacks in her line of vision. Soon these grays sorted out to coherent shapes. She could see the huddled figure of the woman opposite her, and then another woman walked slowly past to another toilet. Maura called out to this woman, but there was no response. As her vision cleared completely, she realized that she could once again find the strength to stand. Slowly, tentatively, not wishing to intrude upon a corpse, she got to her feet and shuffled over to the unmoving figure, taking shallow breaths through her mouth. As she began to bend down to address her, a sharp voice said, "Leave her alone, girl."

Maura turned to see the white-haired older woman who had washed her hair on their first day at sea. She stood at the entrance to the washroom, a pail of disinfectant in her hand. "Just get out of here, girl, and leave her be. She's sick, and ashamed of it, and wants to be left alone."

"I thought she was dead."

"She's not dead, girl. She's just given up. She sleeps in her own mess and won't clean herself anymore. She wants to die, and maybe she will. But you leave her alone. Sure there's an open deck, and you're allowed on it if you want to live. Go on."

"I thought she was dead," repeated Maura dully.

The white-haired woman scattered disinfectant onto the floor of the toilet room. "Don't *you* die, girl," she said. "Get up on deck and breathe deep to get rid of your stink. Go on with you. Sure the only other way is that way." She was looking again at the huddled creature, too miserable to move, to think, to do anything other than rest in her filth, waiting for the next attack by her body on itself.

Maura stumbled past the old lady, into the washroom, inhaling the harsh odor of the disinfectant as if it were perfume.

The staircase to the lower deck was jammed with emigrants on the way to their morning rations of bread and water. Their slow, dogged pace suited Maura; the five minutes more it took to get out into the morning air and light allowed her time to get used to the fact that the pain that had run through her was vanishing, and to rid herself of the fear of its return. Once on deck, she ignored the shoving masses about the steward's kettles of water and bags of stale bread. Quickly she made for the rail, taking careful little breaths. The air was so rich and free and fragrant, it made her feel instantly light-headed. In spite of everything, there was always the sea, endless and pure and beckoning.

"Maura," said her husband's voice, and then she felt his hands on her shoulders, and she turned to look at him at the rail.

"Darling," she said.

Patrick's face broke into a slow, credulous smile. "Last night you told me that you loved me."

"Of course," said Maura. He looked frail and pale in the clear morning light. There was something cleaner about him this morning, something that suggested his ailment was over, or had at least taken a new turn. Still, he was in no sense healthier. He looked as if he didn't have the strength to speak out her name. "I thought you were dead," she said, and the horror with which she expressed this to her groom gave him more happiness than anything he had ever experienced, save for the act of lovemaking itself. "Darling," she said. And she put her arms about his high, skinny neck and rested her head against his thin chest, smelling not the scent of illness and death but the life-giving redolence of the sea.

All that day the two of them nursed each other: They slept at little intervals, they took frequent small portions of hot water and brandy, bits of bread crust, a shared half-cup of watery soup. Maura explained why they both must get well: Only the two of them together could make her dream of success come true. Patrick had another reason for why they both must get well: They were in love, and it was necessary for love to come out of Ireland and establish itself in the New World.

Maura had understood from the first moment she saw him on the deck that all talk of the future was meaningless. She'd been wrong in thinking he'd died in the night, but she was just as certain that his death was waiting for him; he would have a few more hours, a single night, perhaps a final dawn.

"You must rest," he said. "You're very pale. Please look after yourself." All day long he tried to cater to her, as if she were in the gravest danger. But though Maura had been terribly sick that morning, closer to giving up than she had ever been in her life, she was resilient, she was strong, she was certain once again of her life. No matter how Patrick petted her and fed her, no matter how much energy he summoned to create this day of love for her, it was obvious that he was the one who'd be joining

the other Irish men and women dropped in their gray blankets into the sea.

"Good-night, Patrick," said Fiona when the lamps were turned down that evening. "I'm glad you're feeling so much better." Even her widow's grief couldn't blind her. Her voice had the sepulchral tones of a final valediction. To Maura she said: "If it's help you're needing in the night, you only have to shake me once. I mean what I say."

"Thank you, Fiona," she said. But Maura wasn't concerned with a sudden fit in the night, a scream of pain, or a last gasping breath. There was nothing to be gained by dwelling on the inevitability of death. Instead she found herself fondling her husband, initiating a long, awakening kiss, expressing her incipient love with the tips of her fingers, with the tender way in which she held his body against the rocking of the ship.

It amazed her as much as it did Patrick, this capacity for loving. She had been his wife, and she had submitted to his caresses, but she had never been his lover. He had never known what a lover was. In his weak, excited state, her love reached him like a heavenly light, like a pure, unbearably beautiful radiance. Patrick felt as if he were drunk with happiness, flying into the sun.

Where before lovemaking had always been seen as Patrick's right, his reward for having married her, a one-sided assault over a restraining wall, it was suddenly something totally different: two people, already on a plane different from that of ordinary life, reaching out for each other to create a shared moment.

In the close dark, on the hard wooden bunk, in the space shared by hundreds, they kissed, closing out the sounds of the engine, the swaying of the berths, the groaning of old bulkheads as giant waves washed the emigrant ship. No longer did they smell disinfectant, no longer did the twisted turnings of crammed-together bodies divert their attention. Everything was concentrated on the moment—on the touching of lips, the kissing of his neck, of her breast. Maura's fever had passed, and she could feel Patrick's face blazing. In his eyes she could see a vision that transported her to another world, and she was transported: With shut eyes, in the perfect dark, feeling the heat of his fever, of his

love, feeling the rising power of her own heart, she was moved
to a region where she had never been. She allowed her hard,
rigid frame to soften, to blur its outlines to that of a creature
loving and yielding.

There was no thought of making Patrick happy out of gratitude or pity. She was not noble in embracing him, in stripping
away his ragged garments to feel his flat belly, his rising penis.
Everything was mutual, automatic, beyond thought. She had
no need of a fever to exist in his ethereal world. For the first time
in her life, she felt herself a sexual being, and didn't question the
myriad sensations running through her.

He was slow with her, infinitely gentle, not out of art or design but because the rhythm of the world he inhabited was
languid; it was as long as the black night, as long as the fever
would contain him in its fantastic grip. When he entered her, it
was not as it had been: She was wet, she was open, she was shud-
dering with a pleasure that reflected in every corner of his being.
"Maura," he said, and his dry voicing of her name tried to tell
her that he was sorry for leaving her, tried to tell her that their
love was so strong that it must endure in some form, in some
place, in some future time. Maura said nothing. It was no
longer even necessary to say that she loved him; each spoke for
the other, each loved the other as himself, as herself, in the
shared moment, the moment that existed outside of the hell of
the voyage, outside of any real time and space. They made love
in this moment, and their love was good and true and magical,
and without end.

The next morning seven more emigrants were dead of the dysentery, and among them was Patrick O'Connell. Maura made no
protest when Fiona directed the men to take the body up the
staircase to the lower deck. She knew that death was inevitable,
and that all her life she'd have it to look forward to, as a beacon,
as a solace for the cares of the world.

# ❧ CHAPTER ❧
# SIX

Four days after Patrick's death, nine days after having left the Irish coast, the ship came in sight of land. Maura didn't know that the land was an island, Fire Island, a barren and miserable stretch of sand inhabited by fishermen living in huts more miserable than those she'd left behind in Kerry. She only saw the lighthouse glinting in the midday sun, the gulls twisting through the cloudless sky.

The commotion on deck was considerable.

It was, after all, what everyone had been waiting for, this sighting of land, of the New World. Only a few emigrants had to rush down to the steerage to bring up a mob of dazzled passengers in their wake: No matter how sick, no matter how exhausted, no one wanted to miss the sight of what each and every one of them dreamed was the beginning of happiness, the end of despair.

Because everyone crowded the rails, no one noticed the steward and a gang of sailors racing down the staircase from an upper deck and coming up behind them. The crew had seen this moment many times before, and were prepared for it; each held a cudgel, and was prepared to use it. A whistle sounded from the main deck, and before its screech had vanished in the fragrant air the steward had begun to scream.

"Move it, you bastards, get away from the rail! Let's go, you filthy micks! You jump when I say to jump, and I'm telling you to get away from the rail!" Already the sailors, bored with the voyage, predisposed to hate the foreigners flooding their shores, had begun to drag at the women's shoulders and pummel the men with their fists and sticks.

"Let's go—get the hell away from there! Down the stairs, Paddy! Move it, mick! Shake a leg, Brigid, or I'll break you in half! Go back to your puking mess, this ain't for you to see, it ain't part of your ticket!"

Maura, very slow and contemplative in the days since her husband's death, turned her attention from the tranquil sea, its waters leading inexorably to the distant beach, glimmering like an enormous oblong jewel at the horizon. A large red-haired man had turned at the shouts and, without lifting a finger in defiance, was getting beaten to the deck by a wild young sailor. Fury took hold of Maura slowly, seeping into her blood moment by moment, until she had taken in the entire scene: the black-bearded steward, screaming confused commands; the sailors, not giving anyone a chance to obey, bloodying a score of men and women; and the emigrants themselves, more dazed than afraid, more astounded at this latest betrayal of hope than driven into a rage.

But Maura's rage was evident, and powerful. Suddenly, her mind was clear of contemplation. She no longer thought of the meaning of death, the comfort of love, the design of the universe—the intangible inheritance left her by Patrick. Instead, she simply wanted to kill the young sailor closest to her. She grabbed at his cudgel from behind as he flailed it over his head, ready to strike at the redheaded man bleeding and howling at his feet. In her madness she was sure, and strong, and fought like the Dooleys of Kerry had always fought for their rights; more than one man had been killed simply for her father's refusal to shut down his still.

As the sailor turned on her, Maura swung the cudgel up into his jaw. The sailor screamed, shutting his eyes against the pain and reaching both hands up to his face, as if to keep the bones from falling out of his mouth. Maura slammed the cudgel into his belly, into his groin, and, as he doubled over, she drove the hard stick into his back, and across the back of his head. She would have kept on, beating him until he was still, but she was swept up in the crush of passengers moving from the rail to the staircase, pushing past the sailors. No one, not even the sailors, had eyes for what she had done. In the hysteria of a hundred bodies, in the scores of separate blows and screams, Maura's fury had lasted seconds and been absorbed at once by hysteria, confusion, and fear.

A moment later, a series of gunshots rang out, shutting up all noise from the lower deck. The steward and sailors stood erect, their cudgels at their sides, looking forlornly up at the august figure of a ship's officer standing on the staircase to the upper deck.

"You blasted fool," he said, addressing the steward in a low voice.

"I'm sorry, sir," began the steward. "It's only to move 'em down—"

"Shut your trap," said the officer, speaking softly, though loud enough for everyone on the lower deck to hear. For a half-minute he looked about the deck, examining the injured with his eyes. Two of the sailors attended to their young mate, still unconscious from Maura's attack, though the cudgel was now on the floor, kicked toward the rail. "Bloody idiot," said the officer finally. "You know the company has to pay for every one of them sent back."

"I'm sorry, sir," said the steward. "But they wouldn't obey."

"Wouldn't obey?" said the officer. "These are Irishers. Don't make me laugh." He took a tentative few steps down the stairs. "Listen," he said, and his accent was very new, and very grand to Maura's ears. It wasn't English, and it wasn't the ugly American of the steward, but something in between; flat, with neither flourishes nor swallowed syllables. He spoke to the passengers. "You've got one more day on this ship. You're not to stir from belowdecks until you're told to do so. I will remind you one and all that anyone suffering a disability will be judged unfit by the American medical authorities, and returned to Ireland. So do not fight, do not abuse each other, do not make yourselves unfit. Even if it is not your custom, I would recommend a good wash, a good scrubbing, including your hair. The doctors look for

diseases of the scalp as well as of the rest of your bodies. Now
go below at once."

The officer stepped back up the stairs and was out of sight in
a second. But his presence continued to be felt. The emigrants
huddled together at the staircase to the steerage, waiting silently
to go down. About them the sailors stood, no longer threatening, their cudgels firmly at their sides.

"Aren't you going to wash your hair?" said Fiona to Maura
when she had returned to her bunk. Fiona had never gone topside, not caring to look at land until she could step on it. "Sure
I've as much to worry about as you, darling, but I'm looking
twice as lively."

"I'm lively, Fiona," said Maura.

"What?"

"I'm all right," said Maura. "Sure I haven't gone this far to be
sent back. You needn't be worrying about my hair, either. My
hair is fine, and I'm healthy enough unless someone wants to say
otherwise, just because he hates the Irish."

Maura didn't explain that the fury burning in her eyes was
for the sailor she'd nearly killed back on the deck. It was not
enough to survive, she wanted to survive with her dignity intact.
"I'm going to go back up," said Maura.

"What do you mean? No one's allowed up there until we
dock."

"I don't care," said Maura. "I want to see New York from the
sea."

Fiona knew there was little point in arguing. Already men and
women were trying to boost one another up to the open hatches
to catch a glimpse of the land. Someone shouted out the presence
of a small boat, a pilot boat, which had pulled up alongside to
lead their ship to New York Harbor.

"Look here," said Fiona, thinking to divert her friend's attention from running back up to the deck. "Let's go over again
what we're going to tell the inspectors."

"We both know what to say," said Maura.

"But someone told me that it's not good to say you've got a job
waiting for you. There's a new law or something over there, and
you're not supposed to have a job before you even arrive."

"Don't be stupid," said Maura. "They don't want paupers. You tell them you've got family, you've got money, and you've got a job. There's a thousand people on line, and all they want to do is get you through."

"Seriously, Maura. I heard it's better to say that you're only looking for a job, that you don't have it yet. Sure it's a law, and if you've been brought over to work by someone, it's against the law and they send you back."

"Stop it, Fiona. No one's going back," said Maura.

"And twenty-five dollars. Remember, if they ask you, you've got twenty-five dollars all saved up, and all you want to do is look for a job and work hard."

"No one is sending us back," said Maura. "Not for a job, not for money, not for sickness, not for anything."

"Sure if it's the right mood they're in," said Fiona. Maura noticed that her friend's eyes were quite red, either from lack of sleep or from crying. She refrained from telling Fiona to get some rest, however; no one wanted to be told that they didn't look well at this climactic point of the voyage.

"Well, then, we should hope we get a happy inspector, one that likes a pretty Irish girl," said Maura.

Fiona looked at her queerly, surprised at Maura's change in tone. But she relaxed on the bunk when Maura lay down beside her. Neither of them slept, though the ship, guided by the pilot, steamed gently on to Sandy Hook Bar, the berths creaking and sighing, as tired of the trip as their occupants. When the ship's bells sounded six times—it was three o'clock—Maura suddenly got off the bunk and stood in front of Fiona. "Not a word out of you," she said. "Don't be disturbing the others."

Fiona watched in amazement as Maura stepped lightly between the berths and walked boldly up the staircase, while all the steerage passengers looked, their eyes wide with fear.

When Maura emerged topside, she saw a lovely sight: the imposing, freshly painted lighthouse on Sandy Hook, and the six large buoys marking the channel across the sandbar, their red and blue electric lights blinking in the warm sunlight.

"Just the girl I'm looking to see," said a voice behind her. Without turning, she recognized the speaker. It was the steward.

Maura turned on him angrily, determined to remain on deck.

"Now lookit that," he said. "All choked up and ready to rip my eyes out, and what have I even said, I ask you, what have I even said?"

"Don't be making fun of me," said Maura, glaring at him.

"Not of such a pretty girl," said the steward. He forced an elaborate smile. "Even after ten days in the hole, you're looking good, you're looking very good, with that Irish hair and those big white teeth."

"Don't touch me," she said, taking a step back from him. "Just leave me alone. I want to stay on deck."

"You can stay," he said. "I won't chase you. Hey, the trip is over. Don't be snapping at me. I can be of help to you, you know. I can help you get through the inspection all right. There's people I know, and they'll help you out if I give them the word, see?"

"I don't want help. I can take care of myself if you leave me alone."

"If I leave you alone, you're going to be in a lot of trouble," said the steward, doing his best to speak pleasantly. "Look here, do you know where we are? Of course you don't. All you see is Sandy Hook lighthouse and a lot of buoys that don't mean nothing to you, see? But what we're doing here is going north, right along this way, straight on through the lower bay till we get to the Narrows, and an hour after that we dock at the quarantine station, and if you're up here, with no friend to speak out for you, they're going to just send you back where you come from."

"How far is New York?" said Maura.

"Not far. You'll be there soon. Listen, you don't have a husband. Why don't you let me help you? I know a place you can work. I know a guy who can get you a job."

"Please let me just stay here," said Maura. "Please let me just stay here and look out at the land."

"All right," said the steward. Shrugging his shoulders, he left her at the rail and went off to fetch a slice of ham and a bit of brandy. Already her tone was getting softer. With a little food in her, and the freedom of the deck, she'd soon see he wasn't so bad. With no husband, and that pretty face, she'd be the perfect girl to introduce to his friend Mike Kilgallen.

Maura found herself alone at the rail of the lower deck. For a moment, it was like the dream she'd always conjured: herself at the rail, the wind in her face, the promised riches of America spread out before her.

But as the ship entered the Narrows, leading to New York Bay proper, the steward once again made his presence felt, dragging her back to the cold land of reality. He pressed a plate of ham on her, and she surprised herself by eating it, and thanking him for it; she even drank the hot brandy and water he offered as well. As the food warmed her insides, it somehow made her senses less sharp, everything more dreamlike. Even the steward's voice took on a peaceful drone as they passed the huge wooded island that he called Staten Island on their left, and further off on their right another island, Long Island, with a great stone fort catching the last rays of the sun.

It was dark when they reached the quarantine station, and Maura followed the steward's advice and retreated downstairs. Fiona was asleep. Maura took her place beside her, and didn't wake until a crew of half a dozen uniformed men trooped downstairs, carrying lanterns and barking out orders. Even with the delays caused by the unnecessary roughness of the American quarantine officials, each of the immigrants was given a name tag, standing patiently while one or another official pinned it brusquely to whatever ragged clothing covered their chests.

Then the officials left, and the lights in the steerage were extinguished, and the ship didn't move. One bell sounded, then two bells, and finally three bells—1:30 in the morning—before the immigrants, awake in their berths, heard the anchor lift and the engines come back to life.

Maura waited a few minutes, and then once again left the berth and ran up the stairs. This time the steward was nowhere to be seen, though she could hear the cries of the sailors from the upper decks and the rhythmic blowing of the pilot boat's horn as it guided the big ship up New York Harbor. To her right, a dark city, with an occasional distant light, loomed up out of the misty night. This was Brooklyn, but Maura had never heard of such a place, nor had she any knowledge of Jersey City on her left. What she had heard of, what she had been waiting for since the first sighting of land at midday, suddenly came into view directly ahead. There, on a small island dwarfed by the height of its statue, stood the great sculpture: *Liberty Enlightening the World*. Maura shivered as the ship drew near. Only the torch held by the massive female form was lit up, by a great ring of electric lights; this illumination bathed the entire statue in a soft glow, imperfect for viewing it in detail, but perfect for viewing it as a beacon, as a source of joy and welcome.

"Maura O'Connell," said the steward, coming up to her suddenly out of the dark. He fingered her name tag familiarly, as if it gave him new authority over her. "Look here, you pretty thing, this is no place for you to be standing now. I mean it. I don't want you getting in trouble."

"It's so beautiful," said Maura.

"What? The statue?" said the steward with a laugh. "Yeah, it's something. But I wouldn't lose sleep over it." There was enough light from the upper decks to illuminate Maura's face, and the steward saw the tears in her eyes. "Come on," he said. "None of that. I told you I'm going to help you out, didn't I?"

"I don't need help," she repeated.

"And you didn't need my ham neither."

"I thanked you for that," said Maura angrily. He had ruined her moment with the Statue of Liberty. Even now they were drifting away from her bright torch, her bright promise.

"Jesus, all I'm saying is I'll introduce you to my friend who can guarantee you a job so they don't send you back to the pigpen you come from."

"I don't come from a pigpen!"

"I don't mean to be fighting with you," said the steward. "Not when we're becoming such good friends." And suddenly he was reaching for her, grabbing at her shoulders to pull her close, and Maura didn't fight. Ten days of the ship, of dysentery, Patrick's death, the endless uncertainty about what life would hold in store for her, had left her not weak but empty. She was without sensation. She had left her last drop of emotion back with the statue. The steward held her close and kissed her lips, and Maura didn't fight, but she didn't respond either. He pulled at her chin, he touched her breast, he grabbed her throat in a way he imagined would inspire lust in this widow of four days. "What is it?" he said. "Don't be teasing me now—I won't stand for a woman that teases!"

"Let me go," said Maura suddenly, without anger, without fear.

The steward let her go. There was little sense in kissing a corpse. Maura retreated down the dark steps to the steerage, missing the sight of the magnificent bridge connecting Brooklyn and Manhattan. She got into the low berth, trying not to wake Fiona. Soon she, too, was asleep, while the ship continued up the harbor to its North River dock.


At dawn, she was awakened by a great babble of fear and desperation.

The ship was pulling away from its dock, going back toward the sea, going back to Ireland. First- and second-class passengers had been dropped in New York, and now the rest of them, having failed the cursory inspection of the quarantine officials, were obviously being sent back as undesirables.

Even Fiona was mouthing this nonsense, and Maura finally spoke to quiet her: "We're going to Ellis Island," she said.

"No, we're not, they've already landed those who are allowed to stay," said Fiona.

Maura looked at her wonderingly. Only a dozen hours before, Fiona had been calm, telling her of the inspection they'd be going through, advising her on the correct way to behave in order to pass it. Not only was Fiona fast becoming hysterical, catching the madness from the other passengers, but her tired eyes were redder than before; the whole terrified aspect of her face gave her a sickly, failing look.

"Ellis Island," repeated Maura. "The inspection station for new immigrants. What do you think these tags are for? So we'll know our names when we get back to Ireland?"

Fiona stopped short, shaking her head against the force of logic. It was easier to let loose, to accept the release of hysteria, than to understand that they were finally to be reaching their goal. Far easier for all of them to be sent back than for some to enter the country and others sent back.

It took a good half-hour before the steerage was calm. Many others, like Maura, knew that they were not making for the sea, but the immigrant center. When this information became general, and believed, the passengers quieted, waiting for the ship to dock. Even Maura had no interest in going topside now. She had no desire to be on deck with her back to the city, and the immigrant center growing before her eyes. The quiet was broken once again when, more than two hours later, the ship joined a dozen others at the customs wharf, and everyone on board began to search his heart at once: Who would be worthy of entrance to the promised land?

All her possessions—a few articles of clothing, a tin of sugar, Patrick's warm wool scarf—fit into a shawl, and this Maura slung over her shoulder as she joined the exodus from the ship. Fiona tried to stay close, but, because the older girl had more things in her possession, she was clumsier, and unable to fight her way through the crowd like Maura. The ship was disgorging its steerage at the same time as two other ships, and these three human cargo-loads were but another trickle of humanity added to the mad torrent running through the main reception hall.

"Maura, wait for me!" yelled Fiona. "Wait for me when you're through the line!" But her words were swallowed up at once in the polyglot din. All about them, as officials in smart uniforms barked commands, were men, women, and children of a score of nationalities. Polish, Italian, Russian Swedish, French, Yiddish, Hungarian struggled to be heard in the vast room. As the officials forced the mob into a hundred rows, each separated by ropes and railings, mothers howled at their children to stay close, to hold on to each other lest they be lost forever.

"Your name?" said an official, carrying a large writing tablet, looking from Maura's name tag to her face.

"What?" said Maura, amazed that, of all the people in line, she was being singled out for questioning.

"O'Connell—is that your name?"

"Yes, sir."

"Answer sharply, girl, or we'll think you defective," said the official. "Wake up, then, you understand? Answer sharp!" Then he was gone, moving on down the line, to ask the same question of another immigrant.

Maura looked about for Fiona, her eyes searching the bedraggled shapes row by row. A man in a white coat stood at the head of each line, a doctor presumably, and beyond this phalanx of officials stood a wide-open gate to another part of the complex. The line moved swiftly, then slowly, then not at all; then it would start up again. Some lines moved more quickly than others, and some people shouted back and forth to each other from line to line in their native tongues. For a long time she couldn't spot Fiona. There were as many as a thousand different people around her, each wearing the gray, worn clothing of the steerage, most supporting bundles, their heads either bowed, or bobbing for a look at the top of the line.

When Maura finally saw her friend, Fiona was next in line to be examined, four rows away from where Maura waited her turn. She called out her name, but Fiona didn't hear; she was too mesmerized by the questioning of the woman ahead of her. By the time Fiona's turn came, Maura's row had begun to move quickly again. She heard the doctor ask a man: "Nationality? You, healthy? Lift heavy things?" As the man mumbled his answers, the doctor made little checks on his pad. This man was waved through; then another; then a woman and her two children; and then it was Maura's turn.

"Irish?" said the doctor, but Maura's attention had wandered once again; she'd lost sight of Fiona, and wondered where she'd gone, how she'd fared. "Nationality?" said the doctor, speaking sharply.

"Irish."

"Did you ever have TB?"

"No."

"Married?"

"No," said Maura. She looked up at the doctor, examining his face as he ran through his questions. He would have had no interest in the fact that she was a widow, that her married life had encompassed less than a month in her life. His eyes were immune to sympathy. She could be twelve instead of seventeen, a leper instead of a widow, blind in one eye and lame as well, and still nothing of pity would enter those eyes. He had seen everything, and quickly. Even cripples had to hurry past his impersonal gaze.

"Ever have children?"

"How could I?" said Maura, shocked out of her apathy. Even as she looked away from the doctor's face, abashed, she understood for the first time that she could have children. She could be pregnant from Patrick, the same way Brendt was pregnant from Grady Madigan.

"Move that pack!" said the doctor, and he rapped his knuckles against the tin can inside the bundle she carried on her back. Maura was too surprised at the shift of his attention—from childbirth to a bundle on her back—to comply fast enough for the doctor. "Dull-wits! Each and every one of them dull-wits!" said the doctor, and he pulled at her bundle so that it fell to the floor. "Now stand up straight!" he said. Maura did as she was told. "Now," said the doctor, "I can see that you are not a hunchback, my dear. Next!"

Maura picked up her bundle and hurried off toward the mass of people at the gate. If anything, the noise in the next vast hall was even greater than in the first; but through everything, she could hear someone shout out her name. Turning, she saw Fiona at once, one of a group of fifty people, pushed together in a kind of cell, just beyond the gateway. Next to her, an inspector forcibly stopped a woman and pointed her in the direction of the cell.

"No!" said the woman. "There's nothing wrong with me!"

"Move it, hurry, don't waste my time!" screamed the inspector.

Another official was standing beyond them, screaming that all men and women were to separate into two camps in the next series of lines. "*Men*, you stupid Polack!" said the official. "You know what a *man* is?" And he pushed and prodded an old man, afraid to separate from his wife. "Don't speak Polish to me! I'm no Polack, you jerk! Just get in line and let go of your old lady!"

Maura noticed that the men and women being directed to the

cell were all marked with chalked letters: She saw an "X" and an
"I" and wondered what on earth it could mean.

"You can't go there!" screamed an inspector as she started toward Fiona.

"My friend is there," said Maura.

"Move it! Over there, with the women!" said the inspector.

But as he turned to stop another chalk-marked immigrant,
Maura walked slowly over to where Fiona stood behind bars.
Fiona was marked with a large chalked "E."

"What does it mean?" said Maura. The cell wasn't locked; it
wasn't even closed. Its wide entrance was filling with more and
more of the chalk-marked immigrants. Maura didn't know what
they had been selected for, but she knew they had been selected
for no good.

"My eyes," said Fiona. "It's my eyes."

"Your eyes are red, you haven't been sleeping," said Maura.
"Get out of here," she said in a whisper. "Fiona, move. Sure it's
your only chance."

"No, darling," said Fiona. "It's my eyes, and they're sending
me back to Ireland, and sure I'm going to die on the ship, just
like poor Mr. Maloney. It's God's will. I'm being sent back to
die, and meet Mr. Maloney at the bottom of the sea."

Maura moved quickly through the entrance to the cell, ignoring the others, most of whom moved with the slow, self-con-
scious movements of the doomed. She took hold of Fiona and
pulled her sharply. "Come on," she said.

"But they told me to go here—"

"I don't care what they told you," said Maura. "Sure your eyes
are fine, as good as anyone's." Without another word, she tore
off her friend's shawl, letting it drop to the floor.

"It's probably trachoma," said Fiona.

"Shut your trap!" said Maura, imitating without effort the
speech of her new land. "Come with me, and don't look back!"

Clutching her friend, Maura pushed through the confused
masses of people until a furious official yelled at them both to
join the rows of women. It had been astonishingly easy to flout
the authorities, and as Maura dragged Fiona back to that ma-
jority who had passed the first test of entry to America, she was

determined to see that both of them got through the day together.

"Now you listen to me, Fiona Maloney," said Maura, when they had gotten on line, and sat down on their bundles, and brought their tired heads together. "You're here to stay, and I'm going to be with you, and if you go back to Ireland, I won't have a friend in the country. No matter what they tell you, just you tell them that your eyes were examined, that the first doctor said it wasn't trachoma, it was only tiredness and crying from the long, hard trip."

Maura insisted that Fiona go ahead of her on line, thinking that she could be of some assistance behind the weaker woman. But the line soon defeated both of them. Every moment, the din increased—the shouted orders and epithets, the unending screams of infants winding higher and higher, a reflection of everyone's despair. It grew warm, and foul with the odors of the steerage; indeed, the vast complex seemed like nothing so much as an enormous steerage, a steerage in hell, peopled with the doomed from every corner of the earth.

It took three hours for Fiona to make it to the head of the line. When she was ordered past the black-capped official and sent through a doorway to the right, Maura was too exhausted to offer any last encouragement or advice. It seemed another hour— though it was but five minutes—before it was Maura's turn, and when she'd been thrust into the tiny examining room, and had come face-to-face with a tall bony man and an even taller, bonier woman, she was no longer thinking of Fiona at all.

"Maura O'Connell," she said, though no one had asked her. She would show them she was alert, and healthy, and eager to work.

"Married?" said the man.

"No, sir."

"Ever married?" said the woman. "Ever engage in sexual intercourse?"

"I *was* married," said Maura, afraid to look at the woman, whose yellowish eyes seemed to be searching for a flaw, for any excuse at all to send her back where she came from.

"Where is your husband?" said the woman.

"Dead." said Maura. "He died on the ship."

"Wait," said the woman, not to Maura but to the man, who was beginning to draw a rubber glove onto his hand. "How old are you, dear?" she said, but the word "dear," uttered by her thin lips, was no endearment to Maura. Maura told her that she was seventeen. "Have you ever been sick?" asked the woman.

"No."

"Have you ever had trouble with your skin?"

"No," said Maura. "No trouble."

"She's tired, doctor," said the woman. "It's only fatigue."

"I'm not tired!" said Maura. "I'm strong, and I'm ready to work!"

"Pick up your skirt," said the doctor. "Now come on—nurse, show her. Roll it up and get out of those underclothes. Move it, there's a thousand more out there!"

The nurse didn't show her; it was far easier to simply grab the skirt, roll it up, and pull down at her underclothes with vicious speed.

"No!" said Maura.

"*Stop it*," said the nurse to her, and the yellow eyes were hard, and full of hate.

Maura stood there, terrified, looking straight at the doctor as he drove his gloved hand into her private parts, eliciting more shock than pain, more shame than terror.

"Does it hurt?" said the doctor.

"What?" said Maura, not understanding the question, or, for a moment, even where she was. Instead, she felt as if she were once again on the ship, hearing the groans of the steerage, feeling the deck swaying beneath her feet, biting her tongue against the pain in her bowels.

"*She's all right*," said the nurse, and her words were so hard, so full of furious anger, that Maura was drawn back to the present, back to the fact of the rubber-gloved hand, back to the sensation of utter helplessness, her underclothes wrapped about her knees. Looking in wonder to the tall nurse, Maura finally understood that her hatred was not for her, but for the doctor; her anger was not at the immigrants, but at the treatment they suffered. Because every part of her emotional frame had been so battered during the last ten days, the abrupt change from hate to gratitude to love for this unlikely, unattractive creature was natural, easy; Maura turned loving eyes her way, and began to collapse into her arms.

The nurse brought her to a chair and let her sink into it, her head falling over her chest. But Maura was not asleep. "She's not sick," she heard the nurse say. "Doesn't a doctor know when somebody goes into a faint? How would you like it if someone grabbed you there, you filthy old bastard! There's nothing wrong with her, and if you even think of failing her, I'm reporting you—I'll talk to every newspaper in town."

"I'm a doctor," said the other voice, "and you'll not talk to me like that. I have every right to examine her."

"You could change your gloves, you filthy animal."

"My gloves aren't filthier than she is."

"Pass her, you bastard, it's you who made her like this."

A moment later, Maura felt a cup pressed to her lips, and she pulled back her head, and opened her mouth, and let a cool, sugary liquor down her throat. All the while, she heard the doctor ranting—about venereal disease, fauvus, leprosy, tuberculosis, all the dread illnesses that the immigrants brought to America in return for her favors. But the nurse ignored him now, satisfied that he had signed Maura's health certificate. She helped the girl to her feet and squeezed her hands. "You're through with the doctors, dear," she said. "But be bright now, and answer sharply. You've only one more inspector to pass, and you must impress him with your goodness, clarity, and modesty. Do you understand?"

"Thank you," said Maura. "Sure you're the nicest woman I've ever met."

And then she was out the rear door of the tiny room, once again on line, behind a motley assortment of men, women, and children. Fiona was nowhere to be seen, but Maura wasn't worried; surely the nurse had helped her through her examination as well. She found that her legs were shaking, and wanted to sit down, to regather her strength, but suddenly she had a shiver of fear, remembering what the doctor had done to her. What sort of place was this America anyway? Maura reached out to hold on to something so that she would not fall, and this

turned out to be a Chinese woman ahead of her on line, plump
and unsmiling. But the Chinese didn't ask her to let go; she said
nothing at all, merely moved on as the line advanced.

Maura stopped shaking and tried to steel herself, but now the
fact of what had transpired kept coming back, in waves of humiliation: They had stripped her, and he had touched her—he
had prodded and poked her as if she were a slave, or a whore.
And she had done nothing, she had submitted; she had wanted
to enter this place so badly that she had said nothing at all. How
could such a thing be? She wanted to scream at the people about
her. There were thousands and thousands of them, and each
and every one was willing to suffer anything to satisfy the whims
of a few Yankee officials. Where were they all going that it mattered so much to them?

Maura herself wanted to be rich and free, high above the mean
life she had lived at home. But she had never dreamed she'd
marry Patrick only to see him die on board ship. She had never
dreamed of sickness, of humiliation, of terror. What could have
driven this Chinese woman ahead of her on line? Or that family
of peasants, from some nameless country where everyone seemed
dark and spoke in sharp guttural cries? Or that handsome
Swede, big enough to strike down the Yankee forcing him back
in line, but only too eager to comply with the strange English
commands?

How dare that man touch her! she thought, shutting her eyes
so that tears started up and ran through her shut lids as the man
behind urged her forward. How dare they strip her, and touch
her where only Patrick had been, with love.

"Next!" said a sharp voice.

And behind her, a man said: "You, it's you, girl!"

Maura opened her eyes and an arrogant official drummed his
fingers on the counter before her. "Name!" he said.

"Sure it's right here, Maura O'Connell, big as day, if you can
read," said Maura. She wanted to rip off her name tag and
throw it in his face, she wanted to leap over the counter and
pummel the man to within an inch of his life; but some part of
her urged her to hold back, pulled her down, even as her anger
lifted her past humiliation, past fear.

"Look here, Brigid," said the official. "If you want to flash your Irish temper, I'll put you back on the stinking boat you came on. I'm here to inspect your character—and so far, I find your character very bad. Very bad!"

That part of her that wanted to survive reminded her of her dream, of what she had suffered, of the foolishness of letting herself be turned back now. Smile, it told her. Apologize. Smooth your pretty hair. Blink the green eyes. "Sure I'm sorry," she said.

" 'Sorry' don't cut the ice, girl," said the American. "Just answer my questions, and answer sharply."

"Yes, sir."

"Any insanity in your family?"

"No, sir!"

"Are you an anarchist?"

"Oh, no, sir! I'm here to get a good job!"

"Any anarchists in your family?"

"No, sir. We hate anarchists in my family."

"Do you read?"

"Yes, sir. And write, too. Script and print both, and good and clear, my teacher said to me."

"What were you in jail for?"

"I was never in jail," said Maura.

"How much money do you have?"

"Twenty-five dollars," said Maura, remembering what Fiona had told her.

"Let's see it, girl."

"It's under here," said Maura, indicating her belly.

"All right, all right, get out of here, Maura O'Connell, and watch that you keep a civil tongue in your head. You're off the farm now, girl. Go through the last gate and wait for the next boat."

"What boat?" said Maura. "You're not sending me back then? Please, sir, I didn't mean nothing. It was only craziness, wasn't it then? Sure I'm a good girl, honest I am." She had bowed her head, and let the tears come, and there was no longer any anger in her, none at all. She would do anything—she would kiss his hand, she would drop to her knees—if only they wouldn't send her back.

"You blithering Irish idiot," said the official. "Just get out of here. No one's sending you back! It's the boat to the Battery! Get out of here!"

Maura stumbled off, not understanding a word of it. What was the Battery? What boat was she to take? Where was Fiona? What time of day was it? Where would she find money to pay her passage, and where was she going?

"You, girl! Maura!" said a loud, familiar voice, and when she raised her eyes, she saw a man standing in the gateway that led to the outside. Without thinking, she kept walking toward him. "Took long enough!" he said. "I've been waiting all day, and where's the thanks I get? Hey, not even a smile?"

It was the black-bearded steward, and Maura allowed him to take her bundle, allowed him to lead her to the ferry that ran twenty-four hours a day between Ellis Island and the Battery shore.

"Where's Fiona?" she said, and then he told her that Fiona hadn't made it.

"Trachoma," he said. "It's the luck of the Irish, ain't it? They send her back, and when she's better she can try for it again." It was a shame, he added, because he had a good job for her, too.

"Fiona," said Maura, continuing to place one foot after the other as she followed him where he led. The tears wouldn't come, and she was still walking, counting the dead, the lost, the broken.

"Hey, cheer up. You're all right, ain't you? You're going to have a good job, thanks to me. You can send your friend a second-class ticket, sure you can, that's the girl." All the time on the ferry, the steward babbled on about his goodness to her, pointing out the square tower of the Produce Exchange, the starkly elegant spire of Trinity Church amid the endless skyscrapers of her dreams, telling her of New York's "fun" and "class" and how as soon as she was rested she'd look "out of sight."

Maura heard every word, but nothing stayed in her consciousness. The words, like the people of her past and present, ran through her, left her alone, an empty shell waiting to take a new body, a new direction.

"There's my friend, there's your new boss!" said the steward when they'd landed. And even though Maura followed his gaze and tried to take it all in—the fluttering flags, the grand carriages against the mob of people waiting for the cable cars, the great buildings blocking out the horizon—she could do nothing more than nod, and follow, picking up her feet and letting them drop of their own accord. "Look sharp now," said the steward. "Can you at least look a little bit like your old pretty self?"

"Yes," said Maura, remembering that she was at the beginning, that she had crossed the water, that her nightmare was over and something beautiful must now begin. "Yes, sir. Thank you," she said, very grateful as the steward helped her into the grand carriage, and a strong, handsome young man gripped her hands and pushed her into a seat.

"I'm Mike Kilgallen," he said.

"Hello, sir," said Maura.

"Jesus, you stink," said Kilgallen.

Maura didn't answer him. She held on to her bundle and lowered her eyes. The carriage was in motion, and she was on her way in the New World. It took her a night and a day before she understood who Kilgallen was, and how the steward had earned his bounty, and what was expected of her. Maura was ignorant, but in her life she had come to believe in the power of evil, and she knew that Kilgallen was evil, and that he fully believed in his mastery. She had come to the New World, but freedom hadn't been granted her; freedom was somewhere else, off in the future, in a place and time where she would be strong, when the stuff of her dreams would not be stifled by the world of men.

# PART THREE

The House on Spring Street

# ❧ CHAPTER ❧
# SEVEN

She had no eyes for the house when first brought there, no nose for the scent of the East River, no ears for the rhythmic clanging of the presses in the printing shop next door. Kilgallen ordered her out of the carriage and pointed her up a short flight of brown stone steps leading to the front door, then grabbed her elbow and steered her down a dim corridor, deep into the bowels of the large silent house.

She had a moment of rebellion when he pushed her to the first step of the basement stairwell; for a moment she thought she was being put back into the steerage of the steamship *Knickerbocker*. But the room she was pushed into was nothing at all like the steerage, save for the trio of tiny windows set high overhead where the wall met the ceiling, letting in as little light and air as the open hatches of the ship. There was a bed, a real bed with a heavy quilt and a fluffy pillow. The floor was cement, but mostly covered with a bright red rug. On the walls were framed pictures: a bouquet of roses dappled with sunlight, a barking dog, a blond-haired little boy.

Maura took all this in without thought or feeling. She stood quietly in the center of the room, still holding on to her ragged bundle of possessions, listening to the quiet. Kilgallen left her almost at once: He had seen this kind of disorientation a hundred times before, and it no longer had any effect on him. Moments later there was a knock on the door, and a large black-skinned woman with white hair entered the room, leaving the door open.

"Oh, honey," she said. "It's all right, child. Put that down and don't worry about a thing. I'm going to fix you up good."

Maura had seen black people for the first time that morning, when the ship had docked at Ellis Island. In the confusion of nationalities and languages at the immigration center, Maura had hardly noticed them. But now, as the black woman took the bundle from her hand and placed it gently at the foot of the bed, all Maura's attention was captured. Indeed, in an unconscious desire to focus on something other than Kilgallen, other than the death of Patrick, other than the loss of Fiona, Maura found herself sinking into a perfect contemplation of the black woman.

She had never seen anyone like her. Her black skin was so smooth, so young and free of blemishes, that it gave to her presence an air of mystery: How could one be so old, with such white hair, but with the skin of a child? How could those black eyes exhibit all at once love and loathing, pity and contempt? "Come on, child," she was saying to Maura, but Maura responded not to the words but to the touch of the black woman's hands. Gently, beseechingly, she took hold of Maura's wrist. Slowly, with infinite care, she turned her toward the door and led her along a corridor of shut doors to a large bathroom at the back of the house. "You're just tired, darling. You need food and you need drink and I'm going to take care of everything, you wait and see if I don't."

With fascination, Maura watched the black woman pick up enormous buckets from what looked like a stove, and pour steaming water into a white bathtub in the center of the tiled floor. "Come on, child. Don't stand there gawking, get rid of them rags—you're filthier than a pig." The black woman was dressed in fine clothes, thought Maura: a heavy wool skirt covered with a broad apron, and a pretty white shirtwaist. Nonetheless, the black woman didn't seem to mind when water splattered on her clothes, or, when she added powdered soap, that the bubbles ran up her clean white sleeves.

"Darling, you ain't listening, and you've got to listen if you want to get better. Don't you hear me talking to you? You're a pretty thing, but it's hard to see that under all that smelly filth. Come on now, girl, do as I say."

Swiftly, the large black woman removed Maura's clothes, tossing each garment into a far corner. Maura let it happen, as she had let the nurse pull up her skirt to reveal her private parts to the doctor. She watched the black woman's face, trying to understand something of the pain there. Maura wondered whether the woman was herself in pain, or whether what she saw in the black eyes was simply a reflection of Maura's own misery.

"Are you deaf, honey? What is it, are you hungry? No one's hit you—you're as whole and hale as anything I've seen, only skinny and pale, but that's what you'd expect after what you've been through. Are you getting in the tub, or am I supposed to break my back and put you into it? Get in and I'll fix you something hot to eat. Come on."

Maura let herself be pushed up against the hot tub of steamy water. She looked into the bubbly water as if expecting to see a message there; as if it were the surface of the wild sea, with dead men drifting endlessly beneath its waves. The black woman picked up Maura's foot and placed it firmly into the very hot water. It hurt so much that for a moment Maura was fully aware: As the pain fired her senses, she saw the woman's impatience, she understood that she had a desperate need for food, she was certain that she was a prisoner in this room, in this house, and that she was powerless to resist.

"Come on, darling. It's the only way to get clean. Don't you want to be clean and pretty again? Don't you want your red hair to shine for all the boys? Get in, honey." Moving by herself, Maura brought her other leg over the side of the tub and into the hot water.

"It's hot," said Maura, shutting her eyes against the fierce sensations afflicting her skin. Incredibly, the woman took hold of her shoulders and, with a single easy motion, forced Maura flat down on her behind, so that the pain was now everywhere at once—feet, genitals, thighs, belly.

"I'm glad you can talk, I'll say that," said the woman. "Lot of girls off the boat, they don't even know their names. Of course, a lot of them ain't English—or Irish—and that makes a hell of a problem for everyone, especially me. You ever try speaking to one of them Swedes? It ain't easy, I'll tell you that. It ain't easy."

The black woman left her for a moment to go over to the stove and prepare something in a pot, something that Maura couldn't smell because of the scent of the soap. Quickly, the pain subsided, leaving in its place a warmth that Maura hadn't felt since the departed summer, when she had been young and whole and full of dreams. Brendt had been alive then, and Patrick O'Connell had no more chance of marrying either of the Dooley sisters than did the Prince of Wales. Closing her eyes as the hot water relaxed her tight muscles, letting her hands and arms sink into the bath, Maura remembered Brendt's lovely face, when it was wild, and dreadfully serious, imploring Maura never to blame the church on her account. As Maura drifted between waking and sleep, Brendt's face retreated and returned, the fantasy living in the heart of her dream state. But what had Brendt to do with all this? She would have gone to America in any case, with or without Brendt. Whether or not Grady Madigan had dishonored her sister, and the filthy priest had called Brendt a whore, and their father was the worst man alive, and their mother was mad, hopelessly mad—none of these things had brought her to this city, to this house, thought Maura.

Suddenly, she was fully awake. The black woman was scrubbing her with a stiff brush. "You're turning the water black as coal," she said. "I've never seen such a dirty girl in this house. Get under, honey. *Under*, darling," she said and Maura felt her head being forced under water, felt her face smart at the heat. It would be so easy to just relax, she thought. To open her mouth, suck in the water through her nose, to stay there beneath the surface, where everything was warm and dark and silent.

But what on earth was she thinking? she asked herself. If she had wanted to die, she would have done it long since, before all her suffering. No, she wanted to live, in this world, in this country. Her dreams had brought her here, and she could not violate her dreams, for they were the truest part of her self. Brendt hadn't wanted to go to America; but in a way, her terrible suicide had urged Maura on. Their poor mother was alone now, for the ugly old-maid sister and three brothers back in Kerry were but pale, cruel imitations of their loutish father. But it was her mother's money that had helped bring Maura to

America. For them, Brendt and her mother, and for poor Patrick, she must bring her dreams to life; she must survive everything.

"I must eat," said Maura, when the black woman had finally allowed her up for air. "Sure I need a bite if I'm to live at all."

"You'll eat, honey. We're going to fatten you up like a goose. Wait a bit and see if I don't feed you, sweetheart. I'll feed you better than you've ever eaten before." But there was no offer of food yet. Maura's keeper scrubbed soap into her hair, into her ears, under her chin, about her neck. She raised Maura's arms and soaped her armpits, scrubbed the rough elbows, ducking her under the water again and again until the rich bubbles went flat and black scum floated along the water's surface.

"Okay, out, honey, come on," said the woman finally, and because Maura had no strength in her legs, she lifted the young girl like she would a corpse, holding the back of her neck and the backs of her knees.

Maura had a sensation of the approach of night. Looking about her as she stood naked on the tile floor, she realized that the bathroom was also a kind of kitchen, with a narrow cot pushed against a far wall. There were no windows, and she wondered if the early autumn sky in New York was as misty in the evening as in Kerry; she wondered if birds flew in from the sea fogs, catching the light with terrifying suddenness as they emerged from mist to clear air.

The woman dried her with a soft towel; even in her stupor, Maura marveled at the gentle fabric. Behind her, the dirty bath water drained out of the enormous tub; Maura had no idea where it went, or how it left, but she accepted the phenomenon as she accepted everything offered to her the rest of her waking hours.

From the stove—not lit by wood, but by burning gas—the black woman soon began to bring buckets of steaming water to refill the tub. Maura learned that the sink next to the stove was fitted with a cold-water faucet; that the entire house, save for this basement, was lit by electric lights; that the black woman's name was Louise, and that she was a maid, a servant, there to do the bidding of the house's residents.

"Who lives here?" Maura asked. "What am I to do here then?

I have no money—I lied to the immigration. I have nearly nothing, and sure this is an expensive house."

Louise helped her back into the tub for the second soaking.
Though the water was as hot as before, Maura was ready for it;
indeed she was longing for it, for the warmth numbed her
senses, shut up her questions, her fears. This second bath was
far superior to the first. Louise added not only bath soap but
some sort of magical oil; it smelled of roses, as fragrant and rich
as her mother's bushes when the sun returned after a short
summer's rain. Now there was no scrubbing, only a timeless
immersion in the silky, scented water. Louise left her, only to return a moment later with food. While Maura soaked, Louise fed
her soup, not letting Maura hold the spoon, but bringing it to
her lips, like a mother with an ailing child.

"You're a good girl, aren't you?" said Louise. "You're no
trouble, no heartache. Just the best girl, aren't you, sweetheart?
Aren't you lovely, with your red hair and your green eyes. No,
don't sleep, not yet. First you've got to finish this soup, darling,
or you're not going to be well at all."

Maura finished the soup, and she finished her bath, and Louise
didn't have to lift her out of the tub; Maura had enough strength
to get out by herself, shivering against the cold air. Once again
she was toweled dry, and then Louise wrapped her in a long
silk robe that smelled unaccountably of hyacinths. There were
even slippers for her, made of some kind of fur, like those of the
ladies in one of Brendt's romantic novels. Somehow the silk robe,
the warm slippers, made it possible to leave the bathroom; there
was a suggestion of having been dressed for something glorious,
for a dream not fully formed in her mind. And when they
returned not to a palace, but to the little room where Kilgallen
had first lead her, Maura was too dazed to be disappointed, too
tired to try and fathom the series of events that led finally to
this shut-up space. Louise combed her wet hair and wrapped a
towel about her head. She removed her slippers, she sat her
on the bed, she fed her a spoonful of castor oil, and then she
helped her, still in her robe, under the thick quilt.

Maura slept.

Everything came back to her, all at once, crowding together in

twisted shape, in backward form: Brendt leaping into darkness
. . . her mother on her knees, pulling up a weed . . . Fiona at
Ellis Island, bearing the chalk mark "E" . . . Patrick making
love to her, slowly, gently, even as the soul twisted out of his
ruined body . . .

Why was the steward there, his black beard running with seawater? . . . And Kilgallen, the handsome young man in the carriage, what was he doing, speaking in a Kerry accent that he
never possessed? What had they to do with Patrick . . . with
the women in the steerage's toilet room . . . with Fiona in the
wide-open cage . . . with Louise, grinning her white teeth at
her, shaking her head, her smile breaking into a tight-lipped
frown? . . .


"All right, honey, now that ain't going to do you no good, you
listen to me," said Louise, and Maura understood that her eyes
were open, that she had been dreaming, and that she was now
supposed to accept this black face, these American-accented
words, this dully lit little room as real.

"Where am I?"

"First of all," said Louise, smiling once again, "you're awake."

"Louise?"

"Yes, baby, that's me."

"What time is it?"

"It's time to eat, honey. You've been sleeping all night, and
most of the morning."

"How long have I been here?"

"In this room?"

"In America."

"Honey, I don't know when you landed. All I know is when
you got to our house. That was yesterday—getting on to late
afternoon. What are you doing, honey? That ain't right. Stay
in bed, baby. Stay in bed and I'll give you something good to
eat."

But Maura, once started, could not hold back her will. She
had a sudden need to be free of the restraints of the quilt, to cross
the room and look up to the narrow slits of windows, to turn

about and discover her image in the small rectangular mirror hanging on the wall. She was light-headed, but a hundred times stronger than the day before. There was nothing to be seen through the tiny windows but weeds; what was more important was the fact that those windows could not be reached without a ladder—and even with a ladder, no one Maura's size could possibly squeeze through the tiny space to the outside.

But before she could speak, before she could align her fears into a coherent statement, the sight of herself in the mirror took her breath away. Maura looked from the mirror down to the robe wrapped about her thin frame. She touched it slowly, looking at her pale skin against the deep blue silk, at the way her freshly washed red-gold hair fell over the luxurious fabric.

"I'm going to bring your breakfast, honey," said Louise, opening the door.

Maura looked at her wonderingly. "Here?"

"Yes, honey, I'm going to get you some eggs and fried potatoes, you just wait and see."

"Don't leave me here."

"I'll be right back," said Louise, and before Maura could reach her, she was out the door, closing it swiftly behind her. Maura put her hand to the knob, but almost at once she heard the sharp click of the lock, and was afraid to try the door. Instead, she returned to the mirror, looking wildly at herself, trying to understand. Of course she was pretty, even beautiful to some eyes, she thought, remembering the way the steward had grabbed her on the ship and pushed his hateful body close to hers. And, yes, she had heard stories—bits of stories too absurd to believe in, for even among the godless there was *something* decent, *something* civilized.

Maura went back to the door and put her hand to the knob. When she tried to turn it, she felt the resistance of the lock, and all at once the pretty little room began to close in on her.

Maura screamed. She let go of the doorknob and hit against the door, pounding with the heels of her hands, screaming out an indecipherable torrent of Irish lamentations. She kicked at the door with her bare feet; she backed away from the door so she could run into it with all the force of her body; she howled for

Louise, for Kilgallen, for anyone at all, until her voice cracked and she found herself, exhausted, sitting on the pretty red rug in the center of the room.

As her heart gradually slowed to its normal pace, Maura remembered Brendt's admonitions about a wild temper: One couldn't think in the midst of blind rage.

So she remained on the rug, gathering her strength, and tried to put one fact after another in a series of logical steps. The black-bearded steward had brought her to Kilgallen; and Kilgallen had taken her to this house; and Louise had bathed her and fed her; and the robe she wore must cost more than a round-trip first-class ticket to Cork; and the door to her room was locked.

The only thing that made sense was that she was to be a slave. A white slave, sold to a black millionaire from South America. Even Fiona had spoken of white slavery, in the darkest days of the voyage, if only to take their minds off the rocking of the boat. And how else explain the silk robe, the gentle pampering, the locked room? Maura had once again gotten to her feet. Anger was running through her and she felt impelled to move about, to channel the anger into motion, even if it was the useless pacing of a caged animal.

Because she was seventeen and willful, and wild, she couldn't hold on to a core of sense for more than a few moments. She was angrier than before, because now the locked door made sense. Her anger was mad, and murderous, and she wanted only to find Kilgallen and the steward and strangle the life out of them. As she paced faster and faster, and her heart raced, she began to scream, and the screaming led her to the shut door, and once again she was reduced to beating at its surface with frenzied abandon.

But then the lock clicked open, and the door swung wide, and a large man thrust his hand at her throat and threw her halfway across the room. "Shut your trap, you stupid broad," said Kilgallen.

Maura looked at him, feeling her neck where he had grabbed her. Though Kilgallen was lean and handsome, he had the same brutish look about him that her father always had when he had taken it into his head to give her a beating. She stood squarely on her bare feet, watching him as if he were a devil she could make disappear only by the strength of her desire.

"Nobody can hear you outside this house anyway, you crazy bitch," he said, closing the door softly behind him.

"I want to leave this place," said Maura.

"That's only because you're too damned ignorant to know what's outside." He had taken a step closer to her. "At least you don't stink anymore. I hate the way you broads come stinking off those ships. What do they do anyway, roll you in shit?"

"Sure I made a mistake accepting your hospitality at the dock, me not having a penny to my name, but I really have thought it out, sir, and I'm leaving this place. I want my clothes and then I'll just go, and I'll be glad to pay you whatever I owe for the food and the lodgings."

"No," said Kilgallen. He had come close enough to her to strike her, but Maura had refused to retreat an inch. Besides, there was little room to go; if he was going to hit her, he could do it in the middle of the room as easily as he could anywhere else. "I don't want you to talk. I don't want you to move, and I don't want you to talk."

Maura drove her right fist under his chin. She hit him with all her strength. In the space of an instant, she tried to draw power from the thousand oppressions she'd had to bear from her father and brothers, from poverty's endless tyranny, from the miserable steerage, from the steward who'd brought her to this place. It was suddenly clear to her that she was about to suffer at this man's hands, and nothing mattered to her but to show him, even for a moment, that she was not yet his slave.

The blow nearly broke Maura's hand, but it also nearly knocked the big man off his feet. Kilgallen staggered back, blinking at her with astonishment, holding on to his chin.

"I want to go," said Maura. "Sure this is a free country. And you, nor the likes of you, can't tell me what I can or cannot do."

Kilgallen was about to answer this, but stopped himself. For a moment he had forgotten with whom he was dealing; he had almost begun to dispute her assertion as if they were having an ordinary conversation, as if she were someone with whom he'd have to use reason.

He let go of his chin and shook his head, as if to clear his vision. But his vision was fine. She'd caught him off-guard, but the blow hadn't hurt him very much. "I could kill you," he said finally. "I could crack your skull against the floor, I could wring your neck, I could do anything I want with you and no- body would ever know, nobody would ever care."

"Please, sir . . ." said Maura, but she could not go on. She knew that nothing she could say would change his mind about what he would do with her. There was no point in begging when there was no chance of gain. For the first time she moved back from the center of the room. He was coming closer to her, and she wanted to delay his touch for as long as she could.

But now Kilgallen was earnest in his motions, and quick and surefooted. He stepped up close to her and, as she turned to the right, he followed her motion and pinned her shoulders to the wall. He brought his handsome face close, bending low so that his eyes met hers, and then he did an extraordinary thing.

"I love you," he said.

"No," said Maura, in a whisper, for the movement of his lips, the passion in his eyes, were a macabre version of her husband's lovemaking on the night he died.

And though he held her shoulders with an iron grip, he brought his lips to her forehead, to her cheek, to her mouth with such gentleness that the terrible violation he was beginning was magnified by its masquerading as love. She could not move her shoulders, and she could not move her frame from the wall; but she could twist her lips away from his, she could turn her head, she could finally kick into his shin with her bare foot until the smile was driven from his face.

Kilgallen let go of her shoulders and slapped her hard across the face. Maura pressed her back against the wall and began to bring her hands up to protect herself, but Kilgallen grabbed her wrists, brought them together, and held them while he kissed her. Still, his kiss was gentle, tentative, waiting for her lips to respond. But there was no response other than her shut lips.

Every moment drove Maura further away from the reality of

what was taking place. She was angry, of course, but she was confused, too. Sometimes, as she struggled against the wall, she couldn't remember where she was, and against whom she was defending herself. He could have been the black-bearded steward; or Patrick on their wedding night; or one of her brothers, drunk and wild after a night at the pub; or even her father, enjoying the fear in her face, the sense of his power over her life.

"I love you," he said again. "I love every girl in this house, and every girl in this house loves me." If he could not penetrate her shut lips, he simply moved to her eyes, to her neck.

Maura wanted more than anything to move away from him, for her body to be somewhere, anywhere, else than in this room, unable to budge her hands, her hips, her legs. She no longer listened to what he was saying, as the words were vile, without sense or decency.

"I know what you want, you'll get what you want—see if you don't get what you want from me, bitch. See if you don't." He dropped her wrists to place his hands at her neck, to pull back the folds of the silk robe, to tear at the cord that fastened about her slender waist. Still, he was kissing her, his lips ridiculously gentle as his powerful hands stroked her belly and breasts, and Maura felt herself drifting off, aware that her will was crumbling—not from some mad, incipient desire, but from its reverse. What was the prize she was holding back from this man's reach? What did it matter if she opened her mouth, if she allowed her hands to fall to her sides rather than fight uselessly, ceaselessly against him?

"I know what you want," he said. "Mike Kilgallen always knows, and it'll do you no good to pretend that you don't want Mike Kilgallen."

He stepped back from her, as if to look at what he had conquered. Her head bowed, the robe open and loose about her thin body, he examined the revealed curve of her left breast; the sparse reddish-brown patch of pubic hair; the very pale, redhead's skin so shockingly white next to the deep-blue silk.

"Come here," he said, and Maura took a step closer to him, letting the open robe move about her nakedness without shame. Kilgallen opened his arms to embrace her, and Maura allowed

him this pleasure; and when he kissed her, she opened her mouth
to satisfy his desire; and when his tongue beat wildly inside her
little mouth, like a bee in a bottle, she felt his penis grow hard
under his clothes; and when he pulled back from her suddenly,
he was breathing fast, and there was joy in his eyes. Even in her
enervated state, she felt this joy drive out a part of his mastery.
Even in her weakness, she couldn't fail to see this joy starting up
in his body as a weakness that she could use, as a source of
strength she could use to bring back her will.

He opened the buttons of his shirt, but left on his jacket; he
took off his low boots, but left on his socks; he pulled down his
pants and pushed her toward the unmade bed, as stupidly sure
of his power over her as he was proud of his erection.

Maura sat on the edge of the bed, and he joined her there,
holding her head in both his hands, kneeling before her, the
tails of his shirt sticking to the wet tip of his penis. She waited
until he brought both his hands to her breasts, and then she
moved, driving her fist down on his erect penis with all her
force.

She was so shocked that she had been able to do it—that she
had wrung a horrible cry from his lips, that she had been able
to swing off the bed, make for the door, and still no hand reached
out to restrain her, still the man remained doubled up in horrible pain on the bed—that she lost precious moments at the door,
amazed at the fact of freedom. But then her body was alive with
purpose once again. The door was no longer locked, and Maura
opened it, and ran down the dim corridor, remembering to go
right, for to the left was the bathroom, and she remembered no
stairwell from that part of the house.

The stairway was steep, but even as she ran up it, she found
herself tying up her robe. She made it to the top before she
heard the house come alive with shouting. She was not sure
whether to turn right or left, whether to find the back door or
simply run out into the New York street and get on her knees before the first man in a carriage. Her head swam and her legs felt
weak, as if her heart knew that she could never find the front
door, because she had not a clue what to do on the other side of
it.

But then she heard Kilgallen, his voice wild with anger, and

fear drove her away from the banister. She turned right and ran
on her bare feet, and there, in the middle of the corridor, was the
black woman, Louise, looking at her with real terror.

Maura stopped running and fell against the wall. Louise was
not afraid of her, she knew. She was afraid *for* her, for what
Kilgallen would do to her for defying him, for hurting him.
Louise made no move to come toward her, to help her, but it
made no difference, for a moment later two men came running
and grabbed her as if she were still capable of violence. They
pulled her to her feet, and brought her arms behind her back, and
tied her wrists together with strong rope.

"Please let me go," said Maura, not talking to them but to her
image of Louise, as if she were standing there, behind her shut
eyes. "Tell them to let me go, and sure I'll be a good girl, I
won't do a bad thing all my life." If she had spoken loud enough
for them to hear, they would have laughed. But Kilgallen's men
only heard moaning, and they were immune to sentiment, having
long since come to believe that Kilgallen's girls always got what
they deserved.

"You don't want to break her wrists open with that knot," said
Louise. "Mr. Kilgallen wouldn't like that, you can be sure of
that." She used the words to come closer to where the two men
held the girl. Louise wanted to tell her that it would be all right,
but she knew that it would not be all right, not if Maura had
tried to get away. It was not unheard of to try to get away, of
course; it was just extremely unusual. It was never successful.
"It's all right, honey," said Louise to the girl's shut eyes. "Louise
is here. You just get some rest, and then I'll bring you something
good to eat. You've had a long trip, and I bet you'd love some
ham and eggs and hot coffee. Take it easy, darling, and you just
think of that. Think of Louise making you breakfast, just like I
said." Louise followed the men back to the staircase. "That's a
good girl," she said, but Maura still didn't respond, just allowed
the men to drag her dead weight along the corridor, and finally
down the steep stairs.

Even as a very young child, Maura had learned to retreat
into this limbo that was not sleep, not awareness, not a daydream,
but something akin to all three: an oblivion that drifted between

the reality of the moment and the confused fantasies of what she wished to be. Often when her father had begun to beat her, he'd suddenly feared that he had gone too far; that he had whipped her unconscious, or had scared her to death. He could not know that at the first crack of his hand she was already drifting, imagining herself a princesss in a castle, or a fairy that could fly round the world in a minute, or a saint receiving the blessings and tears of every church in County Kerry.

She was aware of Kilgallen when they brought her to him, and he clutched her chin to raise her head. But she was no longer afraid. They had her body, but her body was weak, tired, useless. She could leave it behind. She could imagine the future, the distant future, when she would be free and strong and these men would be dead, and she would wear gowns and furs and step down from a private carriage to a red carpet laid over the snow, and enter a world of music and flowers and light.

They untied her wrists and stripped off her robe and pushed her flat on her back on the bed. She could imagine the future, when she would be rich and she would send for her mother in Ireland. Mrs. Dooley would come first-class, of course, and Maura would meet her at the dock in a coach with four horses, and her mother would exclaim at how grand the world was, how beautiful.

They had removed the quilt, and now they tied her wrists and ankles to the four bedposts, so that her pale, lovely body was no longer hers to control, and even as she tried to drift from the dream of a coach for her mother to the memory of Patrick, telling her awkwardly of his love, someone thrust a rag down her throat and held a hand over her struggling mouth. Against her will, she opened her eyes, and she saw Kilgallen, bearing down upon her belly with a sharp tool, and she could not imagine why they would kill her, why they would take the trouble to tie her to the bed if all they wanted to do was plunge a knife in her breast.

The knife sliced into the soft skin of her lower abdomen; not a killing thrust, but a straight, determined line, to draw blood and pain. Maura fought against the ropes, but the ropes held. She tried to drift back to Kerry, to her mother in the rose garden, to Brendt coming up the hill with a pail of steaming milk, but the knife cut again, and she couldn't howl because of the rag, and the pain was repeated a third and final time, and her mind was so clear, so sharp with the horror of what had been done, that there was no retreat for her, not that day, not that night; no dream could lift her from what Kilgallen had done.

Maura shut her eyes, and someone rubbed something grainy and harsh into her wound, and after a few moments this substance redoubled her pain, and confirmed what she already had supposed: that they had carved a letter into her skin, rubbing in an irritant to try and raise a scar. Maura had heard that the practice was becoming outlawed in most of Ireland—in most of the Empire, for that matter—but that it was still done by the very criminals whom the courts had once sentenced to this marking—to their enemies, and to their unfaithful women.

Maura wouldn't open her eyes; and when the gag was removed from her mouth, she didn't scream. Desperately, she tried again to drift away from them, to make this reality a nightmare and wake up into something without horror and shame. But all she could drift to was Louise's promise—that she would come and give her breakfast, ham and eggs and coffee—and that she had called her a good girl. She wondered what the black woman would say when she saw the letter etched in her skin, saw that Kilgallen had removed her for all time from the world of decent women, that the raised scar in the shape of a "W" marked her as a whore for the rest of her days.

# ❦ CHAPTER ❦ EIGHT

There was no breakfast that day. Maura remained where she was, flat on her back, her wrists and ankles secured to the bedposts, naked and open to the increasingly cold basement room. She tried not to look at what they had done to her, as if ignoring the whole episode might consign it to oblivion. It was an effort to raise her head anyway; it was easier to remain motionless, supine, her eyes focused on the darkening ceiling. She slept deeply that night, her body craving rest, but woke after only a few hours, remembering instantly where she was, why she could not move, what they had done to her.

In the pitch-dark, she raised her head, looking across the pale glowing rise of her little breasts to the black region where she'd been cut. She thought it strange that she had little sensation of pain. The pain had come all at once, rising to a frenzy that had nearly brought her to unconsciousness. Now there was only a dull throbbing, as if the invisible wound were reacting to the beat of her heart. Maura lowered her head to the mattress, waiting for morning to light the room.

She slept again, and dreamed: Her father had come to rescue her from this place. She saw him in the steerage of a filthy ship, sipping poteen. She saw him walking through the immigration authorities, thrusting aside every query with his thick arms. She saw him banging on the door of the house where she was being kept. She saw him coming down the steep stairs to the basement, a terrible frown on his lips. She saw him opening the door to her room, and the room was flooded with light, and he saw her nakedness, her disgrace, and instead of outrage there was only his smile, his leer, as his face grew bigger and bigger, its coarse outlines lit from behind by a hellish fire.

"If you scream, I'll shove this down your bleeding trap," said her father. But it was not her father. And it was not a dream—or, rather, the dream had been beaten back by the beery breath of an ugly man, his face pocked, and marked with red blotches, his sparse hair glistening with macassar oil. The high, tiny windows were still black. A gas lamp glowed in the center of the room. Maura tried to move, but the ropes still held her. The man had a rag in his hand and he was holding it about her face.

"Let me go," said Maura.

"I said to shut your trap," said the ugly man. He put aside the rag and held her cheeks in one huge hand. "You understand English, or do you want me to teach it to you?" He laughed at his own joke, and Maura quieted; for as the man moved back from the bed, she could see the mess left by the knife-cuts in the yellow light. She wanted to touch the wound, to make sense of it, to bend over and study it to see if it could possibly be true that a letter had been carved into her flesh. But the little area of dried blood was again obscured by the pockmarked face, leering at her like her father's face had in her nightmare. He placed a hand on her forehead, another on her breast, and Maura was looking straight up at his thick, blotchy neck, and she felt the skin of his legs touch hers as he swung his awful body on top of hers, straddling her so that his buttocks pressed against the wound in her lower abdomen and weighed unbearably on her pelvis.

It was not worse than her nightmare.

His face was awful, and grew redder and coarser momently; but it was not a dream where the unknown grew bigger and bigger, every moment threatening to overflow the unconscious, to drag something too horrible to imagine into the light of reality. She knew what was happening, she understood that she was helpless, she realized that this was the worst moment of her life; but it was something she would survive.

"You're quiet now—ha! That's better, you're not so wild.

They say you're wild, but you're quiet now, you're nothing to wake the dead, even with all that red hair."

Maura shut her eyes. So much of the last days had passed in darkness, in nightmares, in dreams, that she felt like an amphibian, existing in two worlds. She felt him shift his weight, easing her burden, but at the same moment the pressure increased on her right breast, as if he were holding on to it for support. A hand groped at her vagina, then left it, then returned, even clumsier than before. "What're you, a virgin, a fucking virgin? They told me you were married—Mike says you've been screwed through like a veteran." Against her will, she cried out in pain; the hand at her breast was pinching her nipple as if it were a fruit. "Ha! You like that, bitch? You ain't no virgin, don't give me that shit."

"Please," said Maura, speaking quietly, but he evidently took this for a signal of approval, for he pinched her nipple, and all about the breast, as if it were some exotic way to gratification. Maura began to cry in earnest, keeping her sobs as low as possible, and it was only then that the man's penis began to stiffen, and he swiftly, methodically, began to drive it into her vagina as if it were a ten-penny nail going through stone.

"You dried-up little bitch," he said disgustedly. "What the hell is it, you've got stitches tying up your cunt? Mike ought to thank my ass for this. Jesus, I hope he didn't pay too much for you."

But the man didn't give up. He took hold of her buttocks and tried to push her pelvis against his, as much as the ropes about her ankles would allow. Maura felt a red flash of heat in the back of her head, and she hoped it would grow hot enough to obliterate awareness. The man's complaints grew gradually indecipherable, but her mind was not yet so blurry that she couldn't feel his penis finally enter her, and then, instead of yielding to the rhythm of her body, continue on, like the charge of an army, like a punishing blow. She was dry, and the penis felt enormous, as if it were big and brutal enough to scrape away her insides, but almost at once there was an explosion: The man ejaculated; and he rocked his penis inside her for three spasmodic moments, then withdrew it so quickly that she nearly swallowed her last sob.

Exulting, the pockmarked man knelt over her, exhibiting his shrinking, wet penis, his ecstatic face. "You're all right," he said. "I guess you're all right, and I guess you'll learn a few things real fast." He laughed and patted her breasts with great familiarity. "If it wasn't for Mike, I'd let you out of these ropes right now."

"Please," she said.

"No, can't," he said, and he swung off her, in a hurry to get dressed.

For the first time, she thought she recognized him as one of the men who had captured her. His semen ran through her still body, and she wasn't sure who he was; she was only certain that if she ever had the chance, she'd kill him, she'd murder him as surely as she'd murder Mike Kilgallen.

A moment later he was out the door, leaving the light on for the next man. This man was short and squat, a monkey with muttonchop whiskers, and he said nothing to her as he stripped off his pants over his high-buttoned shoes. The pain of her rope-burned wrists and ankles now claimed more attention than the knife wound. Maura tried her best to be still, to see nothing, and to feel nothing. This man made it easier. He was already excited when he straddled her, and he inserted his penis easily in her vagina, wet from the other man's semen, making precise little motions that caused him to suck in his breath as if he were dying of the exertion. He didn't touch her face, didn't pinch her breasts, didn't place his weight on her wound; he was heavy, though short, but knew how to move so that he didn't disturb her body. When he ejaculated, she felt as if it were an impersonal torrent, mingling more with the pockmarked man's semen than with any part of her own body.

This man left quickly too, as if afraid of lingering in or near her prisoner's body. Though he didn't extinguish the gas lamp, he was the last to rape her that night. Maura wanted to throw up, but she couldn't bring her head far forward enough, and everything rising in her throat slid right back down as she swallowed her sobs, her tears.

The yellow light of the gas lamp finally began to fade into the early sunlight; though the windows let in little light, they faced east and caught the rising sun. Maura prayed for the door to open, for someone, anyone, to come in and let her out of her bonds, even if only for a moment. More than anything in the world, she wanted a bath. She wanted to clean the inside of her body till there was no trace of the men who had defiled it.

"Baby," she heard as the door opened, but before she could fill herself with joy at the sight of Louise, Mike Kilgallen entered the room behind the maid. "Baby, it's a nice morning," said Louise. "You're going to be feeling fine, just you wait and see if you don't." As she spoke, she went round to the front of the bed, behind Maura's head, and began to untie the complicated knot at her right wrist. Kilgallen walked slowly to the foot of the bed, looking steadily at Maura's body—at her legs, her breasts, at the wound. "You're all right, honey," Louise said. "I'm going to put you in that hot bubble bath, and I'm going to wash your beautiful hair, and I'm going to fix you a breakfast fit for a queen."

Since the last man had raped her, the hours till dawn had gone so slowly that Maura was now shocked by the rush of events. She was being freed of her bonds. Her tormentor stood at the foot of her bed. Her comforter stood behind her, at the head. She was naked, raped, marked, a prisoner. Louise talked on of the luxuries of the bath, the quantity of the breakfast. Kilgallen continued to look at her as if she were a wild dog, momentarily obedient after a beating. Maura looked back at him, taking in his physical presence, rather than trying to understand what that presence might represent. She had not yet fathomed what real crimes had been committed against her person, against her liberty; or, if she had, she had placed this understanding deep beneath the surface of thought. It was simpler to remain merely outraged, merely full of hate. It was simpler to look back at the man who examined her naked body, to take in his checked suit, his multicolored tie, his diamond stickpin, his cleanly shaved cheeks, his walrus moustache; to take in every detail and loathe every part, every aspect, every facet of his being.

Suddenly, the right wrist was freed.

"Oh, my God," she said, bringing her hand to her face. Her fingers moved slowly, laboriously, but deliciously. She was able to touch her nose, her chin, her eyes. A moment later, Louise had freed the other wrist, and Maura brought her hands together, and then began to massage her wrists, momentarily oblivious of Kilgallen, of her wound, of her secured ankles, of everything but this sudden freedom.

"Sit up, Maura," said Kilgallen.

She looked at him blankly, lying on the bed, clenching and unclenching her fists. He had used her name, and she had not heard it in such a long time. His use of it shocked her, and the shock drove a wedge of inexplicable terror into her heart.

"Maura," said Kilgallen, "you heard me. I said for you to sit up. When I say for you to sit up, then that's what you do."

If he knew her name, she thought, she could not be dreaming. This was not a vague sequence of nightmare images, with nameless figures confronting her ageless self. She was Maura O'Connell, born Maura Dooley. She'd been married, she'd been widowed, she'd survived the crossing to America, and she was this man's prisoner. This man who knew her name.

"Sit up, honey," said Louise, holding the back of her neck, pulling gently on her elbow.

Maura found herself rising, and as she did, she heard a sickening sound, a release of gas and bubbling of liquid in her vagina. Suddenly, the awfulness of the previous night was driven home to her. She looked from Kilgallen to her wound, to her pubic hair, to her straight legs, obscenely tied to the bedposts, and as she moved slightly forward, rocking on her naked buttocks, she was sure she felt the motion of semen inside her body. She began to throw up, twisting as far as she could so that the thin gruel she vomited ran off the side of the bed.

Maura did not black out, but at least she stopped thinking about the previous night, at least she stopped looking at Kilgallen. Louise finished untying her ankles, and then she was wrapped in the blue silk robe and was taken to the bathroom. Alone with Louise, Maura allowed herself to luxuriate. Her insides were cleansed with scented, soapy water, and Louise washed her hair. Maura drank hot milk with a dash of real coffee, still sitting in the tub. Once she was out of the tub, and Louise had helped her to dry off, she sat in her silk robe before the stove and ate fried eggs and hashbrown potatoes and fresh white bread.

"How do you feel, honey?" said Louise.

"Help me, *please*," said Maura.

"Now, darling, don't go making trouble for Louise."

"I just want to go—sure that's not a lot to ask."

"Let me take a look at you," said Louise. She dropped to one knee before her charge and pulled back the folds of the robe to look at Maura's wound. "It'll be all right, darling. You were crazy to try anything with Mr. Kilgallen. Ain't nothing Mr. Kilgallen won't do if he don't like you, you can believe me. Ain't nothing. I mean to say, the man is a killing man, darling. If you weren't so pretty, you'd be dead now, and that's the truth."

"Am I going to be sold to a black man?"

"What?" said Louise. "Are you crazy? What crazy thing are you saying, child?"

"A black man in South America," said Maura. "Don't you know? Sure that's what they do, that's what I heard, but I never believed it."

"That's crazy. No one's selling you."

"But sure I'm a slave here," said Maura. "Don't go telling me different, I know I'm not crazy. Even if I'm not feeling my best, I'm not crazy, not altogether out of my mind."

"You're not a slave," said Louise. "President Abraham Lincoln freed the slaves, you know that, girl."

"What's this then?" said Maura. She pushed aside her plate and got to her feet, keeping the robe open on her wound.

The dried blood had washed away, revealing a black and purple area of three square inches. At its center were the three joined cuts, already forming a scab, revealing the outlines of the future scar. The block letter "W" was nearly a half-inch high.

"Sure if this isn't the mark of a slave, it's the mark of a whore. And I'm not either, no matter what he does to me. I want to get out of here. Help me get out of here, Louise." Maura's anger disappeared in the face of Louise's sorrow. Neither of them had any power in this house, in this street, in this city. "Please," said Maura. "Sure I'm sorry if I yelled at you. It's not your fault. But please. There's something, there's some way, there *must* be some way to leave this place."

"You shouldn't have tried anything like that," said Louise again, not answering Maura's question.

Maura followed Louise back to the neat little room. A very pretty dark-haired girl was scrubbing the concrete floor on her hands and knees, working with feverish force and concentration. The red carpet had been rolled up and the little room was redolent of flowers, as if the soapy water were perfumed. Maura stood there for a moment, waiting for Louise to explain, but the maid vanished, closing the door after her.

"Who are you?" said Maura, but the girl didn't answer. She seemed to have heard the question, and resolved to ignore it. Maura came closer to where she worked. The girl was barefoot, and her only clothes were underwear. "What's your name?" said Maura, as pleasantly as she could.

But then the door opened, and Kilgallen entered alone. "Finish what you're doing and get out of here," he said to the dark-haired girl.

"Pardon, I no understand, sir," said the girl, speaking with a French accent. She worked faster, as if that might placate the devil in the room, but Kilgallen had already come up to her and grabbed at her arm. "Pardon," she said, springing to her feet.

"Pick up the pail and leave," he said.

"Pardon," she said, still not understanding the rapid English.

Kilgallen picked up the pail and gave it to her. Then he pointed to the door, which he had left open. Bowing two times, the French girl ran out of the room, sloshing water on the floor. Kilgallen shut the door after her.

"All right, Maura," he said. "Let's start again."

"What do you want, sir?" said Maura. It would do no good now to attack him. Even if she could land a single blow, he would surely beat her back down. And this was a prison. There were other men who kept her here. She did not want another night of being roped to a bed.

"Take off your robe," said Kilgallen.

Maura hesitated. It would be easy enough to do. The man had seen her naked, from all sides. He had touched her, and his men had raped her. She was not yet free. What difference would it make if she disrobed now, so long as it prevented another beating?

"You refuse?" said Kilgallen calmly. He sat down in the room's single chair, continuing to look at her. It went against his grain to reason with his girls, but he didn't want Maura to lose her value to him. She was pretty enough to be worth ten thousand dollars a year. He waited a moment longer.

"No," said Maura. "No, sir." But she didn't take off the robe. She remained standing, and then, all at once, she took two steps over to him and dropped to her knees, beginning to cry. It was not an act; she could not have pretended to beg for sympathy from the man she planned to murder. Her tears were real, because for a moment Maura's misery had superseded her strength; she had become a child, railing at the world. "Please, let me out of here," she said, looking at the floor. "Let me go, please, please let me go."

Kilgallen had evaporated into thin air. She was no longer crying from the basement of the house on Spring Street, but from a hidden recess of her childish soul. From the first blow she'd been dealt by her father in Kerry, to the present locked room, she had always wanted the same thing: to be free, to be as careless and unrestrained as an infant, glorified by the universe of a loving mother. She cried so long that the words wouldn't come for want of breath, and every moment she seemed on the verge of breaking; her mind had an urge to fall in on itself, to find bliss in madness. But Kilgallen waited. He still hadn't sent a slap across her face, or spoken a word to break apart her mindless pleading.

When she could cry no longer, she slowly began to come back to her senses. She was on her knees, and she got to her feet by holding on to the legs of Kilgallen's chair. When she stood up, she looked at his impassive face.

"Take off your robe," he said again.

"No," she said. Maura had banished the child. In its place had come a momentary violent rebelliousness. She remembered everything that had happened to her in this place, and she was prepared to die that instant rather than suffer anything further.

"Maura," he said, "you're not to talk, you're not to disobey. Think. Remember last night. I can make it last night all week. I can make it worse."

"What are you going to do to me?" she said finally. The rebelliousness had gone as fast as all her other moods. Now there was only the unknown, the fear that she might be in this man's power forever.

"I'll tell you what," said Kilgallen. "I'll tell you what I'm going to do to you. But first—and this is the last time I'm going to say it—take off your robe."

Maura took it off quickly, with an absurd modesty. She kept her eyes on the ground and held the robe in one hand before her genitals.

"Put the robe down on the bed," said Kilgallen.

Maura turned round and dropped the robe on the bed. She remained across the room from Kilgallen, her hands linked over her pubic hair.

"Come here," said Kilgallen. "Come to me."

Maura walked slowly to where he sat in the straight-backed chair. Kilgallen took hold of her hands and placed them roughly at her sides. "Don't move," he said.

"Please tell me," said Maura. "Tell me what you want from me. Tell me what I have to do to get out of here."

Kilgallen took hold of Maura's sparse pubic hair. He traced a pattern with his right index finger along the surface of her breasts. He pulled some of her red-gold hair from behind her back to across her shoulder, so that it fell over her right breast, the uneven strands of long hair falling to her navel.

Maura remained stock-still. She believed that he would tell her what she must know, and know fast, before she went crazy: why she was here, how long she'd be forced to stay.

"I was told that you were looking for work," said Kilgallen finally. He had moved his right hand behind her back, and now it rested on her buttocks. Because he sat, while she stood, his eyes remained on her breasts and belly, while Maura's now stared bleakly over his head at the far wall, while his words ran on.

"I've got work," continued Kilgallen, "so I made an arrangement with the steward of your ship to get you to work for me."

"Sure I had no idea, sir," said Maura, beginning to spin out an elaborate protest of how she was numbed into following the steward's proposal. All she had really agreed to was to get into a stranger's coach. She was not a whore, she wanted to say— that and a thousand other protests and pleas—but Kilgallen was not interested.

"Shut your trap," he said, pushing her away and getting to his feet. "Don't go too far, or I'll not say another word myself. You'll do what I want no matter what I tell you. Believe me, I know what I can make a woman do."

Maura waited awkwardly in the center of the room. She was afraid to step back, afraid to cover her genitals, afraid to do anything that would anger him further. Kilgallen came up to her and took hold of her chin so that he could point her face up to his. "You cost me a thousand dollars," he said.

"Sure that's impossible," said Maura, speaking out of turn once again.

"You wanted to work," continued Kilgallen, "and you will work. If you want to leave, you will be able to leave. But not until I'm paid back what I'm owed. Do you understand? You can leave when you pay me the thousand dollars. And you won't start earning a penny until you learn to do as I say. Do you understand me, girl? You're not a slave, you're just something I'm holding on to until I get back what I paid for it. And if you don't pay me back, you'll die here. If you give me any more trouble, I'll kill you."

"But I don't want to," said Maura finally. She had stepped back, out of his grasp, and now looked at him with horror. "I don't want to stay, I want to go. This is a free country, let me go! Let me go!"

Kilgallen opened the door and called out to his men. He had lost patience with her, and proven to himself once again that logical talk did little to teach these girls how they were expected to behave. Quickly, Maura was gagged, and tied to the bedposts, naked and spread-eagled as before. That night she was raped not twice but a dozen times, Kilgallen having called on his friends to help teach her a lesson.

But Maura didn't learn what Kilgallen had hoped to teach

her. As before, her nightmares were far worse than the reality of the endless men pumping their semen into her exhausted body. She knew that morning would come, no matter what happened in the night; she understood that the strength of her spirit was more important than the weakness of her flesh; she was certain that one day she would be finally free.

# ❦ CHAPTER ❦
# NINE

Maura lost track of time.

The men came to her, in the light of day, in the yellow light of the gas lamp at night. They were fat, they were old, they were rough, they were clumsy, they were coarse. Some were silent, holding their breaths as if to prove the rape hardly excited them at all. Others were loud, shouting obscenities, huffing and puffing like bulls. A few were gentle. Some were clean-shaven, with a barbershop scent and smooth hands. Many seemed young, frightened, fascinated. All were as quick as possible. None spoke to her. Louise bathed her, fed her, marched her to the bathroom and back to the locked room. After a year, or a month, or a week—sometime, at the beginning of her day, when it was light outside, but darkness threatened—they let her stay in the bed without being tied to the bedposts.

When the door opened that evening for the first man, it was Mike Kilgallen. She was certain that he had not yet been with her, that he had never been one of the many men who had come to her when she was tied.

Maura was amazed that she felt no anger. She remembered, of course, that this was the man she would one day murder, but no emotion greeted his entry to her room. She was simply tired. It was all she could do to lift her head from the bed, to pull the quilt closer to her chin. Kilgallen closed the door behind him, and then began to undress, his back to Maura. She turned her eyes from him to the ceiling, allowing herself the luxury of mov-

ing her legs about under the quilt, of clasping her hands together over her belly.

Suddenly, he was there, looking down upon her. His eyes were
dark, and his handsome, sensual face reminded her of the English
priest she'd caught sight of in her village in Kerry: He had
come, it was said, to study the condition of the Irish peasantry,
and someone had stolen his horse. Kilgallen removed the quilt,
and she shivered at the sudden cold. "No," he said, "you won't be
cold, Maura."

"Don't tie me, sir," she said, speaking so softly that he couldn't
hear her at all. His hands took hold of her wrists and held them
over her head, against the mattress, and for a moment Maura
thought she was back in her bonds, and she couldn't stop the
tears starting up in her eyes.

"You won't be tied, Maura," he said, and she was aware that
his hands about her wrists were gentle, that they moved along the
underside of her arms, that his face was suddenly big and smiling, his enormous mouth covering her eyes, one at a time, as he
kissed her brows, then her shut eyelids, then her open, silent
lips.

Then, like all the others, he was in bed with her; he was
touching her breasts, her thighs, her belly. But she was not tied;
for the first time, she could not take solace in her bonds. If this
was rape, it was not rape as it had been before. Nothing was
preventing her from fighting, from driving her fingernails into
his eyes, from swinging her knee into his exposed groin.

Nothing but a lack of will.

She hated him, she wanted to murder him, she wanted to be
free of this place forever, but she had no strength to combat her
fear, no power to mobilize her exhausted body. Maura was defeated. She remained on her back, understanding this, as the man
continued to caress her. Kilgallen took a great deal of time with
her. He kissed her, and touched her, and moved about her inert
body as if he were her lover, as if he expected some magical feeling to descend upon the two of them. He spoke to her, too. She
was beautiful, he said; he loved her breasts; he adored her Irish
hair. He said that she would be rich as a princess, that men
would worship her all across the city.

But neither the speech nor the caressing concerned Maura.

Kilgallen might as well have been caressing a doll on the other side of the world. He might as well have spoken in Greek. Maura thought only of one thing: that she had come to a point where she had no strength left. That she could do nothing other than accept this violation, that she must simply surrender her will to this man.

Finally, he was done with the love-play. He entered her, hurting her exactly as the others had hurt her. She watched, powerless beneath him, as his face lit up with happiness. Maura did not know what it was that pleased him: that he had ejaculated, or that she had lost her will to fight. After a while, he stopped moving. She felt his semen run through her. He was not in a hurry to leave her body, like the others had been. Kilgallen made himself comfortable, lowering his upper torso so that he covered the length of her body with his heavy muscular frame. She wanted to protest, to tell him that she could hardly breathe, but she said nothing. His penis was shrinking inside her. His heart-beat slowed. A few moments more and the man's breathing assumed the regular, stately pace of deep sleep.

Maura was wide awake. It was the beginning of her day, and she could no more imagine sleeping with this inert man on top of her than she could fly out the tiny windows of this prison. Her hands remained where they had been for the last minutes, flat on the mattress, flanking his hateful body. There was nothing to do but wait.

She began to fantasize: how she might twist the silken belt of her robe lying on a low table across the room, about Kilgallen's neck, until the man would go quite blue-faced, until the blood he'd torn from her belly would come running out of his own throat; how Louise would come through the door, bearing a silver tray, and instead of bowing to the man's sleeping presence, she would simply raise the tray over his head and smash in the back of his skull and save her darling Maura; how Patrick O'Connell, not dead but alive and ruddy with health, would break down the door and tie Kilgallen to the bedposts, naked and helpless and alone—

"All right," he said, suddenly waking, his words coming through clenched teeth. He jerked his head up from her body and looked down at her face, as if to ascertain where he was.

"Please, sir, you're hurting me," she said. His weight was all concentrated now, bearing down on her pelvis.

"What?" he said. He had not yet shaken off the dullness of his nap.

"You're hurting me," she repeated.

Kilgallen, fully awake, rolled off her body and out of the bed. Maura lay still as the man crossed the room and silently put on his clothes. The yellow light of the gas lamp was suddenly brighter, and Maura watched the man adjust his stiff collar in the mirror on the wall. Kilgallen stroked his long sideburns, pulled at the hairs of his walrus moustache, and patted down the wavy hair at the back of his head. His diamond stickpin flashed in a red and green tie—Maura vaguely remembered the man in another checked suit, wearing another flamboyant tie—and then he was coming toward her, buttoning his jacket, his cleanly shaven face pale with displeasure.

"I was hurting you?" he said, standing politely a foot from where she lay naked on the bed.

"Yes, sir. I'm sorry, sir. It's just that you were heavy, sir."

"Cover yourself, you stupid broad," said Kilgallen, and he flung her robe at her and retreated to the chair across the room.

Maura dressed herself in the robe and remained sitting up on the bed. "Come here," said Kilgallen.

Maura got out of the bed, and walked over to him.

"Stand up straight," said Kilgallen. "You look like an opium fiend."

Maura stood straighter, and he began to talk, to rail at her again, the sharp words coming in swift, short phrases: She couldn't move, she couldn't please, she couldn't pretend to be a woman. How did she expect to earn back the thousand dollars he had paid for her if she couldn't make love any better than a cow? She thought it might be a good idea to apologize, but she didn't precisely understand his complaints. She had a mortal fear of being put back in bonds, the men coming through her door one at a time—an endless procession.

Finally, he was through with his speech. He stood up, adjusted his collar one more time, and left her alone in the locked room. Maura remained standing for a few minutes more, unable to make a decision as to what to do next. Idly, without anger, she sidled to the door and tried to turn the knob. It wouldn't budge.

She leaned against the door for minutes, trying to remember what he had told her, trying to reconstruct the meaningless sounds into a communication that would explain the way in which she could be released. A thousand dollars, he'd said. She'd have to pay back a thousand dollars.

Maura returned to her bed, still dressed in her robe, and waited for the men to come. She would ask them for money. If each one gave her one hundred dollars, she'd only need to be raped by ten. If each gave her ten dollars, she'd have to be raped by a hundred.

But it wouldn't be rape, she realized suddenly.

She was not tied. She was going to ask them for money. It was not rape when you begged for a gift; when you opened your robe to bare your skin; when you allowed them, one and all, to do with you whatever they wanted, if only they would help you out of this place.

Maura waited for the men all night, prepared to ask for money, to beg for her freedom in exchange for her body. But the men never came. She fell asleep as the sun began to rise, and, when the door finally opened, it was only Louise, carrying the breakfast tray. The maid didn't speak until Maura had begun to eat.

"You're moving upstairs, darling," she said.

Maura looked up at the smooth black-skinned face. "Upstairs?" she said, with such a dull look to her once-angry eyes that Louise could scarcely recognize the girl who'd been brought to the house only ten days ago.

"Listen, darling," said Louise. "For your own good, if you ever want to get out of here—"

"I want to get out of here," said Maura, interrupting without thought. She let go of the bit of bread in her hand and took hold of Louise's arm. "Sure that's all I want. Please—I've told you— you know I want to get out of here. Please, *I have to get out of here.*"

"Maura!" said Louise, so harshly that the young girl let go of her and jerked her head back in fright. "Stop it! Hush! Come on, hush!" Then Louise took her into her arms and held her till the fear slowly ran out of the young girl, leaving her as quiet as a child waiting to be told a story as complex as the creation of the world.

"Listen," said Louise, "Mr. Kilgallen thinks you've been bad. He says for me to tell you that. I tell him you don't understand, but he says that you're going to understand. Honey, the only way you can get out of here is if you're good. Good his way. Do what he tells you and he'll take you out of here. Otherwise you'll stay upstairs; and if you stay upstairs, you're going to get sick, honey—you're going to get weak and sick and you'll never get out of here. You're so pretty, darling. He won't keep you there long. All you've got to do is behave yourself. Otherwise you don't have a chance. Do what I'm telling you, darling. Listen to Louise."

"Aren't there constables?" said Maura suddenly, her eyes wild with hope, as if perhaps Louise had never thought of the existence of a New York City police force.

"Darling," said Louise, stroking Maura's red hair. "You poor darling, you'd better finish your meal."


"Upstairs" proved to be the fifth—the top—floor of the house, and climbing the narrow back staircase exhausted Maura. Louise had helped her remove her robe, and exchanged it for a rough flannel shirt whose uneven hem ended above her knees. Even in her weakened state, Maura realized that she couldn't possibly run out into the street dressed like that, a foreign girl without money, papers, friends. As she climbed, the rough fabric of the shift irritated the scab where she'd been cut by Kilgallen, reminding her again and again of the extent to which her life had been taken control of.

On each landing there was a narrow window, and every window was barred from the outside. Maura caught her breath as she found herself staring at a brick wall across a narrow yard at the back of the house. *Someone* must notice a house with barred windows, she thought. This was supposed to be an enormous city, teeming with people; she couldn't imagine how a young girl could be imprisoned without a soul knowing about it.

"You—Brigid! Get your ass up here! Quit dreaming and shake it!"

A stout young woman, no more than twenty-five, stood at the head of the stairs calling down to Maura. Maura wondered why she was so angry, but the anger didn't affect her; she simply shrugged and continued the climb.

"You're not so pretty," said the young woman. "You're just another dumb piece of ass, do you hear what I'm saying? Jesus, the clodhoppers they send me. Is that all they have in Ireland, redheaded clodhoppers with little noses? Come with me, Brigid."

Maura was taller than the young woman, but when she grabbed Maura's arm, it was with great strength. "My name is not Brigid," said Maura, the insult awakening her from passivity. She wondered if she was strong enough to twist out of the woman's grip and trip her fat frame down the staircase. But then what? she thought. Even if she broke this new keeper's neck, what would that have to do with her freedom?

The fifth floor was nothing more than a garret, with two tiny rooms leading from the landing. Maura was pushed into one of these, and the door was slammed and locked behind her.

"Thank the Lord—an adult hooker. Sit down by me, love. Come here, don't worry about the kid, just sit."

The speaker was a very thin young woman, no more than two or three years older than Maura's seventeen years. She sat in a little patch of morning light, with thin shadows playing across her features where the bars of the room's single window blocked the sun. Because of the low, sloping ceiling, Maura had to stoop to approach her, but it was only three paces across the whole room, most of which was taken up by an ancient blanket, covering a hardwood floor. Leaning against the wall, a young girl, no more than fifteen years old, kept up a continuous moaning, her eyes shut to the world.

"Come on, good-looking, sit down. Tell me what you did, I'll tell you what I did. Shit, I was stupid. I had it good on Twenty-sixth Street. Servants, silk dresses, champagne, flowers—the

works. Nothing was too good for Ginny, and even Mike Kilgallen gave me my head. I had free rein—no joke, sister. Free
rein with lots of cash, come and go as you please."

"What's wrong with her?" said Maura. It was the first thing
she had said to her new companion. She couldn't understand how
Ginny could ramble on like that with a child moaning all
the while.

"The kid? Screw the kid. I'm fed up to here with that bitch.
Jesus, the fucking kid pisses in my blanket every night. I don't
want to talk about that kid. I've been living with her for a
whole week and I'm off my nut. You Irish?"

"But what's wrong with her?"

"Jesus, what are you, a missionary? She's crying because
she's a dope. Stupid, you know what I'm saying? She ate so
much opium that it was coming out of her ass. She smoked so
much dope that she believed her boy friend was going to marry
her. She's real surprised that she's in a whorehouse now. She
thinks it was a trick. What a laugh! Look at her. She's fourteen,
fifteen—been getting laid since she was ten. Real Bowery rat
gone romantic. What's your name?"

"Maura."

"You all right, kid?"

"I want to get out of here."

"Sure you do, honey," said Ginny. "What is this? Did they
put me in here with a bunch of crazies? What do you mean
you want to get out of here? Where do you think you're going?"

"That poor girl," said Maura, turning from the child moaning
against the wall to Ginny. "Did someone tell her that he wanted
to marry her? Sure that's what they warned us about on the
ship. But who would have thought it possible? And me—I had
a husband. How could anyone do this? I don't understand how
anyone could do this to a child."

"What child? This ain't no child, this is a Bowery rat—
didn't you hear me the first time? You think this was somebody they nabbed in a church? Nobody wants this bitch except
Kilgallen. She'll be smiling as soon as she's out of this place
and gets to a nice house uptown. What's your beef, sister?"

"I don't understand," said Maura.

"What don't you understand?"

Maura looked at her blankly, as if she were about to drift off into a daydream. "Did they cut her, too?"

"What?"

"Cut her," said Maura. She touched the area of her wound through the flimsy old flannel of her shift. "I was cut."

"Let me see," said Ginny.

Suddenly Maura was modest. She didn't want to lift her shift. But Ginny insisted, and when Maura retreated to the wall, she scrambled after her and pulled her flat onto the blanket. "I just want to see, for the love of Jesus," she said, pulling back the shift.

Maura looked at it herself, as if seeing it for the first time. The scab had risen, so that the letter "W" was now quite clear, and Ginny traced her finger along it, very much impressed. "That's going to be some scar, love. I never seen that before."

"No?"

"I mean they do it," said Ginny. "I know some girls who've got cut like that, but I ain't never seen it up close. That's something. He must've been crazy mad, huh? I thought *I* got him mad, but you must've nearly killed the bastard. What'd you do, love? What's your beef, Irish? How'd you end up in the shit-house?"

But Maura had no time to answer, even if she could have fully understood the question. Bertha, Kilgallen's stout keeper of the upstairs girls, returned to order Maura and Ginny to work, leaving the youngest girl to her moaning. On the fifth-floor landing, three tired girls emptied from the other garret room looked out the tiny barred window at the cold gray yard below, at the dull brick wall opposite. One of them was the girl who had scrubbed Maura's basement room on her hands and knees, and who seemed to speak little English. All of them were driven downstairs by a madly pushing Bertha, and directed to a score of household tasks. Maura and Ginny were dispatched to strip the beds in the many rooms on the fourth, third, and second floors and carry the sheets to the basement laundry.

Maura was amazed at Ginny's energy. The girl stripped the beds and ran with the sheets, as if the task had to be accomplished within moments. Maura noticed that she had painted her skin—the black makeup about her eyes was smudged, and her red cheeks began to be diluted by perspiration. "Come on, love," said Ginny more than a few times. "Be quick, or you'll never get out of here."

Maura didn't understand why this was so, but she was soon following the thin blond girl's example. Both worked like demons, running on bare feet, stuffing the stained white sheets, smelling of liquor and smoke and sex, into wooden casks filled with boiling water. Ginny's hardness revealed a hunger that Maura recognized: She would do anything to get out of this terrible place.

"You know this house well?" asked Maura as they turned from the laundry to charge up the stairs for more sheets.

"Later—we'll talk when we're standing still, love," said Ginny.

Maura didn't know when this would be, but she quieted, using her breath for the climb up the stairs. The rooms from which they took the sheets were all small, each with a simple bed and a washstand; even Maura's basement room had been better furnished. There were at least a dozen rooms, Maura thought, perhaps as many as eighteen, and she wondered whether there could be eighteen whores in the house at one time.

"The bastard does this on purpose, you know," said Ginny an hour later, when they were back in the basement, beginning to scrub the sheets against enormous washboards.

"Does what?"

"This. Works us. Not just for punishment, but to put us down, if you know what I'm saying. Take us off the old high horse."

"Sure it's Kilgallen you mean?"

"Mike-the-Pike Kilgallen, may he rot in hell for a thousand years, the son of a cocksucker," said Ginny. Maura kept her eyes on the washboard, unable to look at her new friend while she spoke such words. "They say he's killed a hundred girls, not just from the French disease, but from *this*. No sleep, no food, just slave work and fucking the scum of the earth. It's enough to kill anybody. Do you know I was shopping in Stewart's not a week ago? All by myself, with a hundred bucks in my fist and a cab waiting for me? Jesus, those fucking sales-girls with their noses in the air—I showed them, all right. I had the money right there."

"What's Stewart's?"

"The store, you bimbo—ain't you listening?"

"Sure, Ginny. I'm listening very carefully."

"You never been to Stewart's?"

"I've never been to New York."

"Jesus, where the fuck do you think you are, dopey?" said Ginny, but then all at once she understood. "Hey, Irish, you're steerage meat! They ripped you right off the dock, didn't they?"

"Sure that's what I've been telling you. I had a husband," said Maura, the words growing louder in the steaming-hot room. "He died, they tricked me, I got in this carriage, and that's all it's been. It's not my fault. I didn't do anything, I'm a good girl."

"Jesus Christ, you're a good girl. What am I supposed to be, the daughter of Lucifer?"

"I don't mean that."

"Shit, you don't. Jesus. The same old story. Every whore in New York is a holy saint. Especially the Irish ones. Let me tell you something, bimbo: It makes no difference—a whore is a whore. My mother was as Irish as you, down to her red hair. She had freckles up her arms, she had freckles up her ass, and she went to church, and she was a whore. My father wasn't Irish. Swedish, he was, but I don't remember him. My mother was a whore, see, she had a husband, but she was a whore, and you're no better than she was, don't think you are, don't think you are for a second."

Maura didn't want to answer this. She had been on the verge of learning where she was, what she could do to leave, and she hoped that Ginny would calm down enough to offer her friend-ship once again. Maura scrubbed at a sheet, watching her hands turn red in the hot water.

"I mean, what's the difference, right?" said Ginny finally.

"Right," said Maura.

"I mean, if you want to get out of here, you can't do it by being a saint. If you're a saint, they're going to carry you out of here in a box. They'll put you in Kilgallen's private plot in Washington Cemetery. He's got lots of saints buried there, but no one of them was buried pure, believe you me, bimbo. He just buried the dopes. You want to get out of here, right?"

"Yes."

"You know what this place is?"

"I think it's a whorehouse."

"Jesus Christ, I'm a son of a bitch," said Ginny. "You think it's a whorehouse." She dropped her sheet and pulled Maura close to her, laughing like a lunatic. She kissed Maura's forehead, the black makeup melting along Ginny's nose, running onto Maura's hair. "You think this is a whorehouse, you baby, you perfectly doped-up son-of-a-bitch baby."

"Please," said Maura. "Maybe I'm wrong. I want to know, because I've got to get out of here. I've just go to, do you understand? If I can't get out of here, I'll just die, and I don't want to die. I want to live, but I want to live out of this place."

"You know where I want to be?" said Ginny suddenly, no longer laughing. "I want to be at the Waldorf. I want to have my own room, my own suite—a suite of five rooms, with a servant, a little black girl who can scrub my back, and a real gentleman to keep me. Not another gangster. Some guy without a gat, who knows how to dress and who'll take me to Sherry's. I don't want to be just a dumb broad popping out of cakes while everyone laughs because I'm naked. Shit, I'm pretty. Ain't I pretty, Irish?"

"Yes, Ginny. Sure you are. You're beautiful."

"Damn right I'm beautiful. Jesus, no one can say I ain't got the looks, even after all this shit, even if I'm back in the shithouse again." Ginny turned back to her washboard and began to scrub at a sheet; but then, just as abruptly, stopped. She remembered that Maura was ignorant, and that it wasn't fair to keep her that way.

"Look, love," said Ginny. "Here's the line. This is the shithouse. Bottom of the hill. For the bad girls, you understand what I'm saying? See, Irish, this is how it goes. I'm a hooker, right? I get paid for getting laid, but most of the money goes to Kilgallen. But that's okay, because it's good money, my share. I mean, I ain't crazy—I can make fifty bucks a week. I knew a girl who got out of this scare, and she was rich at twenty-one, just because she was smart pussy. I mean this is the *shithouse*. You're just getting fucked by thumpers and clods and pad-shovers and punks—I mean, don't forget what this is. If you're good—and that means that you do what you're told, you don't complain, you kiss Kilgallen's ass, you clean up his house, and you make his two-dollar boys happy—you'll get out of here. Otherwise you'll be dead. People die in the shithouse. They just give up and die, and Mike takes them away."

"But where—if you're good, I mean—where do you go?"

"Hey, Irish, you're going to be good. Just give them a good time, and they'll tell Mike, and in a few days he'll move you out of here. As soon as he thinks you're the right stuff. That he can trust you. He doesn't want a crazy girl in his hothouse."

"What hothouse?"

"I mean Twenty-sixth Street, love. That's where I was, and I was also in Philly, and he's got places in Pittsburgh, too. And besides that, there's at least four more in the Tenderloin. Mike's got places all over town, and it's some big damn town. Twenty-sixth Street is great. You get senators there, and handsome guys from Columbia College, and everyone's spending money and dropping it for you when Mike ain't looking. I mean, they pay him, but they give *you* something, too, if it's real good. And Mike doesn't give a shit. Hey, listen, I was rich. I had my own clothes, and all the girls get their own rooms, and the rooms ain't bad at all, and there's always a maid."

"What if you want to leave?"

"Leave?"

"I mean—go out of the house."

"Jesus, you just walk out the door, baby. That ain't the shithouse, I'm talking about Twenty-sixth Street. There are no bars on the windows. Everyone's happy, or they ain't there. You know what I'm saying? There's plenty of money, and Mike can be all right if you don't fuck things up. I mean, he'll let you leave if you're not going to work for somebody else. Unless you're trying to take what's his, like some regular, you know what I'm saying?"

"How did you get here?"

"The shithouse? Hey, it was stupid. And I should've known better because I ended up here once before. It's just that a friend of mine got out of the cathouse on account of this gangster with lots of money—he wanted her all to himself. I mean, it happens. He set her up somewhere, and it was okay with Mike, because he knew the guy, and maybe the gangster was a pal, or maybe he just threw some cash his way.

"Anyway, the girl picked me up in a carriage one day, and all day she was talking prices—you know, she bought a bicycle for ninety-seven dollars, a brand new Rambler bicycle, and she got a fur hat, and she got a pearl necklace—fifty-eight bucks, a hundred and eighty-five bucks—you know, money all day. On top of everything, she says she's happy with this guy, he treats her good.

"Well, that same night Mike gives me a guy I didn't want. I had taken this guy on before, and he was heavy, a fatty, and hard to take. He liked me a lot and he wanted me again, but I said no way unless I get more money. Mike was sore—he was in a shit mood, and so was I. I said too much, okay? Mike said too much, I said too much. I ain't going to take the guy on, I said. I was going to work for somebody else—he didn't have to bring me here. But here I am."

"But I thought you said—sure you said," said Maura, very anxious to know, "you could leave the other place whenever you wanted."

"Hey—whenever you want, as long as Mike's not beating the shit out of you. I could have left the day before, but not when I say no to Mike Kilgallen. I mean, he is the guy who's in charge, if you know what I mean. It's a business, right? I just want to get back there so bad, so I can get out of this place. The house on Twenty-sixth is out of sight, love. You'll see when you get there. You'll never want to leave such a class place."


The girls worked all day without a break. There was no food until six o'clock, and by then Maura would have jumped through a fiery hoop for so much as a bit of bread. Six of them ate at once, standing in the basement kitchen, sopping up soup with stale rolls. Louise was nowhere to be seen; the six bare-foot, exhausted girls had to clean up after themselves and then were shouted back up to the fifth floor by Bertha and locked in their tiny rooms. Ginny and Maura's young roommate, who had stopped crying long enough to eat her portion of soup, re-treated to her corner, more terrified than ever. Now that it had grown dark, the only source of light in their cell was a candle, very close to burning to its end. The child watched the flame, shivering against her fear of the dark.

"They'll come for us soon," said Ginny. "Remember what I told you, if you want to get out of here."

But Ginny was wrong. It began to rain violently, and the weather showed no signs of changing for the rest of the night. The candle went out, and Maura held the young girl in her arms to try and quiet her sobbing. All three of them fell asleep in the close, dark room, the even sound of the wild weather prov-ing a sure soporific, even on the thin blanket over a hardwood floor.

But then, at some nameless hour, all three were awakened by the opening of their door. "Brigid!" said stout Bertha.

Ginny pressed Maura's hand, and Maura got to her feet, trying to shake off sleep, and, stooping against the low ceiling, walked out of the room.

Bertha looked at her critically on the fifth-floor landing, hold-ing a large lamp up to her exhausted face. "Stand still, Brigid," she said. Quickly, with evident displeasure, she stripped off Maura's filthy shift, she brushed out Maura's long red hair, she shook a few drops of musk oil onto Maura's shoulders and rubbed it along the girl's neck and breasts and belly. Then she grabbed Maura's chin and pulled her face close, as if she would like to crush her pretty features with a violent hand, as if she would like to devour the beautiful girl with vengeance. "I said be still, Brigid," said Bertha, and she opened a little vial and stuck a finger into it, and then smeared a sweet-smelling sub-stance across Maura's lips and into her cheeks.

"That's the best I can do!" Bertha said, stepping back to examine her handiwork. "Let's see Kilgallen do any better at this hour of the night." And she pushed the painted woman down the steps to a room on the third floor, where a gas lamp glowed and a clean, freshly made-up bed waited. Maura was told to get beneath the sheets, and she did as she was told.

Not a minute passed before the door opened and a young man, only a little drunk but soaked to the skin, entered the room alone. He looked at Maura and liked what he saw. "Out of sight," he said, intoning the latest catch-phrase picked up by collegians in waterfront beer halls, and shared alike by Broadway promoters, daring debutantes, and stevedores. Quickly he shed his wet clothes and got into bed with Maura. "Out of sight," he said again. "My God, you are an out-of-sight girl!"

The slang expression meant nothing to Maura. She was thinking about something else: that she was not tied, and that she would not resist.

Though she felt nothing but the coarseness of his beard stubble, the roughness of his clumsy hands, the insistent hammering of his penis into her unreceptive vagina, she tried to moan with pleasure. "You like that," he said. "Yes, you like that. Hell on roller skates—oh, yes, yes, you like that very much."

After he ejaculated he asked her her name. "Maura," he said. "I'll remember that. I'll come back for more Maura anytime. Gee, you smell like a daisy. Maura! You're beautiful, Maura. I like you—I like you and I'm sure going to remember your name."

She forgot to ask him for money, as she had planned to do all day long. But the young man, the sole customer of the house on Spring Street that miserable rainy night, was a sport—not at all like the regular customers, but a chance drifter from uptown, following the suggestion of a hansom driver after a six-hour poker game in a Bowery dive. Unbidden, he gave her a gratuity: a newly printed greenback dollar.

If everyone is as generous as he, thought Maura, after she had been returned to the locked room by Bertha, the bill crushed in her fist, it won't be impossible to pay Kilgallen his money. She could be free, she thought, clutching at the numbers whirling in her mind: Nine hundred and ninety-nine more dollars and she could pay Kilgallen what he had paid for her. Opening the dollar and flattening it in the dark, she rejoiced, touched by the dream of freedom.

# PART FOUR

## The Tenderloin

# ☙ CHAPTER ☙
# TEN

It grew colder in the house on Spring Street, and Maura grew thinner. Ginny left for the house on Twenty-sixth Street after two weeks, followed by the French girl, and a few weeks after that by an Irish girl, from Galway, who had never spoken to Maura or to anyone but Kilgallen. The youngest girl, the one who had shared the garret room with Maura and Ginny, was removed from the house one night; no one supposed they were taking her to a doctor, and the only other possibility seemed to be the East River, either to drown her or to sink what was already dead.

New girls came and left. Many were from upstate New York, farm girls eager to please their master. A few had been tricked into the house on Spring Street—girls without parents, without husbands, without friends. One of these girls caught a fever before Christmas and died on the first day of the New Year, 1898. Bertha claimed that the girl had been given a decent Christian burial in Kilgallen's section of the Washington Cemetery. But Maura knew that it mattered not at all how one was buried. She remembered how Fiona Maloney's husband had been wrapped in the gray blanket and tossed without ceremony into the sea. Her own Patrick had been given the same service. Such treatment of the dead would have appalled her religious mother, would have shocked even her sister Brendt, whose own death was a suicide that left her battered corpse drifting to oblivion in another part of the sea.

"When will I go?" said Maura to Bertha, time and again, as one girl after another graduated from two or three weeks of confinement, overwork, boredom, and brutality. Everyone moved on, it seemed, except her. She did what she was told, and quickly, as Ginny had urged her. She scrubbed floors on her hands and knees, ran up and down the steps at Bertha's bidding, entertained Kilgallen's customers with as much fake enthusiasm as she could wrest from her exhausted body. She turned eighteen in February, but she told no one on the anniversary of her birth; even at home, in Kerry, no one had celebrated the day with more than a sigh of remembrance.

One morning, in the first week of March, she woke with a start, looking round the garret room with a renewed sense of horror. Two Swedish girls shared her blanket on the floor, and Maura had been unable to exchange a word with them since they'd arrived two weeks before. She had been dreaming of the crossing again: the unbearable stench of the steerage, the endless pounding of the engines, the rolling of the waves. Now, in the near-dark of the tiny room, looking from the sleeping Swedes to the shut door, she saw her present as clearly as she remembered the past: This room, this house, these months, were taking her away from what she had been, just as the steamship had taken her away from Ireland; and for the first time, she realized that she had slowly and imperceptibly begun to submit to the voyage.

Instead of jumping to her feet and hammering on the locked door, she took her new knowledge back to sleep. She had saved twenty dollars in the many weeks she'd been here; most of the men she'd begged for a favor had laughed in her face. Today she would approach Kilgallen, she decided, and offer him the money. She would show him that even in this filthy place she could earn money for him. She would show him that she had changed, that he could trust her; that if only he would give her the chance, she would be beautiful, and men would pay richly for her, and she would never, never try to escape. . . .

"Maura, darling," said Louise, and Maura smiled happily up at the black face and tried to twist more deeply into her dream. "Come on, sweetheart, I'm going to feed you something special. I'm going to wash your hair and I'm going to scrub your back. Come on, darling—that's a good girl."

"Louise!" said Maura, sitting up so fast that she almost banged her head into the maid's. They had seen each other half a dozen times since Maura had been banished upstairs, but they had not been allowed to speak to each other. Other girls had taken Maura's place in the basement room, and every one of them had been sent on to one of Kilgallen's other houses. "I'm sorry, I was dreaming."

The Swedes were gone, the door was open, Bertha was nowhere to be seen. "You're better," said Louise. "You're so much better."

"Sure I'm better. I'm fine and fit and ready to move," said Maura.

The maid looked at her closely, not knowing whether or not to be glad at the change in the girl.

They went downstairs, Maura following Louise to the basement and helping her draw water for the bath. "Am I to be allowed out? Are you putting bubble bath in? I've been here longer than anyone, Louise. Sure it must mean something good. Am I to see Kilgallen? Tell me, *please*. I won't mention what you tell me to a soul."

But Louise didn't want to offer information. Against the fact of Maura's optimism, her eagerness to please, her youthful fancies, Louise grew glum. More than any other girl Kilgallen had brought to her, Louise had been struck by Maura's fierce devotion to freedom, a devotion forged from innocence. Now the innocence was gone, and the freedom sought by Maura was therefore cheapened, impure. Silently, the maid scrubbed her clean, and washed the red-gold hair, and helped her into the new clothes brought to the house that morning. But when Maura was dressed, her face painted, Louise didn't marvel at the transformation of the girlish drudge into a fashionable siren. That transformation was simple. What she marveled at was the ease with which Maura moved on unfamiliar high-heeled shoes, the glad acceptance of a very low-cut dress, the proud preening before the mirror image of a woman whose lips and eyes and cheeks glowed with the man-made colors of the courtesan.

"Sure you're sorry as a dog," said Maura, whirling on Louise. "Is it that you're sad to see me go? Isn't this what you've been hoping for me, to get out of this place?"

"Honey, you're right," said Louise. "I'm just a silly old fool." And she took the girl by the arm and led her up the stairs to the ground-floor parlor, where an oak log burned in the fireplace and Kilgallen sat reading a paper with the latest news from Cuba.

"All right, Louise," he said, without looking up from his paper. "You can go now. Leave us."

Maura squeezed the maid's hand, and Louise went back downstairs.

"Do you realize that there might be war with Spain?"

"No, sir," said Maura, and Kilgallen looked up at her with interest.

"It occurs to me that you've never seen much of this great city of ours, Maura. Perhaps you'd care to take a ride with me."

"Oh, yes, sir," said Maura. The thought of leaving the house so thrilled her that she could barely still her suddenly shaking body. "I would very much like that, sir. Sure I've been a good girl here, as Miss Bertha can tell you. I do what I'm told, sir, and I'm only wanting a chance to show you how good I can be. I have some money, sir. It's not much, but I know from the others that there's much more money uptown, sir, and it's for that reason that I want you to have what I've earned, just so you can see that I'm worth something."

"Where's the money?" said Kilgallen.

"Upstairs. Shall I get it for you, sir? It's hidden in the room where I sleep, in a hole, a crack, right behind where I sleep, and if the rats haven't gotten it—"

"How much?"

"Twenty dollars, sir. Shall I bring it to you, sir? I'm glad to go and get it for you, sure I am, sir."

"No, Maura," said Kilgallen. "Come closer—that's a good girl."

Maura did as she was told, walking up to the man in her high-heeled shoes until he could grab at her tightly constricted waist, or rest his hand on the very pale skin of her partially exposed breasts. But he didn't touch her. He crossed his legs, he adjusted his tie, looked at her from head to toe while she grew more and more afraid; she didn't know if she could bear remaining in this place another day, not when she was this close to freedom.

"So you'd like to come work for me, would you?" he said finally.

"Yes, sir."

"The work may not be very much to your liking."

"Oh, no, sir. It will be, sir. Sure it's only a chance I'm asking for."

"It is the chance," said Kilgallen, "to be a prostitute."

Maura hesitated only a moment. "Yes, sir. Sure I understand what it is I'm asking for."

Kilgallen stood up abruptly. Maura took a step back, sensing his anger and impatience. "Two men have told me about you, girl," he said. "I don't know how many didn't bother to tell me anything at all, but two men told me. They said you were complaining to them, telling them impossible stories. Saying you were a prisoner, that you were here against your will, that the bars on the back windows of the house weren't to keep out burglars but to keep you locked inside."

"Please, sir," said Maura, trying not to sink to her knees, trying to keep her eyes from running with tears. He would never let her out, she thought; he would keep her inside till she went out of her mind, and then he would kill her. All her suffering would have been in vain. "Please, sir," she said again and again, even when he had finished his accusation, even when he had retreated to his chair to study her terrified face. Suddenly he was on his feet again, walking past her and leaving her alone in the parlor. When he returned, he wore an overcoat, and he carried a cloak and a hat and a fur muff for her.

"All right," he said, and he held the cloak for her and she looked at him as if he were mad. "Come on, girl, I thought you wanted to go out."

The cloak was of heavy wool, lined with silk. Maura's heart began to race as soon as it was on. Her hands shook as she placed the hat on her head, and she dropped the fur muff twice before they were out the front door. Kilgallen held her by the arm as she took her first steps in months in the fresh air. She was dizzy with joy, so dizzy that she had to stop walking. She turned

to look at Kilgallen, very handsome in the cold March sunshine,
and was suddenly overwhelmed by the crazy gratitude of the released prisoner for her master. Holding on to him for support,
she looked at the parade in the street before her: new red trucks
with ancient horses, their drivers shouting curses and blowing
horns at the slow-moving pushcarts blocking their way; a cara-
van of young women, dressed in layers of patched-up rags, moving quickly between the vans and horses and whistling stevedores
for a glimpse of the East River before returning to their benches
in the factory after a twenty-minute lunch break; a stray dog
racing across the street a second before the passenger-crammed
horse-drawn streetcar.

There were gulls in the sky, and the wind carried the scent of
the sea, as well as the faint sulfurous odors of the factories.
There was a red-faced, blue-uniformed police officer, walking
with a slow, self-assured gait along the sidewalk, nodding to
porters, to the proprietor of the street's only saloon, to a fat
warehouseman sweeping sawdust into the street. "Ah ho!" he
said, smiling broadly at Mike Kilgallen. "Top of the morning to
you, Mr. Kilgallen!"

"It's half-past noon, Johnny," said Kilgallen. "As you should
be able to tell from your nice new gold watch."

"For which I never cease to thank you, sir," said the police
officer with a grin. "I only said good morning because I know
how late you sleep—meaning no disrespect, of course."

A beautiful black victoria, drawn by two white horses and
driven by an enormous man in tight-fitting livery, complete with
silk top hat, twisted through the traffic and pulled up at the
curb. The policeman helped a speechless Maura into the open-
topped passenger compartment, and, as Kilgallen jumped in after
her, the officer of the peace made a gesture of approbation.

"You like her?" said Kilgallen. "You think she's a looker?"

"Oh, yes, sir. I do indeed, sir. A real looker," said the policeman with mock deference.

"Come around to Twenty-sixth Street, Johnny," said Kilgallen. "This is Maura—remember that name."

"I won't be forgetting, don't you worry, sir."

"I'll be glad to introduce you, Johnny," said Kilgallen. Smiling, he raised a forefinger to the tip of his nose and added: "Oh,

Johnny—you won't be forgetting what you promised? About that basement down the block?"

"Don't worry about it, Mr. Kilgallen. We're not going to allow any prostitutes to move in on Spring Street. Not on your block, sir. We have an agreement!" said the policeman smartly, and Kilgallen ordered the driver forward.

Maura was so radiantly happy that for a moment Kilgallen tried to imagine the scene from her point of view: the snapping of the reins, the stares of the passersby, the intricate profusion of electric wires lacing along the avenues from one high office building to another, bearing light, communication, civilization.

But if Kilgallen imagined that Maura was concerned with such innovations as electric lights and telephones, he was very far wrong. Her thoughts weren't specific; they were general, all-embracing. She didn't isolate electric wires, tram lines, eight-story buildings, the endless congestion of richly loaded trucks, the noise, the myriad races that were all hallmarks of the great city. She took it all in as one. Maura had lived all her life in Kerry, and except for the medieval city of Cork—seen at a disadvantage, along its ugliest waterfront streets—she had seen only the clusters of huts that made up the local villages. Only the ruins of churches and monasteries were magnificent; only the cities spoken of in her mother's tales thundered in her imagination.

Not only was New York her first city, it was a city to which she was released after five months of captivity. As the victoria raced out of the heavy downtown traffic and tore uptown, all her senses were inflamed. The wind tore at her face, bringing tears to her wide-open eyes. The noise of the wheels on cobblestones, the rumble of trains on elevated tracks over her head, the endless honking and whistling of the driver, the squealing springs, the hungry foreigners hawkling rags and firewood and battered fruit, drove a meaningless rhythm into her brain, a pounding that only skipped a beat when the victoria lurched into a pothole and the entire chassis seemed to be bouncing between her teeth. When a train roared by overhead, showering them with soot and the screaming of train brakes, she had no thought in her head as to who she was or where she was going. Her eyes were too greedy for the fresh colors about the next curve, her skin too eager to feel the sun. It was all too much for her. She was overexcited, mad with the joy of being outside in a world that she could never have imagined. It was as if she had dreamed the wild ride, and the dream was going out of control.

Kilgallen was shaking her arm, turning her face so that he could look at her eyes. "Sorry, sir," she said. He had been asking her something that she had not heard.

"Are you all right, Maura?"

"I am, sir," she said.

Kilgallen had to make two stops very far uptown, to pick up cash. In the forty minutes it took to reach One Hundred and Eleventh Street and Second Avenue, he studied Maura closely. It was a matter of pride to him that he should be able to leave her alone in the open car while he went into the narrow five-story tenement house for five minutes. He had misjudged her more than once before, but he was now nearly certain that her will was in his hands, that she would stay where he put her until such time as he would tell her to move.

"Are you cold?" he asked her, breaking apart her reverie.

"What, sir?" She had been looking at a boy with a huge cap pulled low over his eyes, hawking matches from a box strapped to his waist. The wind was rising again, carrying the scent of the East River.

"Put the top up," said Kilgallen to the driver, and he jumped down from the victoria and went into the house on the corner.

Maura watched him disappear without a thought of trying to run away. She was too content to be outside, seated on the comfortable leather cushions, watching the wind bend the branches of a young tree. As the driver fastened the top about the passenger compartment, she felt his eyes on her, intense with longing. She turned to him, and saw his face redden beneath the black hat. He turned his eyes back to his task; and by the time he had finished, Kilgallen returned, a fat envelope clutched in his fist.

"Okay," said Kilgallen to the driver, and as they started forward he smiled at Maura and placed his hand on her knee.

Slowly, the excitement at being outside began to abate. Once again she was able to think. The boys who stopped their ball game near One Hundred and Tenth Street and Third Avenue were not looking at them with kindness, but with hostility; they were poor, and the victoria was a mark of the rich. They continued west on the broad, busy street, but stopped almost at once: An ancient woman, bent over at the waist, walking with the aid of two gnarled sticks, had begun to walk bravely across the avenue, her eyes to the ground. A cacophony of whistles and horns blew up all about her, as horsecars and omnibuses braked, horses lifted their heads, and the green lamps of the Third Avenue tram bore down on her with speed.

"Oh, my God," said Maura, sure that the speeding tram would hit the woman, and powerless to do anything about it. But the three red tramcars rushed by before the woman could step across the tracks; and as cars and vans tore past on both sides of her, their drivers howling curses and blowing whistles and slamming their car-hooks against metal dashboards to punctuate their fury, she paused, her eyes to the ground, her pack heavy on her bent back. When the tram passed, the woman continued her slow trek to the other side of the avenue, once again ignoring the whistles and screams about her.

"Crazy old bitch," said Kilgallen. He lifted his hand from Maura's knee and took out a wad of bills from the envelope he carried. The bills were all of twenty-dollar denomination, and the speed with which he counted them suggested that he had counted them once or twice before.

"What was she carrying?"

"What?" said Kilgallen sharply. She had made him confuse the counting of the bills.

"The old woman," said Maura. "What do you think she was carrying on her back, sir?"

Their victoria passed a hansom cab on the right, and was now tearing down a stretch of empty, badly paved road toward the railroad tracks at the intersection of Fourth Avenue. Maura's attention was suddenly caught by the sight of a boarded-up old farmhouse, not unlike some she'd seen in Kerry, which a developer had bought, intending to put up a score of five-story dull-brown tenements in its place. Next to the farmhouse was a quarry, and next to this an enormous warehouse, and then a tiny one-story saloon with swinging doors, with a drunk asleep on its wooden steps.

"Wood," Kilgallen said. "She's probably coming from the park. There's a lot of them that do that, the old beggars who can't find rags in the street. They pick up deadwood in the park, around Harlem Lake. Some people buy it from them for firewood. There's a lot of them selling it, on First and Second Avenue." He returned to counting his bills, while Maura tried to imagine what it would be like to be poor in such a vast, powerful city.

The scene was changing now, rapidly, and for the better. Maura looked in wonderment at a castle, sitting on a slight rise at the corner of Fifth Avenue, its turrets gold against a suddenly gray sky. The victoria lurched forward, passing a train of furniture vans, the crosstown streetcar, and a slow-moving rag-picker pushing his cart across the broad street. As they sped past the north end of Central Park, a trio of horsemen came out of the park and passed them at a gallop. Maura turned around for a last glimpse of the castle: In a second-story bay window, a young blond girl was bent over a large book.

"Not much money in firewood, girl," said Kilgallen with a laugh. He had counted the bills to his satisfaction, and now placed the fat envelope in an inside pocket. "We're in a much better business, you and me—you listen to what I'm telling you."

They passed New Avenue, coming up fast on another smart victoria, crossing Columbus Avenue where it adjoined the sprawling Morningside Park, and finally pulling up alongside the other victoria as they approached Tenth Avenue. The two young men in the other carriage looked sharply at Maura, and then looked a second time, and laughed to each other, as if there were something contemptible about the girl, something worth mocking. But Maura had little time to dwell on their laughter. Kilgallen's victoria gained the lead, but only for a moment; at the corner of One Hundred and Tenth and the Boulevard, the uptown extension of the avenue whose name even Maura knew—Broadway—Kilgallen's driver had to rein in the horses and force them into a slow right turn, while they wanted to keep racing west.

The driver had his way, and the horses turned up the Boulevard into an amazing parade of bicyclists. They were but five blocks from the new campus of Columbia College, and right in the middle of the latest exercise fad in the city. Though it was a Thursday, there were enough students and downtown dandies, young women without a purpose and young men without a regular job, to fill the Boulevard with bicycles. With the smooth roads of Morningside Heights, the level paving of Lenox Avenue, it was no wonder that Harlem and the surrounding areas had become a mecca for the bicycle faddists. Looking up toward One Hundred and Twentieth Street, and behind her to One Hundred and Tenth, Maura saw hardly a carriage or a horsecar amid the sea of bicycles.

"Don't move," said Kilgallen. "Just look at the students, and don't answer any of them if they speak to you. You got that, girl?"

They had stopped again, at One Hundred and Twelfth, just west of the Boulevard, and Kilgallen was dashing into another house, for another payment—this from a brothel along the Hudson River, frequented exclusively by students.

Maura sat very still, looking at the back of the driver's head, trying to fashion the day's glut of sensations, sights, feelings into a coherent order. Trams and paupers, tall buildings and trains rushing through the sky, a city crammed between two rivers, a city that had no end. An old woman gathered deadwood to earn enough pennies to be able to eat; Kilgallen counted out hundreds, thousands, of dollars in his manicured hands; two young gentlemen had laughed at her, undoubtedly recognizing her for a whore. Even the driver was squirming in his seat, anxious to turn round and look at her again, to taste the shock of her beauty—but now the raised top over the passenger compartment obstructed his view.

I could go, she thought suddenly, looking across the street at the never-ending bicyclists. I could jump down from the carriage, race across the street, and get away.

The thought so terrified her that she had to clasp her hands to still their shaking.

No, she told herself, for the thought of being caught once

again, of being sent back to the house on Spring Street, was worse than anything else her mind could conjure. She must wait, she told herself, wait until it was the right time, wait and not run now.

Her legs stiffened against the urge to flee, and she was within a half-moment of risking a mad dash away when Kilgallen appeared, so suddenly that she nearly threw herself against his body.

But all Kilgallen saw was a nervous girl starting at his entrance into the cab. "Take it easy, dopey, it's only me."

Maura sank back into the leather seat. He would have caught her, she thought, and she would never have been able to tell the bicyclists that she was a prisoner before he'd have had her back in the victoria, racing back downtown to Spring Street.

"You're taking me to Twenty-sixth Street," she said breathlessly, hopefully, nodding her head in anticipation of his assent.

"Jesus, you're a weird broad," said Kilgallen. "Take it easy. Even with that puss, you're going to scare away the boys if you don't learn to take it a little easier."

"Yes, sir. Sure I'll take it easy—whatever you say, sir," said Maura.

The victoria took them east again, back to New Avenue, where a dilapidated tavern hung on the rise overlooking the southeast tip of Morningside Park. Kilgallen dismissed the driver, telling him that they'd take a cab back to Twenty-sixth Street after their dinner.

Inside the tavern were a bartender, a barmaid, and half a dozen out-of-work laborers. One of these began to smile incredulously at the sight of Maura, so pretty, so painted, so voluptuously dressed.

"Mr. Kilgallen, sir," said the bartender with such eagerness to please that the laborers turned their attention elsewhere. The gentleman was not a Fifth Avenue dandy, but a hoodlum in fancy clothes, and it would be better not to stare at his mistress.

It was half-past two when they were seated at one of the four empty tables in the rear of the tavern. Kilgallen ordered a half spring chicken, green beans, fried potatoes, and a pint of beer for Maura; he ordered only whiskey for himself. Maura became hungrier with each bite she took. The chicken was fat, and nicely broiled. She took it apart with her fingers, she dropped the hot bits of potato into her mouth as if she were afraid they'd disappear.

"Slow down," said Kilgallen. "I don't want you sick."

"Yes, sir," she said. But she took so great a swallow of her beer that she nearly choked.

"You know what this costs?" he asked.

"What, sir?" Maura realized she could eat another half chicken, she could devour a loaf of bread, she could eat anything he gave her.

"One dollar," said Kilgallen, waving his hand over the table of food and drink. "A buck, that's what it costs. You know what a dollar is?"

"Sure I do, sir," said Maura. She had finished the chicken, and was now sopping up gravy with bread, potatoes, and green beans.

"Do you know what a factory girl makes working six days a week?"

"No, sir."

"Stop eating for a minute, girl. You're going to get sick, and you're making a mess of yourself." Kilgallen drummed his fingers on the table until she moved her hands away from the plate with its paltry remnants of vegetables and bones. "Three dollars," he said finally. "They make three dollars a week, if they can find a job. Does that sound like a lot of money to you?"

"I don't know."

"It costs three bucks a week to board in the filthiest room in the Bowery. You get breakfast and supper, and you just might die from the food. Some girls don't want to do that. So they live four in a room somewhere else, and buy their own food. They don't even have a nickel for carfare. You know what that hat costs that you're wearing?"

"No, sir."

"Seven dollars. The cloak was eleven dollars. Your dress was nineteen dollars. No factory girl will ever wear that dress or anything like it. No factory girl has any money for clothes unless she marries some poor bastard who's making eight dollars a week clerking, or ten dollars a week pushing paper around in an accountant's office, or fourteen dollars a week managing a posh store. Do you want something else to eat?"

Kilgallen snapped his fingers at the bartender. He turned down her request for more chicken, and ordered her coffee and apple pie. While she charged into this, he watched her closely. She would not run, he decided at last. He would teach her to eat properly, to get rid of her accent, to be alive to the desires of men. When she had finished her dessert, he told her that he'd like to make love to her.

"If it would please you, sir," said Maura. The coffee had begun to cut through the dull glow of overeating. Only minutes ago, it seemed, she had nearly tried to run away. Only hours ago she had been in the garret. "Sure if it would please you," she said, trying to smile the way Ginny had shown her.

"No," said Kilgallen sharply. "You must tell me that you'd *love* to make love with me."

"I would, sir."

"That nothing would give you greater pleasure."

"Yes, that's what I'm saying," said Maura. "It would do me great honor."

"Fucking Irish peasant twit," he said softly. But he was not yet angry; at least she had shown no rebellion.

The bartender took them upstairs to the single made-up room, keeping his manner straight and respectful, even to Maura, at all times. When Kilgallen and she were alone, he opened the window to the view of the darkening park and extinguished the single lamp. Maura wanted very much to please him, and she rode the nervous coffee-energy all she could. He asked her to undress him, to caress him, to be slow with him, to be quick with him, to kiss him, to swallow him, to cover him, to be one with him. The desire for her from men she loathed no longer surprised her, of course. What she did was distasteful, but it was far better than being cut on the belly, than being forced to return to Ireland like poor Fiona in the same wretched steerage in which she came to New York. It was simply a way of going from one place to another—take the fact of one man's desire and work it through, until it was finished—and then she would be that much closer to her goal.

Kilgallen slept a short time, as was his habit, and when he woke he lit up a cigar and sat up in the bed smoking, looking out into the dark room, out into the darker night. Finally, he spoke to her.

"You can be rich, Maura. You can be as rich as a princess, if only you listen to me."

"Yes, sir," was all she said.

It took a long time for the bartender to find them a hansom cab, and when they were finally seated, the driver proved to be surly: He didn't like the way Kilgallen snapped orders, and he made it clear that he had no desire to take the long route to Twenty-sixth Street just so Maura could enjoy Central Park.

In short, he was a typical New York hansom driver: He tried to take turns on two wheels, whipping his horse into a frenzy of speed; every puddle must be run through, every rut must be run over, every bicyclist must be cursed, every pedestrian must be made to race for the other side of the street. The tranquil effect of Central Park's gas lamps, its nocturnal lovers strolling to and from the famous Mall, was vitiated by the clattering wheels, the whistle held in the driver's teeth, screeching at anything that moved. Forced into line by a slow-moving carriage, the driver blew his whistle, kicked his dashboard, yelled across the dark space to where twin red lamps swung from the preceding tailgate. Finally, the carriage pulled over so that their manic cabman could pass.

Maura loved the speed, she battened on the madness. It was of a piece with her being called a princess, being told that she was on her way to riches. It mattered only a little that she was under Kilgallen's control, because she understood that his control would soon be over; his mastery was only a part of her journey. As the cab exited the park at Seventy-second Street and Fifth Avenue, she glowed with happiness.

"It's good to have a full belly," said Kilgallen, patting her knee with a proprietary air. But nothing he said and did within the confines of the cab mattered now. She was dreaming, and he was only a shade, an insignificant character in a mighty pageant. Carriages and cabs clogged Fifth Avenue in both directions, and their driver was forced to slow down. Kilgallen pointed out various mansions, mentioning the sums spent on their construction, the families who lived within their powerful walls.

But Maura wasn't listening to him. She was too alive now with the sense of her dream: This was the America she had dreamed of back in Kerry, the golden mountain, the imperial city. Here the gas lamps were everywhere and the street was brilliant. From the door of a five-story mansion at the corner of Sixty-first Street, a long red carpet extended all the way to the gutter, where a line of carriages were emptying their women in furs and men in silk capes. Servants held flaming torches on either side of the carpet, so that the socialites could flash their jewels and white faces to the curious onlookers outside the pale of fire.

Traffic eased as they passed the Croton Reservoir at Forty-second Street, which the city hoped to tear down to make way for a great library. At Thirty-sixth Street they nearly hit a drunk, weaving his very long way downtown to a bench in Park Row. Ten blocks later, at Madison Square, they turned west, taking giant steps into an area that grew more dismal with every block.

When they finally paused, just west of Ninth Avenue, Maura looked up at an old four-story box of a building, painted gray. Its plain wood door had a large bronze knocker; this, and the fact that it was the only building on the block without a door number, lent it distinction. The front windows were blacked out behind dull iron latticework, and Maura realized that the windows were as effectively blocked as if they had been barred, but as she was helped down from the cab by Kilgallen, she had no sense of foreboding. She was not afraid of this place. And she was no longer afraid of the pimp who took her to its door. Maura knew what was expected of her, and she was certain that her master would be satisfied with her performance.

And when she was ready—when she had money in her pocket and knew where she was and where she could go—she would leave this place. Only a short cab ride away was what she had come to America for, and she was certain that she would get it.

# ❧ CHAPTER ❧ ELEVEN

"Take my arm," said Kilgallen to Maura.

They walked to the front door, and Kilgallen knocked, and the door opened slightly, and then suddenly it opened very wide. "Good evening, sir," said a grave, gray-haired man in bright red wool livery.

They entered the house, stepping from a scarred wood-brick porch onto a gorgeous Oriental carpet. The elegant strains of a piano concerto reached them faintly. As the door closed out the evening behind them, Maura blinked at the rush of light in the small mirrored foyer.

"Please, miss," said the doorman, and he helped Maura off with her cape and handed it to another red-liveried servant. Following Kilgallen's rapid footsteps, Maura crossed a floor of multicolored tile squares and hastened along a corridor lined with English landscape paintings in heavy gold frames. The music of the piano began to wane. Climbing an ornate stairway after Kilgallen, Maura could hear the delicate tinkle of glasses, the scraping of silverware on heavy china plates, the very occasional sound of feminine murmuring, of high-pitched, short-lived laughter.

"Wait till you see the food in this place," said Kilgallen. But he didn't offer to open the door to the dining room, continuing instead to hurry up the stairs. Passing the second-floor landing, Maura saw an enormous Bouguereau canvas of lascivious nymphs and satyrs, resplendent between two gas lamps with red glass shades. "Come on, quit gawking," said Kilgallen. "Hold your head up. Look like a lady." He took her arm at the third-floor landing and led her down a much plainer, serious-looking corridor: a polished parquet floor, a series of fifty-year-old prints of New York Harbor, a dozen shut doors, each with its own bronze plate. Kilgallen stopped at a door marked "312" and turned the knob.

"Your friend will be here in a second," he said.

"What friend?" said Maura. She noted that the door didn't seem to have a lock from the outside.

"Come on, girl," said Kilgallen, opening the door for her.

Maura went in and Kilgallen left, leaving the door wide open. In a daze, she heard his footsteps running down the stairs.

Like the room in the basement of the house on Spring Street, there was a bed, a mirror, a few pictures, some furniture. But here the bed was enormous, covered with a down quilt, crowned by an ornate, regal canopy. Here the pictures were oil paintings, large enough for the room's high ceiling and great depth. There was a chaise longue of red velvet, a tremendous mirror in a gilt frame. There were piles of exotic embroidered pillows, a large armoire, a fruitwood dresser on which rested bottles of French perfume.

"It's like you died and went to heaven, ain't it?" said a familiar voice behind her. Maura turned and nearly shouted for joy: It was Ginny, her frail blond friend from the house on Spring Street. "I mean, look at it, and tell me it ain't heaven," said Ginny, grinning as if about to let some hilarious secret out of the bag.

"I can't believe it's you!" cried Maura as they embraced in the middle of the room. Ginny's blond hair was swept up into a pompadour, lending her beautiful face an aristocratic air. She had gained weight, confidence, radiance. Even in the filmy silk slip she wore in the house—undoubtedly her working costume, thought Maura—Ginny seemed the embodiment of ease and strength. She would not have seemed less vulnerable had she been wearing armor. This was Ginny's home, this was her element, and this was her happiness.

"I kept asking if you were dead, but he said you ain't dead, just slow, just stupid. So I kept asking, I kept asking all the time—Jesus, Irish, you're *here!*"

Maura had a hundred questions, but Ginny hadn't time to answer everything. "I'm telling you, but you ain't listening—you can come and go as you please, dopey," she explained for the fifth time. She showed Maura where the liquor was, and the crystal glasses, and the cigars—all the things she must offer the men who came to visit her. "Tomorrow we'll go downtown and do some shopping. I'll show you the chic stores—you'll be blowing smoke out of both ears."

"We can go out of here?" said Maura. "You and me together?"

"Jesus," said Ginny, "you haven't changed—still as head-in-the-clouds crazy as ever. This is a class place, you've got to pay attention."

"Of course," said Maura. But she was in fact no longer listening. Dutifully, she followed Ginny about as the young woman opened drawers, pointed to linens and wine bottles and ashtrays. A maid would take care of everything the next day, Ginny explained, but it was the girl's duty to attend to the gentleman while he was in the room.

"I had a young guy last week, all he wanted to do was smoke cigars and drink wine. He called me all sorts of dirty names and didn't even touch me once. I wore my slip and sat on the other side of the room and he called me a dirty whore—for hours. He wouldn't leave, he just kept drinking and talking to himself and smoking cigars and once in a while he'd look up and swear at me. It cost him three hundred bucks, I swear to God it did—I found it out from one of the boys. Hey, you want a drink?"

"So we'll go shopping tomorrow, we really will?" said Maura.

"Sure."

"Do you have money? I don't have any money. I gave all my money to Kilgallen."

"I've got money, I've got lots of money," said Ginny. "You can borrow whatever you need."

"You promise we're going to go out tomorrow?"

"Jesus, dopey, I wish you'd quit acting like that! You've got to smile in this place, or you'll end up back on Spring Street."

Maura smiled. Even during Ginny's review of the proper use

of the vaginal sponge—the contraceptive method Ginny had taught her back on Spring Street—Maura continued to smile. It was terrible to hear about the girl who'd died only last month on the abortionist's table, only because she hadn't used her head, had insisted on douching with quinine instead of using a sponge or a diaphragm, but Maura's concentration was elsewhere. She had thought it would be weeks—maybe months—but tomorrow they'd be out, away from the house, and Ginny would lend her money and Maura could run away.

"Are you listening to me?"

"Sure I am, Ginny."

"What'd I just say?"

"About the sponge. Sure I'm using it enough to know what to do with it."

"I asked if you were ready to go downstairs," said Ginny with exasperation.

"Downstairs?"

"Goddamn you, girl! You've got to quit your damn dreaming, or you're going to get us both in a lot of trouble. Listen to me. I'm supposed to get you ready for downstairs. The men start coming in after seven. In the parlor. You'd better take off that dress."

"I'm tired," said Maura.

"Well, hot damn, honey, I'm sorry to hear that, but the night is young. In fact, it ain't even started yet."

"Please, Ginny. Sure it's been all day long that I've been at it. I need to sleep, even if only for a little while."

"You can't sleep!" said Ginny. "I'm sorry if you're tired, but you've got to get down there." There was fear in her voice, as clearly evident as the fear that had run the house on Spring Street. For a moment, Maura was surprised. She had thought Ginny secure, afraid of nothing. "Kilgallen told me to get you ready, and you've got to get ready if you don't want him to be angry. Don't you understand? If you're tired, you'll have plenty of time to sleep. You can sleep right in the middle of it, the way these guys screw, take it from me."

"All right," said Maura.

Ginny helped her undress, helped her hang her clothes in

the armoire, helped her clean her face and reapply the cosmetics that turned her lips an unnatural scarlet, her cheeks a perfect shade of rose. Wearing only a silk slip, a black ribbon tied about her pale throat, Maura followed Ginny down the stairs, suddenly so afraid that she had to clutch the banister all the way down.

Only one more night, she thought; and the fear was so big in her chest, it threatened to burst out of her mouth, to pour out from her eyes. She was not afraid of the men in the parlor, of course; she was not afraid of what they would say to her, or do to her, or ask her to perform. Her fear was that a mistake would occur, a mishap, an accident that would cause tomorrow's outing to be canceled: Ginny could anger Kilgallen, or insist on sleeping all day, or there might be a freak March snowstorm, or someone would decide to lock Maura into her room. Only one long night, and if all went well, she and Ginny would go shopping in the morning. The possibility of being free so soon was what terrified, the prospect of having to hold one's breath, to walk on eggshells so as not to cause a break in the orderly events that would lead to the next day's glory.

"In here, dopey," said Ginny. "And don't be a twit—these guys are just a bunch of bananas waiting to get peeled."

Maura followed her friend into the parlor. An old black man sat at a white piano playing popular tunes, his left foot pressing on the mute pedal. Two other girls were already there, both of them blond, buxom, and short. One of them stood shakily on her high-heeled mules before the piano, pretending to be absorbed in the ordinary music. The other was bringing a tray of drinks to the only customers in the large, wainscot-paneled room—two quiet young men, talking to Mike Kilgallen.

"Jesus," said one of the young men as Ginny and Maura entered. "Come here and let me get a look at those knees."

Maura at once felt Ginny's hand on her arm. "Go on," said Ginny quietly, but fiercely.

The young man who had spoken took a drink from the blond girl's tray and at the same time put his hand on her backside and laughed.

Maura froze.

She didn't understand why, but for the first time she felt shame. It seemed as if everyone were laughing, and all at once she remembered the men who had laughed at her from their victoria, knowing her for a whore. The blond girl at the piano moved over to one of the customers, moving her hips as if all she wanted to do was strip off her negligee and be taken on the floor. Ginny, too, was moving that way, toward Kilgallen, and she was laughing, too—the piano player was laughing—it was funny to see the four whores try to sell their wares all at once to only two customers.

"You—Red," said the young man who'd first spoken. "Let me see you up close. I like the way you look so hard to get." And he was laughing even as he said this, and Maura thought there was a diamond stickpin gleaming in his tie.

Every other time, she had been alone in her room, and men had come to her, and she was a prisoner, waiting to be freed. Now it was entirely different: Everyone knew her for a whore, a woman who sold her own body, a woman who was there to try and please anyone who came through the door. Kilgallen knew what she was, and Ginny, and the blond girls rubbing up against the young gentlemen, and the old black piano player, keeping his music quiet so as not to intrude upon the process of selection.

Maura stumbled forward, taking shallow breaths. She knew it was stupid, but she felt the blood rush to her face, she felt the eyes of the men on her as a disgrace. The other young man, who had not yet spoken, suddenly whispered something in his friend's ear.

"Holy hot shit, lady," said the first young man. "He's in love."

"Oh, shut up, you bastard," said the whisperer. He seemed to be blushing as much as Maura.

"The point, my dear man," said the less bashful young man, "is to get as much puss on your pecker as you possibly can, especially tonight." Turning to Kilgallen, he said: "Especially, Mr. Kilgallen, tonight. You can bear me out. Quantity, not quality."

"Each to his own," said Kilgallen, nodding politely to the quiet young man.

"No, no, no!" said the first young man. "Kevin here is much too romantic for his own good. Imagine how I'd feel if the first time he's in a whorehouse he stays sober all night, if the first time he's in a whorehouse he stays serious. You tell him, Mr. Kilgallen." Taking another long pull on his whiskey, he took hold of one of the buxom blondes and pulled up her slip, so that her pale pubes were exposed to his shocked friend Kevin.

"Excuse me," said Kevin, standing abruptly. "I've asked you a favor."

"Oh, for God's sake, Kevin," said his friend. "I'm just showing you one's as good as another. Come on, Ginny," he added as Maura's friend came within striking glance of him. "Pick up your slip, honey. Show my friend some real hot fudge."

"Go to hell," said Ginny. "You better talk nice to me, or Mr. Kilgallen's going to have to remind you where you are."

"Sure," said Kilgallen. "Talk nice to Ginny, or she's going to charge you double tonight."

"She can charge me whatever she likes," said the young man. Putting aside the blonde, he pulled Ginny onto his lap.

Maura, still halfway across the room, watched in growing horror. At the last moment she remembered herself: Whatever shame had to be endured, she would endure; tomorrow was her chance to flee, and she must not ruin that chance forever.

"Are you free, miss?"

It was the young man named Kevin. He was red-faced, out of breath, looking from her eyes to the floor. He had asked his friend what one must say to one of the girls in the house, and his friend had been flippant: "Ask her to dance," he'd said. "Ask her if she's free, ask her if she'd like to show you her room."

"Please, miss," said Kevin. She was more beautiful than any woman he'd ever seen. Even Milly Arbor, the Broadway actress who regularly bared her calves to her enraptured audiences, was a vulgar, thick-limbed creature next to this ethereal girl with red-gold hair. "I was wondering if you'd care to show me your room."

Maura looked at Ginny, sitting on the other young man's lap, his hands on her breasts, on her thighs. Kilgallen was on his feet and suddenly walking across the room to where Maura stood with the awkward, incomprehensible boy. Somewhere in the house, a clock struck the hour, and a group of four gentlemen were led into the parlor by one of the red-liveried servants. "Everyone's coming early tonight," said Kilgallen, patting Kevin on the back. "Some of our ladies are still asleep."

Kevin didn't know how to respond. Was he supposed to ask Kilgallen for the use of this redhead's favors? Had he already been refused by the young girl with a gesture that he didn't understand? Was it possible that Kilgallen was hinting that he wait around to see the other girls of the house? "This young lady," said Kevin to Kilgallen, "is very beautiful."

Maura looked fearfully at Kilgallen. For a moment it seemed as if the displeasure in his eyes were directed her way. She froze again, certain that he must suspect her plans to run off. But the displeasure vanished. He twisted his lips into a smile and said, "Maura, this is Mr. K. Say hello to Mr. K."

"Hello, sir," said Maura.

"She's shy," said Kilgallen.

"That's all right," said Kevin. "I'm plenty shy myself."

The piano player began to play dance-hall music, and one of the buxom blondes began to dance with one of the older gentlemen who had just come into the parlor. Girls with freshly curled hair began to come down from their rooms, putting on their first smiles of the evening. Kilgallen was wanted on the other side of the room, and nodded briskly to Kevin. Before leaving them, he added to Maura: "You'll be much more beautiful to Mr. K, Maura, if you smile."

Kevin found himself staring at her as she slowly and deliberately tried to follow Kilgallen's suggestion. Only her green eyes remained set, unsmiling; they were seeing something somewhere else than in this room, and the young man realized that it was this strange, indifferent gaze that separated her from the other prostitutes, even more than her beauty.

"I'm sorry if I embarrassed you, Maura. Is it all right if I call you that? Maura, I mean. It seems silly to call you 'miss.' Well, not silly—I'm sorry if that sounded rude. It's just that it's so formal, and I do know your name now, your first name, and it's lovely, if I may say so. I'm a little nervous—you can probably see that at a glance. I'm sorry if I'm sounding like an idiot. I keep staring at you. What I said—I mean, I asked you if you were free. I don't know if that's right—if that's what I'm supposed to say."

He was talking so quickly that his words began to trip up on each other and he had to draw himself to an abrupt halt. Clearing his throat, he said distinctly, slowly, with an almost unfriendly tone: "Look here, Maura. I'd like to know if we can be alone together."

Of course, thought Maura, suddenly calming down. She was simply overexcited from the day's events. There was nothing to fear. She had never been in a situation quite like this, where men selected their women from a roomful of whores. But once she understood that she had in fact been selected, that this nervous young man wanted to make love to her, just like all the other men who had made love to her in the house on Spring Street, she had no more reason to be afraid. If she could keep him with her for hours, perhaps she wouldn't have to endure any more men that night; if she could fire the desire in his eyes, perhaps he'd insist on remaining with her until every other man in the place had gone home.

"Yes, sir," she said.

She hadn't moved, however, and Kevin didn't quite know what to do next. Already he had been braver, more forward, than he had ever been in his life, and this only because of his friend's constant reminder that there was nothing he could say or do in the place that was wrong; the girls here were, after all, nothing but whores.

Kevin reached out and took her arm. "Maura," he said, "perhaps you'd like to show me your room?" He felt his heart racing; felt the full weight of where he was and what might soon take place; felt the touch of her cool, pale skin as something impossibly personal, private, something he could take and violate at will.

"Yes, sir, of course," she said. Maura turned, and he dropped his hold on her arm, and as she walked out of the parlor he looked with amazement at her slender, nearly naked shape in the silk slip.

Catching up with her at the stairwell, he said, "Wait," and he turned her around; and because it was something that he wanted to do, something that he was allowed to do in this place, something that he could never have done with any of the young women he had ever met, he took this strange, green-eyed, auburn-haired beauty in his arms and kissed her mouth, his eyes shut against his fear.

Kevin was so weak with wonder he could barely stand.

He was twenty-one, a Columbia College man, and a virgin.

He felt the girl's frame pressed against his as an inexplicably tender force. His knees grazed her naked thighs, his palm was alive to the warm back beneath delicate silk, his penis swelled uncontrollably with painful desire. She smelled like jasmine, and he didn't care if it was the result of some cheap perfume; she felt as young and innocent as a teen-age bride and he didn't care if she had slept with a thousand hooligans. He had not heard her speak a half-dozen lines, but already, in the space of an embrace, in the mad moments of a lingering kiss, he felt the full power of infatuation. This feeling that threatened to overwhelm him could not be directed toward an ordinary Irish prostitute. This girl must be unique, the product of a tragedy, the complex product of beauty, romance, misfortune, and history.

Holding her hand, looking down on her thick hair, at the slender nape of her neck, he had to steady himself, had to remind himself not to be a fool. This is a whore, he told himself, and you are here to get rid of your ridiculous virginity, and that is all.

Taking a leaf out of his friend's book, he placed his hand on her backside as they climbed the stairs. This was the way one treated a prostitute: not with romance, but with revelry. He could reach out and touch her breast, he could grab at an ankle and trip her laughingly to the floor. This was a whorehouse; for all its fancy servants and elegant furnishings, it was still a place where all the women were for sale; and this woman was now his, he owned her for the duration of the evening. So he took hold of her backside, he squeezed her buttocks, as if to show that they were as much for sale as a pair of ripe plums.

And then she turned and looked at him.

They were just passing the first-floor landing, and Maura was tired. She had begun the day too early, she had seen too much too soon. Every hour had been filled with a hundred hopes, a thousand presentiments. Kilgallen had freed her, had frightened her, had made love to her. She'd climbed stairs, she'd been whipped through the cold air in an open carriage, she'd been starved, she'd been given too much food. She'd been shamed by her nakedness in the presence of whores and their customers. Shame had been followed by fear; fear had been followed by strength; strength had been followed by distaste and resignation. And now this young man, rich and free and bloated with power, had taken her into his arms and feigned an absurd passion. And now this passion was turned about, and he twisted his feelings to exhibit his contempt, and Maura would have none of it, she could bear it no longer.

Without a word, he removed his hand from her backside. It was all he could to do to refrain from expressing a formal apology. They climbed two more flights to her room. When she'd let him inside and closed the door after them, she spoke.

"Why did you kiss me like that?"

"I'm terribly sorry, miss. It was wrong of me to do that. I mean on the stairs, without warning, like an animal. I apologize. Please forgive me."

There had never been a customer like this on Spring Street. Maura looked at him as though he were mad. "You can kiss me when you want to kiss me," she said. "Sure you know that as well as I do, sir. I'm only asking you not to kiss me the way you did, like you were with your wife. I'm not your wife, I'm not anybody's wife, and sure it's better for me if you don't pretend anything you don't feel."

"Miss," said Kevin. "Maura . . ." He had retreated to the armoire on the far side of the room, and he looked at the black ribbon about her pale throat, and the pretty canopy bed, and the auburn hair that caught the gas lamp's light and shifted with every motion of her beautiful head.

"Would you like a drink, sir?" she said, remembering Ginny's instructions, and wanting to break the silence. She wished there were some magic she could perform, something to tear apart the fabric of time. If only he would take his pleasure, sleep his brutal sleep, pay his money to Kilgallen, and leave her alone in the early morning light. If only it could be half-past noon the following day, with her and Ginny sitting in an open cab, racing to Fifth Avenue.

"Please don't call me that."

"What?" said Maura. The young man was smiling, or trying to smile, and he was coming closer to her, his large brown eyes glistening and innocent.

"If I'm to call you Maura, I'd much rather you called me Kevin."

"If it's what you're wanting, then it's what you'll get," said Maura.

He agreed to take a little whiskey, and Maura poured the golden liquor until it filled a large glass halfway. He sat down on the edge of the chaise longue and urged Maura to join him. She sat, and he looked down at her thin thighs, at the gentle curve of her neck, and he couldn't help himself; his hands shook, a few drops of whiskey fell on his lap, words caught in his throat, conflicting visions tore through his brain.

"You're so beautiful," he said finally, lamely.

He didn't know whether he wanted to make love to her, or whether he wanted to take her away instantly, transform her from an unfortunate whore to a lucky young maiden.

But he had to make love to her, he remembered. How could he not? Everyone would know. This girl was a whore, he was a virgin; he had to take her and be done with it. He was not so infatuated with a vision half created from physical beauty and half concocted out of his own wants and desires that he was willing to become the laughingstock of Columbia College. He reached out with one hand to touch her, but this time he was aware of her as both whore and romantic object; he did not grab, did not pinch, did not try to make a joke out of his groping. He placed a finger on her cheek, he picked up a strand of red-gold hair, he ran his palm over her mouth and chin.

Slowly, she seemed to waken to his touch. The girl had the dreamy look of an opium addict, her concentration constantly retreating to some other place, some other time. But now she was looking at him. Her hands remained on her lap, like a little girl at a tea dance, a wallflower waiting to be noticed. Kevin was mad with the luxury of the moment. She was lovely, she was pure, she was whatever he wanted her to be; and she could be touched, she could be made love to as surely as if her flesh were part of his dreamworld.

Once again he was kissing her, and through his shut eyes he had a sense of where he was: alone, in a room that was his for as long as he wanted it, with a girl who would do whatever he desired. The thought rattled him. He believed it, and yet he could scarcely trust that belief. His heart raced; while the room and the girl were his, he had to move quickly, he had to take her to the bed at once; otherwise some part of him warned, this moment would pass, and he would never have another chance.

"Please, Maura," he said, suddenly less gentle, suddenly urgent.

Without a word she left the chaise longue and walked to the bed. He watched her pull back the bedcovers, her thin frame ethereal, dreamlike in his dizzy field of vision. Kevin picked up the whiskey glass and took a sip, but the liquor did nothing to quell his fears. He walked slowly to the bed, as if afraid to fall through the floor, as if the very air he breathed were fragile, as if the dream he was living could be ended by a wrong step, a faulty breath, a clumsy word.

Maura was in bed, the sheet pulled up to her chin.

"I want to make love to you," he said, getting down on his knees on the floor so that his head was close to where hers lay on the pillow.

"I know," said Maura.

"You're so beautiful," he said. If he didn't have this phrase in his mouth, he would end up saying far worse: that he loved her, that he adored her, that he worshiped her, that his only desire was to take her away from this place and keep her with him always.

"You'd better undress," said Maura. She couldn't bear his eyes on her, sick with a passion that made no sense. This whole ceremony of courtship was absurd to her; the whole ritual of kissing her and talking to her and calling her beautiful was but another burden to bear. She was a whore. He was a man who paid whores so he could stick his penis into their vaginas.

"Yes, of course," said Kevin. He rose, turning his back to the bed, and began to take off his jacket, his tie. The minor fear of betraying an etiquette unknown to him—where to put the jacket, whether to fold his shirt, whether to undress completely or leave on his underclothes—was inconsequential compared to the fear now rising in his breast: Would he know what the hell to do? Would he, in fact, be able to do anything at all?

Stripping off his trousers, he was suddenly aware of the gas lamp. "Would you rather," he asked breathlessly, "not have the light?"

"It doesn't matter," said Maura. She wondered what time it was. It was certainly not midnight, probably not even ten o'clock; it might even be earlier. Even with this slow, awkward young man, it would take a miracle to keep him with her all night.

"You're sure?" said Kevin. He left the lamp burning and walked to the bed, dressed in his shorts. "It's just that you're so beautiful that I want—I would like to—I want to look at you, if you don't mind."

"I don't mind," said Maura. He had removed his undershirt, his socks and garters, and she looked at him wonderingly, absorbing his image for perhaps the first time that evening. He had a prominent, attractive nose, a high forehead, dark blond hair. The skin of his arms and chest was pale, and without much hair. He had the flat belly and strong chest of a college athlete, without any of the rough marks of the workingman's life.

Now the blond hair fell across his forehead, the brown eyes grew moist with anticipation, the scent of his sweat was sharp and sudden as he opened his mouth for another kiss. She tried to respond, so that he would be pleased and come into the bed, and make love to her quickly and fall asleep in her arms, so that Kilgallen wouldn't send her any more men that night and the hours till morning would pass like a dream. But Kevin kept advancing, and pulling back; kissing her with passion, and then drawing away from her so that he could look down at her head on the pillow.

"Come into bed," she said, and he hated the words on her

lips, for he imagined she had said them a thousand times, that this moment was not special but simply one in an endless chain of men passing through the experience of her beauty, of her body, of her false love.

Still, he pulled back the sheets and got into the bed next to her, lying flat on his back, until he could stand it no longer and turned to thrust his body against hers. Clumsily, he pulled up her slip, he pulled down the straps over her shoulders, he tried to touch her breasts, first with the tips of his fingers, then with both sweaty palms. He didn't know what to do next. She was against him, her knees against his, her mouth against his, but he still hadn't removed his shorts, he still hadn't had the nerve to touch the unimaginable area below her waist.

"You're so beautiful," he said, saying it again and again, understanding that his body was going through a change, through an experience unlike any other he had ever known. He was happy that he had left the light on, for the girl had shut her eyes and he could look at her at his leisure. He could feel her breasts, so much cooler than the skin of her neck, of her belly; he could stick his face in her hair; he could look at the miracle of her perfectly formed hands. He could lift the sheet; he could pull up her legs; he could kiss her thighs; he could finally bring himself to look at her pubic area, at the reddish-brown hair, so sparse and childlike—yet when he finally touched her there, the coarse, unattractive hair affected him like a fever. Kevin was so sick with desire, so clumsy and inarticulate with passion, that he could do nothing other than blindly grope about her pubic hair, breathing so hard it seemed as if the walls of his heart must break from the effort.

"Wait," she said, opening her eyes, a flash of gray in the green irises. He was like Patrick, she thought. It was absurd, but he touched her with the artless passion of one who wanted to please, one who wanted to be loved. She loathed him, of course. She loathed him as she loved the memory of her husband; for anyone who came to her in this place was an animal, a buyer of human flesh. But still, she needed him at that moment. She wanted to please him, and she understood his need. Quickly, she touched his lips, his hot forehead, she pressed his heaving chest.

"No," she said. "Slowly. Wait. No, you'll see, Kevin. Slowly—just lie back. Don't do anything." And she was on top of him, straddling him so that her coarse pubic hair rubbed his belly. Slowly she lowered her body, moving her light frame on her knees, guiding his penis with both hands so that he entered her, his eyes shut.

The pleasure was so much greater than he could have imagined that tears started up in his eyes. Maura kissed him, so that his passion would stand a chance of living past the moment of orgasm; she pressed her hands against his shoulders, she brought her lips to his muscular chest, she moved and swayed slightly, mechanically, while he sighed with pleasure, opening his mouth wide to breathe in the seconds, to take in the rapture that was all around him. When he ejaculated, he cried out loudly, he opened his eyes to stare at hers, he reached out and clutched the back of her neck, he brought her upper torso flush against his, he sucked in his pleasure as if for the first time in his life he were king of the world.

Maura hoped that he would sleep.

She closed her eyes, she lay on his chest and breathed slowly, evenly, praying that he would catch her rhythm, that he would drift with her tired body into a sleep that would last the night. She hoped that he wouldn't suddenly jerk his head up, look at the time, ask how much more expensive it was to spend the night—a question to which she had no answer anyway.

For a half-minute it seemed as if Maura would have her way. Kevin remained silent, he closed his eyes, he lay still.

But suddenly he was awake, and wild with motion. "Maura," he said, and she could not restrain him. He pushed her away from him, he slipped out from under her, he jumped out of the bed. "Maura," he said again, and he laughed out loud, like a maniac. "Maura!"

"No," she said. "Please. Don't go."

"I have to go," he said, but he was smiling, oblivious to her cares. "I have to go, but I'll be back." He was dressing, looking at her all the while, looking at her as if she were the only source of delight in the world.

Maura begged him not to go, she pleaded with him, she demanded to know why he was leaving, she told him that she wanted only to be with him that night, and that if he left, other men would take his place.

"No, they won't," he said, suddenly serious, suddenly manly. "I'm going for a little while, and then I'll be back. No one will come here but me tonight. No one, Maura."

She didn't understand, and she told him that, and he quickly came over to her on the bed and sat down in his half-arranged clothes. The nervous young man was now self-assured, strong, and knew exactly what he wanted to do. "Look," he said, "I don't know who you are, or what you are, I only know that you just made me feel wonderful, more wonderful than I've ever felt in my life. I'm just going downstairs to get rid of my friend, and then I'm coming back here, and I'm going to stay with you all night."

Kevin wanted to tell her much more, of course. He wanted to tell her that he didn't *care* what she was or who she was, that he would create her, or re-create her: He would salvage her soul, he would educate her mind, he would fill her heart with poetry and knowledge and bliss.

But he couldn't say any of those things, because he didn't know if he would feel that way all night, he didn't know if he would see it all in a clearer light in the morning. For the moment, it was enough to know that he was no longer a virgin, that making love was the most ecstatic thing in the world, and that he would sleep with the beautiful girl in his arms all night.

"All right," said Maura. She hoped it was true, that he would come back; the night would be bearable with only this incoherent young man gripping and poking her. But if it proved otherwise, if Kilgallen sent her back down to the parlor full of whores, she would bear that, too. It didn't matter anymore how many times she had to prostitute herself that night. Every night, no matter how miserable, drew to a close; this one would, too. This night would end, and the sun would rise, and she would leave the house forever.

# ❧ CHAPTER ❧ TWELVE

She was half asleep when Kevin came back, and she kept her eyes closed and lay very still while he stripped off his clothes and got back into the bed. He whispered her name, he whispered endearments; it was obvious he'd keep her up all night unless she responded. Maura let out a little groan, opened her eyes, and turned to him. This time it was he who straddled her. She watched him in the yellow light as he entered her; his brown eyes would not leave her face, even in his ecstasy he could not stop examining her, trying to fathom the secret of her existence, the answer to his incredible pleasure.

Maura fell asleep so soon that when she woke to the morning's light she couldn't be sure whether he had ever come back to her, or whether he had simply been part of her dream. As she raised her head from the pillow, she hoped that he had not been a dream; for perhaps then everything she remembered was an illusion as well—perhaps she was still in the garret, still locked up in the house on Spring Street, and Ginny would not be taking her anywhere that day.

But it had not been an illusion. She was staring at the canopy, feeling the incredible luxury of the mattress, when he spoke to her.

"Maura, darling," he said, coming over to her while he knotted his college tie. "I'm glad you're up. I have to go. It's late."

Maura remained beneath the bedsheet, looking up at him

without comment. His name was Kevin. He had enjoyed her body last night. Perhaps he would give her something extra before he left. She wondered how much she had cost him for the night. Perhaps Kilgallen had taken the boy's last cent.

"No, don't get up," he said, leaning over to kiss her pale forehead as she moved to rise. "I can see you're still asleep. It doesn't matter—I'm coming back tonight. I've arranged it all. We have a date, you and I, just you and I. I've left you something on the dresser. Please don't be offended by it."

"What did you leave me?" said Maura.

"Just a gift," he said. "I wasn't carrying anything suitable, so I've left you some money to buy yourself something."

"Thank you."

"When I see you tonight, I want to talk to you, okay? I want to know where you were born, I want to know how many brothers and sisters you have, I want to know if you like dogs and cats, if you prefer the seaside to the mountains—I want to talk to you. Will that be all right?"

"Yes," said Maura. She wished he would go so she could race to the dresser and see how much he had left. If only it was ten dollars. She could do a great deal with ten dollars. It would give her enough to eat, a place to sleep, maybe some simple clothing—enough to get by until she found a job. Ten dollars, she imagined, and tried to wish the money into place on the dresser.

"I hope you like me a little bit," he said.

"Yes."

"Well, you don't know me. And that's all right, too. We're going to start from the beginning. I'm going to be your great friend, just you wait and see." Again he was kissing her, and she closed her eyes, and then he was finally going, finally out the unlocked door.

The bill on the dresser was for one hundred dollars.

Maura didn't want to touch it at first, afraid it might vanish. But she reached out and hid it under a mirrored tray, refusing to think about what it might mean. Quickly, she took a robe from the armoire, then opened the door, looked down the deserted corridor, and then walked, bold and free, to the bathroom.

One of the blond girls from the night before was soaking in the large white tub. "Come in, Red," said the blonde. "Don't be shy. I'm just getting out anyway. Jesus, you're a quiet one."

The girl got out of the tub, whose water was already being let out. "The water's running out," said Maura.

"No shit! You don't want to bathe in what I just left behind. I wasn't one of the elite last night, honey. The house was crawling with pigs all night. I stopped counting tricks after the fifth guy."

"Where do I get hot water?"

"What?" said the blonde. "Oh, Jesus. Old Mike wasn't kidding—you really are fresh off the boat. Ever hear of hot running water, love? You just wait for this water to empty out, then turn this knob, and you get hot water."

"Well," said Maura, trying to keep the astonishment out of her voice. She had heard of hot running water, of course. But she had never seen it in operation, didn't really believe in it until that moment.

"You're Irish?"

"Yes."

"You don't know much about hooking? Money, I mean. Kilgallen didn't tell you a hell of a lot, right?"

"He told me that I could be rich," said Maura. The water had drained out, and the blond girl turned the hot-water knob and steamy water began to pour out of the tap. "That's hot," said Maura, acknowledging the miracle.

"I'll make it colder," said the blonde, turning another knob and looking at Maura quizzically. "Look, it's a sixty-percent house when you've been here long enough. Mike keeps the sixty, we get forty. For new girls it's seventy-thirty, for stupid girls it's eighty-twenty. Don't be a stupid girl, please, because it makes it bad for us regulars. You know what I'm saying. You got some rights here, it ain't a jailhouse. You just got to speak up, that's all. I mean, don't go overboard, or Mike'll send you up shit's creek. But after a while, I mean a couple of weeks, have a talk with him. Make him tell you about the money, and ask him how much you can keep. He charges us for the rooms and the food, but that's okay, we can still make good money after everything. I made twenty bucks last week. Nothing to sneeze at. Go on, get in there."

The blonde was naked, save for a towel used to dry her chubby little body as she spoke, but Maura was shy about disrobing in front of her.

"Come on, Irish, get in there while it's hot. Sometimes you don't get hot water this easy. Even in America."

Maura took off her robe and hung it on a hook. As she started to get into the tub, the blonde reached out and grabbed her arm. "Wait a minute," she said. "Let me see your mark."

"What?"

"I almost forgot. You're the one Mike cut up. Let me see."

"No," said Maura, and she tried to pull away. But the girl was too strong for her. Maura turned to face her and dropped her hands to her sides.

The blonde looked at the scar, shaking her head from side to side. "That's nothing," she said. "You can't even see it. That's no big deal. That's going to fade to nothing in a couple of years. Go on, quit gawking at me, Irish. Get in the tub, I know what you feel like."

I have to pay attention, Maura thought. She found herself in the hot tub, looking down at where the soapy water covered her scar. She was alone in the bathroom; she couldn't remember how long she'd been in the tub; she didn't know if the blonde had left her a second ago, a minute ago, ten minutes ago. There was a hundred-dollar bill waiting for her in the unlocked room. Enough money to live for six weeks in New York, or six months; one of the girls on Spring Street had once paid ten dollars a month to live in a hole without a window, on the fifth floor of a house near Second Avenue. Enough money to go to Ireland twice and back, and have twenty dollars left over. Enough money to stay at the Waldorf, at four dollars a day, including meals, for twenty-five days. Enough money to buy some modest clothing and find a job as a lady's maid in a Fifth Avenue mansion.

But after all, Maura didn't have any idea what Second Avenue was like, she had only heard of the Waldorf from Ginny, and she had no more desire to become a lady's maid than she did to return to Ireland. Suddenly, though the water was still warm, a chill ran through her. She shuddered, as if fighting a fever. Even if it were true that the scar on her belly was vanishing, she realized that in that moment she had sold herself; in that moment of being pleased at the money in her possession, she understood that she was herself possessed. The gift from the young man was so big, it imprisoned her. How could she run off to freedom when the hundred dollars promised a greater freedom, the beginning of a power that she could not yet fully comprehend?

She sat in the tub, enthralled, not by magic, not by greed, but by the sheer weight of her suffering. She was afraid to take a wrong step, afraid to fall into something worse than what she now endured. Kilgallen had no need of the locked door, because now Maura was free, and working for him, and for herself. She was a prostitute, and it wasn't the worst thing in the world, but it was bad, very bad, and she had given in to its attractions because she wanted money, she wanted to eat, she wanted to be able to bathe in a hot tub; and this mark of her own weakness, her own moral collapse, drove her to tears.

"Maura," said Ginny, entering the humid bathroom and coming up to her. "Honey, what is it? What's wrong?"

Maura told her. She explained that she was a whore, that she was bad, that she slept with men for money regardless of sin. Ginny helped her out of the bath, its water long since grown cold. For once, she didn't tease her, she didn't make a joke of her feelings, but simply took her into her arms and held her.

"It's all right," said Ginny. "Everyone feels like that. It's all right. God doesn't care. He wants you to eat. He wants you to be happy down here, don't He? Don't go and get religious on me. We're supposed to go out and see the shops, ain't we? Don't get religious on me, dopey, it ain't smart, and it don't get you nowhere except the poorhouse, eating garbage and sleeping in filthy rags."

Maura went down to breakfast on the second floor, with Ginny holding on to her arm and smiling. Eleven girls were at breakfast, and Maura found herself staring at them, to see if they were bad, if they had given up the way she had, if their eyes shone with independence or were dull with submission.

"Hey, dopey," whispered Ginny. "Quit staring. Eat something."

"What do they pay?"

"What?" said Ginny.

"The men who come here. What do they pay?"

"It's never the same. It depends on the guy, it depends on who's collecting. Kilgallen's not always here, you know. There's other guys who run things, and some of them get even more than Mike. It's what the johns got in their pockets. It can be five bucks, it can be twenty-five bucks. This is an expensive house, let me tell you, baby. This ain't no four-bit dive."

"What about tips?"

"You don't talk about what you get. You just keep that to yourself, okay? If a guy's going to give you a half-buck or a buck, just grab it and forget it. They don't all tip, and what you get is your business, it's all yours."

"Do they ever tip more than a buck?"

"Sure, honey. I've got more than that lots of times. Once I got a fiver, and I knew it was love. Love is the best thing—you get a steady customer, and you can make him jump through a hoop. I told you lots of times what I want. My dream is to get one of these suckers bats for me, just crazy, so crazy he'll set me up at the Waldorf—give me my own place, and my own little maid. I ain't dreaming, it happens. It's just being there when the right guy comes into the parlor. I'm as good-looking as any of those fancy Peacock Alley girls."

Peacock Alley was the Waldorf Hotel's wide-open meeting ground and show-off place, where unescorted ladies were free to roam and society men compared each other's bejeweled mistresses. But Maura had never heard of it. She tried to follow Ginny's talk, to understand something of what the other girls said to her and to each other, but she couldn't. She was in limbo, lost between opposing shores. The fact that she would soon be outside the house grew larger and larger in her mind, and, with it, the realization that she was not going to flee. But this realization did not soothe her; instead, she was besieged with guilt. She called herself a whore, a coward, a weakling. As the pretty girls in flimsy clothes continued to pour honey on their hotcakes, to chatter at will about hats and jewels and very rich men, she got to her feet, trying to shake off a dizzying confusion.

"What is it, Irish? Where do you think you're going?"

"You said we could go," said Maura.

"I'm not through eating," said Ginny.

"Please, Ginny. I want to go now."

Ginny shrugged, and turned back to her plate for two quick, enormous bites of food. Then she got to her feet and took Maura's arm, as if the younger girl were an invalid, and led her out of the dining room. "You don't have any clothes for the street yet. You'll have to borrow something of mine," she said.

"I have to get something from my room first," said Maura.

"Nobody says you can't. Hey, honey, you're going to have to learn to not be so jumpy. You take all the fun out of everything if you're worried all the time. It ain't natural."

"I'm sorry," said Maura, so quickly that her fear was communicated to Ginny, a fear of being left out, abandoned to a fate she couldn't understand.

"It's okay," said Ginny. "I know what it's like to be a little jumpy. You've been locked up a long time, right?"

"Yes, that's it."

"You go to your room, and then come to mine. I'm in three-nineteen. Will you remember that? Three-nineteen?"

"I'll be there in a minute, Ginny," said Maura, and she entered her own room and shut the door behind her. For a moment, a terrible thought assaulted Maura: The bed had been made up, the chairs had been moved, a clean nightgrown had been laid out on the chaise longue. Maura sucked in her breath and walked quietly to the tray on the dresser and lifted it. The hundred-dollar bill was still there.

Maura folded the bill and shoved it into the pocket of her gown. The money was still hers, and she still understood its power. It was too much strength to turn away from. The young man would come back, he would pay her again, he would fall in love with her whore's body, and she would grow rich. She would grow rich, and her dream would be fulfilled, and everything she'd thus far suffered would make sense.

Quickly, she left her room and went to Ginny's. "Why did Kilgallen take away the clothes he gave me yesterday?"

"Never mind Kilgallen," said Ginny.

But Maura insisted.

"Hey, okay. First of all, it ain't chic to wear the same outfit twice in a row."

"Sure that's not the reason. We didn't have street clothes in the other house, so it was just a little harder to run away. But this is supposed to be different."

"It is, honey. Here, try this on," said Ginny, giving her friend a heavy brocaded blue dress. "You're allowed to go whenever you want. But you don't get nothing for free. That's not your dress, and it ain't Kilgallen's—it's mine, because I bought and paid for it. If you want the dress you wore yesterday, he'll sell it to you. But you won't get it for nothing. Everyone's got to understand that with Kilgallen. He wants you working, he wants you to know what you're working for."

Maura was anxious to go, but first she had to submit to Ginny's ministrations. Once again, lips were painted, cheeks were rouged, eyelids were smudged with kohl. Ginny had a complete set of false diamonds: huge glittering paste earrings; a necklace heavy with crushed-glass beads; rings and pendants and bracelets so large and meretricious that only a country girl like Maura could have mistaken them for jewels of any kind.

"Now, don't you look sharp!" said Ginny, pushing Maura into sight of the room's large mirror.

"Yes," said Maura. To herself she looked harder, more beautiful, more sophisticated. She looked hard enough to willingly stay in this place until the young man, Kevin, came back to her, made love to her, paid her for the privilege, for the service.

"You're sure you're all right now?" said Ginny. "I don't want to take you around if you ain't up to it."

"I am. Sure I'm fine and dandy," said Maura. She put on a false smile and took a half-dozen steps out of a country jig.

"I asked Kilgallen," said Ginny. "I didn't want to get in trouble or nothing for taking you. But he didn't think there was nothing to it. He says you can do what the hell you want. Okay?"

"Okay," said Maura, and they threw on light cloaks for the warm March day, and ran down the stairs, and opened the door to the late morning sun.

"Jesus loves you, poor sinner," said an old woman's voice.

"Damn those bitches," said Ginny. "Don't look at them, just look for a cab."

"Just come on over to me, poor sinner," said a younger woman.

"You'll be free. No one will harm you. Jesus loves you. I love you. Please, just come. I'm talking to you."

"Go to hell!" screamed Ginny. She and Maura left the house and walked to the curb. Ten yards from where the prostitutes waited for a cab, three women kept vigil for their souls. The oldest one ventured closer. "Get away from here, you crazy bitch!" Ginny yelled. "You can't come here, this is private property!"

"The whole world belongs to Jesus."

"Fuck you, lady. Shove that shit. I don't want to hear it!"

Maura looked with amazement from Ginny to the three women, all of them dressed in gray suits with gray-and-black bonnets. She could no more understand their interest in her than she could Ginny's frenzied hate. The two younger women crept a bit closer to provide moral support for their leader, whose eyes now turned to Maura.

"Listen to me, sister. Jesus loves you. Do you know that Jesus loves you?"

"Shut up!" screamed Ginny. "Where the hell is a cab? Get away from us! Leave us be!"

"Jesus didn't condemn the fallen woman. No, he didn't, sister. She was a sinner, but he told her to go and sin no more. It's in the Bible, sister. Are you listening to me? Say that you're listening to me, sister."

"No," said Maura, but so softly that no one could hear. She was remembering Brendt, her poor dead sister, killed by despair. Stupid Brendt, running from the priest's insulting rebuff, running from his refusal to absolve her, could only think of urging Maura, begging Maura, never to blame the church, never to blame the church.

"Jesus allowed the fallen woman to wash his feet with her tears," the older woman was saying. "He allowed her to wipe his feet with her hair."

"No," said Maura, quite audibly now, and she took a step closer to Ginny and held on to her arm.

"If you don't leave us alone, you old bitch, I swear I'll stick my knife in your gut. I swear to Jesus I will."

"It doesn't matter how you came to this place, girl," said the older woman, her face taking on an otherworldly glow. "God loves you no mater how weak you were. It makes no difference if you were dragged in like a slave and kept in a cage. It makes no difference if you fell in with bad company at the five-cent theaters, or if you went dancing every night just to get out of your parents' sight. God loves you. Come with us. Let us show you the Lord's mercy. Let us show you the way back to the Lord."

The older woman took thé last step to where Maura stood and began to reach out, as if to grab at her. Maura didn't hesitate. She swung her fist into the woman's face, she screamed at her and kicked into her shins, she howled at her and would have driven her to the ground if not for Ginny, pulling Maura back and away.

Finally, a cab appeared. Ginny pushed Maura up and into it and directed the driver to Fifth Avenue. "Crazy bitches. Those miserable holy scum. Those filthy fucking broads. Hey, you sure showed them."

"I hate the church."

"Don't say that, Maura."

"I hate the goddamned church. It's the truth. Sure it's the truth and I don't care who knows it."

"Now, Irish, this ain't like you. If I had to guess, I'd make you out for the religious type. Those crazy bitches seemed to like the look in your eyes when the old one got to talking to you. And then you go and wipe her out. You're out of sight, Irish. I never know how to figure you."

Maura didn't respond. The day was fine, and the sun began to have its effect on her wild temper. Once again she was outside, and this time she was on her own, with only Ginny to look after her. Maura reached inside her right sleeve, to feel the hundred-dollar bill folded there, against her forearm.

"They always say the same thing," Ginny was saying. "Every time, it's the story of the hooker wiping His feet with her tears and her hair. Like that's supposed to be a great story. Something to look forward to, if you know what I mean? Get forgiven, so you can get down on your knees and wipe your hair all over Jesus's feet. Why don't they talk about Christmas? Christmas would do it a lot faster to someone like me, ain't that the truth?

Just talk to me about Christmas and the tree and the presents I never got, and, Jesus, I'd walk through hellfire for a pat on the back. But no. These dumb bitches talk about being forgiven so you can be a hooker on your knees. Jesus."

Ginny paid for the cab: They had only been seated for a few minutes, but the fare came to the astounding price of one dollar, and to this Ginny added a tip of ten cents. "It's a buck for the first mile, and forty cents for every half-mile extra after that. And you gotta tip, or they beef like crazy. It's a lot of cherries, dopey, but there's nothing you can do about it. A girl with class can't ride the horsecar, right? You don't want punks to get fresh just because you're pretty. If you want to save money, stay home and read the *Herald*. That's only three cents."

"I've got some money," said Maura, thinking it only fair that she contribute something to their cab fare.

"Forget it, Irish. I don't want you dropping your last four bits on a little fancy dancing. This day's on me, kid. Just stay close and listen to Ginny, and if you say thank you very much, I'll be very glad and think you're a nice kid."

"Thank you very much," said Maura, bobbing her head, as if to a superior creature.

Ginny took her first to a department store, at the corner of Twenty-seventh and Fifth Avenue. Her plan was to show Maura something of the riches of the city's shopping, walking in and out of stores all the way to the towering Waldorf Hotel, at Thirty-fourth Street.

"You never seen nothing like this," said Ginny, pleased with the almost stupefied look on Maura's face as they entered the department store amid a crush of jabbering women, all of them eager to finger everything in the open display cases—though almost never taking off their lightweight kidskin gloves.

The store was immense to Maura. At first glance, the ground floor seemed bigger than her village square, and the people assembled there more numerous than the village's entire population. The ceiling was as lofty as that of an ancient cathedral, and the miracle of electric lights—something she accepted, but could not begin to understand—lit up the endless room as if it were a summer's open-air fair at midday. Everything seemed to sparkle:

the trinkets and baubles in the display cases, the polished knobs of canes in display racks, the spectacles on the smart saleswomen, the brass buttons on children's coats, the polished mahogany of the countertops as greenbacks and silver slid across their wide surfaces.

Ginny pointed to trays of scarves, to stacks of blouses. She dragged Maura over to the glove department, to the shoe department, to look at coats, to goggle at wristwatches, to take a peek at a particularly elegant woman. As if all this material splendor were not enough to entertain her friend—who at that moment could not have felt further removed from the village in County Kerry if she had twisted through the earth and ended up in a Chinese palace—Ginny continually told her of what was to come.

They would go to a much bigger shop, and to a much smaller one, too—the smaller one had much bigger jewels, the bigger one had a much higher ceiling.

They would go one day to the Hoffman House bar, and walk through the white-and-gold lobby of the Plaza Hotel. One of them would find someone with money, who could dress up smart, and they'd dine at Sherry's—Ginny and Maura and their protector—and watch how all the swells ate their canvasback duck and drank their ten-dollar bottles of French wine.

Today they'd make it to Peacock Alley at the Waldorf, seeing if the women there were any better-looking than they. Ginny would buy a pack of cigarettes, and she'd smoke openly there, right at the Waldorf, and see if anyone dared to stop her.

Perhaps they'd even have time to visit the wild Indian Palace, where women were expressly allowed to smoke cigarettes and come unescorted no matter how late the hour. Ginny wanted to show Maura the rich men who bought famous actresses their furs, their wardrobes, their apartments; she wanted to show her the Chamber of Horrors in the Eden Wax Museum; she wanted to give her a glimpse of the famous Stanford White, having a drink at a posh resort, while his fifteen-year-old mistress looked up at him with adoring eyes.

"May I help you, girls?" said a snub-nosed woman with a deep voice, dressed in a tweed jacket with a four-in-hand tie.

"We're just looking," said Ginny, staring down at the case in front of the woman, which contained lace handkerchiefs in snowy piles.

"You're just looking, are you?" said the snub-nosed woman, with anger rising in her voice.

Maura looked at her incredulously, and understood that she, too, knew them to be whores. Suddenly it struck Maura: Everyone seemed to be looking at them, at Ginny and herself, dressed in expensive clothes better suited to a ballroom than to a department store. And it was not merely the clothes, of course. It was their whores' makeup in a place where no decent woman wore anything on her face but powder; it was the fake jewels, where no decent woman wore jewelry during the day, save for a watch, hidden in her bodice, or a simple wedding ring, or a plain gold clasp to fasten the collar of a dress. And not just the clothing, the jewels, the makeup; it was the clumsy youth of Ginny and Maura in these adult trappings; it was Ginny's low-class city accent, and Maura's Irish one. It was all these things together that made it plain to anyone that these girls were cheap mistresses if not whores, creatures from the half-naked chorus lines of sleazy Tenderloin shows if not the common-law wives of murderous gangsters.

"If you're just looking," continued the woman, neatening a pile of handkerchiefs as if the girls' very presence had caused them to sink into sloppiness, "perhaps you'd care to look somewhere else?"

"I'll look where I please, miss," said Ginny. "You don't got no call to tell me where to look."

"Come on, Ginny," said Maura. She felt as if a hundred shoppers had stopped their laborious search for things to buy and had turned to stare at them.

"Now you look here, you," said the saleswoman, her deep voice growing in angry power. "This is not the Tenderloin. You are on Fifth Avenue, in a decent shop, with decent people. Either you leave at once or I'm afraid I shall have to call the manager."

"It's a free country," said Ginny. "Anyone can shop where they please, and that means me, too."

But the saleswoman had already rung her bell, and a great

whispering grew up around where the handkerchief counter stood. There were a couple of very nervous laughs. "Please, Ginny," said Maura, taking her friend's arm and trying to pull her away.

"Screw the bitch, Maura," said Ginny. "It ain't right. I didn't do nothing, and I ain't leaving here. I look as good and decent as anyone in this place, and it's no crime if I didn't get enough school to sound as if I was English or something. I talk the way I please, and I shop where I please, and nobody's going to tell me nothing about where I can go or what I can do."

A moment later, the manager appeared, pushing through the crowd like a police officer on his way to an accident. He was tall, thin, white-haired, and ramrod-straight, dressed in a tight-fitting black wool suit with a thin striped tie. "What seems to be the problem here?" he said to the saleswoman; and then, without waiting for an answer, he looked to Maura and Ginny, the centerpieces of a small, curious crowd. "I see," he said, drumming two fingers of his right hand into his left palm. "Will you please come with me, ladies?"

"What?" said Ginny. "What did we do?"

"Please, ladies, if you will be so good," said the manager, and he pointed to a spot in the encircling crowd, and the whispering women stepped aside at once so that a path appeared, an exit.

"I aint 'so good,' and I won't be good, and nobody's ever done this to me before, no way," said Ginny.

Maura began to speak, to ask her friend once again if they could go, but the shame coming over her was coupled with an impulse so strong that she couldn't speak, she couldn't do anything but touch her friend, and take a step in the direction indicated by the august manager.

"You want me to leave, you get the bulls, or you can try and move me yourself, mister," said Ginny. "What the hell are you looking at?" she added, turning about to the crowd.

Maura wanted to apologize, to explain to Ginny that she was grateful for her friendship and hoped that she would not get in trouble on Maura's account. But she had no words now, only the desire to leave, to hide from the shame of the moment, and the greater shame of the endless months before. "Please, Ginny," she

said, but the words were only in her mind, she never spoke them
aloud, because the impulse that moved her to flee insisted, even if
she had to leave her friend behind.

The crowd buzzed as she moved through it, people standing
aside as if afraid even to touch her dress or her flesh. Maura had
no thought for the manager, or for Ginny, or for the end to this
altercation at the handkerchief counter. What she was fleeing
was nothing so simple as an embarrassing scene in a department
store; she was fleeing for her life. She walked faster—had to
restrain herself from running in her tight, high-heeled shoes. The
noise of the crowd abated, and by the time she found the street
exit on Fifth Avenue, she had a clearer idea of where she was
going, what she was leaving behind.

"Cab!" she yelled, the way she'd seen Ginny do it. But a
doorman, with a silver whistle at his neck, advised her to wait
one moment, and then he blew his whistle, and a hansom cab
appeared from around the corner, and the doorman helped her
into it.

"Where to, madam?"

"Please, sir," said Maura, "would it be all right to go to the
park? The big park?"

"You want to go to Central Park, lady?" said the driver,
turning about to look at the beauty, her painted face garish in
the sunlight.

She remembered the wild ride through the great park with
Kilgallen, the gas lamps glowing in the shadows of trees. "Yes,
please," said Maura. "The big one is the one I mean."

"You got it, lady," said the driver.

Once in motion, Maura sank back against the seat cushions,
beginning to fathom what was taking place. As they drove
north, leaving the commercial district and passing into the realm
of fairy-tale castles and majestic hotels, Maura allowed herself
to smile. She understood that she was not so bad, not so ir-
redeemably immoral. Against all logic, she was running away,
and she would never look back. She was afraid, certainly, but
the day was bright with sun, and when the boundaries of the
great park appeared before her eyes, she felt a surge of courage,
of hope. There would be a hundred worries, a thousand fears,

just to survive the day. But at least for the moment she could walk barefoot through green grass, she could sit on the earth, her back against a tree, looking up through its budding branches at the sky.

Even when Maura began to explain to the cabdriver that she had only a single hundred-dollar bill, and he exploded with hateful passion, reciting all the miseries of driving a hansom, all the insults of the rich, she would not lose sight of her sudden happiness. He let her go, cursing her and her pimp and her female organs in exchange for the one dollar and eighty cents she owed for the trip.

Maura quickly crossed the great Mall, busy with well-dressed strollers, and walked joyfully into the trees.

# ✻ CHAPTER ✻
# THIRTEEN

Maura felt like a child again.

It was too cold to be barefoot, but she didn't care, kicking off her shoes and stepping up and down on her toes in the earth. She wished she could find an apple tree, or a pear tree; she could climb up and grab an apronful of fruit right off the heavily laden branches. Of course it was the wrong season for trees to be bearing fruit, and as the March wind whipped through oak and spruce and elm, she could see that these city trees had been planted to soak up the rains and to provide shade, and for little else.

She scrambled up the side of an enormous outcropping of rock, quantities of which loomed up in odd places throughout the park, giving a sense of prehistoric force to an otherwise civilized enclosure. From the little height, she could see a lake, dazzling in the sunshine, twisting toward the north and west. Rowboats, and what looked like the gondolas she'd once seen in one of Brendt's borrowed books, dotted the water's surface. On the western edge of the park, new buildings, some of them ten and twelve stories high, were in the process of being built out of the surrounding barrenness. The famous Dakota apartment house, already ten years old, looked to Maura like an ancient palace, transported whole from some distant land. Climbing down a few feet on the other side of the outcropping, the rock leveled into a flat gray-and-white table, shielded from the wind by a natural umbrella of smooth stone that diverged from the main body of the rock like an act of God. Maura lay here, the sun's power growing as it moved west, covering her face and chest and gloveless hands.

She slept deeply; but when she woke up, it was with a sense of guilt, and an incipient feeling of confusion. How could she have left Ginny like that, without a word, without an embrace? And now that she was alone, with her one-hundred-dollar bill, with Ginny's brocaded dress, what on earth was she to do?

Maura got to her feet and tried to remember from which direction she'd climbed up the rock: Somewhere below, in the trees, lay her shoes. It was all she could do to keep from panicking. The sun seemed to have accelerated its path toward the horizon; soon the park and its environs would be in blackness. She had to get down, she had to find her shoes, she had to leave the park. She had to find a way to speak with Ginny, to explain to her why she had left, without being seen by Kilgallen.

Quickly, she got her bearings and began to climb down the rock. Near the bottom, she lost her footing and fell half a foot to the ground, landing awkwardly on all fours. Immediately, a young boy, no more than eleven or twelve years old, came running up to her with his dog.

"You all right, ma'am?" The boy, dressed like a little lord in a velvet suit, offered her his hand.

She declined his help and got to her feet. In a moment, an older woman and a younger child, probably the boy's sister, joined them, and the woman spoke to Maura with a heavy French accent.

"You are not injured, miss?"

"No, I'm fine. Sure it's only my shoes I'm needing."

"Shoes?"

"I left my shoes down here, and I fell asleep up there."

The boy found them soon enough, larking about among the trees for five minutes until he spotted them. By that time, the governess had grown noticeably cold. Slipping into the high-heeled evening slippers, Maura felt as if she were wearing a sign that declared her a prostitute. But what could she do? She had no other clothes to change into, no place to wash the paint off her face. The Frenchwoman directed her to the west-side exit of the park, near Sixty-fifth Street, where one might possibly find a cab and where streetcars ran with regularity.

"Do you have any change?" said Maura. "I've only got this one big bill." She held out the hundred dollars.

The governess shook her head firmly, gathered up her charges, and left.

Maura put on her shoes and walked as quickly as she could out of the park. It was nearly dusk, and one or two lights were going on in the houses along Eighth Avenue—which was awaiting a greater profusion of luxury housing before changing its name to Central Park West. A black man with a pack on his back was walking toward the massive, ornate stairway leading to the elevated railway tracks on Ninth Avenue. "Begging your pardon, sir," called Maura, running west to catch him.

The black man stopped in his tracks. He took off his cap, and bowed. "Not at all, miss," he said.

"Do you know where I can find someone who has change of one hundred dollars?"

"You'd better run that one past me again, miss. You done near blew me away the first time round."

"I have a hundred-dollar bill, but no money, and I need some change."

"That's not all you need, miss," said the black man. "Unless you're joking. You ain't? Okay. Now look here, miss. You're a very pretty young lady, and this is a very nice little city we got here, but the first thing you got to keep in mind is never tell anyone how much money you got in your fist. You catch my meaning?"

"But I have to get to Twenty-sixth Street," said Maura, "and I don't have any money except for that bill."

"You can take the El. Or the streetcar. It's only a nickel," said the black man. "Hey, what is it? You ain't crying, are you? Lord, I hate it when you young people cry like that! What have you got to cry about? Ain't you going to be here fifty years after I'm dead and buried?" He had already taken a nickel from his pocket and now he placed it in her palm. "Hey, you lost or something? You follow me, you'll be safe. I'll get you all the way to Twenty-sixth Street, if you want to take the Ninth Avenue El."

"I don't know. . . ."

"Look, miss, it's very simple. Listen to me, and don't you cry. You can take the El on Ninth, or you can turn back to Eighth Avenue and take the tram. The Eighth Avenue's got red cars and red lights. You can't miss it."

"I don't know where I want to go."

"Well, tell me the address, and I'll tell you the best way to get there. We've got horsecars and omnibuses and streetcars, and cable cars and electric cars and surface cars. This is the big time—we've got everything you want here, honey. Just give me the address and I'll point you there."

"Twenty-sixth and Ninth," said Maura, remembering the way Ginny gave the house's location.

Of course, even as she walked with the black man toward Ninth Avenue, she knew that she was not going back to the house, and that she was flirting with danger by going so close to it. But she needed to try to see Ginny, and she had to get back in motion somewhere. Perhaps on the train she would learn of a place to go, a house where she could find room and board, a neighborhood where she could get a job.

"You're an Irish girl, ain't you?" said the black man. "You're a long way from home. And you look like quite a lady for the Ninth Avenue line."

Maura, ever more conscious of looking like a prostitute, asked him what he meant by that. But the man had apparently sincerely mistaken her for a woman of quality. As they climbed the steep staircase, he told her that the "quality" liked to ride the Sixth Avenue line when they weren't in a carriage. There was nothing wrong with the Ninth, he said; it was just more of a working-class group.

Following the man's directions, Maura bought a ticket with her nickel at the ticket booth, and then dropped the ticket into the chopper box, which neatly sliced it in half. She followed the black man to the platform, and looked across the tracks to the uptown side, which was far more crowded. "That's where I've got to go," he said. "Uptown. I'm just going to wait until your train comes."

"You're not coming with me?"

"Hey, honey, I been working fourteen hours, and my missus is waiting for me with a hot supper. But don't be ascared. Look, you listen for the stations, and you get off when it's yours. Fifty-ninth, Fiftieth, Forty-second, Thirty-fourth, and you get off at Thirtieth. Or you can get off at the one after that, Twenty-third, and walk back up three blocks. You got that?"

"Thirtieth," said Maura. "That's the number of the street?"

"Oh, Lordy," said the black man. "Don't they have *streets* where you come from, miss? Now remember what I told you," he added quickly, because the platform began to shake from the approach of the train. "Don't speak to no strangers. Especially about that money. Did you hear me, child?"

Before the train pulled in, a uniformed stationmaster approached them from behind. "Are you all right, miss? This boy ain't bothering you, is he?"

"What boy?" said Maura.

"Good luck, miss," said the black man, taking off his cap and bowing to her once again. "Why don't you let the young lady catch her train, sir?" he said to the conductor.

The train roared in, its red and green signal lamps flashing amid the thunder of its wheels on the tracks. Its cars, painted blue and red, and carrying few passengers, were suddenly opened by passengers waiting to disembark. Maura thanked the black man and ran aboard. On both sides there were wood benches with wicker backs, and she took a seat at once. The three other passengers in the car, all working-class men, quickly took off their caps and placed them in their laps.

"Next is Fifty-ninth!" shouted a great voice from the front of the train, and then they were moving, the cars rattling through the air, on a level with the second floor of the tenements they were passing.

It was Maura's first time on a train, any train, and it thrilled her. Almost immediately, though, they were slowing down, and stopping. Half a dozen men clambered aboard, and the train started so quickly that one of them was flung against the wall. "Next is Fiftieth!" A heavy man in rough work clothes removed a piece of sausage from a twist of paper and bit into it at once. Maura looked from him to the tenement windows and back to the sausage again: She was very hungry, and wondered when she'd get her next meal. Perhaps one of these men could tell her where to get change for her large bill, even though the black man had warned her against speaking to strangers.

"Fiftieth Street!" screamed the great voice, and the cars of the train whipped about a curve and shuddered to a halt. As the doors opened, Maura found herself leaning toward the heavy man with the sausage.

"Begging your pardon, sir—I was wondering if you could tell me where I might purchase a piece of meat like that?"

"No speak," said the man, shaking his head vigorously from side to side. "No speak English. No speak."

"Next is Forty-second! Forty-second Street is next!"

Maura took a great swallow of air, trying to make sense of her situation. This was a great city, famous for its restaurants, cafés, theaters. It was still quite early, not even dinnertime. Surely there were stores where one might buy food, even with so large a bill as she had in her possession. Hopefully she looked out her grimy window, in search of something that resembled a simple eating place, a respectable boardinghouse. But all she could see was an endless collection of broken-down tenements, with a few pushcarts and wagons bearing goods to a ragtag population.

"Excuse me, sir," she said to a worker sitting next to her. "Do you know when we'll get to Thirtieth Street?"

"Thirty?" he said. "Thirty stop?" The man, a Chinese, seemed to be counting on his fingers. "Oh, thirty! Thirty next, after. After this stop, thirty stop. Thank you, miss."

"Forty-second Street!" The Chinese got to his feet, bowing to Maura, and left the train the moment it stopped. "Thirtieth is next. Next is Thirtieth Street!"

Maura understood that the numbers were going down, of course, but she didn't know what that had to do with the geography of the city. And even had she known the shape of Manhattan, the placement of its rivers and parks and grand avenues, she still had no clue as to where to go for a meal, or a place to sleep. All she knew was that there was a brothel near the next stop, a place where she could walk in and be welcomed. As the train picked up speed on its way to the stop, somewhere between

Forty-second and Thirtieth Streets, the vista of streets and
houses began to change. Amid the tenements were large numbers
of people, some of them well dressed; Maura could see the top
hats of gentlemen, and an occasional waiting carriage. In place
of pushcarts, there were brightly lit storefronts, there were
houses with enormous glass panes through which one could see
men drinking at small tables.

The train began to decelerate. "Thirtieth Street! This is
Thirtieth Street! Next is Twenty-third! Twenty-third Street is
next!"

Maura got to her feet and stood near the doors as the train
jerked to a stop, throwing her against a tremendous red-faced
man, smelling of whiskey. The man smiled at her and bowed his
head in mock deference. "Got a match?" he said.

"What?" said Maura.

"Going my way, honey?"

"No, sir!" said Maura, fumbling with the heavy door latches
as the train stopped and no one else prepared to exit.

"Uppity little bitch, ain't you?" said the red-faced man, who
was dressed like a clerk, with a food-stained tie and a frayed
white collar. "Ain't my buck as good as anyone else's?"

Maura finally pulled back the latches, and the doors sprang
open. Turning her eyes to the ground, she left the car and
walked out onto the windy platform. Almost immediately, the
doors were closed and the train took off, leaving her on the
platform with half a dozen men, all of whom were hurrying for
the stairs. She waited for the platform to empty, still shaking
over having been approached as a whore. At that moment she
would have exchanged her brocaded dress for a peasant's rags;
she would have traded her painted face for an old woman's
wrinkles; she would have given up her one-hundred-dollar bill
for a room for one night and a bowl of thick soup.

But the view from the platform gave her renewed strength.
Below were crowds of people moving slowly through the gathering darkness. She would not be on public view in the midst of so
many people. Even from the platform she could see names of
saloons, cafés, and bars. And though the area had a rough look
to it, with workingmen walking in groups of three and four,

there were the carriages of the rich, there were gentlemen in evening clothes, there were hansom cabs stopping and emptying out well-dressed passengers all along the bright, raffish avenue. Surely someone with a coach of his own would be able to change her large bill; surely these brightly lit restaurants would be able to satisfy her hunger. Walking slowly down the stairs, Maura felt that after a few bits of bread, a couple of swallows of soup, she would know what to do. It was only fuzzy thinking that prevented her from knowing how to get a message to Ginny, from knowing where to look for a cheap, respectable room. And food would clear her mind.

At street level, Maura was more optimistic yet. Not twenty yards from the elevated train stop were half a dozen cafés, filled with light and music and men in expensive clothes. She walked toward the first one, her eyes momentarily diverted by a sign affixed to a narrow tenement between two saloons across the way: "Health Massage. Girls of All Nations." A burst of laughter caught her by surprise as a group of boys, perhaps sixteen or seventeen years old, looked her up and down as if she were a pig in the marketplace.

"Hey, girl," said an older man's voice behind her shoulder. "You got a match?"

Maura turned, and caught the intense stare of a handsome gentleman, smiling as he examined her through thick spectacles. "I don't have a match," she said stupidly, instantly aware that it was wrong of her to speak at all.

"I'm a little lonely. Are you a little lonely?" he continued.

Maura took a few quick steps away from him and walked hurriedly past the first cafés she'd seen. She crossed Twenty-ninth Street, and, for a moment, the approach of a man in a checked suit frightened her: She thought it was Kilgallen.

"Hiya, honey," said the man. "How you feeling tonight?"

Maura ignored him, even as she saw a woman for the first time: a thick, slatternly blonde, walking up to the man in the checked suit and whispering something that Maura couldn't hear. "Sure I got a match, baby!" said the man, laughing. "But come into the light, where I can see you better!"

The streets were lit with gas, the storefronts with electricity.

As Maura slowed her walk, out of breath, she saw women, young and old, everywhere. Some leaned against the lampposts; others stood squarely in shadowy doorways; others moved into and out of the yellow and white lights, their painted faces macabre with professional lust.

"Hiya, honey," said another man to Maura; and when she passed him by, another approached, asking for a match; and another, demanding to know the time; and another, calling her by a name that wasn't hers; and another, commenting on the lovely evening air.

Momently more horrified, Maura turned in her tracks and crossed Twenty-ninth Street again, afraid to get any closer to Twenty-sixth Street, and to Kilgallen. She passed the train stop, and on the other side of Thirtieth Street walked blindly into a café, ignoring the whistles of a man on the street and the startled greeting of a drunk inside.

"We ain't open for business, honey," said a waiter.

"I want to eat," said Maura.

"You want to eat, eh? You can eat if you don't bother nobody. This ain't the street, girl. We got gentlemen here who only want to be left alone, you got that?"

"I just want to eat some soup," said Maura.

"All right, all right, don't bust my chops. Just don't bother nobody." He pointed to a tiny table in the rear, and Maura went for it, feeling a hundred eyes examining her, ignoring a dozen compliments. One young man shot to his feet and saluted her, sarcastically begging to have the honor of seating her at his table. Shamefacedly, Maura retreated to the rear of the café, trying to disregard every man in the house, all the while understanding that each one knew her for a whore. When she finally got to her seat, she turned it around so that her back was to the room when she sat down. But though she couldn't see the men, she could hear them.

"What you gonna have, girl?" said a voice at her side, and as Maura turned to the waiter, she could see a young man in a top hat standing behind him, waving to her with a sardonic grin.

"Just some soup, please. Some bread. Sure if you've got some sausage, I'd like some, too."

"She's an Irisher!" yelled the young man in the top hat. As the waiter left with Maura's order, the young man grabbed a chair and dragged it across the sawdust-covered floor, placing it opposite Maura at her own tiny table. "I like Irish girls, it's a fact. Some guys don't like freckles, but, for me, the red hair makes up for it. Red hair drives me crazy, especially under the arms." At this the young man laughed so loud he was forced to remove his hat to prevent it from flying off his head.

"Please leave me alone, sir," said Maura.

"What's that, honey? You want a match?"

"No, please, I don't—please, let me be."

"The thing about Irish girls is that they're strong, you know what I'm saying? Strong. Like your Africans—they're strong, too, but they don't have red hair. Are you listening to me? A pretty girl like you ought to listen to compliments. I could say terrible things about the Irish, too—it's not hard to think them up. You don't have the real Irish red hair anyway—you've got mixed blood, I think. You've got blond in it. I wonder what color your puss is. More brown than red? Or is it blond? Puss is strange. You can have blond hair on your head, and red hair on your puss. What's it going to cost me to have a look-see?"

"Please, sir," said Maura, not knowing whether to beg or to turn the table upside down on this rich, fair-haired boy who so gloried in humiliating her.

"Aren't you a working girl? Why the hell are you parading around with those red lips if you're going to play the little lady? Not too *good* for me, are you? Name your price, I'll tell you if I can afford it. You work out of a house, or do you go to the hotel?"

"I told you not to cause a disturbance," said the waiter, coming over to Maura from behind and depositing a tray before her. On it were a tiny soup bowl, a large plate of bread, and three greasy hunks of sausage.

"Sure it's not me who's making trouble, sir," said Maura to the waiter. "I'm not looking for trouble, but only for a bite to eat."

"You ever see such a ballbreaker, Charlie?" said the young man to the waiter. "All dressed up for a royal fucking, and all she wants to do is suck on some soup."

Maura had already begun to eat, looking at her soup bowl as she soaked hunks of bread in it, and trying to ignore the two men.

"Maybe that's all she wants is to eat. Give her a little breathing space," said the waiter. "I don't want no trouble in the place."

"You're telling me she isn't here looking for tricks? What're you talking about? You crazy, Charlie?" The young man reached into his pocket and took out a fat wallet. Sorting through a stack of bills, he found the one he wanted: a brand-new ten-spot. "Hey, Irish. You with the expensive puss. Take a look at this." He spread out the ten-dollar bill on the table.

Maura took one last sip of her soup. Then slowly she turned her eyes on the young man and, smiling, reached out her hand for the money. The young man allowed her to pick it up.

"We got a date, then," he said. "Isn't that right, Irish? You and me. We'll go wherever you say."

Maura slowly dipped the bill into the greasy soup. "You can go to hell," she said, returning the half-soaked bill to the center of the table.

The young man was too stunned to say anything, too angry to move. "Why don't you leave the girl alone?" said the waiter.

"Stay out of it, Charlie," said the young man, getting to his feet.

"Just leave her alone."

"You fucking whore!" said the young man, suddenly exploding. He slammed Maura's tray off the table and slapped her across the face. "You filthy fucking Irish twat! Who the fuck do you think you're talking to? I'll kill you, you bitch!"

The waiter started to grab at the young man, but wasn't quick enough; the young man threw his chair into the waiter's knees and ran about the table to grab hold of Maura, who had gotten to her feet and was dazedly wiping blood from her nose. He grabbed hold of the low-cut bodice of her dress and pulled her to him with such force that the material tore, leaving part of her right breast bare. The waiter had regained his feet now, and every man in the café was standing, too, watching with the terrible silence of complicity to see what would next take place.

"Maura!" said another voice, a voice of astonishment from

across the room. "My God, Maura!" And the man who spoke didn't walk, he ran, crossing the space with four great strides. Maura's antagonist let her go. "You know this Irish twat?"

Kevin Vane, the tall, handsome young man who had slept with Maura the night before, who had made love for the first time in his life less than twenty-four hours ago, turned away from Maura. The girl had collapsed into a chair, hiding her face in her hands, crying freely, her arms crossed over her chest. Kevin looked at the man and said furiously, "Put your fists up."

"Oh, a sport!" sneered the other young man, and quickly raised his fists in the conventional stance of the time.

Kevin at once stepped inside his guard, feinted with his left, and brought his right fist under and up into the other man's jaw with enormous force, knocking him off his feet instantly.

"You'd better call a doctor," said Kevin. "I think I broke his damn jaw."

The crowd momentarily forgot Maura, who by that time was crying nearly hysterically. Men rushed forward to pick up the unconscious figure, to slap his face, to ask each other to get a doctor. In the brief space of time in which they forgot her, Kevin took hold of her arm and pulled her to her feet. She wouldn't look at him, and she wouldn't stop crying. He had nearly dragged her to the door when the waiter caught up with them.

"The girl owes me forty cents," he said.

Kevin gave him a half-dollar.

"Don't come back here, either of you!" he called after them.

Outside, her limp, disheveled figure drew attention from all sides. But a carriage was waiting, and its driver leaped down from his perch at once. "Mr. Vane, sir, what happened?"

"Help me get her inside," said Kevin.

Maura opened her eyes and looked from the passersby to the driver to Kevin. The inside of the coach was black and smelled of new leather. "There, lean back," said Kevin. "You'll be all right in a minute, Maura."

She looked at him in the near-dark of the passenger compartment. She remembered his eyes, their intent, longing look, trying to discover something that would prove her worth. "Last night . . ." she said.

"Of course," said Kevin, hurt that it seemed to require a prodigious feat of memory for her to separate his face from that of a thousand others; while he had been so longing to see her that her face had come to him from across the café like a siren's beckoning, like an affirmation of love and desire.

"Last night . . ." she said again, and there was fear in her voice, a terror he could sense but not understand. "Please," she said. "Don't take me back!"

"I beg your pardon?" said Kevin. "I'm not taking you anywhere you don't want to go."

"Please," said Maura, not hearing him, the tears starting up again in her eyes. "Please don't take me back. I can't go there, I can't go back—I'd sooner die than go back! Please don't take me back!"

"Maura, please try to listen," he said. "It's all right." Kevin knocked on the glass partition separating them from the driver, and the carriage began to move forward, slowly at first, then more swiftly, driving uptown as a heavy rain began to fall.

Maura wouldn't listen to him; the fear in her was wild, and she tried to get to her knees on the compartment's floor, she bowed her head and clasped her hands in a gesture of abject prayer.

"Maura, please, what's wrong with you? Please don't do that. Don't you know I'd never do anything to hurt you?" Kevin took hold of her fiercely and pushed her back on the cushioned seat, knocking the wind out of her. "Now just be quiet! Listen to me! Quit crying and cover yourself up!"

Maura looked at the angry young man as he stripped off his jacket and extended it to her. "I said cover yourself," he said, more softly than before. Gently, he pulled her toward him, placed his jacket over her shoulders, and pulled it tightly about her chest.

Maura calmed down a bit. She pulled up her torn bodice, and she dried her eyes with the handkerchief he offered her. Looking at him, she sensed a gentleness, a kindness; but she could not trust what she saw. She caught her breath. Through the glass partition behind Kevin's head, she could watch the rain drip off the driver's wide-brimmed hat.

"Are you all right now?" asked Kevin.

"Where are we going, sir?"

"Not to Twenty-sixth Street, okay? Uptown—nowhere. I haven't told him where to go, except away from where we were."

"I only wanted to eat something," she said, looking away from him and through her rain-streaked window. They were traveling in the shadow of the Ninth Avenue El, retracing the route she'd taken from Sixty-fifth Street. In the narrow tenement windows were brightly lit-up domestic scenes: an old man lighting his pipe, a young woman watering plants, children running back and forth playing tag. Suddenly, she had a memory of her mother, on her knees in the rose garden, happy in taking care of what was beautiful, what was difficult to maintain.

"I was coming to see you," he said, taking her hand.

Maura pulled her hand back, away from him. The image of her mother vanished. The coach stopped, caught between two trucks in a line of traffic. Kevin folded his hands together on his lap, berating himself for touching her when she was so obviously still upset. "I told you I was going to come back. Last night was so wonderful for me. I couldn't think of anything else all day. I couldn't wait to see you again. When I saw you in the café, I couldn't believe it. I was only going in to pass a little time before I could go up to the house, and there you were. I hope you feel a little better. I hope he didn't hurt you very much."

"No, sir," said Maura.

"Kevin. Please call me Kevin."

"Kevin," said Maura. She had not thanked him for his hundred-dollar tip, for rescuing her tonight, for the jacket he'd wrapped about her. Slowly, she remembered him: how he had kissed her on the stairs, how he had revealed a passion that was deep and dangerous, that had more to do with love than with lust. But she didn't want to thank him, she didn't want to remember him. He was, after all, another man, another paying rapist, with a different style. Maura didn't want to have anything to do with him. She didn't want to look at his face, be touched by his hands, listen to his false words with their upper-class accent. She wished she could make him vanish, stop the rain, find herself transported to a clean little room in a decent little house

where she could work hard and save her pennies so that she
could one day send for her mother to come from across the sea.

"You're smiling," he said. "You must be feeling better. A
smile is a positive sign."

"Do you know any boardinghouses?"

"What?"

"A simple boardinghouse. I need a place to stay."

"Did you have some sort of quarrel?"

"No," said Maura. She could see his perplexity. After all, he
must be thinking, she is a whore. What does she need with a
boardinghouse? Doesn't she have a space of her own in the
whorehouse? Perhaps the rich boy was afraid. She might be in
serious trouble with Kilgallen, with gangsters who would come
to him in the night with stout cudgels, with pistols, with death-
dealing violence. But what on earth could she explain to him?
He was too pink-skinned and eager-eyed, too rich in his private
coach, his college tie, to understand anything of where she came
from, what she had endured. "No, there was no quarrel."

"Oh. I only asked because—well, I assumed you lived there.
On Twenty-sixth Street, I mean. Or nearby."

"I don't live anywhere."

"I don't understand," said Kevin. The night before he had
imagined her to be something different from what she'd appeared
to be—or at least to have come from someplace that justified the
low station she had fallen to. But now, listening to her Irish
peasant's accent, observing the hard edge that threatened around
the corner of every spate of tears, he wondered again if he was
trying to create something—or, worse, to imagine something
coarse and vulgar to be delicate and fine.

"I haven't lived anywhere since I left Ireland."

"I'm afraid that doesn't make sense to me. How long has it
been since you left Ireland?"

"I don't know."

"You don't know how long you've been living in America?"

"No!"

"But how, if you don't mind my asking—how long have you
been in the house? How did you happen to get there? That *was*
your room we slept in last night? That wasn't simply a dream?"

"No, it wasn't a dream," said Maura.

"Well, if it was your room last night, why isn't it your room tonight? Look here, I'm not trying to be awful about this—you needn't tell me a thing if you don't want to—but if you're in some sort of trouble with the men who run that place, tell me, and I'll do what I can to help."

The kindness was still there, but was being swamped with exasperation. He was one of the men who had used her, but he had also offered his help at a time when no other help was available. Maura tried to explain herself, but she knew that he would believe almost nothing of her story.

"I need help," she said. "I was not there in that place of my own free will. They will want me back."

"What do you mean—not of your own free will?"

"Sure it's what I said. Kilgallen is the worst man alive. If you want to help me, help me stay away from him. Find me a place where I can stay."

"I will," said Kevin. "I'll find you a place." He didn't want to question her further, not at that moment. The part of him that so urgently desired her to be a princess from a fairy tale, a lady in distress, did not want to be shaken. He had wanted her to say that she was not like all the others; in essence, that was what she had already said. But he was afraid to ask more, just then. He wanted to hold her in his arms that night, to make love with her, and not be forced to pull apart an obvious, flimsy tissue of lies.

"All the money I have is your money, what you gave me last night. One hundred dollars. I want a place, and I want a job, and I don't want them ever to get me in there again."

"They won't get you, Maura," he said. "And money is not something you have to worry about, not with me."

Something was going wrong in the way he looked at her now, she thought. As if the blindness of love were turning to calculation. Perhaps he was trying to figure out what she would cost him, how many dollars would have to be spent before he could be certain that she was his property.

Kevin knocked on the glass, and the driver slid open a shield that covered a screen in the partition. "The Waldorf," said Kevin.

"Where are you taking me? I don't want to go to the Waldorf. I don't want to go to a hotel. I want to go to a boardinghouse, a decent boardinghouse that I can afford."

"Maura, that's out of the question," said Kevin. "Not tonight. Young women don't look for rooms after dark. Especially not on a night like this. And, I'm afraid to say, you're not dressed in a very appropriate manner for getting into a respectable boardinghouse."

She grew quiet after this, seeming to shrink in size against the seat back. He tried to pass the time with superficialities: telling her of his college, how he was in his last year, how the boardinghouse he lived in was run by an Irish harridan who allowed no other women but herself into any of her boarders' rooms. The Waldorf was very grand, she would like it very much, he told her. He would send her a dressmaker the first thing in the morning, he would arrange for a proper dinner that night, he would grant her anything and everything in his power.

Maura listened to every word. It was not impossible that the things he said he'd do for her would come to pass. It was not suspicion that made her want to leap out of the carriage, jump through the puddles in her torn clothing and painted face; rather it was the certainty that he knew not a thing about her, that he never would, that all he could desire her for was her flesh. She felt a revulsion for him—and for herself, because she remained where she was. No matter what he told her, it was clear that he wanted to make love to her. No matter how generous he might prove to be, he was seeing her as a woman without a will of her own.

The driver pulled up at a private entrance to the famous hotel, and a porter was given Kevin's card. Maura had no notion of the world that Kevin's family inhabited. She had no idea that the Waldorf was always booked up, that a suite at a moment's notice could only be obtained by a few influential men—or, as in Kevin's case, the son of an influential man. The shock of an alien culture was less awesome than the artifacts of that culture: She had that day taken her first ride in an elevated train; she would now ride the first elevator of her life to a floor—the tenth—higher than she'd ever been.

So it was not the ease with which a suite was obtained that

amazed her. Neither was it the deference shown Kevin by
servants in flamboyant hotel livery, nor the back corridors of
the grand hotel that led to a luxurious private elevator. And the
fact that countless dollars had been spent by the hotel's man-
agement in stripping Europe of eighteenth-century antiques to
fill their New York hotel rooms made no impression on her
at all.

What made Maura gasp was the view from the suite's living
room: a northward vista of mansions beneath the towering hotel,
their lights blazing against the rainy night. From the bay window, she could look up Fifth Avenue as far as Sixty-sixth Street,
and every black carriage swinging its lanterns, every spire and
battlement and rooftop garden, every lady passing into a palace
under a porter's umbrella, was like a memory of what her dreams
of the city had been.

Once again, hot water was available at the turn of a knob.
Maura marveled at the sinful ease of such living. Here she was,
sitting in the largest bathtub she'd ever seen, soaking in hot
water and French bath oil ten floors above the ground, while
people outside struggled to get in from the cold, driving rain.
Once her father had taken the stick to her because she had eaten
more strawberries than her share. Now, in the bowels of the
hotel, men labored to make her a dinner—to cook meat that had
traveled the continent in two days, to prepare fruits from sunny
Florida, cheeses that had crossed the ocean in better style than
she had.

Kevin did not intrude on her privacy. He had obtained a robe
for her, and a maid had brought fresh towels, soaps, perfumes.
She was a long time in her bath, relishing the privacy, the
chance to dwell on her comforts and not her troubles. When she
had washed her hair, scrubbed her face, brushed her teeth, and
combed back her wet, red-gold hair from her child's face, she
put on the robe and walked through the enormous bedroom into
the adjacent living room. Kevin sat before a large fireplace, contemplating the burning logs with a glass of Cognac in his manicured hand.

"Kevin," she called to him, because he had not heard her light
step.

He turned to look at her, and was shocked at the intensity of her gaze. She had the look of a child who had been wronged and was determined to speak her mind about the injustices of the adult world, knowing in advance she would not be heeded.

"What's wrong, Maura?" said Kevin, rising from his comfortable chair, wanting simply to take her through the connecting foyer to the tiny, candlelit dining room where a butler waited to serve.

"Kevin," she said again, and he wondered at her scrubbed-cheeked beauty, at the fine, haughty planes of her face. Why not believe her a princess? Why not fall in love with a creature whom he could create? "Sure it's not that I'm angry, or being the least ungrateful," she said. "But it's fair and proper for me to explain who and what I am, whether or not you're believing me. My name's Maura O'Connell, born Dooley. I'm eighteen years of age, from County Kerry, a poor girl, with a blackguard father and no money. But my mother is of fine family. There's priests in it, and teachers, and nuns—educated people that would be shamed to see me standing here like this. My mother is a good woman, and I swear by her life that everything I'm telling you is the truth.

"I married Patrick O'Connell, of my own country, and we left Ireland to come to America. My husband, of blessed memory, poor dear Patrick, he died on the ship, and they threw his body to the fish. Just like they do to all the stinking Irish. And when I came here, more dead than alive, my only friend was sent back and a blackguard of a steward tricked me into a stranger's carriage, and I ended up in the basement of a house with locked doors and barred windows. I was raped and I was starved and I was cut, and they made me into a whore. I wanted to leave, you see, but I couldn't. I just wanted to go, but I was never allowed. I was locked in.

"They did it to me, because I'm a good girl. Even if I don't believe in God, even if I hate the church with all my heart, I'm a good girl. Do you see what I'm saying? It's not me. I'm not bad. I'm a good girl, and I swear on my mother's life I'm not a whore. On my mother's life. I know you're a rich and well-bred gentleman, but I've got a family, too, and mine is nothing to be ashamed of. I can read and write, and so can all my family, and so they have on my mother's side for five hundred years. I'm a good girl, Kevin. Please believe me. Please don't think I'm a whore."

She had more to say, of course, and the scar to show him, though it was by no means as clear as it had once been. It was a mark of his infatuation, if not his esteem, that he never once interrupted her speech, never thought of questioning it. When she began to cry, it was the high-pitched, uncontrollable wailing of a child, and he took her into his arms, not like a whore, but like a younger sister, like a friend.

But none of this meant that he believed her. Certainly, she might have been married, the name of the county from which she came might have been Kerry, and perhaps her mother was alive and well and a good woman. But there was no such thing as forced prostitution. There were no white slaves in this city, the capital of the world. No one had held a gun to her head when he had made love to her last night, and she had not offered to return the hundred-dollar bill he'd left on her dresser.

Kevin held her in his arms and allowed her to sob out her fantasy, to reshape the structure of her life. It was all right with him if she wanted to destroy her past history and create another one. It was all right, because he was determined that the beautiful young girl would be his mistress, and his alone.

Maura understood something of this. But she knew that he had heard every word, and that the words would be remembered if not believed. He treated her with great kindness at the dining table, talking to her about the way red wine was stored in cellars, explaining the way Manhattan was laid out in a grid pattern, telling her of walking along the dunes on Long Island. When the waiter was dismissed, he still said nothing about her speech, but his talk grew more serious.

"I want to help you," he said. "I'm very rich. I want you to live here for as long as you want. I like you very much, Maura."

But she knew what he wanted, no matter what he had said: He wanted her to rise, with great passion, throw her arms about his neck, bring her lips to his, cling to him while he carried her to the bedroom, to the bed.

Maura would not do this.

She wanted to say something, to explain to him without wounding his pride, or insulting his kindness. She could no longer agree to an artifice, to a convention that had no hope of lasting. He wanted to help her, he claimed to like her, when in fact he was sick with lust, wild with the first love of his life. How could she explain to him that, now that she was clean, no longer hungry, safe from Kilgallen, all she wanted was to be left alone, to find her own way, to be free of help or hindrance?

"I like you too," she said. "You're the kindest man in America. Would it be too much trouble if I slept on your couch? And then in the morning I'm off, and I'll never be forgetting you, never."

Kevin didn't answer. Maura hadn't broken his romantic mood. She was tired, her cheeks flushed from the bath and the wine. He didn't think her coy, or teasing; he preferred to think of her as exhausted, and overwhelmed with a sense of a new direction to her life. He took her hand, and she didn't protest, and he led her not to a couch but to the bedroom. He helped her out of her robe, helped ease her tender frame beneath the bedsheets. And then he joined her, pulling her body close to his, kissing her shut eyes, touching the delicate skin of neck and breasts.

Maura wanted to be good, she wanted to bury the life of a whore, a life that had been forced on her. But already she was compromising, blaming her nakedness on exhaustion, and a desire to be kept rich with hot water and good food and a view from the sky of the golden city. "No, please," she said, pushing his hand away from her thighs, twisting aside as his knee moved slowly into her groin.

"Maura," he said, growing stronger as she grew weaker. "Maura." And his hand found her genitals, and he forced his lips on hers, and the whole weight of his athletic young body pressed against her, throbbing with anticipation, with a desire that insisted on being met. Through her fear, through her weariness, through the enticements of clean linen sheets, through the resolve-weakening sense of having accepted this violation of her person endless times before, she revolted.

"No," she said, speaking softly, looking for the strength to push him away. She had made no compact with him. He had

helped her out of kindness, she told herself. There was no understanding that she was to go from one form of servitude to another.

But her gentle movements, her mad thoughts, didn't deter
the young man. He didn't know her, he didn't believe her every
word, but he was sure of one thing—the power of his desire.
If she struggled, it was playful; if she protested, it was to dif-
ferentiate between the night before, when she was a whore, and
this night, when she had become his mistress, his lover. Kevin
held her shoulders to the bed and entered her with clumsy
urgency. He had raped her, and not known it to be rape. But for
Maura, as she submitted, it was exactly that. Kevin, who had
begun as her hero, ended now as just another exploiter in her
life.

Kevin held her in his arms until she was still. He imagined
her grateful, romantic, full of dreams both childish and voluptu-
ous. A few minutes later, he wanted her again, and thought himself romantic, decadent, and very much the hero as he made love
to her shut-eyed, unresisting form. Once more, Maura had retreated to a dream state, removing herself from the bed, from
the smell of his body, from the desperate rhythm of lust. But this
time her dream wasn't childish; she didn't take the route to her
mother's stories, to the touch and the scent of County Kerry, to
the familiar vision of castles and queens. Lying perfectly still,
she remembered all the nights and days she'd spent in five months
in America, all the men who'd used her body, all the hate that
had been directed at her in the name of love. As Kevin made love
to her motionless form, she conjured the lines of Kilgallen's
face, she saw the brutish mouth and eyes, she felt the powerful
hands that had never ceased to hurt her. And in her dream
she was not afraid. She was big and strong and full of power
and dignity. In her dream she slowly, methodically pulled out
his hair, she ripped off his ears, she tore off his nose, she shut
his mouth so that his face was smooth, featureless, invisible.
There was no blood, there was no struggle, but as Kevin Vane
ejaculated for the second time that night, Maura murdered
Mike Kilgallen. It was only then that she was able to sleep in
Kevin's arms.

# PART FIVE

## The Factory

# ☙ CHAPTER ☙
# FOURTEEN

Maura tried to put herself into a state of suspension. She attempted, if only for an hour, a half-hour, to remove herself from the world of decisions, goals, ambitions. What was happening to her was so out of the realm of her experience that she was content to watch. Like the dimly realized figure at the periphery of a dream, she wished to make no comment that would rupture the moment, that would return her to reality.

She knew that she was awake, and alone in bed. A maid had blown out of the mists of sleep and was walking toward the bed, a tray in her hands. "Good morning, madam," said the maid smartly. A Tiffany clock on the night table revealed the time to be half-past ten. "Will madam permit me?" said the maid. Maura sat up against the headboard, and the maid set the tray up, opening its collapsible stand. She showed no reaction to the girl's nudity. In a rich man's hotel with a thousand bedrooms, she had seen everything, and more than once.

"Would madam like a newspaper?" said the maid.

Maura didn't answer for a few moments. She was too absorbed in the contents of the tray: a boiled egg, a French roll, a few pats of butter, and a dish of jam. Beside this were a silver coffeepot, an eggshell-thin cup and saucer, a single rose in a crystal vase. A piece of blue notepaper, folded in half, rested against the coffee cup.

"Yes, please," said Maura, looking up at the maid. Slowly, she grew more aware. The note was from Kevin. She remem-

bered the night. She had not wanted him to make love to her,
but he had done so nonetheless. The maid was standing over
her, offering her the morning *Herald*.

"Will that be all, madam? Shall I pour for madam?"

"No, thank you," said Maura politely, though she could see
the contempt in the maid's eyes. Maura picked up the coffeepot
and poured a steady stream of the aromatic, steaming liquid
into her cup. Not till the maid left did she reach for the note,
written in black ink under the hotel's majestic crest.

Darling,

You are far too beautiful to wake in the morning. I've
ordered you a light breakfast for half-past ten. I shall be
back from classes at one and want you to be starved. We
shall go somewhere smashing for lunch. A dressmaker will
be coming to you at eleven, so you shall be fully occupied
until my return. I'm so happy I found you. Last night was
wonderful.

                                        Kevin

Maura took a sip of the coffee, after she'd read the note for
the third time. It was twenty-five minutes before eleven on the
Tiffany clock, and she needed a bath, food, clothing. Though
she was not hungry, she ate every bit of her roll, her egg, her
butter and jam. As she swung her legs out of the bed, she
thought angrily of Kevin. It was simple to kindle her anger
against him: He had crushed her when it would have been so
easy to offer kindness; he had given her so little regard that he
could not even imagine that she might have hated him for what
he had forced upon her. "Last night was wonderful," he'd
written, and she remembered how he had enjoyed her, refusing
to listen to her; or, if he had listened, refusing to believe her
words.

But getting into her bath, she found herself wavering. Whatever he was, Kevin Vane was not a Mike Kilgallen. However
insensitive to her own desires he might be, he was not a pimp,
he was not truly cruel. Still, if last night was wonderful to
him, it mattered little that he had rescued her. Rescued her for

what? To pull her into his coach and rape her in this hotel? So
what if he was better than Mike Kilgallen? He was still a man
who promised slavery, no matter how comfortable the surroundings.

Maura dried herself with thick towels. She wrapped herself
in the robe he'd gotten for her last night. The seductiveness of
the situation was not the possibility that Kevin Vane was truly
fond of her; it was simply that here was a respite from the storm.
Had Kevin not found her in the Tenderloin, she might have
ended up on Twenty-sixth Street, in Kilgallen's house, or even
back in the house on Spring Street. Some part of her had impelled her back to the district from which she'd wanted to flee.
Here, at the Waldorf, she was clean and safe and warm, but still
Maura knew that she would not stay. She had not traveled from
Ireland, had not suffered the loss of her husband, had not
endured the life of a whore to become the painted mistress of a
college boy. Somehow she would swallow her fear of either
being found by Kilgallen, or forced to return to him in order to
survive in the great city. She would begin to make her own way,
and succeed.

The dressmaker was prompt, and came with an assistant, a
Jewish immigrant girl who understood little English. Maura
nodded at all the dressmaker's suggestions, agreeing to fabrics
and styles for morning, tea, and evening dresses that she would
never see. All she wanted to get her hands on was the simple
shirtwaist that Kevin had asked the dressmaker to bring so that
Maura would have something "decent" to wear at once. Maura
started at the sharp words thrown at the Jewish girl by the dressmaker. As the seamstress hemmed Maura's dress, silently suffering the insults of her employer, Maura wondered if that was
the sort of job she'd get—working on her knees, sewing, serving,
scrubbing. The seamstress's large black eyes, rimmed with exhaustion, seemed like a promise of what Maura would soon have
to learn.

While the girl hurried to finish the hemming of Maura's dress,
Maura wrote a note to Kevin. Having no pen at hand, and no
notepaper, she used a stub of pencil from the dressmaker and
simply wrote on the bottom of Kevin's note. Her large, firm

hand, made rougher by the thick lead of the pencil, was in
marked contrast to Kevin's elegant writing.

> I am leaving here. Someday I will pay you for the dress.
> I thank you for helping me get away from that blackguard.
> I do not thank you for after. You say nice things to me, but
> you think me a prostitute, no matter what you say. You
> treat me like you paid for me, and you did, but never again.
> Please, can you bring this dress I leave to Ginny? The
> blond girl? She did no wrong to me or you, and lent me this
> and her jewels, too. Dress and jewels are on the bed.
>
> Maura

When she read it over, she thought it would anger him, but
she decided to change nothing. She could have written far
worse. She could have called him whoremonger, rapist. It was
a mark of how far she'd fallen, she told herself, that she could
actually wonder if she had been too harsh in her note. She had
begun to think of herself as others thought of her—as a whore.
So what if he had taken what the night before she had sold?
Maura added to the bottom of the page:

> No matter what you think, I am no whore. I was never
> a whore, and one day you will know that I am no whore.
> And what you did to me, in Kerry they'd kill you for sure,
> even with all your money.

"Thank you very much," said Maura to the Jewish seamstress when she'd finished her work. The dressmaker insisted on
helping Maura into the shirtwaist, fussing over the prim white
collar, straightening the accompanying jacket with its mother-
of-pearl buttons till Maura looked for all the world like a
Barnard College girl. "Sure it's late I am," said Maura when the
dressmaker began to take out thick catalogs of bonnets and
shoes and gloves. "I have an appointment. We will have to wait
till the next time, if it pleases you."

"If it pleases *you*, madam," said the dressmaker, finally allowing a hint of sarcasm into her fawning tones. To the seamstress

she hissed: "Let's go, lazy thing. Pack up, pack up, we don't have all day! Madam is in a hurry and you're keeping her!"

"You don't have to rush her so," said Maura, trying to send a smile into the downcast eyes of the girl.

"Madam, if only it were so. With the sort of trash one finds to hire these days, if I didn't hurry them on, no work would ever be done. No work at all. Have a good day, madam."

When they were gone, Maura brushed her thick hair into a pompadour, left the note for Kevin against the Tiffany clock, extracted the hundred-dollar bill from Ginny's ripped dress, and rushed out the door. Only when she was in the elevator did she remember that she had not written a note to Ginny, to send with her dress. And she had not made clear to Kevin that had he simply rescued her last night, and not taken his pleasure with her as if she were a whore, she would have remained eternally grateful to him. But it was twelve-fifteen, and she had to be gone before his return.

The elevator stopped on three and an elderly gentleman got on. He asked Maura if she was on her way to the famous free lunch in the hotel's bar.

"No, sir," said Maura, wondering at the question, hoping that it was not yet another way of insinuating that she was a whore. If anyone could be so bold to her when she hadn't any paint on her face and was dressed so demurely, she must be carrying the mark of a prostitute in some invisible, inescapable manner.

"Wherever you're going, my dear," said the gentleman with great courtesy, "it is very unwise to carry any sort of greenback in your hand. Even at the Waldorf. If you'll pardon me for saying it to such a bright and beautiful young lady."

"Yes. It's all right. Thank you," said Maura.

"From Ireland!" said the old gentleman. "Your daddy better stay close to you this trip. It's your famous complexions, you know. Here on vacation, are you?"

They arrived on the ground floor, and Maura nodded at the gentleman and fled. She stumbled through Peacock Alley, not recognizing it from Ginny's descriptions, ignoring the lunchtime crowd of actresses and courtesans and their rich protectors. Even with her limited knowledge of the world, she realized there must be someplace in this grand hotel where one could change a hundred-dollar bill into notes of smaller denomination. Off the ornate main lobby she saw a clearly marked cashier's counter, and could hardly believe her good fortune. It seemed to Maura that if she could only break this great sum of money down to usable size, she could do almost anything: find a boardinghouse, ride a hansom or a trolley in search of a job, pay for a sausage or a newspaper or a coat.

"Begging your pardon, sir," said Maura, holding the bill up to the cashier's window. "I would like smaller money, if it pleases you, sir."

The cashier looked at the pretty young girl in her brand-new clothing, wondering at her peasant's accent. "One hundred dollars," he said. "Certainly, miss. How would like you that, then?"

"Please, sir, if it's not too much trouble, I would like one hundred one-dollar bills."

"What are you doing, miss, starting up your own bank?" said the cashier. Then, seeing that she did not realize that he was joking, he explained that he couldn't possibly let her have that many one-dollar bills. He gave her instead two twenty-dollar bills, four ten-dollar bills, two five-dollar bills, and ten one-dollar bills. These he placed in a pale blue envelope, imprinted with the hotel's crest. "It's a lovely day for shopping, miss," said the cashier. "But take care to count your change. Not everyone in New York is as honest as I am."

Maura took the envelope and, holding it tightly, walked out the Fifth Avenue exit of the hotel. A doorman bowed briefly, offering her a cab, but Maura simply shook her head and turned to her left, joining the incredible mass of people heading downtown. It was warm, far warmer than yesterday, as warm as a summer's day in Kerry, though it was still only late March. Afraid to attract attention, Maura at first kept her eyes to the ground. She had not yet gotten used to the idea that she attracted attention not as a prostitute but as a well-dressed, pretty young woman.

In spite of her self-absorption, she tried to take notice of everything she saw. Women wore brightly polished oxford shoes,

some with pointed patent leather tips. Men carried canes, or
furled umbrellas. Omnibuses clattered by, jammed with well-
dressed people. Streets of shops were interspersed with magnificent churches. Four blocks from the Waldorf stood the Dutch
Reformed Collegiate Church, and Maura wondered what sort
of people prayed there—whether they were Dutch, or members
of a college, or reformers, or perhaps all three.

Becoming overheated, Maura realized that she was walking
faster than most of the strollers. Trying to copy the style of the
natives, she slowed her pace, and looked up more boldly at her
fellow pedestrians. Every class seemed to be lumped together
indiscriminately: Men in rags looked fearlessly at gentlemen
in Prince Albert coats and silk top hats; ten-year-old ragamuffins
begged for pennies from cold-eyed women carrying pink para-
sols. Coming from a world where a single stranger on the road
to town could elicit talk for a month, Maura marveled at the
perfect equanimity of the city's inhabitants. Few stared, except
to smile at a pretty girl; no one seemed surprised by the sight of
a police officer dragging a disheveled young man from the
steps of the Union Club to a police wagon.

Though she had experienced the mad rhythm of the Tenderloin streets, and had been driven wildly about the city in
Kilgallen's carriage, and had followed Ginny into Stewart's
department store, this was the first time that Maura, alone, with
open eyes, had walked the city streets as a free woman. Suddenly,
she smiled. In spite of herself, she was happy. In the space of minutes she had seen a thousand faces, and every one of them lived in
this crowded place, every one of them had a place to sleep, a job,
a friend. Away from the terrible noise of the trams and elevated
trains—these weren't permitted on Fifth Avenue—Maura felt a
joyous atmosphere overpowering everything else in the city.
Here, anything was possible. One didn't have to dream of skyscrapers and fine ladies and bookstores the size of a cathedral;
everything she had ever wanted was here. All she had to do
was be bright, and strong, and hold on to her purpose.

Just off the avenue at Eighteenth Street, in the shadow of
a huge concert hall, she caught sight of an ice-cream parlor.
Maura had never tasted ice cream, though the descriptions of

the stuff in letters from America to family in Ireland had always intrigued her. A friend of Brendt's had a brother in Pittsburgh, and Maura had once agonized over his lengthy description of cold, sweet, creamy mountains, washed down with bubbling water. In Ireland only the very rich ate ice cream. That it was a dessert for the masses in America seemed symbolic of the riches awaiting Maura on the other side of the sea.

Impulsively, she turned off Fifth Avenue and walked into the ice-cream parlor. For the moment, she resolved to forget about where she would sleep that night, where she would find a job. All she wanted was to sit at a table and eat a dish of ice cream.

"Over here, miss," said a gruff waiter, pointing to a small table at which three women were sitting, two of whom had already been served. Maura took the last chair, and sat down uncomfortably, wondering what strange etiquette she'd have to summon to buy and devour the fabled dessert.

"He's the nicest sort of young man," one of the women who'd been served was saying to her friend. "Parents are both from Philadelphia. His father's line is railroad ties. His mother's people go back to the Quakers, but they're not even Quaker. And he's tall, he speaks like a politician, and all he wants to do is buy her red roses."

"Yes, miss?" said another waiter, swooping low over their table. Turning to the woman sitting on Maura's right, who was also alone, the waiter asked: "You together?"

"No," said the woman, speaking loudly enough to interrupt the conversation of the two women who'd already been served. "We are not together, and it might interest you to know that I have been waiting for service for a quarter of an hour."

"It don't really interest me, madam, but thanks for letting me know. You're too kind," said the waiter.

"You're too fresh," said the woman, who was big-boned and fortyish, and looked like she was about ready to strike the waiter with her bag. "Bring me a strawberry ice cream before it's melted to a puddle."

"And you?" said the waiter to Maura.

She had only just noticed the bewildering profusion of choices listed on a far wall: phosphates, soda supremes, frappés, Broadway fudges, chocolate sizzles—she had no idea what any of these were.

"Please, sir, the same for me," said Maura.

"Not very original of you, my dear," said the fierce lady, snapping on a kindly look. Maura kept her eyes on the table, not realizing that the woman was lonely and bored and eager to talk to anyone. When the two other women at the table finished their ice cream and left, she turned to Maura and tried again: "One more word about that prize pig from Philadelphia, and I think I would have had to strangle her. You're not a New Yorker, are you, dear? You're Irish, of course, but where do you live? I only ask because it's a sort of hobby of mine. Accents. I run a boardinghouse, and I've got Germans and Swedes and Irish and Italians all packed in together. You give me a few syllables, and I'll tell you where you're from. It's a talent. You're from Boston, right? Mother born in Ireland, so you get your accent from her, but your father's native American. Maybe his people are Irish, but, from the looks of you, his family's been fine and prosperous right here in America since the Civil War. What do you say? Am I right, or am I wrong?"

"Wrong, ma'am," said Maura. "My father's Irish as well as my mother, and I don't know a soul in Boston."

The waiter returned, feigning great exhaustion. From his tray, he deposited two dishes of strawberry ice cream, each topped with a cookie and a swirl of whipped cream. "Fifteen cents, ladies," he said, punctuating the remark with the ungentle placement of two tall glasses of soda water alongside their ice cream. "That's not together. That's apiece. Tipping is permitted."

Maura reached quickly into her Waldorf envelope and pulled out a bill—a ten-dollar bill.

"A sawbuck? I'm asking you for fifteen cents and you're giving me a sawbuck? I didn't ask you to sit down here at my table, miss. I'm giving you the best seat in the house, and you're trying to pass a sawbuck on me? Do I look like the Bank of America?"

Maura put the bill back in the Waldorf envelope and, opening it wide, looked through a few bills until she found a single dollar.

"You always carry your loot around like that, miss? Didn't you never hear of the word 'thumper'? You don't got by any strange chance a miserable little two-bit piece in that fancy envelope of yours?"

"No, sir," said Maura, holding out the dollar bill with embarrassment.

"You may take mine as well, waiter," said the boardinghouse landlady. She put eighteen cents on the table.

"Well, aren't we generous today!" said the waiter. He took their money and gave Maura her change. Maura nervously slid over a nickel from her pile of coins. "My God, I'm getting rich fast here! This Fifth Avenue trade is spoiling me for the world, I can tell you. Thank you, ladies. Thank you for your generosity."

"Eat your ice cream, dear," said the landlady.

Maura picked up the spoon and took her first bite. It was sweet, far sweeter than fresh strawberries, and cold. It slid down her throat with a delicious rush.

"That oaf of a waiter said one thing that made sense," said the landlady, watching Maura closely. "It's absolute folly to be carrying such a lot of money about in the open like that. I'm surprised your parents let you stroll about like that."

Maura nervously took the envelope off the table and onto her lap. Then she took another bite of the ice cream, trying to relax enough to taste it, to savor the moment. But she was afraid of the woman. What if she were to grab at her money and run off into the crowd? Or worse—what if she were to ask her how she had come by so much money?

"Do you stay at the Waldorf often?" continued the landlady, taking a spoonful of whipped cream into her mouth.

"How did you know I was at the Waldorf?"

"Your envelope, dear. I'm not prying. But I couldn't help but see, could I? All those bills staring me in the face. You should really carry a bag."

"I didn't think," said Maura, feeling more and more worried about the money. What did all her plans mean if someone came along and grabbed her envelope and knocked her down? The boardinghouse landlady was looking at her queerly, and Maura tried to compose her face.

"I didn't mean to upset you, my dear," the woman said. "Just to caution, if you'll forgive me. Also to entertain. Make a little conversation. It's lonely for me when my boarders are out to work. I enjoy a nice ice cream and a bit of talk with a visitor to the city. Perhaps you'd allow me to suggest some attractions for you to visit. Do you know Saint Patrick's Cathedral? Every Irish girl must see Saint Patrick's. It's cost two million dollars already, and they haven't finished, not completely. It might cost another half-million. Can you imagine how much ice cream one could buy with so much money?"

"Excuse me," said Maura, standing up abruptly. She had taken only two bites of her ice cream. "I have to go," she said, and she turned about and walked quickly out of the store, holding the envelope against her belly.

Once again she joined the stream of people moving downtown along the great avenue, reveling in the invisibility offered by the mob. Perhaps she'd been unreasonable to run off like that. The boardinghouse landlady might have proved to be a friend. If only she could have trusted her, how easy it would have been! She would have loved to have been able to hand over her money, take a room in her boardinghouse, ask her where she might be able to find a job. But she couldn't trust her. She couldn't trust anyone in this city, not until she understood what was meant by a smile, by a raised eyebrow, by a confidence, by a joke, by a frown. This was not Kerry, and everyone and everything was foreign to her—Kilgallen had taught her that. There were whores in Ireland, but there were no farmer's daughters dragged off into brothels in the middle of the night. There were hoodlums in County Kerry, but they weren't tolerated by the people, weren't allowed to walk about the village in the light of day. Maura resolved to find her own boardinghouse, locate her own job, and select her own friends.

Maura passed two more churches, an enormous hospital named after the city, and the imposing towers of the Judge Building, before stopping at an enormous newsstand at the corner of the madly congested Fourteenth Street. She hadn't kept the copy of the *Herald* that the Waldorf's maid had brought with her breakfast, and the sight of so many journals arranged before her eyes reminded her that in one of these would be listed a proper lodging place, a decent job. In Ireland, every American newspaper was valuable, even if months old, for it provided readers with a chance to live vicariously the lives that their emigrant relatives were living in fact. Even her dull and brutish father had enjoyed hearing her mother read out the "help wanted" columns from the scraps of American papers that came their way. Though he had no interest in leaving Kerry, it amused him to hear how much the Americans were willing to pay some Irishman to carry a load of coal on his back.

But which newspaper must she choose? There seemed to be dozens of them— the *Herald*, the *Times*, the *Tribune*, the *World*, the *Sun*, the *Star*, the *Press*, the *Telegram*, the *Post*, the *Mail and Express*—an endless number displayed behind the wizened old man at the counter and arranged in piles before him. Maura carefully found a nickel in her envelope, took one *Herald* (three cents) and one *World* (two cents), and dropped the nickel in the change bin on the counter, as she had observed a dozen others do within the last half-minute. Clutching these papers, she crossed Fourteenth Street and joined the crush of people walking east toward Union Square. Ignoring the manicured pleasure grounds, the rushing fountains and newly erected heroic statues, Maura took possession of a bench, and began to search the newspapers.

There were many listings, and she found the categories confusing. Under "Boardinghouses," the listings were few, advertising only the address and the prices. Under "Rooms, Board Available," the listings were many, and the advertisements mentioned "genteel boarders, immaculate furnishings, French-cooked meals," and other extravagant claims. Under "Rooms, Light Housekeeping," the listings ran for two pages in the *Herald*, and one and one-half pages in the *World*, and there were no descriptions as to what one might obtain for the generally minuscule prices.

Turning to the "Help Wanted—Female" section of each paper, Maura tried to get an idea of how much money she could earn from what was offered. But here, too, the choices were bewildering. There were listings for "day labor," at three dollars a week, with no indication as to what the labor might be. There

were listings for "articulate young ladies—earn fifteen dollars
a week and more!" There were listings for cape-makers cigar-
makers, flower-makers, box-makers, picture-frame-makers, but
none of these indicated what wage they were paying, and whether
or not apprentices were accepted. Some listings asked for replies
"in person"; others demanded replies "by mail only." Every
listing for servants demanded a minimum of two references.
Several asked for "young attractive ladies"—mostly receptionists
in photographers' studios and dental parlors. Two asked for
readers—one for a "blind lady," another for an "invalid gentlewoman." This last listing Maura found especially attractive. It
offered "generous terms," and suggested itself as an "enriching
opportunity." Maura resolved to find herself a place to board,
and then go at once to this "invalid gentlewoman" in Washington
Square.

Turning back to the "Boardinghouse" section, Maura looked
for something near the numbered streets she'd just passed:
Fourteenth, Fifteenth, Sixteenth, and quickly found one for five
dollars a week on Seventeenth Street, "only steps from Fifth
Avenue." This wasn't the most expensive boardinghouse listed—
two others had rooms for seven dollars a week—but it was far
more expensive than the one-dollar "light housekeeping" rooms
on streets she had never heard of. Still, as Maura had no pecuni-
ary experience to go by other than that of the brothel, she didn't
think of the sum as an impossible obligation. As she walked back
uptown with a light step, she divided the ninety-nine dollars
and change she had left by five, and arrived at the relaxed notion that she had nineteen weeks in which to find work that
would suit her.

Why, nineteen weeks was an eternity! Maura found it difficult to believe that it would take her longer than a single
week to find work. Even if she spent half her money on clothing
for work, she'd have nearly fifty dollars left—two and one-half
months' room and board. Other than clothing, she would have
no expenses. Surely she would have enough to begin to send
money home to her mother. Surely she would have enough to
save for the future, when there would be enough money to
bring her mother over to America to live with her.

The boardinghouse was more than a few steps from Fifth Avenue—it was actually close to the corner of Sixth Avenue. Maura walked down the stairs to the basement door. She had to ring four times.

"Who in the name of Jesus is that?" said the landlady, one Mrs. Saunders, five feet tall and two hundred pounds, with a large rolling pin in her fist.

"Mrs. O'Connell, if you please," said Maura politely, explaining that she had come in answer to the advertisement in the *Herald*.

"You're sure that you're a Mrs.? said Mrs. Saunders, stepping out into the sunlight to get a closer look at her prospective boarder. "What's your husband doing, if I may be so bold as to ask? This ain't no home for runaway newlyweds."

"My husband is dead," said Maura.

Mrs. Saunders stepped back across the threshold, put down her rolling pin, and pulled Maura inside. "You poor baby," she said. She wanted to sit Maura down in the kitchen and fill her with tea and cake, the better to extract her story. But Maura had no time, she explained. She had an appointment to see someone about a job, in Washington Square.

"What kind of job? You don't go answering no ads for canvassers, you got that? That's the only job they've got nowadays, canvassers, and they don't pay nothing but commission, and you can't eat commission. I need two weeks in advance, that's the way things are, deary, and I hope you got the ten bucks, because you look like a nice sort."

"Oh, yes," said Maura, and too quickly she took first a twenty, then a ten-dollar bill from her envelope and gave it to the watchful landlady.

"You ain't even seen the room."

"May I see it later, if it's not too much trouble? I want to go quickly about this job."

"Hey, deary. Never let it be said that Ethel Saunders takes advantage of nobody, least of all a poor Irisher widow girl. You come on upstairs and look at the room, and if you don't like it you get your ten bucks back, right? Where's your trunk?"

The room was on the third floor, and Maura looked at it

perfunctorily. It was small, clean, private, and there would be three meals a day with it. Mostly single men lived there, said Mrs. Saunders, aging clerks making as much as fifteen dollars a week. Even in spring and summer, everyone was in their beds by ten o'clock.

"I'll be back later with my things," said Maura. "If it's all settled then." Though it was almost two o'clock, Maura thought it possible to get a job, buy a trunk and some clothing, and return to the house before dinner. Filled with optimism at having found a place to sleep so easily, she hailed a hansom instead of inquiring how to take the Sixth Avenue Elevated downtown. The driver charged her one dollar for the short ride to the foot of Fifth Avenue. Even Maura was able to realize that paying one-fifth of her weekly room and board to take a ten-minute ride was absurdly expensive, and she resolved never to do it again. Still, it was nice to be met at the curb by a liveried servant from the house she had come to.

"May I help you, madam?" said the servant.

"Please," said Maura. "I'm here about the advertisement in the *Herald*."

"Oh, yes," said the servant, looking at her closely. How could an Irish girl expect to get a job reading aloud to Mrs. Crimmins? The old lady hated the Irish, the Greeks, the Swedes, the Jews, the Germans—she even hated people from upstate. Two words out of her mouth, and that would be the end of the interview. Like her few friends left alive, Mrs. Crimmins lived in a house left her by Dutch New York forebears. She never ventured above Fourteenth Street, never being able to face the fact that the rich now lived in a part of the city that had been farms and wasteland in her youth. An invalid confined to her chair, her eyesight failing, she loved only one thing—playing the aristocrat.

"Look here, my dear," said the servant. "I'm afraid Mrs. Crimmins is with her doctor now and really can't be disturbed."

"I can wait, if it's all right with you, sir."

"This job calls for reading aloud, for many hours," he continued, opening the door to a dark entrance foyer whose walls were covered with dull prints in heavy frames.

"I like to read, sir."

"You're from Ireland, I see," he said brightly, wishing that the lovely girl's accent could vanish before it was too late. In a softer voice, he added: "Please don't call me 'sir,' madam. Mrs. Crimmins very much stands on ceremony, and if you are to be hired, you'd better realize that at once. How shall I announce you?"

"What?" said Maura. A white-haired lady was being wheeled into the foyer by a nurse.

"What is your name, please?" he whispered.

"Mrs. O'Connell," she said.

Turning round, the servant made a little bow and said to his employer: "Mrs. O'Connell is here to see you, Mrs. Crimmins."

"*O'Connell*," said the gentlewoman. "I don't know anyone named O'Connell. What is she, a politician's girl? Someone from Tammany Hall? Or did she came over on a potato boat?"

"Mrs. O'Connell is here to see you about the reader's job, madam."

"Is she? Is that absolutely a fact? Here to see me about reading? Just because I'm too old to see fine print and the squinting's driving me mad? *Move!*" This last injunction was to her nurse, who had refrained from bringing the harridan any closer. Maura felt herself turning red as the wheelchair was pushed up to where she stood, and the old woman screwed up her cataract-clouded eyes at her. "You came here to read, let me hear you read!" she said, slapping a little leather volume into Maura's hands.

"Yes, madam." Maura looked at the gold letters embossed on the cover in a great shield: *Childe Harold*, by Lord Byron. "What page, please, madam?"

"What page?" said the gentlewoman, trying to imitate Maura's accent, laughing at her own joke. "Any page, Irisher. Page twenty. Twenty will do me fine. Go ahead. Let's hear your dulcet tones."

"Childe Harold was he hight: —but whence his name
And lineage long, it suits me not to say;
Suffice it, that perchance they were of fame,
And had been glorious in another day. . . .'"

As Maura read, Mrs. Crimmins laughed. She laughed so hard that it became difficult to hear Maura's words, and finally it became difficult for the old lady to breathe, and the nurse asked Maura to stop.

When Mrs. Crimmins stopped laughing and caught her breath, she turned round to the servant. "What's wrong with you, are you deaf or something?"

"No, madam."

"You might as well bring Negroes in to read to me. Zulus from the bush would be about the same, don't you think?"

"Yes, madam."

"Can you conceive of that pig-and-potato accent reading Shakespeare to me? Is this city so far gone that all that's left is foreigners who want to work? Why not bring me a China girl? Why not bring me a monkey, for that matter? I don't even let Irishers do the laundry in this house! Throw her out! The nerve!"

Even the servant's whispered apologies to Maura couldn't stop the pounding of her heart. Of course, she knew that she had an accent, but wasn't it a far sight prettier than anything the natives spoke? Her father's side of the family was common, but not her mother's. And she and Brendt had always tried to imitate their mother's lilting, musical speech. Though she was the daughter of a poteen-maker, she could speak as well as a priest, everyone in Kerry said so. That had been her mother's legacy—that and her stories and her love of beauty. And now, to be treated worse than a whore only because of the sound of her voice. Here, at the beginning of her search for employment, to be met with such contempt was too much for her. Her confidence was dashed. She could envision an endless succession of employers calling her similar names, laughing at her accent, demanding to know how she dared to enter their presence. In the back of her mind she remembered a column of advertisements in the *World*: "Girls Wanted—Figure Models." And another, longer column: "Girls Wanted—Masseuses, Experienced and Inexperienced." Perhaps those would be the only sort of jobs open to her. What was wrong with being Irish, she wanted to know. Weren't Irishmen quicker and braver and stronger and smarter than anyone else in the world?

Maura walked back uptown, dropping her two newspapers into a garbage can. A department-store window filled with life-like mannequins caught her eye at the corner of Broadway and Thirteenth Street. Suddenly determined to be treated with respect, she walked into the store and demanded service from the first saleslady she saw.

"Yes, madam," the saleslady said. "It's a pleasure to serve you."

Maura bought a trunk far more elaborate than she needed. It was fitted with a parasol case, a dress tray, a hinge tray, a bonnet box, and iron corners. It cost six dollars, but Maura didn't flinch at the price. She would find work, she told herself. She would refuse to let anyone intimidate her. There was money in her pocket, and she would show the world that she was not afraid to spend it. And so she bought underwear, two shirt-waists, a dark trained skirt, a bonnet, a fan, a pair of oxford shoes, a hairbrush, a cape, a purse, a beautiful lace handerchief; and together with the trunk, her bill came to thirty-nine dollars and seventy cents.

But Maura felt strangely better. The demon of fear that had risen in her belly in Mrs. Crimmins's foyer had been mo-mentarily banished. She put the more than forty-eight dollars left her in her pretty little purse, and watched with satisfaction as the saleslady packed her new things into her new trunk, and had a husky boy deliver them to a hansom. The new boarder arrived at the house in style.

Mrs. Saunders emerged from her basement domain, leading a wild-haired young girl in a maid's uniform. The maid was put in charge of the trunk, and Mrs. Saunders took Maura back up to her room on the third floor. "Didn't get the job, did you, my dear?" she said, reading the girl's expression. "I bet you ain't even eighteen yet, are you? You poor baby. What a miserable world. Dinner is at seven sharp. There's a bell at five minutes of."

Maura, alone in her room, kicked off her high-heel shoes, washed her face in a tin basin, turned on the electric lights in two ornate sconces on either side of a mirror, and examined her pale, tired face. There was another light, also electric, on a night table next to the low, narrow bed. From the mirror to the head of the bed on the opposite wall was five paces, and this was the length of the room. The room's width was a little less than four paces, from the washbasin to the single window, looking out onto West Seventeenth Street. The dresser was old and heavy, and took up much too much space; the armoire's door was cracked, and the mirror inside it black and distorted. The warm air in the room refused to move about; the lone window brought no breeze, but only the occasional clatter of a horsecar, or the song of a drunk walking east from Sixth Avenue.

Maura quit pacing to sit on the edge of the bed, then tried one hard-backed chair at the window, one broken-backed wing chair under the mirror. She got up again to find her purse, to check its contents, to count the money once, twice, three times. She found some paper and a pencil stub left by a previous boarder, and made a chart of expenses for one week, for two weeks, for three weeks, trying to calculate how much time she had to find herself a job. Then she was up again, sticking her head out the window into the darkening afternoon. The maid brought up her trunk, hung her few garments in the armoire, and left in silence. If not for the sound of the dinner bell, Maura might have remained at the window half the night, looking into the hazy glow of the gas lamps for some glimpse of her future.

# ❦ CHAPTER ❦
# FIFTEEN

Long before the breakfast bell at five minutes to seven, Maura was up and dressed, in a new pale blue cotton shirtwaist, and had written to her mother. Brendt was fine, she'd written in her strong hand, as was Patrick, both of them working hard to try and make something of themselves. If she had not heard from them, it was because Brendt had taken a schoolteacher's job in the faraway West, and mail from that region was desperately slow. Patrick was too tired to write. He asked Maura to send his regards.

Folding the fantasy-filled letter, Maura joined the other boarders in the basement dining room. As had been the case the night before, none of them took much notice of her. There were eight men and three women, not counting the overworked maid and the ever-supervising landlady. Most had already bought a morning paper, and ate their eggs and sausages from behind these barriers to conversation.

"A nice morning for job hunting, Mrs. O'Connell!" said Mrs. Saunders as Maura took her seat. "If you need any directions downtown, you just ask, my dear. I know every tramline from here to the Bowery! Eggs and sausages go down with you? Good! You eat hearty when you're going to be out pounding the streets!"

Even this outburst produced no commentary from the boarders, all of whom sat at the single long table and whose slightest signal—for salt, or the butter tray—was swiftly picked up by a neighbor, long accustomed to each other's dining habits. The night before, Maura had learned that the youngest man was twenty-eight and engaged to be married; he was waiting to save up the sum of five hundred dollars with which to furnish a rented two rooms for himself and his bride. Like the other men, most of whom were in their late forties, he was a clerk. Some worked for a bank, others for an insurance company, another for a great department store. One of the women was a saleslady in a jewelry store; another worked as a bookeeper in a paper-box factory; and the last, the youngest, worked as a stenographer.

"That's the ticket, Mrs. O'Connell," she had said to her the night before. "If you're wanting work, you get yourself to night school and learn stenography. Otherwise there's nothing out there, not for a decent woman."

But this morning Maura wasn't thinking about going to school. The letter of lies to her mother had put her one step back onto the road of wishful thinking. Even through the basement windows the sun shone brightly. All these gray people about her earned a living, a good living, and she could do no worse than they. Mrs. Crimmins's anti-Irish tirade had been an aberration. This morning she would walk into an office where her services would be welcomed and well paid, she told herself, finishing her breakfast before the others and rushing off.

She bought the *Herald* at the newsstand on the corner of Sixth Avenue and Seventeenth Street. From a bench on the corner of Fifteenth Street, she began to circle possible jobs with her stub of pencil, looking up from time to time at the church of Saint Francis Xavier towering over the neighborhood. Before setting off on her first attempt, Maura walked to the post office on Seventh Avenue and bought an envelope and stamp for her letter to Ireland. She was so full of irrational confidence that she wrapped a ten-dollar bill in the folds of her penciled letter, to which she added a postscript: "I hope to send much more very soon!"

The long morning did much to return Maura to the real world.

Her first circled employment ad took her to an address just west of Union Square. The short walk was tiring in her new shoes, but she found the rush of people getting to work by eight o'clock exhilarating. Clocks stood on every other corner, were mounted in the facades of banks, featured prominently on the walls of stores: Maura had not yet gotten used to this city-bred obsession with the passage of time. She hadn't learned what every working girl already knew: the way to count the minutes from eight o'clock in the morning to six o'clock at night. Daylight was irrelevant; sunrise, sunset, summer, winter meant nothing in the regimen of the city. Only the beating of the clock had meaning. Only the hours measured by man determined when one would rise, when one would eat, when one would sleep.

Maura climbed four flights of a dingy stairwell to a dimly lit corridor. After peering closely at a half-dozen tiny signs on as many doors, she found "Fortune Imports" printed in gold on a green door and began to knock. Immediately, the door was opened and a young woman walked out, passing Maura in a huff. "Five bucks they're paying! Might as well give it away—those skunks!"

Maura walked into a tiny room where four young women sat on a single bench, hands folded over their pressed-together knees. There were no other chairs in this reception room, save a deserted desk chair behind a desk covered with stacks of paper. As Maura began to strike an awkward pose, leaning against the wall, a thickset blond man of about fifty came out of the adjacent room and called out, "Next!" One of the girls stood up quickly and followed the man into his office. Maura took this girl's place on the bench.

Through the door Maura could hear the questions, but none of the responses. "Are you married?" he said. "Name? . . . How old are you? . . . Parents alive? . . . Ever do office work before? . . . You don't know shorthand, do you? Let me see you write this down. 'Mr. Graham is very fair. He treats his girls with the utmost courtesy.' *That's* too fast for you?"

The man was back at the connecting door, ushering out the young woman and calling for the next. Maura felt his eyes on her, and she looked up at him. "Who are you?" he said to her abruptly.

"Mrs. O'Connell is my name, sir."

"Mrs. O'Connell, is it?" he said, affecting a comical brogue. "Well, it's Mrs. O'Connell I was expecting. Why didn't you mention you were here? Come on, come on, my dear." Brushing aside the young woman whose turn it was, the man helped an astonished Maura to her feet and pulled her into his office.

"Sit down," he said, the brogue gone. "My name's Graham, Mrs. O'Connell. What's your husband doing that he's putting a pretty young thing like you out to work in the world of men?"

"My husband is dead, Mr. Graham," said Maura.

"Well, that puts a different light on things, don't it?" he said. The man's clothes were cheap, his shirt collar turning yellow, and his watch chain wasn't even gold. Graham's office was small, the desk old, the walls in need of paint. "I'm a bachelor myself, so I know what it's like to be alone in the night, Mrs. O'Connell. Tell me about your office experience."

"I can write a good letter, and in a good hand," she said. "I used to work in my father's business, and I'm good with figures. Sure it's hard work that I'm willing to do, that I'm glad to do. I don't tire easily, and long hours don't bother me at all, sir."

"Excuse me, Mrs. O'Connell," said Mr. Graham. "You don't have any office experience, is that correct?"

"Yes, sir."

"Are you engaged to be married, by any chance?"

"No, sir."

"I only ask because it's important to know. Nobody likes to hire some pretty young thing and the next day she's gone with a feller and you're out of luck, looking for a new girl."

Maura sat still, waiting for him to offer her the job. It was clear that she had no qualifications to work in this place, save the fact of her youth and beauty.

"So you've got no feller, is that it, Mrs. O'Connell? You're not an *attached* girl? You're not *spoken* for, so to speak?"

"Excuse me, Mr. Graham," said Maura, "but this job doesn't appeal to me." And she was on her feet and out the door before he could cross the room. She ran down the stairs and walked quickly, straight to the park at Union Square. She had not quit life as a prostitute to be ogled by a dirty middle-aged man in an office without decent work.

For a few moments the terrible rejection of yesterday afternoon returned to her. If this man hadn't insulted her Irishness,
he had insulted her womanhood instead. Why would one place
be any different from another? Any good job would be taken
by a no-nonsense woman with experience: one who could take
shorthand, who could even type-write letters. No one would
trust her to handle the myriad details of office life. Any man
who would hire her would want her in the office for the same
reason that Mr. Graham did. The young stenographer in her
boardinghouse was right—only with training could she get a
decent job. And since she had neither the money nor the time for
such training, it was all she could do to restrain herself from
throwing away her newspaper in despair.

But Maura quickly pulled herself back together. Two interviews with two such different prospective employers meant
nothing. A gentleman on the street doffed his hat to her, and she
felt young and charming and free. She got directions from a police officer on how to take the elevated train to a photographer's
studio on West Twenty-eighth Street, and even when the door
to this faraway studio proved to be posted with a disappointing
sign—"Receptionist's Job Taken. No More Need Apply"—
Maura held fast to her optimism.

The next job advertisement was for an office on Whitehall
Street. A policeman directed her to a streetcar and advised her to
ask someone for more exact directions when she'd arrived at
Bowling Green. But Bowling Green was a long way on the slow-
moving horse-drawn car. It seemed to stop on every corner,
joining and rejoining the ever-worsening downtown traffic. By
the time she'd gotten to Bowling Green, it was noon. Maura had
chanced on the glorious moment when most of the office workers
were being let out for their half-hour lunch break.

Once again, the late March day was like summer. Young
women in shirtwaists, young men in rumpled suits, older men in
stiff collars, laborers and clerks, receptionists and secretaries
and bank tellers, all descended on a few park benches. Oblivious
to the noise and traffic, they opened lunches carried in bags and
boxes and pails. There was a chattering, a joyousness, that
Maura associated more with work than with having been let out
of work for a respite.

After months of enforced passivity, she wanted what she thought they had: self-directed lives. She wanted to be able to go to an office, do a good job, and be paid for it. She wanted to know that if she learned more, and worked harder, she'd be promoted, she'd be given a larger salary, she'd be rewarded according to her deserts.

Mrs. Saunders had offered to pack her a sandwich for lunch; it was part of her board. Now Maura regretted that she hadn't wanted the bother of carrying lunch around with her all morning. Checking the address she needed on Whitehall Street again, she asked three people for directions. Only the third one bothered to answer her, so in a hurry were the others. The downtown area she found herself in was far more congested than Fifth Avenue. Crowds seemed to occupy every bit of space between the tall buildings. She could never have imagined anything so chaotic in the world of free men. Only at Ellis Island had she witnessed such pandemonium, but that had been among immigrants, clamoring to get into their dream. Here, on Wall Street, she was at the heart of that dream, and the pace, the mad urgency, the barely concealed terror in the sharp, rude movements of the masses of people made little sense to her.

The Whitehall Street office building was very grand, all of twelve stories, with uniformed elevator men as smartly mannered as those at the Waldorf. She found the office she was looking for on the third floor, and was told to wait in a bright, airy room until the manager would be back from lunch. The manager's assistant came over to her a few minutes later, apologized for having to keep her waiting, and asked her if she'd like to fill out an application form. Maura took the form, together with a lapboard and a pencil, and began to write out her married name. Beneath the space for her name were a score of queries: age, state of health, primary and secondary schools from which graduated, previous employers, personal references, business references, special skills, and on and on. Maura quickly blacked out her name, and waited for the manager's assistant to leave the reception area. When she had, Maura nodded at the receptionist, and got to her feet and walked out, leaving the lapboard, pencil, and uncompleted application behind her. Blindly, she groped for the elevator button, afraid that the manager would arrive, or his assistant, demanding to know why she'd had the audacity to appear there in the first place.

"Yes, madam," said the elevator man, and Maura got in and whispered her desire to go to the ground level. Looking at her feet, she saw that the bottom of the elevator cage was covered with pennies, thousands of them, glued to the floor. My previous experience, she thought, was as a maker of illegal whiskey—and very good whiskey it was at that, sir! And afterward I was a wife, I was a whore, I was almost a mistress. Maura walked quickly out of the building, into the crowds and the summery weather.

Crossing the street, she was nearly hit by a sedately walking horse. As its driver shouted at her, she continued west, crossing Bowling Green, ignoring the inviting tranquillity of Trinity Church to her right, crossing Washington Street and West Street against the onrushing traffic of produce-laden trucks, and made for the water's edge. More than the sight of tall ships, unloading their wares from every port in the world, she wanted the scent of the water, the winds of the sea. The piers were numbered, and she stepped up her pace to put the numbers behind her. Pier 8 was tiny, with a single small ship getting ready to sail. Pier 9 was huge, loaded with crates that were released from giant cranes by sweating, bare-chested men. Across the Hudson, Jersey City sat in a humid haze. Looking up the river, she could see an endless line of ships hugging the shore and steaming up and down the western edge of Manhattan. Tugboats and freighters, sailing yachts and steamships mirrored the confusion, the energy, she had seen on the streets. It was these men of muscle—powerful black men and frail old immigrants, young Irish and German men from the Bowery, Italian boys refusing to spend another day of their lives in school—who handled the grain and the gold, the lumber and the bananas, the copper and the cloth and the steel that fueled the work of the men in the offices only blocks away.

Past Pier 11, the traffic along West Street became oppressive. Washington Market, the great produce center of the city, dispersed its least desirable, and cheapest, fruits and vegetables at one o'clock in the afternoon, and every truck in town seemed to be converging on that space of earth. The smell of horses, the never-ending curses of their drivers, drove away any tranquil blessing of the water. Men called out to her—from the piers, from the trucks, loading ships—and they looked at her, and they whistled at her; this was their world, and she was out of place.

But wasn't the world of the office just as much a world of men? she thought. Wasn't she welcomed there just as she was welcomed here? Maura knew that if the world allowed it, she could drive a truck, she could lift a crate, she could hawk bruised vegetables with a great voice. If the world allowed it, she could do whatever it was that Mr. Graham did, or that Kevin would do, or that Mrs. Crimmins's husband must have done. But the world did not allow it. She was pretty, so she could aspire to the lofty position of receptionist. She was clever, so, if she could find the time and money, she could learn to be a stenographer. With her beauty, she could become the mistress of a wealthy man. With great fortune, she could even become somebody's wife.

"Gee, but ain't you a mark!" said a familiar voice, an Irish voice, coming from behind a stack of curbside barrels. Maura turned at the words, and an old woman lurched toward her, smiling ludicrously. "Pretty as a rosebud," said the old woman, coming closer. Her gray hair was red at the temples, her eyebrows were red and black, her skin was white and freckled with age spots, and she didn't have a tooth in her mouth. "Come on, give an old working girl a hand."

Maura backed away, her heart rising to her throat, the ground heaving beneath her. The derelict's resemblance to her mother was so strong that Maura felt as if she were going mad. This toothless hag could be her mother in ten years, or twenty years; it could be herself in a generation more.

"Cab!" she called out, suddenly finding a reckless hansom twisting through the vans and the trucks. She didn't care that she couldn't afford it, or that she hadn't decided where she wanted to go. She simply had to leave this apparition behind.

The cabdriver didn't bother to pull over; he halted his rig in the middle of the traffic and waited nonchalantly for Maura to dodge through the slow-moving mass of horses and giant wheels.

Maura looked down at her *Herald* and gave the driver an address
on Broome Street. When she had settled down in her seat, she
realized that the advertisement she'd selected had been one of
her last choices: "Girls wanted for cape-making," it had said.
She had been reluctant to circle it at all that morning, so
optimistic had she been about finding a job in an office. Well,
she was less optimistic now. She had marked it as a last resort,
but the cab was already hurtling her to Broome Street, so she
might as well take a look at what the job had to offer, she
thought.

The ride removed two more dollars from her pretty purse,
and as Maura climbed the steps to Gotham Capes, on the top
floor of a six-story loft building, she began to understand how
much faster than she'd imagined her money could run out.

Pushing open a huge, heavy door, Maura found an old German man sitting on a crate next to the time register. "Pardon me,
sir," she said.

"See the foreman," he said, not looking up from his newspaper. There was only one place to go, and that was through the
next door, just behind the German. Maura walked through, and
was immediately assaulted by the sound and heat of two-score
sewing machines jammed onto three tables. In the small space,
the noise was deafening, and the place was much too bright.
Hot sun came from the skylight, and gas jets burned over the
heads of the stoop-shouldered girls at their machines.

"Yeah?" said a very short young man, coming up to her with
a pencil behind his ear and a large pad in his hands.

"If you please, sir, I would like to see the foreman."

"If you please, Red, you're looking at him. 'If you please'—
I like that."

"I'm here about the job," said Maura, exhibiting the folded
*Herald* in her hands to him.

"You don't look the type, sugar."

"I would be pleased if you would tell me how much you
pay."

"Three-fifty, honey. Ain't enough to buy you that fancy dress.
Ever work a Singer, Irish?"

"A Singer?"

"Wait a minute," said the foreman, suddenly enjoying himself very much. "Let me get this straight. You come here to see about cape-making, and you never heard of no Singer, right?"

"I'm sorry, sir."

Straight-faced, the foreman sidled down a row of enormous levers and switches and quickly slammed down the master switch. Immediately, the power to the forty machines was shut off, and the humming, and the pounding, and the whirring wound down to a whisper, and then vanished altogether. Forty girls looked up in the sudden silence. Two dozen much younger girls, runners and cutters and bundle-makers, came out of their cramped corners to see what was happening. Maura faced the curious stares of the brightly lit workers.

"Okay," said the foreman, strutting his sovereignty over the silent girls, "I want you to take a look at this girl." They were still staring at her, and now Maura was beginning to see individual faces in the crowd: One girl had a harelip, another was partially bald, a third was missing an eye. But most had no deformities, other than the bad teeth and rough skin of poverty. They were all tired, pale, filthy with sweat. She understood that they hated her for her clean dress. They didn't know her for what she was, what she had been; her clothes, her clean hair, her beauty were all they saw, and they loathed her.

"She comes over to me and she says," the foreman continued, "she says to me, she wants to see about a job here in this place here, and I says to her, I ask her if she ever worked a Singer, and she says to me—get this—she says to me, she don't know what a Singer is!"

The laughter that followed was worse than the silent hatred. It swelled up, a release of the backbreaking tension of work and boredom and resentment; it grew like a beast in a nightmare, battening on Maura's humiliation as she fled through the door. Even before she was out the second door and beginning to run down the stairs, she heard the power turned back on, the machines alive again to their task, their monotonous strength overriding the ravenous hilarity of the girls.

Once again Maura found herself walking along the water's edge, letting the wind whip through her. She was facing south-

west, but didn't know that; she fancied that Ireland was directly
ahead, on the other side of the filthy water. For a moment she
wondered whether it would have been better to remain in Kerry:
to have returned home with the story of Brendt's death, to have
never married Patrick, to have run off to a servant's job in Cork
or Dublin. Then, at least, she would never have had to hear the
words men direct at a whore, the insults flung at foreigners, the
hate-filled laughter of workers at their own kind.

But thoughts of Ireland quickly faded. She left the waterfront and walked east, looking up at the grimy windows behind
which labored men, women, and children for ten, twelve, fourteen and more hours a day. Maura found herself on Chambers
Street, removing a nickel from her purse for the electric car line.
After a half-hour of standing in a crush of workers—mostly
office workers—she stumbled off the car at the corner of Sixth
Avenue and Seventeenth Street and walked the final few steps
to her boardinghouse, and to her landlady's much too loudly
sympathetic greeting.

The next day Maura learned what a Singer was. She saw
Singer sewing machines in underwear factories, in shirt factories,
in handkerchief factories. In the next week she was to see the
machine in its many guises: the older, smaller home models
turning up in the tiny three-girl sweatshop; the larger, ter-
rifyingly fast industrial models turning up in factories the size
of the Gotham Cape Company. As she grew more desperate, she
went to more factories, and fewer offices. After a while she
stopped answering ads for lady's companions, practical nurses,
and receptionists. While the rich people who needed a girl in the
house loathed her Irish accent, the office managers who needed
a pretty girl in the reception room were willing to pay only
three dollars a week; besides, none of these offered her work in
any case.

It was in the factories that she felt she had a chance.

As exhaustion and worry drove her from the sweater district
to the coat district, from the makers of artificial flowers to the
makers of bandboxes, she began to look more and more like she

belonged with the workers whose ranks she hoped to join. She slept badly, dreaming of Patrick dying in the miserable steerage. She suffered the constant rejections of foremen who refused to take on apprentices. She had little appetite in the evenings, and seldom took more than a bite of the sandwich she now took from the boardinghouse when she set out looking for work each day.

The other boarders began to give her pitying looks, as if they knew she had little chance to survive—as they all survived. With this pity came its natural concomitant, condescension, and Maura found herself the first to leave the dinner table, rushing upstairs to count her slowly dwindling supply of dollars.

Worse than the interviews, when she would be asked if she had ever worked making music boxes, jewelry cases, shirt collars, and the like, were the hours spent killing time between interviews. Faced with an empty bench and a pencil-marked newspaper, she began to look through the "Boardinghouses" section, wondering what sort of place a dollar-a-week house would be. It seemed more and more inevitable that she would have to leave her current home. And not in two months, but in two weeks, unless she wanted to see her reserve of money disappear altogether.

Two weeks after she had begun life in the boardinghouse, she was prepared to tell Mrs. Saunders she would have to leave. One job had been offered her in a sweater factory: It promised four dollars a week, if she survived a three-week apprenticeship for which she would not only not be paid, but would herself have to pay a fee of twenty-five dollars!

"There's always the laundry," another disgruntled job hunter told her. "If you're starving, it's three dollars a week, and it's always open. There's never a problem about getting a job."

But Maura still had enough money left to refuse to take a job that everyone said was unbearable, and which wouldn't even cover her room and board. She gave Mrs. Saunders five dollars for the third week of her stay, and told herself that she would find a decent job that week or take a bed in a girls' dormitory and a job in the laundry.

But that week, she found a job.

The foreman of a twenty-girl handkerchief-and-underwear

factory took a liking to her and offered her four dollars a week. The shop was on Franklin Street, a ten-minute walk from where the Sixth Avenue Elevated left her off on West Broadway. The nickel carfare added up to sixty cents a week for the six days she would have to put in, and it was clear to Maura that even with this job she would have to move, and quickly.

"I'm going to take good care of you, Mrs. O'Connell," said Mr. Marandino, the foreman, on the day she was hired. "Maura, I mean. We don't truck to no formalities in this place. We all know each other too good for that. And I'm going to look forward to knowing you real well, ain't that right, Maura?"

He knew she was a widow, and she knew that he was a low sort, eager to touch her and ogle her as she moved about the room. But she hadn't the luxury of picking the foreman she wanted for the job she must take. He hadn't actually touched her. He had simply looked. If the price of gaining a job was being looked at by the foreman, so be it, she thought. Tomorrow she would be put in the hands of one of the experienced girls and taught how to use her sewing machine. If only she could keep this job for a little while, long enough to learn a skill, she would be satisfied.

The job hunt had been so long, and so full of worry, that Maura wasn't surprised at the anticlimactic depression that set in that afternoon on the way back to Seventeenth Street. She didn't even mention to Mrs. Saunders that she had finally found a job. The cooking smells in the basement kitchen made her nauseous, and she refused to come down for dinner. Taking a little tea and toast from Mrs. Saunders's hands, she sat alone in her room, wondering if she would be able to bear the work of the shop, if she would be able to stand the new boardinghouse to which she would have to move.

The night seemed to last forever. The boarder beneath her, a fiftyish bank clerk with unusually quiet habits, had chosen this night to initiate his brand-new Gramophone. Though he quit playing his American Negro music well before ten o'clock, the strange rhythms ran through her nervous frame for hours afterward. She remembered a job hunter's description of the laundry: a hellish room, filled with steam and black bodies. The Negro music affected her as if it were an omen. She thought it more and more likely that she would be unable to work the sewing machine, and be forced to take a job in the laundry after all.

She was dressed and at the breakfast table before seven. Mrs. Saunders gave her breakfast before the others came down, and Maura hurried to finish and leave. The Sixth Avenue Elevated got her to West Broadway in thirty minutes. Out of breath, nervously trying to best the Yankee clock watchers, she was at the time register at the entrance to the factory at fifteen minutes to eight.

Five girls were there already, turning their register keys to mark their time cards. A diminutive girl with a great mass of wavy black hair showed her how to do this, with great good humor.

"I'm supposed to learn you," she told Maura. "Marandino says you're to be doing fifty specials before noon or that's it for the job. So we best get to it. Okay?"

"What's a special?" asked Maura.

"That's what makes you blind as a bat and crippled in the neck," Jenny said cheerfully, but then she was an unusually cheerful girl.

The other girls in the loft were less cheerful. Few spoke to each other, and one was so thin that Maura thought she must be starving herself to death. Jenny explained that the worst thing was to let the work get you so depressed that you quit washing, and talking, and eating. "It's easy for me," she explained. "I know what I'm here for, see? I got three kid sisters, babies really, and I want them to eat. I got a ma who ain't feeling so good, and a pa who's never too happy he came here to this country in the first place. My brother's okay, thank God for that. But the rest—my money is what they're eating. So it's easy for me. I mean I see what I'm doing, what I'm here for. It's the others, who ain't got no one, you know what I mean? Who are alone here, with no friends, no family. They're the ones you got to watch out for. I mean they don't know why they're working like that. Just so they can go to church Sundays and have a filthy bed to sleep in? It ain't enough, you see what I'm saying?"

Jenny showed Maura her machine. They were to sit side by side on a little backless bench at the head of a narrow table shared with a dozen other workers. As in many other factories, the lights were bright and the ventilation was awful. The factory was on the second floor of a four-story building, and there was a factory below that made ornamental boxes; the stink from the glue they used rose right through the thin floorboards and added to the nauseating effect of the still, warm air. Jenny showed Maura the lace-edged handkerchiefs—"specials"—that she would be expected to produce at great speed after her training. Carefully, she guided Maura's smooth hands on a cotton square, placing lace along one edge and showing her how to slip it under the needle. When Jenny turned on the power and the needle began to jump up and down, Maura's hands began to shake uncontrollably.

"Hey, it's nothing to get crazy about," said Jenny easily. "Don't be afraid of it. It's all right."

But Maura was afraid. And nauseous. She got off the bench and ran for the tiny toilet room and threw up. It was not yet eight o'clock, and she already felt defeated. She knew that the needle was nothing to worry her, that the fact of the electric power would become commonplace to her, that she could do anything that all the other girls in the place could do. But still, she couldn't explain the physical fact of her terror. Her head ached. She was nauseous. She felt as closed in as she had in the steerage crossing.

"Hey, Maura, come on!" said Jenny from outside the toilet room. "We ain't got all day!" And when Maura came out, Jenny squeezed her hand and told her that she had nothing to worry about. "Everyone gets a little spooked at first. That ain't the hard part. The hard part is sticking to it. The hours, I mean. But you're going to be all right, and I'm going to tell you why. Because it's me learning you how do it, and there's no one better at that than Jenny Newman. You got that?"

"Thank you," said Maura. She went back to her machine and pulled the little lever beneath it that activated its power. Carefully, she pushed her cotton square with its lace edge under the needle, and watched in amazement as the needle sewed the lace to the cotton with incredible speed.

"No, no," said Jenny laughing. 'That's all wrong." And she showed Maura how to feed the fabric under the presser foot, concentrating intently on the seam being formed, to insure that the stitching was straight and evenly spaced. Maura tried again, bringing her fingers so close to the needle that Jenny had to slap away her hands. "You don't want to sew your finger up, girl!" she said. Maura tried again, clumsily twisting the lace so that the flying needle sewed together a crumpled corner. "That's beautiful," said Jenny. "You've got the artistic touch. Come on. Try again."

Maura's fearful nausea was passing. Her hands grew steadier, and her headache passed. This was simply a physical task: Open your eyes, smooth out the cotton and lace, match up the edges, slowly guide the fabric under the needle. She had to concentrate, and the concentration precluded all thought.

"How're we doing here, sugar?" said Marandino, the foreman, coming up behind Maura and placing his large hands on her shoulders. Maura started violently.

"She's quick, Mr. Marandino," said Jenny. "She gets the idea, you see what I'm saying. You don't got to tell her twice."

If he doesn't take his hands off me this second, Maura thought, I am going to tell him to take them off, even if I lose this job.

"Good, good, girls," Marandino said, taking his hands off her shoulders and patting Maura's head. Then he was off, and Maura looked up at the white-faced clock across the room. It was 8:30. There were nine and a half hours to go.

By 10:30, the concentration had begun to create a muscular tension at the back of her neck, and by 11:30 her hunching over the machine had twisted the pain from the neck along her spine to the small of her back. Jenny helped her thread the bobbin and needle, and smiled sympathetically. "Hey, believe me, I know what it feels like. You ain't used to the work, so it ain't easy. Think about lunch. It's almost time."

But Maura couldn't think about lunch. She had to think about what she was doing, step by painstaking step. In place of fifty finished handkerchiefs, she had two or three acceptable ones, and all these had been done with Jenny's hands over her own. She had to learn or she would not be able to keep this job. Somehow, the heat of the packed-in bodies, the din of the machines, the glare of the gas jets, the stink from the factory downstairs must become inconsequential to her. The throbbing in her neck, the ache in her back must be ignored.

"Are you all right, girl?" said Jenny. The master switch had been shut off, silencing the machines, and all the workers had fled to familiar positions on the floor, where they opened their lunches. "Come on, Maura, you'd better get something down you." Jenny helped Maura up from the bench and brought her over to a quiet corner. "There, you see? Twelve o'clock already. It's not so long, see? You're getting the hang of it, ain't you?"

Maura took a bite of the sandwich prepared by Mrs. Saunders, and remembered that she would have to find the time to look at some of the cheaper houses listed in the *Herald*. She wondered what sort of place Jenny lived in with her brother and three sisters and parents. Maura's family had been cramped in their cottage in Kerry; but they'd had the land, and the sky, and the distant, mist-shrouded horizon.

"It's time, Maura," said Jenny.

Maura looked up at Jenny. Twenty-five minutes had passed. The master switch had been turned back on. Jenny was standing, and offering her a hand to get up.

"I don't know why I'm so tired," said Maura.

"You're going to get used to it real fast, see?" said Jenny, and Maura accepted her hand.

"Sure this isn't the way I usually am. I'm usually strong as a horse," said Maura. Even her voice sounded weak, she thought.

At the machine, her work grew a bit neater, but she had no speed; she would have to learn to work more accurately, and at five times the rate. She remembered her pride at being the best at turning the grain during the whiskey-making for her father; even he had had to acknowledge her skill. Maura wondered when her mother would get the letter she'd sent. She tried to imagine her mother's surprise at seeing the ten dollars Maura had enclosed; her mother would imagine Patrick working at some fine job, Brendt dressed like a great lady, teaching in a California school.

"Catching flies?" said Marandino about Maura's open mouth. "Are we keeping you awake, sugar, or is it that you're dreaming of your foreman?"

Maura didn't answer. Instead, she redoubled her sleepy efforts, and shoved a bit of cloth too quickly under the presser-foot. The flying needle tore right through her skin.

There was hardly any blood. Jenny reached over and turned Maura's machine off, and gripped the wounded hand, holding fast to where the needle had penetrated. "You got to pay attention, Maura," she said, smiling from her to the foreman. "You do that at one of the cutting machines and you'll end up missing a few fingers, see?"

Maura washed the blood off her hand and went back to work. She tried alternating her position on the bench—now hunching her shoulders, now sitting very straight-backed, now leaning so far forward that her chin nearly reached the base of the machine. All the while the tension in her back and neck increased, the neat little holes just below the line of her knuckles grew more and more sore, the queasy feeling from the glue smell and the heat and the din grew worse.

For most of this, Maura blamed herself. She was weak, where she had once been strong. The dream that had kept her alive crossing the ocean had been so beaten down that she was cowed by this simple task, she told herself. If she felt sick, it was because she had hoped for too much, too soon. Because she had wanted an office job and had not been able to get it, this simple work exhausted her. Perhaps, she thought, she was sorry that she hadn't stayed at the Waldorf. That rich boy with his extravagant talk would have done anything for her, and knowing this, she imagined her body to be in rebellion. She could be eating cakes and drinking tea in bed, served by a maid who came at the press of a button.

"Two o'clock, Maura," said Jenny. "See how the time's running? Before you know it, the day's gone. This seam ain't straight. Let me do another with you, all right?"

How could it be two o'clock? thought Maura. The only windows in the loft were so far removed from where she sat that it was easy to imagine the April day long since gone, the drizzly afternoon turning into a crisp, bright evening. Lunch seemed a

lifetime ago. Jenny's hands on hers, holding the cloth, guiding
her clumsy movements, seemed as familiar to Maura as if she
had known them always. How long did they actually expect her
to sit there, in the same place, doing the same endless task?
And for four dollars a week? Sixty-seven cents a day? How could
she earn so little when ice cream in a nice parlor was fifteen
cents? When a cab was one dollar for the first block? Why, if
all she did was take the Elevated train and buy the *Herald*,
she'd have three dollars and twenty-two cents left over for room
and board. And she needed clothing. She needed to buy postage
for the letters she would send to her mother. She needed to go
to night school so she could one day get out of the factory and
into an office.

"That's a real good one, and I ain't just saying it, see?" said
Jenny. "I swear you got the eye for it. You take it in fast, and
I'm going to tell Marandino that, if he gives you any truck."

An hour later, Maura began to feel better. The glue smell
lingered, and the heat and noise were just the same, but she
felt stronger, less nauseous. Everything came into sharper focus.
She asked Jenny questions about the machine, about the place
where she lived, about the other girls who worked there. Maura
worked more quickly now. The pain in her neck and back was
still there, but she accepted it; it was a very little thing weighed
against other pains, other experiences. She couldn't understand why she had felt quite so bad, why she had allowed herself
to be so self-pitying. When she looked at the clock now, it was
to get used to the passing of time, not to feel defeated by its
slow passage.

At five o'clock, Marandino returned his hands to her shoulders
and leaned low to inspect the work at her machine.

"Please don't do that, sir," said Maura.

"What's that, sugar?"

Jenny turned off her machine, and so did Minnie, a pretty
blond girl sitting on Maura's left who looked no older than
sixteen.

"Don't touch me, sir," said Maura.

"Her neck hurts, Mr. Marandino," said Jenny brightly, as if
this were a happy thought.

Marandino removed his hands and turned on Jenny. "Just because I give you an Irisher to learn a little don't mean you can't finish your work. What the hell did you do today anyway? You call this a special handkerchief?" The foreman picked up the last of Jenny's work and tore off the lace. "Anything this Irisher ruins I'm taking out of your paycheck, you got that?"

"Yes, Mr. Marandino," said Jenny.

"Your neck hurts," said Marandino to Maura with great sarcasm. "Better take care of your poor neck. You sure know how to thank a man for giving you a job."

As soon as he walked off, Jenny put her machine back on, lowering her face to her work. But Maura saw that tears were beginning in her new friend's eyes. "Sure I'm sorry if I got you into any trouble," said Maura.

Minnie reached over and tapped Maura's hand. "It's okay. Let her be."

"Why is she crying?" said Maura.

"You're going to cost her money, girl. Foreman's going to make her pay for all these you ripped." Minnie exhibited the many ruined handkerchiefs. "She could lose a buck this week. Wouldn't you cry if you lost a buck?"

At six the machines were shut down. Marandino walked over to Jenny and told her that it was her turn to sweep up. He said nothing to Maura, but Maura quickly took a broom, and stayed an extra half-hour with Jenny, feeling stronger and more clearheaded with each passing minute.

She would have loved to have been able to sit somewhere with Jenny, in a cheap dairy restaurant or an ice-cream parlor, and get a chance to talk, away from the noise of the machines. But Jenny had to rush home to help her mother with supper, and Maura hoped to be able to use the time after dinner to look at some cheap boardinghouses.

"Hey, we'll see each other every day," said Jenny. "You're going to make out good, girl, see?"

"I hope so. I'm sorry about Marandino."

"Forget that bum. Maybe he'll drop dead tonight. Maybe he'll fall off the El and we'll have a party, right? You look better now. You don't look so sick like before. You're going to be fine.

It's a good job when you know what you're doing. You can stay
here steady, you can work for a hundred years making hankies.
It's a good job, see?"

The other boarders were at dinner when Maura got to the
house at 7:30. Once again, her body was behaving strangely.
She thought she had felt better, but now, looking at the half-eaten
roast on the table, she felt weak and nauseous all over again. And
there was absolutely no glue smell in the air.

"Well, come on and wash up, my dear," said Mrs. Saunders.
"Everyone's waiting to hear. You got a job, didn't you? Come on,
darling. Tell us, we're your family!"

"I got a job," admitted Maura, but then she hurried past the
anxious face of the landlady and the condescending faces of
the boarders, and rushed upstairs to her room.

Mrs. Saunders followed almost immediately. "Now, Mrs.
O'Connell, I don't think that was very polite! What is it with
you? Don't you feel well?"

"I'm tired, Mrs. Saunders," said Maura.

"Well, of course you're tired, that's only natural. You found a
job! Did you already put in a day's work?"

"Yes."

Maura had sat down at the foot of the bed, trying to ward
off the sensation of a fever that seemed more a product of her
mind than of any disease. Mrs. Saunders took hold of Maura's
hands and looked at her crossly. "Your hands are freezing, Mrs.
O'Connell. Did you know that? It's drizzling, and I didn't see you
come in with an umbrella." The landlady now touched the back
of her hand to Maura's forehead, eliciting an even angrier response: "Mrs. O'Connell! Even at your age you should be taking
better care of yourself! Under those covers! Right now! You've
a fever, you've a fever for sure, and you've nobody but your
foolish self to blame!"

Maura did as she was told that evening. She wasn't delirious,
but she could make no sensible comment about her condition, so
she answered all of her landlady's harsh queries with silence.
Her head was burning, her hands were cold, her feet were cold,
and she huddled deep in the blankets. She was sick, as sick as a
young child with a high fever, as sick as she'd been when Brendt

had nursed her back to health when she was a little girl. But she was no longer a little girl. For a moment she forgot about Mrs. Saunders's presence. The room was black, and the only noise was that of an unfriendly, wild rainfall. She was alone, utterly alone. She had no sister, no mother, not even a father to comfort and care for her. She needed to work to make the money to keep herself in this bed, to feed herself during the day. Tomorrow she would be too sick to work and then she would be without a job.

"Get me a nightcap," Maura heard Mrs. Saunders say in the tone reserved for her maid. "Wool socks. Bring up my heaviest nightgown. Not the new one, the older one. Boil water for the hot-water bottle. Prepare some tea and bring the brandy and lemons. Don't mix them in—that's for me and nobody else to do. Now go on with you, hurry. Can't you see how sick our Mrs. O'Connell is?"

Maura tried to speak, to tell the landlady that she would soon be leaving her house, that it was too expensive, that she must seek out a dollar-a-week house so that she could save some money, so that she could make something out of her life. But she had no strength. She couldn't understand why she was so weak, why her strength had waxed and waned throughout the first day at work. She hardly followed Mrs. Saunders's lecture: How could she have gone off on a rainy day dressed as if it were the Fourth of July? This was only nature's way of teaching her to respect her own body. She was lucky she had fallen ill in the home of an educated woman, one who was used to treating the sick. If Maura followed all her directions, it would be a matter of a few days before she was well. "Now," said Mrs. Saunders, "do you understand what I'm telling you, dear? You'll be all right sooner than you know!"

But Maura didn't know that. She didn't know what had possessed her body to behave this way. But no matter what was wrong with her—whether it was fatigue, fever, a cold—Maura knew that she would have to ignore it. She would not lie back and accept defeat. No great weight of despair, not if it descended on her chest and threatened to press the life out of her frail frame, would keep her from rising.

She woke before the breakfast bell, surprised to find herself in Mrs. Saunders's enormous nightgrown. Slowly, she got out of bed and walked unsteadily to the window. She was tired, she was nauseous, but at least her fever had passed. She washed her hands and face, trying to draw strength from the tepid water. On top of everything else, her stomach was bloated, signaling the approach of her menstrual period. But Maura counted her blessings: She was well enough to walk down the steps, to face the warm April morning, and take the Sixth Avenue Elevated to a job.

# ❧ CHAPTER ❧ SIXTEEN

Maura held up for three more days.

She had begun work on a Tuesday. Wednesday night she found a fifth-floor room in a boardinghouse on Fourteenth Street and Second Avenue for one dollar a week, without meals. Thursday morning she told Mrs. Saunders that she would be leaving for a less expensive house the following evening. Friday afternoon she turned in her time card, as did all the girls, to Mr. Marandino. When the workweek was finished, at six o'clock, paychecks were distributed by Mr. Barker, the owner of the factory, who was otherwise never there.

Maura's envelope contained two dollars and twelve cents. More than fifty cents had been deducted for her slow output. Jenny received three dollars—losing one whole dollar due to work ruined by Maura. Even in so short a time as four days, Maura understood with great clarity what fifty cents meant in her new world, what one dollar signified. The five-dollar-a-week boardinghouse would soon seem absurdly expensive, she realized. A hansom cab would be something to look at, like the outside of a church on a sunny day. The notion that a young man had given her the sum of one hundred dollars for a night's pleasure reached her like a memory from some tawdry dream.

Maura tried to give Jenny a dollar to make up for the loss, but Jenny wouldn't hear of it. "You're going to need every penny, girl. I'll get over this. I got a brother, I got family. It's bad, but it won't kill me, see? Ain't you moving today? How can I take a buck from a girl living by herself? I ain't no monster."

Maura didn't argue. She would get the dollar back to Jenny in some way, sometime in the future. Jenny had helped her through these past four days, had done as much for her as a sister. She had instructed her at the machine, advised her how to talk to Marandino, told her which of several dollar-a-week boardinghouses was in the most decent neighborhood. And most important, while she was sick, Jenny had encouraged her to remain at work, not to give in to weakness. She knew that even a half-day's absence might cost her her hard-won job; and without a job, Maura would not be able to survive.

"Hey, Irish, hold your horses," said Minnie O'Neill, the blond, childish-looking girl who sat on Maura's left at the machine table. Jenny had just left the building, taking great strides through the April drizzle, anxious to get to her family's tenement flat just north of Canal Street, on the East Side. Though it was a forty-minute walk through a jungle of factories, slums, and saloons, Jenny never considered wasting a nickel for a tram ride.

"I'm in a hurry, Minnie," said Maura, as the blond girl took hold of Maura's arm at the threshold of the gray factory building and walked with her into garbage-strewn Franklin Street.

"I know you're moving. I want to help," said Minnie.

"Thank you, but it's not necessary," said Maura. In the last few days, Minnie had taken as strong an interest in Maura's welfare as Jenny had, but with a different emphasis. Minnie didn't like how Maura looked, how she came into the loft with a greenish pallor nearly every morning, and had thrown up in the tiny toilet room with punctual regularity at half-past ten for the last three days. While Jenny insisted that Maura ignore her illness, Minnie had insisted the opposite: Maura must see a doctor, the sooner the better; and if she lost her job, that was a small price to pay for insuring her health.

"Irish, I'm helping you and that's the long and the short of it, see?" said Minnie, playing her Bowery-rat stance for all its toughness.

Maura tried to explain that there was really nothing to do: Mrs. Saunders, convinced that Maura could no longer afford her room, had sorrowfully arranged to send her trunk over to the new, much rougher address, refusing any payment for the task. Maura had few belongings. It would take her a moment to unpack.

"Irish, I says I'm going, see? You ain't going to stop me if it's what I want to do, right?"

Minnie lived a block away from Maura's new address. Those half-dozen blocks of Fourteenth Street, between Third Avenue and Avenue D, were lined with countless boardinghouses, all of them cheap. The red lights of working-class brothels and the plate glass of saloons were all that broke up the monotony of crumbling tenements, ancient fire escapes, and yellowish laundry flapping from sagging lines. Still, the neighborhood was better than the Italian-German-Jewish slum where Jenny lived, where diphtheria and typhoid fever ran through the windowless, impossibly crowded rooms of the immigrants.

"I'm not going to see a doctor, Minnie. Sure it's the truth I'm telling you. I won't see a doctor. You're just wasting your breath on me."

"Come on," said Minnie. "We'll take the El to Fourteenth Street and get a transfer to a streetcar."

"A transfer? You mean free?"

"You don't think I'm going to spend ten cents getting to work each way? I ain't Frick's daughter. And I don't know none of the Morgans neither."

Minnie made no further comment until they had walked to West Broadway. "Now let's see you make it up the stairs," she said.

Maura frowned, and walked quickly up the steps to the Elevated train's platform. She actually felt pretty well at the moment, not as tired as she had been that morning and in the middle of the afternoon. As they boarded the mobbed train, she tried to smile at Minnie to show her that she was feeling fine, but Minnie didn't respond. At Fourteenth Street, she took Maura by the arm and walked her quickly down the stairs. "Are you on the rag?" she said.

"What?" said Maura.

"The rag. I mean, is it your time, Irish?"

"Sure I don't know what you're talking about."

"Jesus," said Minnie. "You know. What do you call them? The monthlies. Have you got the monthlies?"

"Oh," said Maura, suddenly abashed. She was astonished at such a personal question, no matter how well meant. Even after sitting between Minnie and Jennie for four days, they knew little enough about her. The girls in the factory came from so many different backgrounds, immigrant as well as native-born, had endured so many different kinds of hardship, some from parents, some from husbands or "gentlemen friends," that personal questions were avoided. Maura never asked Jenny if she had a "gentleman friend," never thought of inquiring after Minnie's parents—who lived in Vermont—until Minnie herself had mentioned that she lived alone on Fourteenth Street. And so Maura had simply explained that she was a widow, that her husband had died during the crossing to America, six months ago. No one had asked her to explain about the last six months. Maura couldn't imagine volunteering the shameful information.

"You can get your behind off that high horse, Irish," said Minnie. "I'm asking you a question, see? That means I want an answer, right?"

"No."

"You ain't on the rag?"

"That's right."

"Are you late?"

The streetcar came, and Maura swung herself on into the crush of workers heading home to their single day of rest. Minnie pushed in after her. "Yes or no?" said Minnie.

"Maybe," said Maura. "I think so."

Minnie didn't smile at this either. She simply nodded, satisfied that Maura was talking. Minnie had no proprietary interest in Maura because of their shared Irish background; Minnie had never even known the grandparents who'd left Ireland for America three decades before she was born. She had another reason for taking such an interest in Maura's state of health, but she waited to tell her that until they were alone in Maura's new room.

"You're right on the avenue, ain't you?" said Minnie as they walked from the streetcar to the tenement that was Maura's new home. The entrance was on Fourteenth Street, but Maura's room on the fifth floor looked out on the Elevated train on Second Avenue. Even Minnie was tired out by the climb up the narrow, slippery wooden steps.

Maura opened the window in the tiny room and lit the single oil lamp. Her six-dollar trunk was on the floor. In place of an armoire, a series of nails had been hammered into one bare wall. Some filthy pots and pans rested on the unlit coal-burning stove. The bed was very low, supporting a bloodstained mattress without sheets. There was a kettle, and Minnie announced that she would make some tea.

"I don't have tea," said Maura.

"I got a tin right here, Irish," said Minnie, patting her bag.

While Minnie busied herself with shoveling coal from the closet into the stove and setting the kindling on fire, Maura stepped to the window, trying not think. An approaching train blew up out of the dark, its lights red, its wheels flashing. The train was so close to the window that Maura fancied the sparks from the tracks might set her tenement on fire. As it was, smoke and dust blew into the tiny space, and the vibration set up by the train rattled the pots and pans, the kettle on the stove, the tin basin on its ancient stand.

"Shut the window when you see one coming. It could be worse. The Third Avenue runs all night, right through. Just like the Sixth Avenue. This one stops running at midnight. You can open the window then. You can fall asleep at least. And when it starts up in the morning, it'll wake you for sure. You don't even need a clock."

"I'm sorry there's no food I can offer you. After we have some tea, maybe I'll get something," said Maura. "Maybe you'll eat with me. I'd like that."

"I'm seventeen," said Minnie. "How old are you?"

"Eighteen. Last February."

"Jenny is fifteen."

"What? Sure that's not possible! Only fifteen?"

"She looks older. You can't really tell. Angela—the dago girl—she's thirteen."

"I had no idea," said Maura. "I didn't think anyone that young worked in the place."

"She's the youngest. She's lucky she got the job. Marandino

likes her. He likes you, too. He likes pretty girls. But forget
that. That's not what I wanted to tell you. Jenny's fifteen. That's
why she don't have any idea why you're sick, see?"

"I'm not sick."

"You ain't sick, that's right," said Minnie. "You're pregnant."

Maura heard the word, and took it like a blow to her face.
Of course she had thought about it. But she had also deliberately
shunted it from her mind. If her breasts were tender, it was
because her period was due. Being nauseous in the morning
proved nothing. Weren't old ladies often nauseous? Hadn't she
been far more nauseous on the boat to America?

"Listen to me, Irish. I don't know you, see? You look like
an okay girl, but I don't know you. I don't know your folks, and
I don't know your people. But what I figure is you're all by
yourself, see? And I remember last year the same thing happened
in the shop. Maybe it was Marandino who knocked her up,
maybe it wasn't. She was a kid too, younger than you, maybe
seventeen. A Swedish girl, her English wasn't good. And she
was scared, just like you're scared, because all you greenhorns
are scared of doctors."

"Sure it's no doctor that I'm scared of," said Maura, remembering the one who had touched her on Ellis Island, who had
probed her most private parts like a foretaste of her time with
Kilgallen.

"Jenny's telling you not to go to no doctor because she's
fifteen and she don't know nothing. Her people still act like
they've got one foot on the boat, even if she speaks like an
American. But last year, with the Swede, when she got knocked
up, she was nauseous, she was green, she was tired, she was
scared, and nobody said nothing to her until it was too late.
I mean, when it showed, she knew—that's how smart that
Swede was. When she missed her monthlies twice, and her
belly was getting to grow, and she was crying all the time, not
working right, and Barker fired her. See what I'm saying? She
had no people here neither. She had no choice. I had nothing
to do with it—she wasn't my friend. But I should've told her when
I had an idea, just like I'm telling you. I mean I should've told
her that there was ways to help her, if she didn't wait too long."

"I'm not pregnant," said Maura very quietly. "That's all there is to it, Minnie. I'm not going to a doctor."

"They don't send you back to Ireland for being pregnant, Irish," said Minnie. "Doctors see plenty. They know girls get in trouble. I'm not telling you what to do or not to do, right? Hey, don't get me wrong. If it was me, I know what I'd do. But you, you do what you want."

Maura remembered Ginny talking to her constantly about how not to get a baby. In the house on Spring Street, all she talked about half the time were the whores who'd killed their babies after they'd given birth to them. In that brothel, and in the elegant one on Twenty-sixth Street, Ginny had shown her how to use the vaginal sponge to avoid getting pregnant. But it didn't always work, Ginny had said. Half the abortions in New York were performed on prostitutes using sponges or diaphragms. Besides, that night with the rich college boy, the night he helped her out of the Tenderloin, only to put her into his bed in the Waldorf—that night she'd used no sponge, having left it behind in the brothel, having no thought of ever needing it again. Kevin, his name was. The handsome rich boy who was so self-absorbed and infatuated that he couldn't imagine her not wanting him. Kevin. If she was pregnant, she thought, it was Kevin whose fault it was.

"Are you listening to me?" said Minnie.

"Yes."

"I'm saying that the Swede waited too long to know what was happening, see? If she'd known right off, she would've done right. I mean she was fired, she got no money, just a few bucks, no gentleman friend around, naturally—she must have got knocked up all by herself, see? So she's three months, maybe three and a half months along when she goes for an abortion, and she's dead the same day, bleeding to death, right? And whose fault is that? I'm not saying it's mine, Irish. But I'm saying if I see a good girl, and she looks like she's pregnant, and she's sitting next to me, I'm going to tell her, like I'm telling you.

"Listen, I think you should see a doctor—just so you'll know. Now, not next month. It don't make sense to wait. I don't know a thing about criminal abortion, except that it's all over this neighborhood, and the newspapers say it's on Fifth Avenue, too, and maybe they do thousands a year that nobody gets hurt from. But I don't know. I mean I can ask if you want. But all I know is a doctor. A good doctor, so you can trust him. I'm taking you there, Maura. I don't want you to die on me next month, and have it on my head, see? You're doing this for me, and that's all there is to it, right? Ain't there no teacups in this joint? All this talk's making me thirsty."

Maura didn't answer Minnie's speech for a long while. She found one cracked cup and a filthy glass and washed these out in the tin basin, drying them with a handkerchief remnant from the factory. Minnie poured the tea, and then surprised Maura with a small piece of chocolate. The two of them sipped their tea, nibbled at the chocolate, and smiled as another train tore into the station not fifty feet from where they sat.

"What was her name?" asked Maura finally.

"The Swede? Karin, I think. We always just called her 'the Swede,' see? She was pretty, real wavy blond hair, thick as yours, and the saddest pair of eyes you ever saw. The doctor is close by my place, Maura. The next building. We can go as soon as you finish the tea. He's got a woman with him, his nurse, and he don't do nothing but examine you, just so you can know, right? That's all. Just so you can know."

Maura finished her tea, and without a word the two of them got up and left the tiny, shut-up space, and walked down the five flights to the street.

Maura's new landlady, red-nosed and balding, sat on the stoop bundled in three layers of sweaters, looking out at the thin stream of pedestrians passing by in the dark. "That room's only for one of you, you got that?" said the landlady. "If it's the both of you, there's an extra two bits a week—that's the law of the house. And I close up tight at ten, for the night, and it ain't easy to wake me after that. I charge you a solid dime every time you do it. This is a respectable house."

Minnie held Maura's arm and set the pace for their walk. She cautioned Maura to keep her eyes to the ground, as half the men on the streets were on their way to brothels and saloons, and merely meeting someone's gaze would be enough to be thought of as a streetwalker. They crossed under the Elevated tracks at Third Avenue, and Minnie pointed out the dark tenement where she lived. The doctor's office was in the basement flat of the tenement next door. There was a bellpull, but Minnie ignored this, opening the door for Maura to get in out of the dark, damp night.

Three women were waiting in the small entrance foyer, sitting on two chairs and a stool. Maura and Minnie stood in the corner, as there were no other chairs. The other women were Italians and they spoke in their native language, whispering in short, fierce bursts, and retreating to gloomy silence.

"You know, I was the eighth kid in my family," said Minnie softly. "The last. I doubt if ma wanted me either, see? But I remember what happened the last time she was pregnant. It was maybe six years, maybe seven years ago. I didn't know much then, see, but you should've seen what she did to get rid of it. My ma ain't so big or so strong, but all of a sudden she was out back of the house chopping wood. Every day, morning and night. We never had so much firewood ready to burn. She was sweating and cursing and chopping till she nearly dropped. One of my sisters told me why, see? It's the exercise she wanted. To get rid of the baby."

"Did it work?"

"I don't know," said Minnie. "But there was never another kid after me."

The nurse came out of the inner office soon afterward, leading a terrified and downcast girl of fourteen or fifteen, obviously related in some way to the three Italian women. A single question was asked by the oldest of them, and when the nurse responded with a slow nod of her head, the woman slapped the young girl across the face. The nurse began to remonstrate, but the women had already grabbed hold of their wayward teen-ager and quickly pulled her out with them into the street.

Minnie went up to the nurse and explained why they were there: Mrs. O'Connell thought she might be pregnant and would like the doctor to examine her. "All she can pay," said Minnie, "is one dollar, and that won't be easy, see?"

The nurse reassured Maura. She was a big woman, with

large, capable hands and enormous brown eyes. "Mrs. O'Connell," she said. "Such a pretty young bride."

"Widow," corrected Minnie. "She's a poor working girl and
her husband's dead."

The doctor was a Russian Jew, with framed degrees on the
wall from universities in Germany. He was pale, with bloodshot
blue eyes and sparse white hair. His accent was similar to that
of one of the youngest girls in the factory, the daughter of Jewish
immigrants from Odessa.

"Nurse will help you take off, maybe?" he said to Maura.

She was glad Minnie hadn't come in with her. Now that she
was alone with the doctor and the nurse, she was glad she had
come. Instead of struggling against Minnie's good-heartedness,
she could surrender to her own feelings. Yes, of course she might
be pregnant. Yes, she had to know. Yes, this old man with the
tired eyes who had seen everything in the world would tell her
at once what she would have to do.

The doctor touched her gently about the breasts, asking when
her last menstrual period had been. He asked about her fatigue,
her morning nausea, her vomiting. He noted the darkness of
the areolae of her breasts, and asked her if she'd felt a heaviness
in her pelvic region.

When Maura was being helped to lie down on the examining
table, she was sure that she must be pregnant. Already the
questions were forming in the back of her mind: Could she
really lose a baby by chopping wood? Was it true that hot
baths taken three times a day would bring on her menstrual
period? And as the doctor gently probed her abdominal region,
then slowly brought his light close to her vagina and with
great care examined the vulvar and vaginal tissue, Maura
understood that she would do anything not to be pregnant.
Where before she wouldn't even consider the possibility that she
could be pregnant, now she couldn't conceive of the possibility
that she was anything but; where before she wouldn't mention
the idea of abortion, now she understood that she would rather
do anything than allow her body to bring an unwanted child
into the world.

"It is a shame, Mrs. O'Connell," said the doctor, "that your
husband isn't alive to be with you at this time."

"I'm pregnant?"

"Yes, my dear. Unless you are a very unusual body. But the signs—you have the signs. Some have one thing but not the other. I can take some blood, some urine, but you need your money, I think, and it's not necessary. The vulva is almost purple. The uterus is big. Your breasts, look how dark it is around the nipple. It is a shame you are not too happy. But I hope to God that someday this child will bring you happiness."

"If I exercise, doctor—what if I exercise?" began Maura.

"That's all right, Mrs. O'Connell," said the nurse, helping her to dress. Maura realized that there were tears in her eyes and that she had little control over her voice.

"Mrs. O'Connell," said the doctor. "Please. I know you are not happy. But I do not want you to injure yourself. I want you to think, and not to be like a little girl who knows nothing. You can come to talk to me if you want to. But not now. Now you must go and think first."

"There's nothing to think about," said Maura. "Sure it's very plain. If I'm pregnant, I don't want to be. And you say I'm pregnant. Please, doctor, I only want to know what I have to do to not have a baby. How can I have a baby? My husband's dead, I live in a filthy hole, I work all day long, and I've got no money. I'm only asking you because you're a doctor. If I exercise all day, will that help? Or hot baths? Or something—what? You're the doctor, you know how to help me."

"Mrs. O'Connell," he said, "I tell you what I tell everyone. It's not the end of the world, believe me. All I say now is don't do something stupid. Don't chop wood. Don't fall down stairs. The only way you get rid of a baby that way is you kill yourself too. You understand?"

"You'll get rid of it for me?" said Maura.

"No," said the doctor. "I am not allowed. It is against the law, and it is against my medical oath. You are not very advanced, Mrs. O'Connell. Another few days won't make a big deal. Please. Think. Wait. Be smart. Maybe you have a relative, a friend with some money. There are people who want babies and can't have them. If you can't take care of it, someone will. It is something to think over, not jump into. There are people selling drugs to kill the fetus. This is not true, do you understand? Don't buy anything. It will either not work or it will only work if it kills you too."

"How do I get rid of it then?"

"Only a doctor can do it, Mrs. O'Connell."

"You're a doctor!"

"I am not an abortionist," he said, his patience beginning to wear thin. "There are one hundred thousand criminal abortions a year in this city, and I do not do one of them, not one. I want you to think, young lady. Think of how many criminal abortions end with deaths. Think before you buy some stupid magic medicine. Think before you let some friend talk you into putting a sponge or a needle up your vagina. I am sorry for you, Mrs. O'Connell, but in the long run it will be safer if you go ahead with it and have the baby. Anything else is a risk to your own life."

"You said only a doctor can do it," said Maura. "I don't know why you won't do it. Sure I don't. I don't."

The nurse took her back to the waiting room, where Minnie remained standing in deference to three very pregnant women accompanied by what looked like a mother and a pair of husbands. "Remember what the doctor said," the nurse told Maura. "He's telling the truth. There's no magic medicine that can cure what ails you, no matter what they claim."

Maura waited until they were alone, walking back along Fourteenth Street in the dark, before she spoke. "Remember what you said to me? That you know what you'd do if you were pregnant?"

"Yes."

"Well, I'm pregnant. Tell me what you'd do."

"I'd get rid of it, see?" said Minnie. "Any way that was possible."


Maura got little sleep that night, and the trains that pulled into the station so near her window were only partially to blame. She was conscious of wanting to commit a terrible crime, the murder of a living thing within her womb; and at the same time, she had no idea how to go about accomplishing this. When she was able to calm her conscience by assuring herself that there was no baby within her, but only a seed that had not yet shown true signs of life, a terrible agitation set in. She must hurry. She must swiftly rip out this seed before it sprouted. The longer she delayed, the greater her crime would be. If only it could be done at once, there would be no crime, no sin at all.

When the last train pulled out of the station going uptown at midnight, Maura brought her hands to her abdomen and pushed down. It was not a sin—she could not think in terms of such moral classifications, not when this pregnancy was the result of rape, whether the gentle rape at the hands of her college-boy hero or the paid-up rapes of Kilgallen's clients. And even if it had not been rape, she realized, even if by some miracle this pregnancy was related to poor dead Patrick's making love with her, even then it would not be a sin to end it at once. She was only eighteen, without money, without support, and she must first make a life for herself. No accident was going to determine her fate. Her fate was to make her own way, create her own world.

Like a madwoman, she got out of bed. She reached her arms high overhead, then quickly bent at the waist and brought her fingertips to her toes, keeping her knees straight. Then she did it again, and again, until the dark room, lit only by the electric lamps from the deserted elevated train platform, began to whirl about her in a dizzying dance. Yes, she told herself, this was what Minnie meant. This was what she needed, to do this until she dropped. To push herself to the limit of endurance, until whatever was locked within her was suddenly let free in a spontaneous flow of blood.

But the blood wouldn't come. When her back ached so much that she could not bend at the waist, she began to flap her arms, like a scarecrow come to life. When her arms grew too stiff to move, she let them fall to her sides and began to jump, unmindful of the noise, until the boarder beneath her woke and began to beat at the ceiling under her feet.

Exhausted, she went back to bed. Perhaps the bleeding would start in the night. Perhaps the doctor had lied to her and the medicines advertised in the *Herald* really did work: PORTU-

GUESE LADIES' PILLS. DO NOT USE DURING PREGNANCY, OR IMMEDIATE MISCARRIAGE WILL RESULT. Or THE WIVES' ELIXIR: PORTUGUESE REGULATORS, FOR MARRIED WOMEN. CAUTION: NOT TO BE USED DURING PREGNANCY, OR MISCAR- RIAGE WILL SURELY RESULT.

A miscarriage wouldn't be so bad, she thought. If it was in the paper, it couldn't very well be that dangerous, no matter what the doctor said.

All night she slept fitfully, imagining a full-grown baby twisting and turning inside her, imagining a tiny infant twisting out of her vagina covered with gore. When the trains returned outside her dark window at five in the morning, she was awake and already getting dressed. She would walk to work, at a fast pace, and if along the way she found a pharmacy that was open, she would buy a bottle of "woman's pills."

At half-past five she found a drugstore at the corner of Fourteenth and Third Avenue. A light burned from behind shut curtains, but the door was locked, and when she knocked on the glass pane there was no answer. "Hello!" she shouted, feeling suddenly quite ill. She'd eaten nothing but tea and chocolate the night before, and nothing since. But she blamed everything— her fatigue, her dizziness, her foul mood—on the foreign body within her that must be expelled.

"What in tarnation is it?" said a thickset old man from behind the door, pulling aside the curtains to get a look at her.

"Please," said Maura, but he couldn't hear her suddenly weak voice, and he opened the door. Looking down at his feet, she asked: "Have you any of those pills for ladies? Portuguese, I mean? The Portuguese Regulators, I think they're called."

"Are you a student?" he asked, looking at her exhausted face.

"No."

"I don't sell to no students whose daddy's going to come after me with a gun, see?"

"Sure I'm no student, just a poor working girl, sir, and if you've got them for sale, I'd like very much to buy a few."

"Not married? Of course you're not. Where are your parents?"

"In Ireland."

"Do you mean to say there's some Irish who ain't left to come to New York City and grace us with their presence?" He smirked. "You're all alone, right? If I sell these to you, I never seen you, I never heard of you, you never been here, you got that?"

"Yes, sir."

"It's ten bucks."

"Oh," said Maura. That was two and a half weeks' work. She had the money, she had nearly three times the money, but that was all she had left. If she gave him ten dollars, she'd be down to eighteen dollars, and that was including the two dollars and twelve cents she had made at work.

"If you ain't got it, kid, you ain't got it. But do yourself a favor and don't go buying no umbrella ribs. They're perfect to tear yourself to pieces, and you'll never stop the bleeding."

"I have ten dollars," said Maura.

"Wait here," said the druggist. He came back to her a minute later with a small glass vial. Inside were four large pills.

"That's all I need?" said Maura.

"You take one every hour until you start feeling cramps. It's just like when you have your monthlies, just the same, there ain't no trouble, not with these." He didn't hand it over until she had placed the ten-dollar bill in his hand. "Remember, Irish, you never been here, I never seen you, you never gave me no money, and I never gave you no pills." Then he shut the door in her face, and Maura opened the vial and took the first pill greedily into her mouth, and swallowed it down her dry throat.

She followed Third Avenue downtown to the Bowery, waiting for her body to react to the pill. The rising sun filtered through the tracks of the elevated railroad, but the light did nothing to cheer her. Every time a train went by, she stood rooted beneath the tracks, hoping the vibrations would find their way to what she wanted to lose.

It was just after six when she got to Canal Street. She turned west and saw a small group of workers shuffling into a dairy restaurant which was at that moment opening its doors. Understanding that she had to stop and rest and put something into her belly, Maura walked in and sat at a table with three old women who looked like they'd been wandering the streets all night. For four cents, Maura bought a large bowl of coffee and three small hard rolls. Unlike the others at her table, she ate slowly, without appetite, attentive only to what might be happening within her womb.

But there was nothing happening.

A clock on the wall inched its way to half-past six, and Maura wondered if an hour had passed. The druggist had been quite clear: She must take one pill an hour for four hours. It was too soon then to be expecting anything. She picked up her bowl of cold coffee and filled her mouth with the dregs; through pursed lips she pushed in her second pill, and swallowed, momentarily reassured. There was no need to feel worried, not until she had finished all the pills.

It took her an hour to walk along Canal Street to Hudson Street, to Franklin Street, following the direction of early-morning workers. She knew they looked at her strangely. Several of them asked if she was sick. And Maura herself knew that her feet were dragging, that her morning nausea was worse than ever, that the sharp pain that threatened to split her in two was coming not from her womb but from her stomach. This didn't worry her, however. She had paid ten dollars for the powerful pills, and she had expected to have to put up with discomfort. Instead of giving in to her body's demands for warmth and rest, she plodded on to the factory, intent on the coming of half-past seven, when she would take her third pill.

The door to the factory building was open, but the door to the handkerchief factory on the second floor was still locked, and this was maddening to Maura. Usually someone had opened up by half-past seven, so the early girls could get a half-hour more on their time registers. And she was sure it must be half-past seven, no matter that the door was still locked. Maura walked downstairs, ignoring the terrible pain jumping in her stomach, and opened the door to the box factory.

"Please, sir," she asked a man sitting at that establishment's time register, "would you know if it's half-past seven yet?"

"I would know and I do know, honey," he said. "It's half-past seven and five minutes more, Irish."

"Yes, sir," said Maura, turning round and rushing back up the stairs. She sat down heavily in front of the locked door to the handkerchief factory and swallowed the third pill. All right, she was only five minutes late, she thought; surely that made no great difference. There was only one more pill, and that would be taken at twenty-five minutes to nine. By then she'd be at work in front of her machine, a clock staring at her from across the room. When the cramps started, she would be surrounded by friends, good friends: Jenny on one side, and Minnie on the other. Marandino wouldn't fire her. Not for getting sick for a few minutes on the job. She would be in the toilet room, and it wouldn't be anything worse than when she usually had her menstrual period. There was nothing to worry about. Now she simply had to ignore the pain in her belly and wait for the others to come and open the door.

Angela, the thirteen-year-old Italian girl, got to her first, only a minute later. And moments later she was followed by Beryl, the Jewish girl from Odessa, by Katie and Lucinda and Rose and Virginia, and finally Mary, whose job it was to open the door. It was still twenty minutes before eight o'clock, but the mild poison Maura had been swallowing in small dosages since half-past five that morning was running through her body. She was hot, her eyes were glassy, her stomach tried to throw up its contents.

The girls spoke to her, asked her what was wrong, wondered if they could get her to a doctor. "No, no," said Maura, smiling weakly against the pain. She could feel herself drifting, to a region beyond pain, where she could sleep and the red heat behind her eyes would let up, where there would be no more worry about whether or not she would succeed in this terrible world. And she cried out, against her will, letting out a scream that was the more terrible for its short duration. She had to be strong, she reminded herself, trying to hold on to consciousness. More than anything else, she had to remember to take the fourth, the last, pill.

Then Jenny arrived, and took her in her arms, and tried to speak to her, but Maura only nodded her feverish head, trying to keep her eyes open, waiting for the hurt within her to travel to her womb. Minnie arrived a moment later and took Maura's cold hands and asked her what was wrong. "What did you do,

Maura? Irish, I'm talking to you. Did you take something? Speak to me, girl. What did you do to yourself?"

"You took her to the doctor," said Jenny accusingly. "This is the doctor's fault. This is what happens from going to doctors."

"The doctor didn't do nothing but tell her, see?" said Minnie, roughly searching Maura's purse, and finding the little unmarked vial with its single remaining pill. "What's this, then? What the hell's this, Irish? She's gone and poisoned herself, see? We got to get her to a hospital. She's pregnant and she's tried to do herself in."

"No!" said Jenny. "No hospital. All they want is to let you die, so they can have your body to cut up. Everyone knows that."

"Please," said Maura, trying to get back her vial. Opening her eyes, she could see nothing but hazy reds and blacks. The vial had gotten out of her possession and was now drifting through a space she could not see. "I have to take the last pill," she begged.

But Jenny and Minnie weren't listening to her. Together with the others, they helped her down the stairs to the street. Little Angela quickly found a hansom cab, with a good-hearted driver who lifted Maura from their hands and into his passenger seat.

Even Minnie was terrified of hospitals. When Jenny proposed to take Maura to her family's apartment, no one could think of a better idea. At least Jenny had a mother. No one could doubt that the sick girl had need of a mother's experience, far greater than any of their own. They were all of them, after all, just young girls.

# ✿ CHAPTER ✿
# SEVENTEEN

Maura noticed nothing about the trip by cab to an enormous tenement building on Elizabeth Street, just north of Canal Street. She had no eyes for the peddlers, Germans and Swedes and Jews, already out on the early-morning streets, pushing their carts to the pedestrian thoroughfares most likely to crave buttons, apples, or cloth. She didn't hear Minnie demanding to pay for the ride, and she didn't notice the stench of garbage as Jenny and Minnie both dragged her up four flights of stairs to the three-room, one-window apartment which had been Jenny's home for the last ten years.

The Neumanns—renamed Newman by a decisive Castle Garden immigration official—had emigrated from Bavaria, with short moneymaking stops in Frankfurt, Antwerp, and London factories, and arrived in New York City eleven years before. Jenny had been four, her brother Jake nine, her father twenty-eight, her mother twenty-six and pregnant for the third time. Eleven years later, Mr. Newman was sorry he'd ever left Europe. He was now thirty-nine, and made his living pushing a cart of pots and pans into the adjacent Jewish neighborhood. His twenty-year-old son made more money than he, but only at the expense of sleepless nights and endless work. His fifteen-year-old daughter worked in a factory, his ten-year-old daughter Andrea worked at sewing buttons for a neighbor on the third floor; his six-year-old and four-year-old daughters walked around in shapeless, cheap clothing, while their mother tried to shop and clean and cook for the family and its two boarders, trying to ignore the pain of her arthritic knees.

"She's sick, ma," said Jenny, by way of introduction, pushing Maura into Mrs. Newman's arms.

"She's pregnant, and she took this," added Minnie, exhibiting the lone pill in its vial. "She's a widow, see? She's a good girl."

Mrs. Newman didn't hesitate. She sat Maura down in that small square of living space she had designated her kitchen, and forced a spoonful of castor oil down her throat. From the depths of her stupor, through all the levels of pain in her stomach, Maura's repugnance to the taste brought her, gagging, to her feet.

"Bringing the bowl," said Mrs. Newman, and Jenny did so quickly. But Maura didn't throw up. She allowed them to lead her into the next room, a small windowless box, lit only by the light from the first room coming through the door. There was a small couch that ran the length of the room, facing a sea of bedding on the floor. Maura was helped onto the couch, and as Jenny's two youngest sisters watched, their mother bundled this strange, auburn-haired girl with half the blankets in the entire flat. Mrs. Newman sent everyone out of the room and, alone with Maura, she stroked her hot forehead, she rubbed her cold hands, until the poor girl fell asleep.

The Newmans rented their flat for eight dollars a month. The tenement building was five stories high, with two water closets on each floor and one sink with cold running water. Each floor accommodated ten three-room apartments. With their two boarders, the Newmans had nine people in their three rooms—more than some, less than others. But whether there were ninety wretches sharing the lone sink and the two water closets, or eighty, or even one hundred, made little difference; people used pails and discarded their waste when and how they could. This was not, as some landlords claimed, because immigrants were not used to living in civilized surroundings; it was because their surroundings were uncivilized that they had to learn to survive like animals. The smallest boys and girls were sent to bring water from the sink, and quickly learned to fight for their place in line. Neighbors who piled their garbage in the hall were forced, at knifepoint, to remove their garbage to the street.

Children described the mating habits of parents, uncles and aunts to their friends. Fastidious housewives learned to ignore the stench of boarders who were too tired to wait on line for water to wash themselves or their clothes.

But Maura was aware of none of this. Jenny and Minnie went back to work, and she slept in the dark room. In the late morning a sudden spasm shook her awake and she cried out involuntarily. Hardly knowing where she was, she let Mrs. Newman help her to her feet and squat over a pail. The pills had had a caustic, cathartic effect on her intestinal tract, but after her bowel movement, she felt infinitely better. Her hands were getting warmer, the pain in her stomach came back only when she moved. For now, she was content to lie still, to sleep.

Mrs. Newman woke her in the late afternoon and helped her to sit up and drink some broth. "You'll be all right," she said, her German accent strange to Maura's ears. For some reason she had thought she was back in Mrs. Saunders's boardinghouse. But she resolved not to think, but to sip the broth, and then lie back and close her eyes and wait for enlightenment.

Jenny and Minnie visited her, and she smiled at them, and they spoke softly, and the words went right past her, unnoticed. Other dream figures appeared: three little girls, all with dark, wavy hair and enormous eyes; a tall, middle-aged man, carrying his own sewing machine on his shoulder; a short young man with a blond beard and a worried expression; a thin man of forty or so, with watery eyes and an apologetic look. This last man was Mr. Newman, and he spoke to her briefly, apologizing for the lack of comfort he could offer, and then vanished into the third and smallest room. Here he and his wife slept, accompanied by their four-year-old, in perfect darkness, this windowless room getting even less light and less air than the one in which Maura, Jenny, and two of her sisters slept. The two boarders slept in the first room. Here was a window, a table in Mrs. Newman's "kitchen" area, a cot, and two thin mattresses on the floor, as well as the door to the fourth-floor hallway. The cot was for Jake, Jenny's twenty-year-old brother, when he was there overnight. Otherwise, the boarders flipped a coin for it; less for the pleasure of the bed than the joy of gambling.

"Please to get up," said Mrs. Newman late Monday morning.

Maura had slept through half of Saturday and all of Sunday, and was still tired. She opened her eyes and looked at the German lady wonderingly. It was true then. She had left Mrs. Saunders. She had gone with Minnie to the doctor. She had bought pills.

"What happened to my pills?" she said.

"You ate them," said Mrs. Newman. "All except one, thanks be to God. Please to get up."

"I'm afraid I don't remember your name, ma'am," said Maura.

Mrs. Newman told her, adding that everyone had gone off to work hours ago. Maura noticed two little girls with black wavy hair watching her shyly from the corner of the room.

"I want that you should get up and walk, Maura," said Mrs. Newman.

"I'm sorry," said Maura, doing as she was told. There was little dizziness when she stood, just a sense of fatigue that even the day of sleep hadn't been able to dispel. "Sure I want to thank you for everything," said Maura.

"You will eat some oatmeal, yes? Hot," said Mrs. Newman, leading Maura to the table. In place of chairs, benches flanked the table's length. As soon as Maura sat before the steaming cereal, a chain of associations started up: from the bench in this flat, to that in the factory, from the factory to worry about the time she'd lost from work, from worry about work to remembering why she was absent. The pills hadn't worked. She was pregnant. Another day or more had passed, and whatever was in her womb was growing still.

"I want you to eat, Maura," said Mrs. Newman.

"Thank you," said Maura, but she wasn't looking at the food, but off into space. She had only taken three pills. Perhaps the fourth one would have worked, she thought, realizing in the same instant that four pills would have only taken her that much closer to killing herself. The doctor had been right. But he had said that a doctor could do an abortion. If she couldn't get rid of her problem with pills, she had to find a doctor who would do what the other doctor refused.

"Your husband, he is dead," said Mrs. Newman. "I am sorry. Please to eat."

"He's dead, and I'm pregnant." Maura forced herself to take

a bite of the cereal. At once she realized how empty her insides were. The oatmeal slid down deliciously, with only the barest bit of discomfort. This was mostly fear, coming from her mistrustful stomach.

"You can't get rid of the baby with those pills," said Mrs. Newman. "And if you listen to some stupid girl at work, it is worse. No needles, you understand? No sticks, it's dangerous. And rubber, too. Even that can tear you to pieces. Please, it's not safe."

"Do you know a doctor, Mrs. Newman?"

"No. That's not the way. They're not doctors. Not the ones I hear about. They might be anyone. A shoemaker. They can kill you just like a friend, and it's expensive."

"I have to find a doctor."

"There are things you can do without a doctor," said Mrs. Newman.

"What?" said Maura, her face lighting up. Was it possible that this woman knew a secret, a trick, an easy way to rid herself of this burden? If only it were simple, she thought. If only a few words had to be said, a priest give his blessing, a doctor give his pill, and that would be the end of it. But it wasn't simple. She had nearly died, she had probably lost her job, she had thrown away ten dollars, and still this thing inside was growing, against her will.

"I'll boil some water, if you want to try," said Mrs. Newman.

"Yes," said Maura. "Please."

"If you're strong enough," Mrs. Newman added, but she knew how Maura felt, she knew the girl would stop at nothing until she had rid her womb of its contents. Mrs. Newman had once tried "Portuguese" pills; the result had been Jenny's ten-year-old sister. She had tried the same time-honored method she was about to use on Maura on herself as well: Twice her pregnancies had survived intact and uneventful to term; but once, two years ago, sufficiently savage heat and exercise had, she was sure, brought on a blessed miscarriage.

"If you are strong, it is all right if you are tired," she said. "It is better if you do not go to sleep at all until it happens, if it's God's will. Do you understand?"

Mrs. Newman sent her six-year-old for water from the hallway sink and lit the stove. She explained to Maura that what
would take place would be difficult for her, and that it might
not work. It would be God who would decide, she explained. "I
love my Martha the same as my own life," she added, gesturing
toward the door through which the six-year-old had vanished.
"It was God's will that I should carry her, no matter what. You
must know that before you start, so you will not be too sorry, you
understand? Even a poor girl can find time to love a child if
there is no other way."

"But it can work?" said Maura, watching as the German
woman put the kettle up to boil. "You have seen it work?"

"Yes. For myself and others, too."

"Sure I will do everything you tell me. I am strong enough,"
said Maura.

There were no bathtubs in any of the flats in the tenement.
People bathed with water out of pails, washing themselves with
sponges and soapy water. But Mrs. Newman explained that the
method of sitting in hot water for long hours was not as good
as her method: It was the steam, not the hot water, that was
the key to success, she said.

For the rest of the afternoon, the six-year-old was kept busy
fetching water from the floor's communal sink. Mrs. Newman
heated the water until it was steaming, then poured it into a
large tin pail, over which Maura squatted, without underclothes,
her skirt pulled over the pail so that the steam bathed her private
parts. Every few minutes Mrs. Newman poured fresh steaming water into a second pail, pouring what water was left from
the first pail back into the kettle. The six-year-old enjoyed the
water-fetching game immensely, as there were blessedly few
others waiting at the sink. Preparing for any contingency, she
filled every pail and bowl and cup in the apartment, lining them
up one by one in her mother's steaming "kitchen."

The steam didn't bother Maura. It was the squatting that
threatened to break her. Even after the first few minutes, the
muscles in her thighs began to shiver and shake. But Mrs.
Newman wouldn't allow her to rest. This was only the beginning,
she said. If it was too much for her already, she might as well

give up altogether. There would be no rest until the cramps began, or until Maura decided to have the baby. Maura's knees threatened to crack. She wondered if it was this endless squatting that had given Mrs. Newman arthritic knees. Only when the pail of water was exchanged did Maura have a chance to stand, and this getting up soon proved more painful than simply remaining in her squatting position.

At half-past six, Mrs. Newman took Maura into the innermost chamber of the three-room flat. Here, in the tiny space where she and her husband and their youngest child slept, she put Maura to work: Standing barefoot on the floor, she was made to jump, throwing her legs out to the sides, then bringing them back together like a giant human scissors. The Newman six-year-old was left alone with Maura, making sure that she took no period of rest. A single candle burned on a small clay dish, lighting the cracked walls, the low bed, the tiny roll of bedding on which the four-year-old slept. Maura jumped, alternately landing on her toes and her heels, trying to enjoy the respite from the steam and the squatting, but the pain in her knees only intensified with each jump. And the little girl who watched her, so eerily lit by the flickering candle, was like a living rebuke of what Maura was attempting. A perfect little boy or girl, indestructible, was being formed even as she ruined her knees and broke her health, she thought. This was all useless, she felt, every time she caught the eyes of the little wavy-haired girl.

Jenny came into the room soon after. Maura had long since lost track of time, though she understood that Mrs. Newman was busy feeding the boarders and her family as they all straggled in from the day's work. But this little room in which she exercised was so dank and airless that she felt as if she had danced herself into a nightmare.

"You will have this room for the night," said Jenny. "Ma will keep you at it, if you can take it, okay? No, don't stop. You're not to stop until you drop."

But of course Maura couldn't go on much longer, no matter what reserves of energy she tried to dredge up. When she faltered, Jenny held her up, refusing to let her sit down, or lean.

"Come on, girl, you're only just starting," she said. "You're going to be all right if you see it through."

Soon Maura found herself on the floor, flat on her back, looking up at the ghostly features of Mrs. Newman and Jenny as they bore down on her in the candlelight.

"Don't sleep," said Mrs. Newman. "You're not to sleep." She had a rolling pin in her hand, a tremendous rolling pin, and Maura looked from this to the little girl, whose huge eyes were wide with wonder. Then she saw Mrs. Newman and Jenny, on either side of her, bear down with the rolling pin on her belly, and push.

"You're not to sleep," repeated Mrs. Newman, pushing down hard with Jenny on Maura's abdomen. Maura opened her mouth to ask her what she was doing, but she was too tired to speak. She shut her eyes, and immediately felt the heat of the room, the stifling closeness of sweating flesh, the hiss of steam. "You're not to sleep," said Mrs. Newman again, and Maura opened her eyes, and saw that Jenny was looking at her with terrified eyes, and felt a sharp pain in her belly that was nothing remotely like a menstrual cramp. It was more like an iron nail passing through her stomach and suddenly turning its sharp end into the inside wall of her body. But this passed. The passage of the rolling pin along her abdomen began to be pleasant. At least she was allowed to lie still. She opened her eyes and smiled lovingly at Jenny, at Mrs. Newman, at the little girl.

But then she was pinched, and the pain brought her more fully awake. Mrs. Newman told Jenny to do it again, and Jenny grabbed the soft flesh of Maura's underarm and pinched hard, so that tears came to the exhausted girl's eyes. Then the rolling pin resumed its course, up and down her abdomen, and the mother and daughter pushed harder, but still there was no stirring from within, except the pangs of hunger and the occasional aching cry from the walls of her stomach where the "Portuguese" pills had inflicted their damage more than thirty-six hours before.

Because she could no longer squat, they put her on her knees over a smaller pail, so that the hot tin wouldn't burn her flesh. Maura noticed that the candle had almost burned down to noth-

ing, but couldn't remember whether it was the first candle or
the second; she couldn't remember when it had been lit, and
why she could see no window in the black little room.

Jenny was sweating now too, her eyes red and tearing. Mrs.
Newman leaned against a wall, exhausted, holding her six-year-
old on her lap, rocking her gently, all the while watching Maura
where she knelt, in a sullen stupor, over a steaming pail.

"Again," said Mrs. Newman, and Maura, to her amazement,
found that she was standing up, her feet spread far apart, her
skirt gone.

"Jump," said Jenny, blowing up out of the steamy darkness.

"I'm naked," said Maura, speaking to herself wonderingly.
Mrs. Newman slapped her across the face, hard, twice. "What?"
said Maura, suddenly bursting into tears. What had she done
wrong now? She was so young, and wanted now to be much
younger, in her mother's arms, being comforted by an Irish
song. This woman's harsh accent angered her. She wanted to
be spoken to gently, to be fed and clothed and cared for. Even
Mrs. Saunders was kinder than this woman, but Mrs. Saunders
was only for the very rich, after all. Five dollars a week.

Jenny pinched her and told her to jump. "What?" said Maura
again, and she slowly brought her feet together, launching herself a few inches into the air with an absurd smile on her face.
She remembered that these were her friends, and that she had
better do what they said. Again and again she jumped, scissoring
her legs, remembering the pills she paid ten dollars for, and
feeling so sorry for the money she'd lost that tears began to roll
down her face.

"She can't do it, ma," said Jenny, but Mrs. Newman snapped
something at her in German and clapped her hands in Maura's
face, setting up a rhythm for her jumping.

How would her mother write to her? thought Maura suddenly,
remembering that she had not sent her new address. What if her
mother had never even gotten her letter, with its gift of cash and
its lies about dead Patrick and Brendt? She was jumping now so
listlessly, with so little motion, that Mrs. Newman brought her
back to her knees over the steaming pail. Maura looked up at her
without comprehension. The steam, the position on her knees, the

eager talk from Jenny to keep her awake, all retreated for the moment. She remembered being this feverish before, when Brendt was there, bathing her forhead with cold towels, telling her that all would be well. Flat on her back once again, she caught sight of the candle, but now it was big, brand-new, and she remembered that it had been smaller and near to going out, and so took assurance that the night was passing, that the ordeal of her life would soon be over.

Slowly, she felt awareness return. They were pushing down on her abdomen to kill her baby. She had been jumping up and down to destroy the terrible seed. They had been sending steam up her vagina to somehow destroy the inside of her womb. But it was no use. Nothing was stirring. Only her dreams were coming to life, hunting her with their irony: She would emerge from a carriage, wrapped in silks and furs, stepping on a red carpet to the majestic entrance of a Fifth Avenue mansion. Maura remembered the Waldorf then, how its trappings fit the contours of her dream. But the dream was dead. All she had wanted was to leave the Waldorf, and the rich boy who wanted to keep her, as now all she wanted was to leave this gift of a new life behind, so she could somehow go on with her own.

In the steamy room Maura continued, blindly going from station to station: flat on her back, jumping in place, kneeling over the hot water. Time stood still, or else rushed backward—to the house on Spring Street, to County Kerry, to Fiona Maloney bemoaning the death of her husband. Mrs. Newman became Mrs. Saunders, and Mrs. Saunders became Louise, and Louise became Fiona, and Fiona became Brendt, and Brendt was flying, flying off into space because she had allowed Grady Madigan to make love to her, and the church hadn't forgiven her, but Maura was never, never to blame the church.

"It's God's will, Maura," said Mrs. Newman, her voice clear as a bell to Maura. "You are not to lose the child."

Maura heard this, and understood that they had failed, and refused to accept it. She struggled to her feet in the near dark; she began to jump up and down; she begged them to hit her; she asked Jenny to boil water; she asked Mrs. Newman if they could throw her down the stairs. All this energy kept her going for another half-minute. She shouted, she jumped, she begged them to continue, and then she collapsed. It was near five in the morning, and no one in the little apartment had been able to get much sleep; Jenny and her mother had gotten no sleep at all. But Jenny went off to work, leaving shortly after seven so there would be ample time to walk. Maura would be causing enough extra expense in her family's household without squandering nickels and dimes on trolleys and trains.


Maura slept in the dark room where she'd spent most of the night. Her sleep was fitful, because she knew she'd been defeated; and knew, too, there was a way to win. But her waking moments weren't lucid. And her dreams only roiled the peaceful waters of sleep. She dreamed of the house on Spring Street, how the men had tied her down, and she grew angrier and angrier, until her body lurched her awake.

Mrs. Newman was there, having heard her cry, ready to comfort her.

"Where's Ginny?" asked Maura.

"Jenny is at work, Maura. You'd best eat now. Come on, I'll help you up."

Ginny, not Jenny, thought Maura, smiling crazily. Her friend from the Tenderloin. Ginny, who had done everything, who knew everything. Ginny would help her. Doctors did abortions, and Ginny would know who they were, and how to get to them. Ginny, she thought, and, smile intact, she followed Mrs. Newman into the first and largest room of the flat and sat down on a bench at the table.

"I have to send a message, please," said Maura.

"You're not to talk yet," said Mrs. Newman. "You're to eat, then you're to talk. You understand?"

"I have to send a message to a friend. It's very important," said Maura. Once again she was stricken with a terrible, manic urgency. What was growing in her womb yesterday was with her still, but a day older, a day closer to disaster. She had tried so hard to end it, but it hadn't worked, and now only Ginny could help her, and she must get a message to her at once.

"I said not to talk!" said Mrs. Newman. "Be a good girl!"
Both the six- and the four-year-old began to giggle at this, but
Maura took no notice. "Please, Mrs. Newman, you don't understand. Sure there must be someone, some boy who can carry
a note for me. Please. It's a matter of life and death, don't you
see? Please."

Mrs. Newman took her hands and tried to comfort her, letting
Maura lean her head against her shoulder and cry.

"I'll take the note," said a strong, slightly accented male voice.
"Give me the note and I'll take it wherever you want."

Maura turned round and saw a young man of medium height,
with the same wavy black hair as his sisters. He was dressed in
the rumpled, stained clothes of a workingman. His eyes were
bloodshot, his color pale, but he was certainly the most beautiful
man Maura had ever seen.

"This is our Jake," said Mrs. Newman, trying not to sound
proud. "He does us this big favor of coming home this morning.
Look what he brings us. Potatoes, milk, cheeses—three kinds—a
fresh chicken, look how big." Mrs. Newman brought the bowl
of hot oatmeal to Maura and put a spoon in her hand. "Now come
on. If you have a note, our Jake will take care of it. He can take
care of anything. But first you eat, you understand?"

"I don't have a note," said Maura. "I have to write it."

"If you don't eat first," said Mrs. Newman, "I kill you, you
understand?"

"Say, ma," said Jake. "I'll sit down here next to your patient,
just like this. And then she eats, and she tells me what to put
in the note, and everybody's happy. I can write anything, and
faster than most."

"First she puts something into her mouth," said Mrs. Newman.
But she brought paper and pencil, and Maura told the beautiful
young man to write that she needed to see Ginny at once, it was
a matter of life and death. Then she told him that she wanted
him to go to a brothel on Twenty-sixth Street, and apologized
for the shame of it in front of his mother, and for speaking of it
in a decent house. But she needed to see Ginny, and that was
where Ginny could be found, and he should please be very careful, because it was a terrible place—not just the house but the

whole Tenderloin; it was filled with gangsters and dangerous.

"Look," said Jake, "you want me to find this Ginny and bring her back to see you. No problem."

"Thank you," said Maura, understanding at once what lay behind his beauty. He had perfect confidence in his future. Everything was possible. The best of all things could be his, *would* be his. She didn't know why he made her feel so ashamed. He hadn't blushed at the mention of a brothel. If he had been shocked by what had transpired in his parents' bedchamber last night, he didn't show it. "It's very good of you, it's very kind."

"Sister, it's nothing," said Jake Newman. He got up to go, and Maura understood her shame. This young man didn't desire her. He looked at her with kindness. She was another victim of the misery all around them, but in his eyes she was still guilty of crimes: She had tried to induce a miscarriage, she knew of brothels and whores, she spoke of the Tenderloin as if she knew it well. Imagining herself through the young man's eyes, Maura found herself cheap, degraded, a woman to help out of pity, never out of desire or love.

She couldn't have been more wrong. Jake seldom made a move out of pity. Everything in the world around him was pitiable, and he couldn't hope to right every wrong, destroy every evil on the Lower East Side of New York City. He worked demonically, intelligently, shrewdly. Nothing diverted him from his ambition to be rich and powerful, save for the love he gave his family. He carried the note from the auburn-haired beauty to the Tenderloin brothel, amazed at the strength of this new desire.

# ❧ CHAPTER ❧ EIGHTEEN

Ginny arrived at the tenement flat three hours later. She wore a red dress, a hat with peacock feathers, a necklace of large paste jewels, and had painted her pretty face as if it were midnight on Twenty-sixth Street. Mrs. Newman served Maura and Ginny tea, as if she were a servant in this one-window room. Jake had vanished upon depositing Ginny at the door. The four- and six-year-olds were banished to the innermost chamber.

"Talk about dopes," Ginny said. These were her first words to her friend, and she didn't have to elaborate. Maura had abandoned Ginny in a Fifth Avenue department store, leaving her to explain to Kilgallen what had happened to one of his most uneager prostitutes. In exchange for the glories of the brothel on Twenty-sixth Street, Maura had managed—in only a month—to end up pregnant and half dead in a miserable flat on the Lower East Side.

"I'm sorry," said Maura.

"You ain't sorry—don't give me none of that," said Ginny.

"For leaving you in that big store, I mean," said Maura.

"I forgot about that. That ain't nothing. I bought myself a handkerchief, a silk handkerchief, and the bulls never came. They had to eat crow. It was out of sight, see? They all looked like dirt when I was through with them, and that ain't no lie. Nobody throws me out of no store. It's a free country." Ginny leaned forward and smiled at her friend, speaking softly so Mrs. Newman couldn't hear. "This ain't tea, dopey. She's done made up some hot piss, the old beggar."

"Please, Ginny. She's been very good to me."

"Yeah? Like I was to you? Jesus, dopey, I'm the dope, ain't that right? I'm here, ain't I? You just whistle and old Ginny comes back to her high-and-mighty Irisher. I could've been killed for what you done. You left me, girl. What was I supposed to say to Mike the Pike? He could've broken my ass, you know that? You leaving me like that, just because they were crumbs in that store."

Maura had thought her friend might have forgiven her, but now, the vehemence of Ginny's reply was terrifying. In her high-strung emotional state, Maura felt that her last hope of getting rid of her pregnancy was gone. She began to cry.

Ginny put down her teacup. "For Christ's sake, dopey," she said. "I'm a jerk. I didn't even ask you how you feel or nothing. Would you quit crying, or am I going to have to smack you? What do you think I came to this joint for, just to drink tea? Come on, let's get out of here."

"I'm pregnant," said Maura stupidly.

"No shit, dopey," said Ginny. She took hold of her friend and, making abrupt apologies to Mrs. Newman, took her out of the flat and down the four flights of stairs.

"What are you going to do, miss?" said Mrs. Newman, who had accompanied them to the street. Maura, dazed by the sunlight, looked in awe at the teeming population.

"I'm going to help her," Ginny replied.

"You can bring her back here, afterward," said Mrs. Newman. "Do you understand?"

"I get you, ma'am," said Ginny. "But it won't be till tomorrow. We ain't visiting a butcher shop, see? This is safe, as safe as when it happens to a regular nob. This is where the knocked-up ladies all go, see? And nothing never happens to them rich buggers."

Ginny waved her courtesan-red furled umbrella at an off-duty hansom and told the driver to take them uptown. Maura had stopped crying and sank into her seat, close to Ginny's exotic, scented form. "You want to tell me what you been up to?" said Ginny. "No, I guess you don't. You don't want to talk, so I'll talk. I made an appointment for you. We got a couple of hours first, so I'm taking you for ice cream, and then we'll get you fixed real good."

"I don't have much money," said Maura.

"You never did, dopey. And by the looks of things, you never will, neither. But it ain't that expensive. There's a place on Fifth Avenue that charges three hundred bucks—they must give you champagne instead of ether. But this place is fine. It's fifty bucks, and it's very clean, and the doctor's a lady, a real doctor, and she ain't American—she's got a European accent, and very nice manners. That bohunk you sent, he's that woman's son, ain't he? Pretty good-looking clodhopper, and he knows it, too. You stuck on him?"

"What?" said Maura, not taking in her question about Jake Newman, still too upset at the mention of the fifty-dollar cost of her abortion. "Ginny, I don't have fifty bucks. I don't have nearly that much."

"Listen, dopey, if you listen to me, you'll have a hell of a lot more than that in a week's time, see? If you play your cards smart, instead of jumping ground, going here, going there . . ."

"I can't go back to the house, Ginny," said Maura. "I can't."

"No one's telling you to go back to the house," said Ginny. "This Kevin Vane guy's hooked on you, see? If you're smart, you'll have him keeping you in style. That guy can buy skyscrapers with what he keeps in his pants pockets. He gave me twenty-five bucks when he dropped off the clothes I lent you. And he gave me another twenty-five bucks today, just like he said he would, just for letting him know I heard from you."

Ginny paid the driver and guided Maura into an ice-cream parlor under the Sixth Avenue Elevated. She ordered two "specials"—monstrous mountains of vanilla and chocolate ice cream, drenched with syrup, flecked with nuts, and topped with whipped cream and chocolate shavings. Maura ate greedily. It was simpler than talking. How could she explain to Ginny that in the space of a month she had traveled a thousand miles from the whorehouse? How could she tell the happy prostitute that she would never again take money for giving herself to a man? Nothing must get in the way of the next few hours: Maura was afraid to question, to complain, to give an opinion. She had one goal for the moment, and that was to end this pregnancy. So she stifled her questions about Kevin.

"What do you think about Kilgallen, eh?"

"What?"

"Kilgallen. Mike—Mike the Pike. Say, don't tell me you ain't heard?"

"Heard what?"

"Jesus, you're kidding me. Don't you read the newspapers? How long you been sick for? Hey, when I tell you all this, you're gonna be too sick to finish your ice cream."

"Ginny, please," said Maura. "I don't want to think about anything until after it's over."

"Just tell me one thing. Do you know about him getting screwed by the bulls on account of the little Jew-girl?"

"What do you mean 'screwed'?" said Maura, suddenly curious in spite of herself. What was growing in her womb had begun not with Kevin but with the man who had forced her into becoming a whore. She hoped to hear that he was hurt, that he could no longer harm her.

"Jesus. You ain't heard. Shit. Me and that Kevin Vane, that's all we talked about. You play your cards right, that rich man's boy is going to be lapping champagne out of your shoes. Dopey, it was on the front page of the *Herald* only two days ago."

"Please, Ginny. Just tell me, okay?"

"There was this Hebrew girl, didn't speak no English, you know. Mike the Pike, he picks her up, he takes her to Spring Street, he tries to get her into the life and everything, and in less than a week she's dead. It happens, we all know it, you know what I'm saying?"

"Yes."

"But it don't end there. She's got a brother, see, and he goes to one of the Hebrew gangsters and tried to find out is she alive or is she dead. The Hebrew hood knows Mike, they're in the same business: They both pick up girls at the dock, and the Hebrew ain't exactly thrilled that Mike the Pike's picking up on Hebrews. That ain't Mike's territory, if you see what I'm saying. They spread it around. And this is in an area where these Jew-boys are strong. I mean, they've got the biggest houses in

the Tenderloin, some of these guys, and their Italian friends.
So Mike the Pike, he's out of line. So when Mike is fingered
as the guy that picked up that girl, the Hebrew girl, they don't
finger him for a murder, they just pull him in as a pimp. The
Hebrew pimps—listen to this—they've got the Irish cops in
their pockets, so the bulls gotta break Kilgallen's chops, even
though he's been paying them through the nose for years."

"*What happened?*"

"Take it easy, dopey, I'm getting there. You want some more
ice cream?"

"No."

"Can I have a bite of yours?"

"*Yes.*"

"He got six months."

"What?" said Maura. "Six months in prison?"

"Well, it wasn't six months' vacation in Asbury Park, dopey."

"For murder?"

"Not for murder, Maura," said Ginny. "They only got him
for procuring. The bulls picked him up as a procurer, and that's
all you can get for it here, just the six months. And that was
only because the Hebrew pimps had it in for him for moving in
on their territory, see?"

"He's in prison, then? Kilgallen is in prison?"

"He's dead, Maura. That's what I've been meaning to tell
you. Mike the Pike is dead, honey."

Ginny didn't speak in riddles, but she had little sense of
clarity or chronology. Maura pinned her to that spot in the
ice-cream parlor until she had the story straight: The brother
of a Jewish girl who had been picked up by Kilgallen at the
Battery, after arriving from Ellis Island, found his way to the
Jewish white slavers on the Lower East Side. These hoodlums
knew Kilgallen, and agreed to help their coreligionist find his
sister. By the time they did, she was dead—whether from
starvation, or shock, or a beating, no one knew.

Coincidence saved Ginny from Kilgallen's ever discovering
Maura's disappearance. The day she returned to the brothel with-
out Maura, Kilgallen had already been picked up by the police.
The Jewish white slavers had decided it was vastly preferable to

have him picked up for procuring—an occupation shared by
ten thousand men in New York City—than to close up the house
on Spring Street. After all, they were in the same business.
Jewish, Italian, and Irish gangsters saw to a speedy trial by
one of their paid-for judges. Kilgallen was sentenced to six
months. At the moment of sentencing, just two days ago, the
brother of the dead girl walked up to Kilgallen in the courtroom
and shot him once in the head, killing him instantly. This
spectacular murder was still being played up in the newspapers.
The young man's trial was to begin next week, and this was
what Ginny meant when she said that the world was going
to know about Spring Street.

"The churches are going to have a field day," said Ginny. "I
was telling all this stuff to your Mr. Vane—"

"He is not *my* Mr. Vane," said Maura.

"I beg your pardon, dopey."

"And I'm happy that son of a bitch is dead."

"Hell, you're a tough broad, ain't you? He wasn't as bad as
some others, let me tell you. If you played by his rules, you
made a good living. He ran some good houses, he kept order, and
that's important. You need some order, or the place goes right
to hell."

"For the love of God, Ginny, the man turned me into a
whore," whispered Maura, clutching her friend's soft hand. But
Ginny's eyes went quickly cold.

"If that's how you feel about it, dopey," she said. "I tell you
what. You're a saint. It's only me who's a whore. But maybe we
better get a move on. It's almost time for the saint's abortion."
Ginny's anger quickly died down, replaced with a smoldering
sense of having been wronged. She had no shame at being a
prostitute, but she had considerable shame at being thought
inferior or base by her friend. Maura had refused to hear about
Kevin Vane. She'd acted as if the idea of being kept by one
of the richest men in town was some sort of sin.

"Please, Ginny, don't be angry at me. I think you're the best
friend I ever had. I only meant to say that I hated Kilgallen,
nothing else."

"What about Kevin Vane? If you hate him so much, why

don't you let me have him? I could use him, let me tell you. I
could do wonders with a guy with that kind of cash. I want you
to know something: For all your talk, he's the one paying for it
all. I like you, dopey, but I wouldn't spring for fifty bucks you'll
never pay me back for. It's him who's given me the money to
take care of what ails you. So when he comes round to whatever
joint you go back to, remember to say, 'Thank you, sir.' Remember it's him who's paid."

Once again Ginny found them a hansom, and gave the driver
an address on West Thirtieth Street, next to an abandoned gas-
house. Maura realized that a combination of fatigue and revela-
tion kept her from dwelling on her fear. Had she not been so
battered from the night's desperate attempts to force a miscarriage, she would have been far more shocked at the news of
Kilgallen's death. Had she not been so eager to rid herself
of her pregnancy, she would have tried to resurrect the rich boy's
face, tried to imagine why he would have paid Ginny fifty
dollars to help find her, and why he cared enough to pay for
the abortion.

But since everything had come at once—the useless night of
exercise and exhaustion and pain, the appearance of Ginny, the
news of Kilgallen's death and of Kevin Vane's continued attraction—everything blended into a dreamlike fabric, serving
to insulate her from the frightening moments to come. Even
Ginny's talk of botched abortions drifted into the weightless
film about her consciousness. Ignorant girls who tried to manip-
ulate sticks or sponges through the cervix, fake doctors who
inserted stiff rubber tubing without thought of washing their
hands, inexperienced midwives who tried to inject soapy water
into the womb, held no fears for Maura; she was near to
somnambulism.

The lady doctor's nurse met them at the door and smiled
grimly at both of them. Maura examined her coarse face with
its trio of warts under the left part of her mouth, as if these warts
might be a key to understanding the significance of her dream-in-
progress. Soon the lady doctor herself drifted in from the next
room. Maura returned her smile. She was a very pretty older
woman, with gray eyes and a prominent, aquiline nose. Ginny
said something to Maura that she didn't hear, and then repeated

it: "I'm going now, honey. The doctor says you're going to be fine, see?"

"You're going?" said Maura, and Ginny's smile ran right through her sleepy bubble, letting out every bit of soporific calm. "What do you mean you're going?"

"She must go, Mrs. O'Connell," said the lady doctor. Maura heard every word now. She was no longer looking at the nurse's warts but at her red scrubbed hands. Ginny's face was white under the red paint; she was scared, for all her brave talk. The room was lit with gas, not electricity, but it was very bright, and warm, and Maura was sitting up on an upholstered table. Ginny backed out of the room with an apologetic nod at Maura, wishing her luck.

"Wait, Ginny," said Maura, but her friend was gone.

*She was going to have an abortion.*

Yes, this was the lady doctor, this was her nurse, and she wasn't dreaming. She was flat on her back on an operating table, and she was suddenly awake, she was suddenly aware. The lady doctor spoke to her gently, despite an accent as harsh and clipped as her eyes were soft and her hands warm.

"What are you going to do?" asked Maura. Quickly, she began to tell the doctor the story of the night before—of the boiling water, the endless exercise, of Mrs. Newman explaining that it was God's will for her to have the baby. "I don't want the baby, but I don't want to die, either. What are you going to do?"

"Please, Mrs. O'Connell," said the lady doctor. "It will be better if you take deep breaths, one, two, one, two."

"Why?" said Maura. "What are you going to do? How are you going to take it out of me? Are you going to cut me? Sure I only want to know. It's not trouble I'm asking for. Please, just tell me."

"I've performed more than two thousand abortions," said the lady doctor. "No one's ever been hurt, not by me. Don't get up. You're going to sleep, and you won't feel a thing."

"But I'm not asleep," said Maura. "Please don't start until you're sure I'm asleep."

The nurse held a wad of cloth under a small bottle and poured out a few drops. Swiftly, she took the wet cloth, placed it in a kind of mask, and brought this to Maura's face.

"What are you doing?" said Maura. "I told you I'm not asleep. I'm not sleepy, and sure it's the truth that you're not to start until I'm asleep. It's your own words, it is. . . ."

But the mask fit snugly over Maura's nose and mouth, and when she opened her mouth to protest, she sucked in the ether-like odor of the chloroform. The doctor looked calmly into Maura's frightened eyes and spoke softly, evenly: "I'm not going to hurt you, my dear. It's very simple. You're going to sleep. This is what they used when Queen Victoria gave birth to Prince Leopold. She slept through everything. So will you."

But Maura didn't want to give birth. She wanted quite the opposite. She hoped the doctor hadn't forgotten this, and wanted to remind her, and tell her to please not begin anything until she was sure she was asleep. But she couldn't talk. Terrified, Maura tried to raise her head, to pick up her legs, to strike out with her arms, only to show that she was still awake. But the nurse held her arms, she stroked her forehead, she wouldn't allow Maura's legs to rise. Maura shut her eyes and tried to fight. She would struggle with every ounce of her strength until she lost consciousness, so they would know not to begin.

"She's out," said the nurse.

"She went fast," said the doctor. "I've never seen anyone go under that fast."

Fifty dollars was the equivalent of three months' work in the handkerchief-and-underwear factory, but for that much money Maura received expert care. In 1898, at least one hundred thousand criminal abortions were performed in New York City; and of those, six thousand were said to have ended in the death of the patient. Of course, statistics about an illegal operation were unreliable. There were those who claimed that twice as many abortions were being performed, with a much lower fatality rate; there were those who claimed that most abortions were performed without doctors, and few were successful. But Maura's doctor knew from daily practice the realities behind all those sets of statistics. There were deaths, but these were the result of ignorance. Abortion, performed in the way that she and other qualified—if criminal—doctors did it, had a lower fatality rate than childbirth.

One clumsy butcher would manage to perforate the uterus, and let his patient bleed to death; another might inject some irritating substance into the uterus to bring about the death of the fetus, often leading to embolism and a quick death. Half the barbers and druggists and greedy midwives who opened abortion mills knew nothing about disinfecting their hands or their equipment, leading to infections that couldn't be cured in the surroundings of poverty. None of the uneducated criminals who specialized in lacerating the fetal membranes with pins and needles—or worse, inserting rubber tubing through the cervix, and leaving it there in order to prompt premature labor— used anesthetics.

Maura's doctor had performed her first abortions because she had need of patients in her newly adopted country. She had become a specialist in abortion because her patients had come back to her, and had brought friends, and friends of friends. When at first she had refused to help them, because of the law, some of these women chose to bring unwanted children into the world; other women went to abortion mills, and died. Now she refused only those who were more than three months pregnant, and these she begged to go through with childbirth, explaining why their lives were at stake if they attempted an abortion elsewhere.

With Maura, the procedure was simple and swift: The doctor dilated the cervix with sterilized instruments so that she could bring her semisharp curette into the uterus. Curettage was done quickly, with the expertise of experience. The same scraping motion, performed too slowly, or too clumsily, could lead to hemorrhage instead of the simple expulsion of the uterine contents.

But there was never any danger of this with Maura. After fifteen minutes, when the chloroform began to wear off, the bleeding was under control. Maura felt a sharp pain that took her quickly from a daze to awareness. She opened her eyes and saw the nurse bring a wet cloth to her forehead. The lady doctor smiled at her, and spoke. "All done," she said. "You're fine now, my dear."

Then she felt a duller pain, and it repeated itself deep within her womb in rhythmic fashion. But the doctor smiled again and took her hand, and said that all her pain would soon go away.

Almost as bad as the lack of sterilization in the abortion mills was their lack of bed space. Hardly had a patient undergone the abortion when she'd be sent off in a hansom, often to bleed to death a half-hour after coming home. Maura was told that she'd be staying overnight, and that all she had to think about was rest.

The nurse helped her to an adjacent room, whose windows were covered with black shades. There were three beds, all of them empty, and Maura took the one farthest from the window and allowed the nurse to settle her beneath the covers. "If you feel a little nauseous, that's all right," said the nurse. "That's normal, and it will go away. The chloroform makes you a little groggy, but that's fine too. It will make it easier for you to sleep, and that's what you need."

She didn't remember falling asleep. The next thing she knew the nurse had brought a lamp close to her and was replacing the bloody cotton plugs the doctor had inserted in her vagina to help stop the bleeding. "It's all right," said the nurse. "Just the same as your monthlies."

It was true, in a way. Maura felt the uncomfortable cramps of the first day of her menstrual period. She lifted her head, and felt weak, but well. The sharper pain she remembered from before was gone, completely vanished. A young woman now slept in the bed next to her, her face in shadows.

"Did she also?" said Maura.

"Yes," said the nurse. "Just after you. Now sleep."

Maura returned to sleep almost at once. She had no idea how much time had elapsed when she woke again. It was dark in the room. If the nurse had come back once more, she didn't remember it. In the adjacent bed the young woman seemed to be crying, and so rhythmically that Maura thought the woman might be sobbing in her sleep. Maura wondered what man had brought her here: whether she was a whore or a wife, an unmarried lover or a mother with too many children.

It was then that she remembered Kevin Vane.

Not his face. Not his voice. Not even the size of him, nor the

color of his hair, nor the way he had kissed her. She remembered what Ginny had said: that he was rich, and that he was
paying for this abortion; and it was because of these memories
that Maura remembered his forgiveness.

There, in the dark, with the cries of her fellow patient for
background, she remembered how he had forgiven her, without
saying the words. He had been her protector, without being her
champion, for she knew that he hadn't believed the story she
told him at the Waldorf. Perhaps, if he had shared her visions,
her sense of self, if he had even *imagined*—like the brother of
the murdered Jewish girl—that Kalgallen should be killed,
Maura could have loved him.

But there was no possibility of that now, no matter what
Ginny had told her of his wealth, of his infatuation. She had
never been a whore, only a victim. Even in the house in the
Tenderloin she hadn't been a willing, cognizant prostitute, eager
to ply her trade, but an automaton, able to accept the rules of
the macabre world in which she'd been placed. When Kevin had
looked at her and told her that he liked her, that he wanted
to care for her, she knew that he hadn't believed her story.
Rather, he had accepted her story, was willing to let it stand,
was willing to allow her this fantasy. Maura felt this forgiveness
like an accusation, felt his compassion like the blind feel mis-
placed pity.

Now that Kilgallen was dead, she thought, even Kevin would
learn that she had told the truth. If what Ginny had said was
true, when the Jewish boy who had murdered him was put on
trial, he would tell the story of his sister, of what Kilgallen had
done to her, what Kilgallen's stock-in-trade had been. There
would be witnesses. Kevin Vane would know that her wild story
had been true. Kevin Vane would know that he had treated a
decent girl like a whore.

The young woman in the adjacent bed suddenly stopped crying. Maura spoke to her through the dark: "Are you all right?"

"No," she said, after a long pause. "I am not all right. It hurts,
it hurts terribly. Doesn't it hurt you?"

Maura said that it hurt only a little, and that it was getting
better all the time. She wondered whether the girl cried because

of the pain or because of the sin and the shame. Maura had only
to remember Brendt leaping to her death to know that she cared
for no religious opinions; as for shame—there was no shame in
being alive and whole with her body coming back to its normal
state. Soon, the young woman returned to her sobbing, and
Maura went back to sleep. When she woke again, it was daylight, with the shades pulled up a half-inch. The young woman
was gone, and the nurse was entering the room, carrying her
breakfast.

"The gentleman is here to see you home, Mrs. O'Connell,"
said the nurse, after inquiring about her aches and pains.

"What gentleman?"

"I'm afraid he hasn't given us his name," said the nurse. "He
says not to hurry on his account. He is waiting in his carriage.
The doctor will look at you after you've eaten."

The reality of what had taken place began to set in after she'd
finished her breakfast. She felt remarkably well. It had been a
long time since she'd enjoyed breakfast. The nurse showed her
how she was to change the cotton plugs, cautioning her to wash
her hands with great thoroughness. The lady doctor asked her to
walk, and to sit, and to stand, and asked her how she felt. Then
they helped her dress in her bedraggled shirtwaist, and gave her
a supply of the cotton plugs, and cautioned her not to exert herself for the next three days. But all the while, Maura was occupied with only one thought: She was no longer pregnant. The
terrible spirit that had taken possession of her body against her
will was now banished. Her life was hers once again. She need
go to no lengths of self-abuse and humiliation to get rid of what
she had never wanted. She had nothing to cry about, unlike the
woman who had shared her recovery room. There were no
regrets; there was only the joyous release of having been returned to her normal physical status.

"You're all right, dear," said the doctor, and she kissed Maura
on the top of her red-gold head and sent her out the front door
into a morning bright with promise.

She recognized Kevin at once.

He was dressed foppishly: black Prince Albert coat, light
gray trousers, silk top hat, a rosebud in his buttonhole, and he
was very straight-backed and handsome and awkward. There was

something boyish about him, naïve, that exaggerated the man's frame, the gentleman's clothing. He was embarrassed even before he came up to her, removing his hat and shaking his dark blond hair out of his eyes.

"Please take my arm, Maura," he said.

She took his arm without a word, and he walked with her to the carriage, very slowly, as if he thought her an invalid. He helped her into the carriage, and then for a moment was at a loss for words.

"I'm so terribly sorry that you had to go through all that," he said finally.

"Thank you," said Maura. "For helping me."

"I would have done much more for you if I had known where to find you. I'm sorry, I'm so sorry about our misunderstanding. In spite of everything, you look very beautiful."

Why hadn't he said something about Kilgallen? she thought. Was it possible that he was still sitting in judgment of her, was looking down at her from some great plane of wealth and breeding?

"I'd like to go home, if you please," said Maura. "I would like to change my clothes and spend the day resting."

"Of course," said Kevin. "Perhaps there's something special you'd like your landlady to make—I could get some food."

"My landlady doesn't cook," said Maura. She gave him the address on East Fourteenth Street, and Kevin in turn shouted it to his driver.

"If your landlady doesn't cook, perhaps I could bring you some prepared food. I only want to help. You must feel as weak as a kitten."

"Sure I don't feel anything like a kitten," she said. He was not going to apologize, she realized. He had come back to her, through Ginny, and he was sweeping her away once more, eager to spend money and make her life pleasant, never once stopping to consider who or what she was.

"I only meant that you must be a bit weak after—the experience," he said. "Look here, Maura, I want to say this once and for all so we can cast it aside and go on as if it never happened. About your note—the day you left me—"

"I haven't paid you for the dress yet, but I will," said Maura.

"Forget the dress!" said Kevin, letting his frustration loose for half a moment. "I'm sorry, I didn't mean to shout. I just want to say that you made a mistake."

Maura looked at him now, wonderingly, and Kevin was struck by the full force of her beauty. It frightened him, it silenced him. It was a face that couldn't be put on canvas, he thought, remembering how he'd tried to describe to a friend the image of Maura he carried with him in his mind. The long red-gold hair, the green eyes, the pale skin somehow translated into something of ordinary beauty in only two dimensions—a vision of blooming youth, of a beauty that was powerful, perhaps even dangerous. But these weren't the qualities that brought him to silence, that had obsessed him for a month, that threatened to break the back of his patience. Especially after her ordeal, he could sense the fact of an inner fragility, a residue of pain, that fired all the power of her face. It was the sense of suffering that tore through the substance of youth, the lovely perfection of her flesh.

If she was strong, if she was dangerous, if she was potent, she had a right to be: This was the message of her beauty. She was not simply pretty features, grown up in an elegant hothouse, a delicate female flower. The experience of tragedy, the knowledge of cruelty, was at the core of her being. Her eyes were lovely, lovable; but they had once burned with hatred. She looked so pale and delicate that one wanted to rush up and support her; but she looked like one who would trust few offers. More than caution, more than pain, more than strength, she radiated a longing. It was as if her eyes were searching her memory, and could never quite let go of what she had lost, could never quite give up her earliest dreams.

"Sure I don't mean to be ungrateful," said Maura, "but it was not me who made the mistake, I'm thinking. It was you who made it, thinking of me the way you did."

"I only meant that you made a mistake by leaving," said Kevin quickly. "I'm sorry for mentioning it, since I can see it's upsetting you. I'm behaving like an idiot, and I apologize. I'm sorry that we couldn't have talked before you left. I was frantic with worry about what would become of you."

"I'm all right," said Maura. "You see I'm all right."

"Yes," said Kevin, but his eyes were full of pity.

She examined him carefully now, trying to still her anger. He had apologized for speaking too quickly, but not for the night he had rescued her from the street and then raped her in his hotel room. Now once again he had rescued her, after a fashion, paying for the abortion that Ginny had set up. Maura had a vague awareness that this power of his—to put her into the Waldorf, to pay out fifty dollars without a care in the world, to be ready to supply food and clothing and anything and everything she might require—repulsed her as much as it thrilled her. She knew he would find her room a horror, her job in the factory beneath contempt, her plans to one day go to night school a useless dream. And worse, far worse, was the secret, tiny longing within her eighteen-year-old soul to just give up, drop everything, and let this handsome young man sweep her away, let him take her anywhere he wanted, just so she would no longer have to think.

This is what she rebelled against.

She loathed the factory, she loathed her room, she loathed drudgery and poverty and exhaustion. This handsome young man could end it for her. But Maura didn't want this young man to sweep her into his arms and re-create her life. She had to make her own way, or else understand that everything she had managed to endure on her own had been pointless. She would have no worth, other than the worth that this rich young man assigned her.

The carriage stopped in the filthy shadows of the Second Avenue Elevated, and Kevin escorted her into the rooming house. He tried to think everything out that he was about to speak, so as not to anger her unintentionally; but the poverty and filth of the hallways, the slippery, steep stairs, the odors from the myriad rooms, and the noise of the adjacent train made him blurt out his pity.

"It must have been hard for you," he said.

"It was all right."

"Ginny said that you found work."

"Yes."

"In a factory," said Kevin. "I didn't know you knew anything about factory work."

"I didn't," she said. It would have been simple to add that he didn't know anything about her at all, except for the color of her hair and eyes, except for the knowledge of her flesh. But they had come to the top floor, the fifth, and she was out of breath. "Thank you for taking me home," she said, thinking that perhaps he'd go away without seeing the bloodstained mattress, the filthy pots and pans in the tiny soot-filled room.

"May I come in?" asked Kevin. "Perhaps I can help light the stove, or make some tea?" Maura pushed open the door and turned slowly to catch his pained expression.

"I only just moved. I had a better place. Sure it won't be so bad when I've cleaned up. It's only one night that I've slept here. I stayed with a friend's family when I wasn't feeling well."

At that moment, a train came screaming into the station. The noise of the brakes obliterated the last few words of her sentence, and when the train had stopped, Kevin went to the filthy window to look at the platform.

"What sort of factory is it that you work in?" he said.

"Sewing. I work at a machine, making handkerchiefs."

"Did you sew in Ireland?"

"Yes, of course. But not with a machine. It's not the same at all. It's so fast, it's like a miracle really."

The train started up again, and Kevin turned around, watching the room shake as the train left the station. "I would like very much to help you, Maura," he said when the great noise abated.

"You have already helped me," said Maura. "I did not have fifty dollars to pay the doctor."

"I would like to help with much more than that," he said.

"Why?"

"I like you," he said lamely. "It's simple for me to help. You can't work now. Factories don't hold jobs open when girls are sick, you know that. There's nothing wrong if I lend you some money, is there?"

*Factories don't hold jobs open.* Maura was suddenly very tired. She sat down on the stained mattress, wondering why she hadn't thought of that terrible reality. Once again she'd be without work. The thought of going around to a string of new factories, learning a new task, talking to new girls, was so depressing that she began to cry.

"What is it?" said Kevin, very much alarmed. He had no understanding of the mechanics of an abortion, but imagined that it was physically painful and emotionally devastating. It made perfect sense to him that this girl should cry, either from the memory of her operation or the contemplation of a child she had destroyed. Just as he never once thought of the possibility that her pregnancy could have had anything to do with his love-. making, he never once tried to imagine a moral justification for her wanting the abortion. Kevin truly wanted to help this girl, to understand her, but he never looked at her without a filter before his eyes. He thought it likely that she was good and kind and gentle, and so he sat next to her on the mattress and put his arm about her slender shoulders to comfort her.

There was no specific plan in Kevin's mind. He did not think of himself as a corrupter—not with a girl who had been a prostitute, and who was still the only woman with whom he'd made love. She was poor, and he would give her money. This room was vile, and he would find her a pretty suite of rooms, with a maid, and they would dine out every night. Certainly he had no interest in making sexual demands on the poor girl just after an abortion. But eventually, in a week, or three weeks, she would be back in his bed. In his fashion, he loved Maura. After a short period of time, he would have her whenever he wanted her. She was lovely enough, unique enough, for him to put up with a period of waiting, of romancing. Ginny's prattle about the murder of Kilgallen had not, of course, convinced him that Maura was an angel who had stumbled into a devil's den; Kevin was still sure that no decent girl would ever descend into prostitution, no matter what was done to her. Still, there could be no doubt that Kilgallen was a mean sort who'd kept a tight lid on his girls. Perhaps Maura had wanted to get out of the brothel, and Kilgallen had made that difficult for her. If that was so, so much the better. He would do his best not to think of her as a prostitute. She would simply be his lover, in a way that no girl of his class could ever be.

"I can't stand to see you crying," said Kevin.

"I'm all right," she said, surprised by the kindness in his face.
He got up, and tried to smile at her. "Let me make some tea,"
he suggested, looking for the coal closet, but Maura shook her
head.

"No, thank you. There's no tea. I'm not thirsty anyway, and
I have to get going, actually. I only wanted to change my
clothes."

"Where are you going?" he said. "I thought you were going
to rest. You shouldn't be going anywhere."

"I'm fine," she said. "And I must go to work."

"To work? That's crazy, Maura. You can't be on your feet all
day."

"We sit. There's no standing."

"But you can't, and that's all there is to it! How much do
you make there anyway? In all likelihood the job is gone. I'm
happy to let you have whatever you need. If you need a week's
salary, it would be a privilege for me to help pay it. If you need
more, say so. I can't be responsible for letting you harm yourself."

"You're not responsible," said Maura. Her desire to get to the
factory was growing. It seemed that if she could get there instantly, there'd be a space for her on the workbench that would
otherwise be gone forever.

"May I ask what they pay you for a week?" he said, taking a
wallet from his coat. "Ten dollars, fifteen? I have no idea, Maura.
Please, just tell me what you need. I want to help, I want to be
close to you. Don't you understand that?"

"Yes," she said. "I do." He was coming back to her on the
mattress, so handsome and beautifully dressed and clean. His
hands were large and strong, but without calluses. The fingernails were immaculate. His brown eyes were shining, clear, exhibiting their goodwill. She understood. He wanted her to rest,
and he would take care of everything. He sat on the mattress, he
placed his hands on her cheeks, he looked into her eyes, and
he kissed her forehead.

"There's no need for you to stay here, you know," he said.
"I could get you rooms anywhere. With a maid to look after you.
It's not expensive. I won't bother you at all. I still have school

till June, you know. After that there'll be lots more time. We can go anywhere, we can do anything. We could go to France. Have you been to Paris? Of course you haven't. I would show you Paris. It would give me joy to show you Paris, Maura. Imagine, you in Paris, you'd be the most beautiful girl in the entire city."

"I can't go to Paris with you," she said, speaking softly but emphatically. "I'm not a prostitute, I'm a working girl."

"My God, I didn't say you were a prostitute," said Kevin.

"I have to get to work," she said, standing up, so that he was forced to do the same.

"Please, you're not going to be angry with me again, are you? I want to see you. You're not going to just walk out on me again, just like before? It's not being fair to me, can't you see that?"

"Thank you for all your help," she said. "But you really must go now. I have to change, and I have to get to work."

"You're crazy," he said. "Do you know that you're crazy?" He still believed that the right word or phrase would send her gratefully to her knees, begging him to stay, admitting that he was far too good for her but that she wanted to be with him, to be his lover. But he held himself back from saying something worse. He had not found her after all this time to lose her in a fit of pique. She wanted to go to work—he would stand back and let her. Perhaps it was the aftermath of the abortion that was making her act so ridiculously. He knew where she lived. He could come back in a day—or, better yet, in a month and a day. She would miss him, and what he had to offer.

"If that's what you want, I'll go. But let me leave you my card. If there's anything I can do for you, let me know. Please."

He stopped himself from kissing her hand, and instead grabbed her shoulders and brought her lips to his. He kissed her mouth, and when she didn't respond, he let go of her and stepped back. Then he nodded briskly to her and walked out of the dreadful room.

Maura closed the door behind him and waited until she could no longer hear his descending steps. For a half-moment she regretted his leaving. He was kind, she told herself. She had never realized how kind he truly was.

But what was she thinking? Just as clear as his kindness was the fact that he still regarded her as a woman he could purchase. He had paid for her abortion, and an hour later was telling her he'd like to take her to Paris. He wanted to pay for her apartment, her clothes, for her person. Maura resolved to put the handsome young man out of her mind. He had not redeemed himself, she reminded herself. He had still not understood that she was not for sale.

Maura changed her clothes, wondering when she'd get a chance to wash them. She needed to buy soap as well as food before she returned to the fifth floor. There was a cold-water tap in the hallway outside her door, and she ran some water into her tin basin and returned to her room to wash her face and neck and hands. There was no mirror in the room, and her hair felt wild and dirty to the touch. But Kevin Vane somehow found her beautiful, and Maura resolved that Marandino would find her appealing enough to give her back her job.

Maura took the streetcar from her corner, remembering to ask for a transfer to the Elevated on the West Side. A gentleman on the train took off his hat when she entered the car, and Maura felt better. There was a difference between looking pretty enough for the foreman to be charitable and simply accepting the favors of a rich man. Maura knew that if she could get her job back, she would do well at it. She would learn to be fast and accurate, and she would be strong enough to spend her evenings in school. She could go forward in life, on her own steam.

Afraid of being disappointed, she built her fantasy block by block as she walked from the train to the factory. Her friends were there, Minnie and Jenny, and they would urge Marandino to hire her back. All the other girls would be for her, too, she imagined, and Marandino would have to give in to their combined desires. Maura would be welcomed back, and she'd do such a good job that soon she'd be making four-fifty, then five dollars. Soon she'd have enough saved to send more money to her mother in Ireland.

She hoped that if Marandino refused to hire her, she wouldn't rush back to look at Kevin's card and send him a request for money. How could he have imagined that a factory girl made fifteen dollars a week? Or even ten? The sum was so ludicrous that as she walked through the door to the factory it was all she could do to keep from laughing.

Marandino saw her at once.

It was just after the lunch break. There was the terrible feeling that the only break of the day was over, and that all that could be looked forward to was the closing bell, so many hours away. The smell from the glue factory downstairs didn't bother her now, nor did the heat, nor the noise of the machines, nor the glare of the gas jets. There, between Minnie and Jenny, both of whom looked up at her with wondering eyes, was a machine, her machine, without an operator.

"What's so funny, Irish?" said Marandino.

Maura reined in her smile. There was nothing funny about Kevin's thinking these girls were paid ten dollars or more. It explained why there were so many brothels in the city, why men like Kilgallen were able to flourish. "Nothing, sir," she said. "Only that I'm glad to be back to work."

"That's pretty funny, Irish. You don't show up for work Saturday, Monday, Tuesday, and you come walking in here Wednesday afternoon ready to get right back to it. What do you think this is, a home for wayward girls?"

"I was sick, sir," said Maura. "Didn't the others tell you?"

"Well, they said you was here Saturday and went home sick. I know all about it. Ruined the morning for me, if you want to know the truth. And Saturday's never any damn good because you all get paid on Friday and you're all still half pissed from Friday night. You don't look sick to me."

"Well, I was. I would like to come back to work, if it's all right with you, sir."

"It ain't all right with me, Irish. You cost me too much already. You got everyone too upset to work on Saturday, then I got to hire someone else on Monday because you ain't here again—even with Sunday to rest all day, for the love of God— and she ain't no better than you. All thumbs and whining all the time, can hardly speak English. Jesus, I got rid of *her* yesterday. I hired a new girl yesterday afternoon to come in today, and she ain't even here. I don't want to hire nobody who don't appreciate this job."

"But I do appreciate it, Mr. Marandino, sir," said Maura.

"You sure as hell never showed *me* no appreciation, girl."

"I'm sorry, sir."

"I'll bet you're sorry," he said, looking at her green eyes, at the pale young face. "Jesus, what am I thinking? I'm too damned good, I am."

"Please, sir," said Maura, "I just want a chance to work. I'll never miss another day. I swear it."

"I don't know," said Marandino. "I just don't know."

"Please," said Maura. She would have gotten down on her knees if she'd thought it would help. And she would have driven a stake through his heart rather than be sent back on the streets without a job, without a trade. "I'm begging you, sir. Give me another chance. I won't be sick again."

"Okay," he said finally, looking up and down her thin frame as if it now belonged to him, for four dollars a week. "You can get back to work. I'll even give you a half-day today if you really move it, see? I mean move it, now!"

"Thank you, Mr. Marandino," she said.

As she turned around to go to her table, the foreman smacked her backside with a satisfied laugh. But she didn't care. In a moment she was sitting on the bench, smiling back at Minnie and Jenny. Never stopping their work, they asked her how she felt, if it was over, if she was herself again.

"I'm fine," said Maura, grabbing a handful of unfinished handkerchiefs. She slammed on the power lever and smoothed out the cloth beneath the presser foot. There was no baby growing within her, the smell of the glue from the first-floor factory didn't make her nauseous, and she felt rested and strong and free. She had a job, she had a room to sleep in that night, and she owed Marandino nothing more than good skilled work. This she would give him. For the rest of that day, Maura thought of nothing but work, giving all her concentration, all her attention to the machine, to the factory that would sustain her, that would define her place in the world.

# PART SIX

## The Type-Writer

# ❧ CHAPTER ❧ NINETEEN

Maura learned to sew.

In a month she was producing fancy handkerchiefs, their seams flawless, as fast as Jenny, and faster than Minnie. In two months she was transforming muslin and lace into piles of frilly underwear. She learned to concentrate all her attention on the point of the jumping needle, so that the ache in her neck or her back wouldn't distract her with a twitch or a shudder and ruin five minutes of painstaking work.

Maura kept thinking that her aches and pains were the products of inexperience. One day, she imagined, her body would have become so used to hunching over her machine that it would no longer rebel at its treatment. She was so glad to be feeling stronger, and not nauseous, that the fatigue and aching muscles she took home every night seemed like the smallest part of an illness that would soon fade to nothingness. But she was wrong about this. All the girls, from the youngest to the oldest, felt the pains. They all sat at their machines from eight o'clock in the morning until noon, and then from twenty-five past noon till six o'clock. There was no other way to sew accurately, and speedily, than by hunching forward, with perfect concentration, squinting through the glare of the gas jets at the dancing needle, hands tense, pulling the fabric tight, right knee prepared to shut off the power lever at a moment's notice.

By nine o'clock in the morning, everyone's body craved a minute of rest. By ten o'clock, backs begged to be stretched out,

necks yearned to be massaged. By eleven o'clock, the muscles
about the squinting eyes had tightened every face at the worktables; it looked as if everyone was either smiling insanely, or
leering, or frowning, or twisting her mouth in agony.

At twelve, when the machines were shut off, there was little
joy at the short break. Lunches were consumed, conversations
started up, romantic novels glanced at. But everyone was dis-
pirited. The morning had been so long, and everyone knew how
much longer the afternoon would be. It was almost as if the
lunch break reminded everyone of how much more time remained to be lived through.

Even the final bell at six o'clock had its sadness. There was
only a long walk or a miserable crowded ride on a streetcar to
look forward to. By seven o'clock, most of the girls would either
be home or at a grocery store or pushcart selling bruised fruit
at cheap prices. And everyone seemed to live up countless stairs,
in dingy flats without sufficient ventilation, with smoking oil
lamps, with the smells of a thousand adjacent tenants and their
troops of squealing infants. Only two of the twenty girls were
married, and both of these had babies kept in a charity nursery
and husbands who never came home. The rest lived like Maura
or Minnie, in miserable single rooms at the tops of tenements, or
like Jenny, surrounded by family and boarders in a miserable
succession of crowded, dark spaces. Home meant only a chance
to peel a potato, drink weak tea, look out a cracked window at
scenes of desolation, listening to the roar of the elevated trains
until it was time to sleep. It was difficult to say whether it was
better to live alone in an unfriendly rooming house, trying to
linger more than two minutes over a scanty meal without conversation, or with a crowded family, where every move one made
would be monitored, and commented on, by a sibling or a parent
or a boarder.

Friday was the most awaited day. It was payday.

Friday made Thursday endurable, even lent a tinge of hope to
bleak Wednesday. At six o'clock on Friday, Mr. Barker would
appear, always nattily dressed, always enjoying the feeling of
power that paying the girls gave him. Marandino, the foreman,
would have enjoyed paying the girls himself; but as it was the

factory owner's prerogative, Marandino made it up to himself by letting the machines run a minute or two after six, or demanding a better and longer period of sweeping and mopping after the final bell. Like the owner, the foreman looked at the wages as gifts, as largesse bestowed by a master. After all, Marandino had the right to fire anyone he pleased during the week, without paying her for the days she'd put in since the previous payday. And Barker could suddenly announce that all four-dollar-a-week girls were going to get three-seventy-five, and no one could demand the extra quarter. Owner and foreman both knew that there was an enormous class of young girls to draw from, products of huge, impoverished families, immigrants from Europe's poorest countries, or refugees from failed farms in New England and upstate New York. These desperate girls were joined by hordes of orphans, runaways, abandoned wives between the ages of twelve and twenty, forced into the lowest types of work by the masses of unemployed men and boys, by black sharecroppers up from the South, by broken men who spoke no English and were willing to work for next to nothing so that their children would have something to eat.

Most of the girls accepted this state of affairs. No one liked the notion that their six full days of work were granted to them as a boon from a benevolent despot, and that their wages were dropped in their hands as if they were beggars. But all of them knew what it was like to be hungry, without money, without hope of food. All of them knew the haunted faces of the unemployed, of tramps and beggars and derelicts. Four dollars a week wasn't much, and the work wasn't easy; but it was far easier than the laundry, and it paid a dollar more than that hellish place.

If Friday was the most awaited day, Saturday was the happiest. The anxiety over whether or not they'd be paid, and how much of their four dollars might be deducted for damaged materials, was ended for a while. Each girl had her money, and at the end of Saturday they'd be let out, free to roam the shops, the streets, the ice-cream parlors. Saturday night was wild with the released tensions of six days of work: Music halls, dance halls, social clubs rioted with the youthful working class, so

pleased at being able to put down a nickel for a beer, to smoke
a cigarette, to get into bed past midnight and sleep till the middle
of the next day.

Not all the girls in Maura's factory went out dancing and
drinking and smoking on Saturday nights. Some, like Jenny,
were forbidden to go out by strict parents. Others, like Katie
and Lucinda, were already too tired and jaded at twenty to give
a thought to anything but getting to bed after the heaviest meal
of the week. But Minnie went out, sometimes with Mary and
Angela from the shop, sometimes with a nice young man from
her rooming house who never so much as tried to kiss her—and
never so much as paid for a cup of tea for her, either.

The girls who lived alone had to contend with the problem
of shopping, especially if they planned to go out Saturday night.
A small percentage of lucky workers were let out of their factories at half-past four on Saturdays, and this group converged
with others let out at five, five-thirty, and then finally the largest
group, at six, to create a mad crowding at every shop and cart
and stall in the poorer sections of the city. Most stores stayed
open late to accommodate the workers. Maura couldn't understand how anyone found the strength to first go up five flights
of stairs with a quart of potatoes, a loaf of bread, a container of
milk, and a string of sausages at seven-thirty at night, and then
begin to get dressed to go out for the evening.

Of course, this was partly due to the fact that Maura, more
than any of the other girls in the factory, had no desire to run
riot on Saturday night.

Only a week after she'd gone back to work at the factory, the
trial of Moses Pollack—the Hebrew who'd murdered Kilgallen—
began. All the papers ran lurid headlines: WHITE SLAVERS
THRIVE IN NEW YORK, and PROCURERS TORTURE IMMIGRANT
GIRLS, and POLLACK A HERO TO ENEMIES OF SIN. Kilgallen's
history as a procurer was presented in black and white, and
the testimony was reported everywhere for all the city to read.
Church groups, who had been publishing unread pamphlets on
the white slave trade for the past twenty-five years, attended the
trial, appeared as witnesses, and demanded Pollack's acquittal.
A Jewish benevolent society marched on the courthouse, and

sermons raged from every pulpit in the city to let Moses Pollack free.

During all this time, Maura expected Kevin Vane to appear on her doorstep, top hat in hand, apology prepared on his lips, begging her forgiveness.

But the young man didn't come.

April gave way to May, and the New York summer arrived six weeks early, bringing sticky heat to the factory and sleepless nights to Maura's top-floor room, the hottest in the house. Moses Pollack was acquitted, and carried out into the streets on the shoulders of his supporters. But still Kevin Vane didn't come back to her room, didn't send her a note, didn't acknowledge that he had been wrong. All Maura had of him was his beautifully printed personal card—his name in black letters in the center, his parent's Fifth Avenue address in the lower right-hand corner.

In truth, she knew as little of him as he did of her. And in the workaday world, where each girl had her romantic hero, bold and dashing and very rich, secreted behind eyes wearied by squinting at the jumping needle, it was not so strange that Maura's mind began to refute the indisputable fact of Kevin's insensitivity. As the heat and humidity increased with each passing day, as the trial of Moses Pollack finished and began to recede in the distance, as Maura's confidence at the sewing machine became less of a novelty and the work more of a disheartening drudgery, it was no wonder that Kevin Vane began to be transformed in her memory. While the other girls had their books and newspaper stories about the rich, Maura actually knew the son of Edward Vane, one of the two or three richest men in the city of New York. She knew Kevin Vane very well, in fact: He was kind, he was handsome, and he loved her. This she told herself at the sewing machine, as it became more and more apparent that she would never have anything to do with him again.

It wasn't impossible to live as if the months of prostitution had never happened. The noise of the machines made conversation difficult, and one had to be very skilled to talk and work at the same time. It was far easier to dream. Let the body go to rack and ruin at the task of sewing; all the while the mind could drift to lands of riches, lives of ease. Often Maura found herself believing the story she had told to her friends at the factory: She had been pregnant when she'd arrived in America, already a widow. She knew nothing about men, save what she had experienced from her poor husband, dead in the crossing to America.

And Kevin Vane—how did she know Kevin Vane? She just knew him, she told herself, trying to dream away the way they had met. Besides, no one at the factory knew about the rich young man. Only Jenny's brother and mother had seen Ginny, and no one from the Newman family would be so indiscreet as to ask how the modest little Irish girl knew such a flamboyant prostitute.

And so Maura was looked on by most of the other girls as a quiet young widow, too prudish to join the fun-lovers on Saturday nights, even if Jenny and Minnie suspected that their friend knew much more than the others imagined. Maura shopped with Minnie sometimes, and occasionally they'd go to a dairy restaurant under the Elevated on Third Avenue and talk softly over coffee and rolls and butter. Jenny brought her home more than once to share in a Sunday dinner with her family, where everyone would ask her about Ireland, about the life she'd left behind.

Maura didn't open up to either of these friends: The story of her time in the house on Spring Street, and in the posh Tenderloin brothel, was locked within her. In the months since she'd left that life, she'd become more and more horrified at what she'd experienced, so she either denied the experience totally, or let it come back to her only when she lay down at night. Like most victims, she'd begun to see her own suffering as humiliating, something she must hide, as if she were the one responsible for the horror.

Thus, in the space of two months, Maura had created a new life for herself, a new identity. She worked six days a week, traveled home by train and on foot, ate a simple meal, went to sleep, and slept like the dead. Though she had plans—to go to school, to save money, to better herself—for the time being, these were kept in abeyance. The factory work shaped her. The drudgery had its compensations: In some part of her consciousness, it was like a punishment for her sins. The repetitive, concentrated work brought her back to earth. She was reminded of her dreams of the New World, and now understood them as absurd, as simple girlish vanity. The work that all the others accepted, the long hours, the lack of rest—this was her lot, and she accepted it too, for the time being, letting her muscles ache like those of all the others, letting her aspirations suffocate into the same nothingness like those of all the other girls.

"When are we going to try the night school, Maura?" asked Jenny, time and again, reminding Maura of her promise to go there with her. But Maura was too tired. She had to eat, didn't she? When were they supposed to go to school anyway? Someone had to buy food, prepare it, and then she needed sleep for the long day at work. No, she wasn't ready for night school yet, she thought. It was enough just to keep up with the work, with climbing the stairs to the fifth floor at night, with saving eighty cents a week out of food and transportation expenses so she could buy herself a summer-weight dress.

"You can go yourself if you're so anxious, then," said Maura.

"Hey, I'm not going to let nobody make a jerk of me all by myself," said Jenny.

The free night school had a terrible reputation among the factory girls. All the teachers were old ladies, with iron-gray hair and pince-nez glasses, and they hated all the immigrants, and all their children, and all the native-born who couldn't speak like perfect ladies and gentlemen. But this was not what prevented Maura from making good her promise to Jenny and to herself to go to school. She was simply not ready to leap into another sphere in life. In the space of a year she'd been virgin, wife, widow, whore. She was comfortable with these girls for the moment, comfortable in sharing their hardships. About the only time she broke out of her modest, complacent shell was when Marandino bothered one of the youngest girls with his attentions: a pat, or a squeeze, or a fleeting touch.

"Sure this isn't a brothel you're running here, Mr. Marandino," she'd say in a loud voice that always surprised the others.

"What's it your business, Irish?" he'd say, growing angrier and angrier each time she managed to bring the attention of the twenty girls to his petty lechery.

"My business is working the machine, sir," said Maura. "But

I know well enough that it's not *your* business to be bothering the girls."

"Am I bothering you, Irish?"

"No, sir."

"Then shut the hell up and get back to work, or you'll be out of here on your ass, see? You sure sing a different tune since I let you have your job back. You sure do, girl."

But he didn't fire her on the spot. He had gotten it into his head that the pretty Irish girl was jealous—that she stood up for the other girls because she wanted his attentions all to herself. And not the kind he gave the others; Marandino fancied that Maura wanted him to take her to dinner, to the theater, to buy her sweets and flowers and tell her he loved her. Well, if that was what she wanted, maybe he'd just do it one day, just for the hell of it. One time when his wife and kids were off to Coney Island for the day, that is.

"Come to dinner tonight," Jenny said to Maura one hot morning at the end of May.

"What do you mean? It's Tuesday, Jenny."

"It doesn't matter. You'll get back fast enough. Jake is home. He'll get you back all right, you know that."

"I don't think so," said Maura.

"He's not going to talk about night school," said Jenny. "I'll see to that, okay?"

Maura had seen Jake only once since the abortion. She was certain he was indifferent to her, and she felt uncomfortable in his presence, as if he were a link to the months of prostitution. It was Jake who'd brought Ginny to her, who'd made the abortion possible. And his cockiness, his great good looks, his large plans always made everyone else around him feel small. He had spent the last five weeks traveling with his pack of household goods into the hamlets and villages upstate, and Jenny was sure that he was dying to see Maura.

"If he's just come home, it's not right for me to be there too. Your mother and father will want him to themselves."

"It's what Jake wants," said Jenny slyly, but Maura simply shook her head at this. It was all in Jenny's mind, Maura felt sure. Her brother was interested in one thing: making a million dollars. Even his lectures to Jenny about going to night school were part of his larger philosophy of life. He wanted everyone to be like himself, pushing and striving and dreaming.

That night, when Maura went home to her lonely supper of fruit and bread and tea, there was a letter waiting for her from Ireland. By some miracle of communication, the letter had traveled intact across the ocean, and gone from Mrs. Saunders's boardinghouse to her new address without mishap, in the space of five weeks. Her mother had touched this paper with her hands, with her lips, she'd held it to the clear air of County Kerry in the month of April. Now, not yet June, in New York City, Maura tore open the envelope and recognized the dear handwriting, spidery as a child's.

Her mother thanked her for the ten dollars. It was a grand gift, a tremendous gift, and she hoped that Maura and Patrick could afford it. She had not spent a cent of it, she said. There was enough to eat, thank God, and one never knew how bad things might become. Things were not good now, she was sorry to say. She didn't want to burden Maura, but the truth was Bill Dooley was sick. The truth was Maura's poor dad was dying, and it wasn't easy dying, it was long and slow and full of sadness.

Maura put down the letter and listened to the latest of a series of early-evening trains pulling into the station. There was more in the letter, much more, but she didn't want to read it all at once. She felt an urgency about her own situation that she must think out at once. It was almost June, and she needed to get to night school, she needed to learn to be an office worker and get a good job very fast. By September, perhaps, or October, she might be working in an office, she might be making five dollars a week. And if she could somehow learn to be a type-writer, how wonderful that would be! She could be paid as much as eight dollars a week. She could find an apartment for the two of them, her mother and herself. Ma could cook, and Maura would work, and the two of them would be together and console each other for the loss of Ireland.

Her father was dying, Maura read again, and she tried to feel something for him, for the man who had given her life, but

the most she could feel was an emptiness. It was all she could
find to replace her deep hatred for the man. He had beaten her
and threatened her and misused her, but with great effort she
could clear her mind of a hundred incidents and try to imagine
his face in repose, in death. Her father was dying, she read on
the page, and she found a kernel of sadness there in the fact
that he was her father but had never shown her love, shown
her kindness. Her sadness, she realized, was not for him, not
for his death, but for her own life, her own troubles. She walked
to the grimy cracked window and looked down at the train platform, the hub of so many struggling lives. She was through
feeling sorry for herself, she thought. Her father was dying, and
he would soon be dead, and she would mourn for him in whatever way she felt when she heard the news. But his death meant
that her mother would be free. She would not belong to the house-
ful of children who despised her. Her mother would be free to
join Maura in America, and it was this fact, more than anything, that made it so difficult to grieve for her ailing father.

There were other things in the letter that troubled Maura.
Her mother had asked about the health of Brendt and Patrick.
She had asked what sort of job Maura had taken that she could
send so much money to her old mother. She had asked if Brendt
had written to Grady Madigan. Why hadn't Patrick written to
his father, and why hadn't Brendt even added her name to the
bottom of Maura's own letter? She hoped that nothing was
wrong, and that no one was angry with her. She should tell
Brendt that she was not angry at her for having fallen in love
with a bad man. Maura's mother signed her own name with a
flourish, adding that she prayed for all three of them every day,
prayed for a time when they would all be together in health
and peace and prosperity.


Maura and Jenny joined a night-school class ten days later. The
class was free. Its teacher, Mrs. Partridge, drew a supplemental
salary from an amalgam of New York charities, and the city's
public-school system donated the use of a classroom on Henry
Street, on the Lower East Side. Twenty-five pupils showed up

for the first class, and there were thirty-five desks; but the desks were meant for grade-school children, and these were twenty-five adults. At eight o'clock, Mrs. Partridge entered, and found the room full of immigrants standing or leaning against the tiny desks. Many of them were eating the remains of a quick dinner. Most of them were talking, and the disharmonious mix of a dozen unfamiliar languages grated on Mrs. Partridge's sensibilities.

"You will remain standing for the Pledge of Allegiance," she said, by way of introduction. This was her classroom by day, as well as by night, and unconsciously she was reaching for the long wood pointer in its resting place under the blackboard. The class turned to her at once, quiet and cowed. She raised her pointer.

"I pledge allegiance," she said, pointing to her chest, and then to the class, waiting for them to answer. "*I pledge allegiance*," she repeated steadily.

Someone spoke up, an unkempt Russian Jew: "I pledge allegiance," he said, and a few others joined in: ". . . allegiance."

"That's right, boys and girls," said Mrs. Partridge, looking at them bitterly—the Poles, the Russians, the Greeks, the Jews, the Irish, the Italians, the Germans—the immigrants whom she had to teach the rudiments of civilized behavior. "Repeat after me. This is the famous 'Pledge of Allegiance' written by Francis Bellamy in 1892, and something that you will all have by heart before too long. Listen and repeat, and be grateful for this country and its flag." The pointer reached up to the American flag hanging behind her back over the top right corner of the board.

"I pledge allegiance to the flag of the United States of America and to the republic for which it stands, one nation, indivisible, with liberty and justice for all."

Mrs. Partridge kept them at it for forty-five minutes. She sat herself down after a few moments, but she kept them standing: It was better for maintaining discipline, and these immigrants needed all the discipline they could get. The cacophony of accents grew more and more confident as she kept them going at the unwieldy, majestic sentence, over and over again, never forgetting to point to the flag toward which they faced.

"You may sit down," she said at last.

Jenny, at fifteen, was the youngest one in the room, and one of the smallest. But even her knees were jammed up against the tiny desk's underside. The backless workbench in the factory was more comfortable. Like the others in the room, she'd been up at six, at work since eight. Mrs. Partridge called the roll of foreign names.

"Isaac Wolinsky!"

"Yes, madam, yes?"

"You need only say 'Present, Mrs. Partridge.' This isn't Poland, and we've very simple here, as you'll soon learn."

"Present, Mrs. Partridge."

"Jenny Newman!"

"Present, Mrs. Partridge."

"Speak up, girl. Take the marbles out of your mouth."

"Present, Mrs. Partridge!"

"Michael O'Malley!"

"Present, Mrs. Partridge."

"You have two choices, O'Malley. You can either remove that stupid smirk from your face or you can leave this classroom forever. Is that quite clear?"

"Yes, ma'am."

"It had better be. Maura O'Connell!"

"Present, Mrs. Partridge."

"Two Irish in a row. This must be my lucky day. Ah—Casimir Antonovich. That's more like it. Speak up, Antonovich!"

But Maura had gotten to her feet. "Mrs. Partridge?" she said.

"Have I called on you, girl?"

"No, Mrs. Partridge. But I would like to speak, if you please. These desks are very small. Isn't there another classroom in the building where the desks are bigger?"

Mrs. Partridge smiled, enjoying the silent anticipation in the class. Here was gentle rebellion, and the perfect opportunity to quash any more dangerous rebellion in the future.

"O'Connell, do you know what a roll call is?"

"No, Mrs. Partridge."

"A roll call is what you have just interrupted. During the calling of the roll of names in this class, I expect silence from each and every one of you, regardless of your previous homelands, no matter how primitive. This is a civilized city in the greatest country in the world, and the sooner you learn to follow its rules, the sooner you will be able to participate in its bounty. Is that quite clear, O'Connell?"

"I'm only thinking that we're factory workers here, ma'am, and our backs ache bad enough as it is. And if there are bigger children who use bigger desks somewhere in this building—"

Maura's speech was cut off by the pointer smashing down on the teacher's desk. "You may stand in the far corner, girl. Face the corner and say nothing further until I speak to you. Go. To the corner."

Maura had to hold herself back from walking out the door. What did this nonsense have to do with getting an office job? The electric lights brightened the hot sticky room, but everything else about the school promised disappointment. Everyone here was a victim. There was no one here that wasn't exhausted. Everyone wanted the same thing: a little knowledge, and not for the soul but for a chance to nourish the body. This teacher didn't seem to promise anything but a reinforcement of what they all already knew from the factory: Don't question, don't challenge, don't step out of line.

Class was dismissed at 9:15, after the roll call was completed and the students instructed to purchase notebooks and pencils for the next class. Maura was allowed to turn round and approach Mrs. Partridge at her desk.

"All right, O'Connell. You have earned yourself a homework assignment. Take this, put it in alphabetical order, and make me twenty-five copies, one for each of you. If it's not neat, you're going to have to do it over. If you don't want to do it, don't bother to come to class. Is that quite clear?"

"Yes, Mrs. Partridge," said Maura. She smiled at the teacher, taking solace in a sudden epiphany. Of course she would do the absurd assignment. She would stand in the corner and sit at the desk of a child. This woman had a power over her, but it was an ephemeral power, based on the scanty knowledge that she possessed. Mrs. Partridge knew a few things more than Maura did: She spoke in a fashion that was acceptable in America, she

knew the Pledge of Allegiance, undoubtedly she knew other
things as well—how to write a business letter, how to speak on
a telephone, how to fill out an application for an office worker's
job. But she was stupid. She was petty. She was mean-spirited,
and therefore not to be feared. This was Maura's sudden understanding, and it supported her well throughout the night-school
experience. She was eighteen, and not sufficiently educated
for the job she wanted. This woman was older and could teach
her what she needed to know. But there was no reason to fear
her; Mrs. Partridge was not her better. And every slight and
insult confirmed this feeling. In a country where Mrs. Partridge
was given the sacred task of teaching, Maura could be anything
she wanted to be.

The class met Monday through Thursday nights for seventy-
five minutes, and led to a Certificate of Completion. Maura
couldn't imagine what one was to have completed, other than
the year that the course ran. Homework was invariably copy-
work: Writing out the Gettysburg Address in script, and then
printing it, and then memorizing it for recital was typical of a
Partridge assignment. But Maura knew that she wasn't hanging
on for the silly certificate. Even with all the impediments that
Mrs. Partridge threw in her way, she was learning. Her spelling
improved; Mrs. Partridge made a particular mockery of anyone
in the polyglot class who confused the three words "there,"
"their," and "they're." Maura struggled with a conscious effort
to strip the lovely Irish lilt from her speech, and an unconscious
effort to preserve it. She learned to mimic her teacher's syntax,
rather than that of the girls in the factory. Mrs. Partridge affected a hundred mannerisms of the gentlewoman she wished to
be, and Maura imitated the way she sat in a chair, the way she
handed over a book or a paper, the way she held a pencil in her
plump right hand.

Though Maura was perfectly happy to maintain the frosty
atmosphere between herself and her teacher, Mrs. Partridge
couldn't help but be flattered by Maura's attentiveness to the
lessons she taught. By August there were fifteen left in the class,
and by September only ten. Besides Jenny and Maura, there
were three Russian Jews who struggled on despite Mrs. Par-

tridge's indifference to their small grasp of English, and five single representatives of Italy, Poland, Greece, Germany, and France, whose English consisted almost entirely of phrases relating to the use of the Second Avenue Elevated.

"I can't keep up with it," said Jenny after class one night. "I'm thinking of just forgetting the whole thing, see? It's no use for nothing."

"What do you mean?" said Maura. "You're the one who wanted me to go, and now you're going to leave me all by myself?"

"What do you mean by yourself? You got old Partridge, ain't you? She'll keep you company. She knows a good head when she sees one, and she sees you real good."

"Can I help it if Mrs. Partridge is easing up on me, Jenny?" said Maura, but she knew her protestations were in vain. It was early September, and the summer's miserable heat had not yet passed. Tensions in class and in the factory were higher than usual. Not only Jenny took Maura to task for her proficiency in class; Minnie and the other girls were quick to see that she was learning manners and ways that were foreign to them. Carrying a grammar book was enough to incite half the girls in the factory. More than one began to imitate her straight-backed walk, copied from prim Mrs. Partridge.

"When are you leaving us, Irish?" Marandino would say to her, catching her studying during the lunch break. "Any day now you're going to be too good for the likes of us, right? You going to work for the Morgan bank? They're looking for red-heads, I hear. You just got to work on the accent, so you can answer the phone real snooty, see? It's the snoot that's everything in the business world. You just got to work on keeping it high in the air."

Marandino's remarks bothered her much less than those of the girls. They acted as if she had betrayed them, and in a sense she had. Mrs. Partridge spoke to her after class, encouraging her to work on her penmanship, to think of studying shorthand, to save her pennies for some new clothes so she could make a good appearance in the business world. Maura told herself that there was nothing wrong in wanting to better herself.

She wasn't doing it to leave Jenny and Minnie and the others behind; she was doing it to bring her mother over to America, and to try to create a decent life for the two of them. Still, when Jenny quit the night school in October, the daily factory ordeal grew a hundred times worse. Maura felt excluded from the grumbling of the others, as if she were beginning to believe what the girls said of her—that she was uninterested in the factory because she would not be staying there long.

One day toward the middle of October, she felt particularly awful. She had not had a letter from her mother in more than a month. She began to feel sure that her mother had seen through the letters she'd been sending to Ireland, detailing Brendt's adventures as a schoolteacher out in California and Patrick's work in the West Side rail yards. She had a terrible dream that her father had died, and that her mother, instead of following Maura to America, jumped off the same cliff that Brendt had so many months before. At work, the lovely cool weather that had brought even tempers back to the factory had been broken by a sudden hot spell. During the lunch break, Maura tried to interest Jenny in the latest work from class, but Minnie cut her short: "She ain't interested in that stuff, and neither is nobody here, see?"

"I wish you'd come too, Minnie, only to one class," said Maura.

"Look, Irish, why don't you mind your own business? I'm not asking you for nothing, so don't you ask me for nothing neither no more. I'm tired of you and your ladylike airs, okay? I'm just tired of it and I don't want to hear it, and that's the end of it."

This outburst from her friend and comrade of the worktable almost drove Maura to tears. That afternoon she was clumsy at the machine, and Marandino was loudly insulting to her, but no girl came to her defense. She tried to retreat into a fantasy as she concentrated her fingers on the cloth, her eyes on the needle, but the image she conjured of Kevin Vane was mocking. She felt as if she'd lost the goodwill of her friends and gotten nothing in return. Kevin had never gotten in touch with her again, and why should he? What was so special about her after all? She felt as if her prettiness were fading into obscurity, her strength and intelligence vanishing into thin air. With all her care, with all the trams she'd skipped, the meat and cheese she hadn't purchased, the newspapers she read only after they'd been discarded, she still had hardly any money saved. What if her father was dead? How could she possibly bring her mother to America? She hadn't even enough money for the steerage crossing, and she had long since sworn to herself that her mother would cross second-class, or she wouldn't come at all.

"Maura," said Jenny, toward the end of the day, pressing Maura's knee so that she would know to turn off her machine. "Are you all right, Maura?"

"Yes," she said. But she was not all right. Maura could feel the tears running down her cheeks, and she could do nothing to stop them. Jenny took her hand and squeezed it, told her that it was okay, not to take it like that, that everything was going to be fine. But Minnie, on Maura's other side, never said a word, just kept her machine running, aloof in her anger.

When the final bell rang, Maura was the first out of her chair and the first out of the loft. She didn't even have the strength to wait for Jenny, to thank her. She wanted to be alone, on the street, where she could cry in the presence of no one who knew her name.

"Maura!" said a voice from behind her back, a male voice that she didn't at first recognize. She didn't want to turn, she tried to hold back her tears, but Jake Newman caught up with her and took hold of her arm, and she began to cry in earnest, she began to cry as if she had lost every friend she'd ever had in the world.

"Okay, one leg after the other," he said. "Step wide, move it. We want to get out of here, right? You don't want to see none of those other mugs, right? Hurry, hurry, let's go. Jake Newman's buying you supper, and you can cry all you want, you can drip in your soup, and I ain't going to care."

Jenny's brother got her off Franklin Street and into the mob of pedestrians shuffling uptown on Hudson Street.

"I can't afford to go out for supper," said Maura finally, catching her breath as she dried her eyes and nose on the thin cotton sleeve of her shirtwaist.

"Hey, you deaf or something?" said Jake, his American speech comically leavened by a slight German accent. "I'm buying, I said, and all you got to do is appreciate it, see?"

He hadn't changed his clothes for this chance to meet her, she noticed, but she was warmed by his concern. In the months she and Jenny had been going to night school together, he'd show up afterward once every few weeks, and buy them ice cream, and escort first Maura, then his sister, home. Now, with all her friends in the factory growing cold toward her, she took Jake's offer with gratitude and noncomprehension, a boon she didn't quite deserve.

"I have school tonight," she protested weakly.

"Say—you ever been to Coney Island?" he asked, ignoring her words.

"No," said Maura. The famous resort on the ocean was all the girls talked about during the summer. It seemed everyone but her had gone there on Sundays, either to gape at the Ferris wheel or flirt with young men in the beer gardens along the boardwalk. But she had been too tired, too eager to study her lessons, too worried about spending money she needed to save. "I've always wanted to go."

It was mid-October, well past the end of the season, but the Culver Line still ran a few steamers from the Battery. Maura surrendered herself to Jake for the evening, leaning on his shoulder as he fought for a space for them on a downtown electric car, letting him place his arm about her shoulders as they sat on the open deck on the steamer to West Brighton. She thought of him as a brother, so unlike her own brothers back in Ireland, for Jake was always eager to help her, and never wanted anything in return.

"You're very tired," he said. "You can sleep for a bit. I'll wake you up in time for your eats."

But Maura didn't sleep. Jake kept showing her sights on the retreating downtown shoreline, and the sun was setting over the Hudson, and a delicious breeze woke her work-numbed senses. Jake told her about Coney Island in season: how ten million people came to its beaches every year, both rich and poor, flocking to pavilions and racetracks and hotels; how strong men drowned fighting the powerful undertow; how guest houses and cottages were rented to the rich for the entire miserably hot New York summer.

They were going to West Brighton, in the middle of Coney Island, because it tended to be the most lively after the close of the season. Before they landed, Jake asked her if she was quite awake, and when she said that she was, he brought his face close to hers and said, "This is going to be our evening, see? So I'm going to get Jenny's part of it out of the way. Jenny asked me to talk to you. That's how I came to be there."

"What did Jenny want?"

"Jenny never knows what she wants. She ain't so fast as her big brother—not yet. But she knows she ain't been so friendly to you lately, and she knows you ain't been so happy, and she feels bad about it and she wants you to know it, see?"

"She didn't have to quit night school."

"Sure she didn't, but she did. So don't give yourself a bellyache about it. She ain't sixteen yet, she can change. It was too much for her, but that ain't your fault. I'm too much for my pa, but I don't take that to heart. It ain't my problem that I want more than he does."

"But she really asked you to talk to me?"

"I ain't making it up. I mean, I wanted to see you anyway— I got my own reasons. But Jenny asked me. She wanted me to see if you were okay. And she told me to tell you that Minnie likes you too. It's true. It's just that it's hard for her. She can't even read, Minnie, she never learned how, and she can't stand to hear you talking about night school when she can't even look at the newspaper."

Maura didn't dwell on what Jake could mean by saying he had his own reasons for wanting to see her. She was dazed by the fact that poor Minnie couldn't read, and began to formulate ways to approach her, to gain back her friendship so that she could teach her to read. No wonder Minnie had been so unhappy!

It had grown dark by the time they climbed up the steps to the boardwalk at West Brighton. Jake told her that the next stretch of beach, Manhattan Beach, was frequented by rich families in season, and for their amusement there were fireworks every night over the ocean, and the beach itself was lit by electricity. But he liked West Brighton best. Even now, off-season, the board-walk was crowded in the unusually warm mid-October weather. He walked with Maura to the rail overlooking the dark waves. Below, they could see the ghostly figures of a few walkers on the sand. Jake told her to try to imagine the beach, brilliant under a summer day's sun, with a hundred thousand people swarming over it in an endless variety of costumes.

"And every year it's going to be bigger, see?" said Jake. "That's one sure thing about New York—it's getting more and more crowded, and it ain't getting any cooler in the summertime."

They walked past the famous iron piers, each nearly a fifth of a mile in length, and the mammoth hollow elephant, which Jake told her was five stories high, with restaurants and dancing-rooms on each floor. But the elephant was closed for the season, as was the observation tower, and two out of three of the beer gardens and restaurants. Sandwiched between two closed restaurants was a small shop, also boarded up for the season, and Jake pulled Maura tighter to his side as they approached it. "How do you like it?" he said.

"It's wonderful," she said. "It's so lovely to walk near the side of the sea."

"Not that," said Jake. "This here." He pointed to the boarded-up shop, and Maura looked at it uncomprehendingly. "I got a twenty-year lease," he said. "Yesterday."

Laughing, Jake pulled her along to another boarded-up shop. "This here I got for twenty-five years. And one more—wait a minute, just a little." He showed her the last of his newly leased tiny shops. "Twenty-two years. Sixty bucks a year, Maura. They think of it like twenty bucks a month for the season, but listen to me, in twenty years these little dumps are going to be gold mines. And this is just the beginning."

Jake dragged her into a beer garden and sat her down in the enormous, nearly empty hall. A waiter brought them beer and "hot dogs," the New York sausage wrapped in a bun that Maura had always promised herself to taste. She found herself guiltily calculating what all this must be costing Jake: fifty cents for each of them for the round-trip steamer from the Battery, the double carfare from the factory to the steamer and back to her rooming house, thirty cents for the hot dogs, twenty cents for the beer; between the two of them, he'd end up paying out nearly half her week's wages.

"You know, everybody thinks I'm crazy because I ain't in school like you, and I spend so much time on the road, and I ain't got a girl friend or nothing. But look, I'm young. And if you don't do this when you're young, when're you going to do it? This is all we got, just a big ugly city and everybody trying to make a buck, and I don't want to be an old man without a pot, if you know what I'm saying. I don't want to be impolite in front of somebody I respect, see?"

Maura listened to Jake explain. He had a desire to spread out the numbers in his head before her. He had traveled five hundred miles, he had sold forty-two frying pans, he had bought up a cheap lot of wool cloth, he had sold seventy cans of stove polish he carried in his pack on consignment. "But I ain't stupid, see? I'm saving everything. I got three hundred dollars. Do you have any idea what that means? Do you know how much money that is, and how long it's taken me to put it togther?"

"Three hundred dollars," she repeated wonderingly. Why, it was sixty-five dollars to travel second-class from Ireland to America. It was twenty dollars to go like a slave in steerage. It was four dollars she got paid for working a sixty-hour week. It was three dollars a week they paid in the laundry. It was a dollar a week to sleep in her room at the top of a tenement. It was five cents for a bowl of coffee and three hard rolls on Canal Street.

Jake was twenty years old and he was rich, and she wanted to know how.

"Peddling," he explained. "I'm good at it. The ladies feel sorry for a poor boy with a heavy pack. Even the bad peddlers make five dollars a week. I can make that much in a day if I just keep on pushing, pushing."

Jake had saved everything, had spent nothing. He had gone to Coney Island and looked at the prospects for a store. At the end of every season, a few merchants always went out of business, and the owners of the stalls were often glad to lease the property at any price, just to have it off their minds for the

winter. By next summer, the owners of the stalls might have demanded eighty dollars a year for the leases. They might have
insisted on a five- or even a four-year lease. Jake would sell
hot dogs from one stall, souvenirs from another, soda pop
from a third. He'd put his sisters to work, even Jenny if she
wanted to get out of the factory, and he'd make a fortune,
or at least the beginning of a fortune.

"Are you finished with the hot dog? Forget the beer—you
don't like to drink it, I can see that. I'll get you a coffee." Jake
took her hand and pulled her excitedly from the beer garden.
The boardwalk was a little less crowded now, and the breeze
had picked up so that the scent of the sea embraced them. Maura
loved the weightless feeling that walking on the wood boards
gave her. The moon had risen, and the boardwalk's tall gas
lamps, and the hundred cigars burning like beacons in the mouths
of gentlemen, and a trio of police officers on bicycles equipped
with lanterns all seemed to merge into a fantasy of light and
freedom and promise. She asked Jake if they could walk out on
one of the piers, and he held her close and they walked far out
over the water, listening to the waves crashing on the rocks,
and Maura felt so happy for Jake, and happy for his having
shared his story with her. Jake would be rich, certainly. And if he
could save so much money, she could get an office job, she could
get paid enough to bring her mother over to America. In
America, all things were possible.

"Aren't you cold?" he asked her as they approached the wind-
swept edge of the pier.

"No, I feel grand. Sure there's nothing better than a breeze
from the sea, and the night air."

"You're very beautiful, Maura," he said suddenly, letting
go his hold about her shoulders and looking into her eyes.

Maura looked at him wonderingly. Every girl in the factory
who'd seen Jenny's brother had fallen in love with him at once.
If one of the two of them on the pier was beautiful, thought
Maura, it was he, not she.

"It is a little cold, actually," she said, turning to go back.

"I never got you that coffee," he said.

"No." She was glad that he didn't return his arm to that

brotherly position about her shoulders; she was becoming confused about his role in her life. How could he be interested in
someone like herself? A widow, without a penny, and one who
had gone through an abortion arranged by a whore.

They walked quickly back to the boardwalk. Jake bought her
coffee at one of the few open stalls, and as she drank it he
changed the drift of his conversation. He spoke about how
expensive it was for the restaurants to pay their help and their
rent on the boardwalk, and how the little stalls would undersell
them, selling hot dogs for a dime and beer for a nickel. And he
would use this same technique in other places. He had a dream
of putting stalls together in the cheapest parts of the city, creating a department store grander than Stewart's, but composed of a
hundred merchants, each in their own space, selling their own
merchandise at prices far below those of the uptown stores.
From all these merchants he'd get a percentage, and he'd one
day take his family out of that tenement and get them a house on
Manhattan Beach, near the water, with sea gulls screaming and
waves crashing and a bathroom and a sink for every single one
of them.

"I would like to know more about you, Maura," said Jake
suddenly.

"About me? There's not much to know." Once again the
uncertainty was raising, and, with it, fear. She didn't want to believe in this young man's attraction to her. She wasn't ready for
it, there was nothing she had done to merit it. "I'm a poor girl
trying to save some money and get an education, and one day
I'll send for my ma to come over."

"That's nice," he said, and his eyes showed her that he was
idealizing her, that he was creating worth for her out of some
irrelevant fantasy. "I want to know about your ma."

"Ma? She's very pretty. She has a garden, and she likes to
tend it. I don't know what you want to know."

"Everything," he said. "I don't understand you, I never did.
You seem like a kid, see? More than Jenny even, and she's
younger. But you're a widow. How old were you when you were
married? What was your husband like? What did he die of? I
mean, there's a lot I'd like to know, because it don't make any

sense. That you know that Ginny, a prostitute—all that. You seem like you're about fourteen and no one's ever kissed you, not on the lips. But you're a widow. You're eighteen, you know things, and I know what you went through when you learned you were pregnant. I'm sorry for talking like that, but I just have to know."

Maura didn't answer him. She didn't want to ask why he wanted to know. She asked if they could start walking back to where they could catch the steamer to New York. It was late, and she had work the next morning, and she was cold.

"Hey, finish your coffee first." He watched her drink it, the warmth spreading from her fingers to her cheeks as she cradled the cup in both hands and tipped it gently to her parted lips.

Later, when they were on the boat, he sat on a bench opposite her on the quiet, nearly deserted deck. "I hope you ain't sore for me asking a lot of questions, it's just that I like you, okay?"

"I'm not sore, Jake."

"I'm not ready for nothing, not me. I mean, like a girl friend. Look at me, I dress like a bum. I live on the road, or else in my folks' place, which is worse. I got money saved, sure, but it's all spoken for. I got to buy goods for the road, and I want to get off the road soon anyway. I got to rent some place, maybe on Canal, maybe on Fourteenth Street. I'm good at selling. And next summer—hey, next *spring* I'm going to open. As soon as it's a little warm, I open three stalls on the boardwalk, I put the Newman girls to work, and the money comes back like crazy. Maybe I'll have three stalls in the city then, too. I always go for the long lease, see? I figure it's got to be worth lots of bucks, because every year everything's going up. As soon as I get some real money, I start buying, not renting. That's the ticket, if you got any brains. What I'm saying to you is I'm kind of busy, but I'm busy for a good reason, and I wanted you to know that I think a lot about what I want for my life later on, too. When I'm older. More established."

It was very late when they arrived at the Battery, and Maura was tired. She watched Jake try to keep his eyes open as they speeded uptown in an empty electric car. If she'd been up since six, he must have been up since five. She tried to imagine him all cleaned up, dressed like Kevin Vane in a rich man's suit, a silk tie, a silk hat. At the Fourteenth Street stop she touched his shoulder because he seemed to be asleep, but he grabbed her hand immediately and smiled, fully awake. They had to walk a few blocks along the tenement-lined street, and now Maura did most of the talking. She thanked him for showing her Coney Island, for giving her Jenny's message, for buying her supper, for paying for her fare.

"You're going to live better than this one day," he told her when they'd come to the front door of the rooming house. Maura understood what he was saying: He wasn't so much giving her a proposal as making a statement of a future alliance. But when he took her in his arms and kissed her, she responded in kind. Not because of the late hour, or the walk so close to the edge of the sea, or the promise of being lifted off her feet in some nebulous future. Maura kissed Jake because she loved him at that moment. Not in the way she'd loved Patrick before he died, nor in the way she'd imagined romantic love to be. She loved him for the strength of his dream, and because it reminded her of how deep and strong her own dream was—how much it had in common with his, and how different it was, too.

It surprised her, this sudden rush of feeling, this sudden desire to bring his beautiful face close to hers, to hold him the way he held her, to want to stand with him in some place of shelter against the black night. But she pushed him back after a little while. "No," she said, and he understood nothing. He knew only that he had kissed her, and that she had kissed him, and that was enough for the moment. Maura would have liked to explain why she had kissed him, why she had wanted to stop.

"I'm going places," he said. "It's the truth, see? I'm going to be rich, and I'm going to make you happy."

Later that night, after the midnight train had come and gone, leaving her in peace until the five o'clock train would arrive, she found herself smiling. I'm going places too, she thought. And it's me who's going to make myself happy.

# ❧ CHAPTER ❧ TWENTY

The next day was Friday, payday, and all the girls had a happier look about them. Minnie was civil, telling Maura that she really hadn't meant any harm by what she'd said the day before. Maura responded by squeezing her friend's hand and kissing her cheek. "You saved my life, Minnie. You don't have to explain anything to me."

"I heard you skipped school last night," said Jenny, smiling at Maura as Marandino flicked on the main power switch and all the girls set their machines in motion.

"Sure it was nobody's fault but your own," said Maura.

"Where'd he take you to eat?" asked Minnie.

"He took her to Coney Island," said Jenny loudly over Maura's head to Minnie, through the growing noise of the machines.

"Coney Island in October? The guy must be in love. Nobody goes to Coney in October unless they're crazy for somebody, right? Hey, he ain't so bad to look at, Irish. He's even prettier than you."

Soon their concentration on their work stopped them from talking. Maura assumed that Jenny must have taken Minnie aside after work and told her how much Maura was suffering from the two of them. She felt tired from staying up late the night before, but far less troubled and anxious. Instead of feeling surrounded by a hostile environment, living only for the chance to break away from the machines and the noise and the unfriendly girls, she found something enjoyable about the morning.

Her back hurt, but it was not unbearable, and she took pleasure in the way her fingers remembered their tasks. Marandino managed to spend a few moments leaning on her shoulders, examining her work, but she shouted him off, and Minnie told him to go bother his wife.

At the lunch break, she chatted with Jenny and Minnie about Coney Island, and asked them if they'd like to join her for supper —there was no school on Friday evening. For the first time in weeks, she let herself be absorbed by the concerns of the girls about her—new "gentlemen friends," the massive unemployment in the city, the price of winter coats on Dumont Avenue, the best place to find remnants to sew into skirts and blouses.

All right, she told herself, she would leave this behind. But for the time that she was here, she would let their concerns be hers, their dreams be part of her own. No wonder there had been a current of feeling running against her. She had been guilty as charged. She had transported herself to a different sphere of existence, and in her heart had despised the pettiness, the lack of ambition and drive of the girls around her. Without thinking, she had put her nose up in the air, and they had been offended. All she had offered them was lectures on why they should be attending night school, as if her concerns were the only ones that had validity. She had been too blind to guess that poor Minnie couldn't even read.

The afternoon went swiftly. Jenny couldn't join her for supper, but Minnie said she'd be glad to. The weather had shifted suddenly, growing colder throughout the afternoon, but in the factory the machines and the proximity of so many workers kept everyone pleasantly warm. Everyone worked smoothly, anticipating the coming of Mr. Barker, with his little envelopes and lord-of-the-manor smile. Maura found herself thinking about Jake, wondering when he'd appear at the factory door once again. Saturday would fly by at the factory, thinking of the joy of a day's rest on Sunday. Perhaps she'd run down to Canal Street after work Saturday and buy a hat from one of the stalls. Minnie had promised to show her a shop on Delancey Street where factory-made shirtwaists could be bought at half-price. She had homework to do for class on Monday, but she knew she could speed through this on Sunday night. Maybe she and Jenny could take Jenny's little sisters off her mother's hands Sunday afternoon, and take the streetcar uptown to Central Park.

"His Highness is here early today," said Minnie in the late afternoon. Maura half turned to see Mr. Barker in serious conversation with Marandino. It was only four o'clock. Marandino shook his head, seemed to contradict the factory owner, but quickly did an about-face as Barker reprimanded him. Maura couldn't hear a word of their conversation, but it worried her nonetheless. Anything that broke the rhythm and regularity of factory life was dangerous. She tried to concentrate on her work, to ignore the sense of unease rising in her belly, but almost at once Marandino shut off the master switch, and all the machines slowly ground to a halt.

"All right, you girls, Mr. Barker's got something to tell you, and I want you to keep it down, see? I don't want no loud noises, no whining or moaning or groaning, you hear me?"

Barker moved to a position from which he could look at the faces at all three long worktables. He did not look as if he were about to dispense some favor to his serfs. On the contrary, he seemed to be trying to compose the lines of his face into a sorrowful mask. Even before he spoke, Maura felt the falseness of what he was about to say. He was like a bad actor who was trying to get out the lines he'd memorized and have done with them.

"All right, girls," he said. "Maybe you've heard, and maybe you haven't, but times in ladies' fine handkerchiefs aren't exactly booming. I've done what I could, but my only alternative—seeing as how you're all like family to me and it would be a shame to have to fire anybody—is a pay cut, right across the board. It's not anything to worry about—only two bits. That's nothing for each one of you, but added up in this factory, and my other factories, it lets me keep you on. I don't want to let anyone go, even though times are bad, and so I'm doing this. I'm doing it for your own good, because I want to keep you all, just like I've always done. I hope you understand what I'm saying and can appreciate it."

There was perfect silence after this while all the girls tried to understand what the loss of twenty-five cents a week might mean: It could be offset by walking instead of riding to work, by giving up newspapers, by forgetting about a ferry ride on a Sunday or buying a new paperback romance. Of course, there were some who couldn't offset a twenty-five-cent cut in any of these ways, for they were already walking to and from work, had already given up newspapers, never took a ferry ride unless a "gentleman friend" paid for it, and never bought a dime novel. Jenny thought at once of the blow to her mother's finances, wondering if she could tell Jake about it in secret, so he could make up the difference without their parents knowing. Minnie thought at once of the twenty cents a week she'd been saving for months, trying to build up a few dollars for a winter coat. Now she'd have nothing to save, and would have to cut out something else as well. Angela, the youngest girl in the shop, was the first to break the silence.

"Excuse me, sir," she said, her words shocking after the long moments of quiet and contemplation, "but business seems real good to me. I mean, we got orders for hankies like crazy. I ain't never been so busy in my life."

"Who is that girl?" said Barker, not deigning to talk to her directly.

"Angela Minucce," said Marandino. "She's thirteen and don't know what she's saying."

"You tell her for me, if she doesn't like working for three dollars and seventy-five cents a week, that I can replace her in one minute—no, in one second—at three dollars a week. You tell her that."

"You got it, Angela?" said Marandino. "You want to make some more trouble for everybody? You just keep it shut when Mr. Barker says something. What do you know about business? If he says business is no good, show a little appreciation. You know what it's like out there on the street. Just keep it shut."

"I'll leave these with you," said Barker, dropping the envelopes on a bench next to Marandino. "Make sure they put in the full day. And if anybody wants to leave, that's fine with me."

Then Barker was gone, and Marandino was left to face them. "If you got any other complaints," he said, "I suggest you talk them over with the girls working the laundry shifts, see? What's wrong with you, Angela, talking back like that to Mr. Barker? You want to get us all fired or something?" Without waiting for further comment, he turned on the master switch and ordered them back to work.

"Hey," said Minnie before any of the girls had gotten back to work. "What about this week?"

"What?" said Marandino, coming over to where she sat. "You still have questions? You're really looking for trouble, ain't you?"

"Hey, I ain't looking for trouble," said Minnie, standing up in front of her machine. "But I ain't no idiot, neither, see? I ain't a slave, I ain't even a nigger, and I can talk if I want to talk. It's a free country, okay?"

"Sit down," said Marandino.

"Like hell I'll sit. I'm talking. I want to know about this week. Is he stealing two bits for this week, too, or is the bastard cutting our pay starting tomorrow?"

"I told you to sit," said Marandino, and he grabbed hold of her shoulders and pushed her down in her bench.

"What are you doing?" said Maura, getting out of her bench. "You don't touch her!"

"I'll touch if I want to touch! And you'll all shut up if I tell you to shut up! And if there's another word out of any of you, I'll fire the first one who peeps. You got that? You want to get fired, just open your yap!"

"Go to hell!" said Minnie, getting up again and backing away from Marandino. "I just asked you a question, and I want to get an answer. We all worked for four bucks this week, and I want to know if we're getting four bucks or if we're getting three-seventy-five."

"I told you to sit down," said Marandino. It seemed to the foreman that if he couldn't reassert his authority at that moment, he would lose it forever. He didn't want to fire this girl, but if he couldn't force her to obey him, he would have to fire her, and at once. He grabbed Minnie's right wrist and twisted her close to him. "Now, you sit, girl, and you get to work, or you won't get paid a cent this week, or any week."

"Let go of her," said Maura, standing behind his back. "You let go of her!"

But Marandino wasn't listening. He twisted Minnie's wrist until she cried out in pain, and when he pulled her back to the bench, she began to follow, her eyes tearing.

Maura picked up a fine-work sewing needle from the work-table and, without thinking, jabbed it into Marandino's arm. Immediately, he let go of Minnie's wrist, and, as he did so, Minnie swung her open hand across his face. Marandino staggered back toward Maura, who quickly got out of the way.

"Who stuck me?" he yelled. "Jesus Christ, I'll kill you, you bitch!" he said, seeing Maura turning from him.

"Stay away from me," said Maura.

"You heard her," said Minnie.

Marandino looked from one to the other. They had each assaulted him. They were young girls, but they were threatening his control. He had to put them in their place, but he didn't know if he should first physically knock them down or simply fire them immediately and get them out of the shop before their hysteria spread to the others. He hesitated.

"You don't touch either one of us," said Maura. "You don't touch anyone in this place, or, so help me God, I'll stick this in your heart."

"You're fired," he said to Maura, finally acting. Turning to Minnie, he repeated the words. "You're fired, too. You're both fired, and I want you out of here this second. You lost your places, you're out of work. Get your asses out of my shop. Move!"

But it was too late for the foreman.

The dreaded words—"You're fired!"—could hardly be heard, much less drive home their message of terror. Even as he'd started to speak, Angela, the thirteen-year-old who had dared question Barker, had gotten to her feet. And she had been followed by little Beryl from Odessa, by big-boned Mary, by frail little Lucinda, her bloodshot eyes wild with purpose.

And then all at once the benches were moving, scraping the floor, as all twenty girls got to their feet and advanced on Marandino, a menacing semicircle of young women and girls. Before anyone had vocalized it, had created the concept around which they needed to rally, they understood what was happening.

This was their shop, more than Marandino's. The fact of their hours of labor, their weeks and months of ceaseless work, must amount to something. It could not be severed so simply. They had rights, and if he didn't recognize them, they would force him to understand.

"You don't fire nobody," said Angela.

"You fire one, we're all fired," said Jenny.

"If anybody gets out of here, it's you," said Minnie. "What the hell do you do all day except grab at us girls? We ain't meat, see? I ain't leaving. *You're* leaving."

"Yeah," said Angela. "Why don't you take a walk?"

"This is your last chance, girls," he said. 'If you're not back in your chairs and at work in two seconds, you're all through, the lot of you, you get me?"

Maura said it first. They were already on the way, of course, sent there by Angela, by Minnie, by the point of Maura's pin. Perhaps Barker started it. Or Marandino, with his insistence on mastery, his reluctance to look at the workers as human beings.

But Maura said it first, and the others remembered her for it.

"Strike," she said, as if discovering the word.

It was a frightening thing to say.

To every girl there, the word conjured policemen clubbing workers who tried to hold a picket line. Strikes meant a total loss of wages, and therefore hunger, the threat of eviction. Most had experienced strikes through a father, a brother, a sister. Begun in anger, continued with hope, they usually progressed to worry, fear, and desperation. Factory owners found it easy to hire scabs from the enormous numbers of the unemployed. Men had begun to organize, but the factory owners made them suffer for each little gain. Women, who often had far worse grievances, found organizing still more difficult. They worked at jobs that most men didn't want. Their employers looked at them as replaceable cogs in a vast machine, not as skilled entities, worth treating in any decent fashion. Every girl there heard the word, and understood that they were about to take a terrible step, and that they would almost certainly lose their jobs, and never get them back.

"Strike," said Maura again. "We strike."

"Yeah," said Minnie, agreeing to a fight whose goal she didn't quite clearly see.

"Strike," said Angela.

"Strike," said Jenny, speaking softly, wonderingly.

No one had asked for a vote, but as they stood around Marandino, the chorus of girls' voices seemed like a vote against this man.

"You don't know what you're doing," he said. "You're screwing yourselves, and you're too thick to see it, you jerks. You're going to be eating dirt in a couple of days. You're going to come back begging, and there won't be no job. I can stand out in the street and hire myself twenty bohunks in ten seconds and pay them peanuts, and they'll be happy, they'll be very happy to do whatever I say."

"Strike," said Beryl.

"Strike," said Mary.

And then they were all saying it, as if the word gave them strength, as if the united outpouring of the single syllable would somehow right all the wrongs under which they suffered.

"Look, for Christ's sake, I'll forget the whole thing," said Marandino. "If you get back to those machines this instant, I'll even give these bitches another chance, see? Just get back to work and I'll make believe it never happened."

"Over on Houston Street," said Angela, "I got a friend in a shop like this. They make hankies too. They get off at four-thirty on Saturday, and she's getting four-twenty-five."

"So what?" said Minnie. "I know a girl in a place where they get paid extra for wiping up the floors after six. It ain't included in their week. If she cleans up every day, she can make four bits extra a week. And everyone's out of there on time. No one cleans up the floors and everything unless they get paid for the extra time."

"Hey, what the hell is this?" said Marandino. "This ain't a social hall. If you want to stay in this place, get back to your machines, or else get the hell out of here."

"We're on strike," said Maura softly to Marandino, wondering at her bravery. "You don't tell us what to do now."

Mary, the oldest and the biggest of the girls, took a step closer to Marandino, and so did three or four others. In the sudden shifting of events, from a deadening sadness at losing twenty-five cents a week and having their insecure status reaffirmed, they were becoming drunk with a new power. They outnumbered this man. They were on strike. If they wanted, they could force him to leave, they could knock him down, they could stand him on his head.

"First one who touches me gets this in the face, see?" said Marandino, raising his fist to Mary's face.

"You're not going to touch anyone," said Maura, continuing to speak softly. It seemed to her as if every girl in the place were looking to her for direction, and this worried her. She was not the oldest there, and hardly the most popular. Almost every other girl had been at the factory longer. She had no special desire to lead anything. Still, she had been the one to stick a pin into Marandino, the one to first say "Strike." Perhaps rebellion had always been a part of her: in Kerry, where she had rebelled against her servant's role in the family; on the ship to America, where she would have gladly led the steerage to revolt; in the whorehouse, where she had never been truly conquered. Somehow, the confused amalgam of love and pity for the workers she would one day leave behind had urged her to be the first to speak. They had all seemed to despise her yesterday, for her new manners, her night-school speech. Today she had been given a new chance. Jenny and Minnie had both made her feel welcome. This spirit had seemed to be shared by all the others. Here, in a new world, was family. Maura's anger and strength rose momently. She must return their love and acceptance. Better than any of them, she knew what it meant to be a slave, a captive of a system.

"You're going to shut up," said Maura. She took a few steps closer to Marandino, and the others let her through. "Listen. We're on strike, you heard it. We'll leave at closing. But we're not working. And the money in those envelopes belongs to us."

"If you ain't working, you ain't getting no money, bitch," said Marandino, and he started to push Maura out of the way so he could get to the bench where Barker had dropped the envelopes containing their week's wages. But Mary reached out and grabbed the man's wrist, and two other girls blocked his way, and Minnie pushed him hard into the back wall.

"Who do you think you're pushing?" she said, smiling at Maura.

"Someone get our money from the bench," said Maura, watching Marandino.

Jenny at once went to the bench, and took all the envelopes into her hands. "What should I do with it, Maura?"

"Give it out," she said. "It's ours, right?"

"You can't give that out!" cried Marandino, still not believing that he was being held in check by girls. "I'm warning you to get out of my way!"

"Shut your trap," said big Mary, "or, so help me, I'll fold you under my machine."

The girls laughed at this, and the rebellious mood grew more and more festive. Jenny distributed their money, and the fact that Barker had already deducted twenty-five cents from the week they'd just finished only added to their reckless spirit. If they were to be treated this way, they might as well strike. And if they were going to strike, they might as well make a series of demands.

"Why don't we throw him out of here?" said one of the girls.

"Yeah, let's put him out on his ass, like he's always saying he's going to do us. Let's learn him something good."

"I'd like to break his fingers. What's a matter, Marandino, you don't want to touch me all of a sudden?"

"Get away from me," said Marandino, suddenly frightened at the appalling prospect of a beating at the hands of girls. Mary had picked up a plank from under a worktable, and another girl had a metal pole used to brace one of the machines. They could actually kill him. "I said get away from me!" he said, and his voice cracked, and someone laughed, and then they all joined in, and Marandino pressed his back against the wall and looked wide-eyed at the hysterical faces around him.

"This is stupid," said Maura. "We don't want to hurt him. Sure that's the way to get the police on us, and we won't get a thing out of this except a broken head."

There was a brief moment of resistance to Maura's interference, but the girls quickly agreed with what she had to say. Marandino sidled out of harm's way into a far corner of the room; as much as he would have liked to leave, he could not bring himself to flee from a pack of females. Already he was composing in his mind what he would say to Barker after he had locked up the shop and gotten safely away.

"Now what do we do?" said one girl.

"We start looking for jobs!"

"He's never going to give in, this Barker. The problem ain't that business is bad, it's all the girls that'll work for nothing. Tomorrow morning there'll be fifty girls here looking for work, even if he's paying three bucks, wait and see!"

"Hold your horses," said Minnie. "We didn't even try nothing yet and you're already running scared. I say we let Maura talk, see? She's the only one here who's got her head on straight and ain't about to go chicken the first copper comes in here with a stick."

"I ain't chicken," said big-boned Mary.

"But you ain't so smart, neither," said Minnie.

"Okay, maybe I ain't," said Mary. "So now what do we go and do, hey? I'm ready for anything, but what's it going to be?"

Once again they were all looking at Maura. Softly, without trying to play the role of leader, she suggested that they all think out loud about what they wanted to get out of the strike.

"You mean like a raise!"

"Getting out early on Saturday!"

"Extra money for extra work!"

"No more being pawed by that punk foreman!"

Jenny took Maura aside. "You've got to help put it down, Maura. On paper I mean. Real neat and formal like. A list, okay? A list to give to Barker, and then we'll just wait until he gives in. Just wait and hold on tight."

"All right," said Maura.

The next hour was a slow awakening to the gravity of their situation. While the girls all called out complaints, Maura wrote them out in her neat hand. But she was not merely their secretary. Once she would put something down on paper, the girls would ask her how it looked, whether she approved of the demand. If some of the girls resented her sudden prominence in their midst, most found it comforting to have a calm center. Maura modestly wrote down everything, answered all questions, gave her opinion when it was asked for. She thought it was unrealistic to ask for four-fifty a week when Barker was trying to lower their wages; instead, she suggested four-twenty-five as one of their strike demands. Everyone agreed that the shop should close at half-past four on Saturdays, and that girls asked to clean up should be given ten cents an hour for this extra task.

"What about Marandino?" said Jenny. "Shouldn't you put down something about him? How he's always touching and grabbing?"

Maura added the demand that Marandino be fired. And then she suggested further demands: that the lunch break be expanded to forty minutes; and that, in addition, two five-minute breaks be instituted, one in midmorning and one in midafternoon.

Maura then read out the whole list of strike demands, and the girls listened in silence. Little Angela spoke first after Maura finished. "Wouldn't it be great?" she said. "I mean, just imagine!"

"Yes," said Maura. "And just maybe we can do it."

There was little more to be done after that. The girls arranged to return to the shop the next day at fifteen minutes before the usual hour. If Barker and Marandino tried to bring new girls in, the strikers would be there, ready to shout and hold hands.

Maura took the paper with the neatly printed demands of the strikers to Marandino and placed it in his hands. "This is real funny," he said. "You'll all go far with this." He waited until they were all out of the shop before crumpling the paper into a little ball and locking up the factory.


Though it was more than an hour before their usual quitting time, all the girls seemed in a rush to get home. There was time for a little shopping, but no one bought more than a few items. They didn't know when they would see another pay envelope.

The next morning they woke to a cold October rain.

It was Saturday, usually a happy day, the last workday of the week, but there was nothing happy about the girls who showed up at the loft building on Franklin Street. Mary no longer had the key to let them into the factory, so everyone huddled on the stairs, waiting for Marandino or Barker to show up.

By 9:30, some of the girls wanted to leave; if they were going to be broke and out of a job, they said, they might as well enjoy the free day while they could. But Maura insisted that no one leave. This was what being on strike was all about, she said.

But by eleven o'clock, she couldn't hold them back. In twos and threes the girls went off to coffee shops, to bargain-hunting, to their homes.

Barker and Marandino came at half-past eleven. With them were a dozen girls, all of whom kept their eyes on the ground and said nothing. Out of the twenty girls in the shop, seven were left to guard the locked door to the second-floor factory.

"Don't go in there, we're on strike," said Maura.

"She's the one causing the trouble," said Marandino to Barker. "If it wasn't for her, this whole thing would have never happened, I swear it."

Marandino brusquely pushed one of the strikers away from the door. "This ain't your door, girl, see?" he said. "Get out of my way."

"You can't go in there!" said Maura as the newly recruited workers were ushered past her by Marandino.

But they all went in, and Marandino and Barker followed them, and shut the door on the strikers. Maura began to hammer on the door with the heels of her hands. She wanted to speak to Barker, to explain to him that their demands weren't excessive, that if he would at least give them the opportunity to discuss their grievances, the strike would be settled to everyone's satisfaction.

But no one answered her knocking. Instead, she soon heard the machines starting up. After a few more hours, even Maura had had enough. The strikers left, resolved to return on Monday, and this time form a human chain in front of the factory door.

The rain didn't let up the rest of the day. Sunday was lovely, but few of the strikers felt like observing the autumn leaves in Central Park. Everyone tried to rest, to forget about the next day's confrontation.

On Monday morning, all twenty girls showed up, grim-faced,

and stood four deep in front of the door to their place of work.

Marandino came at five minutes to eight, bringing with him the same cowed dozen girls. But this time he could not get to the door.

"If you don't move out of the way, I'm getting the coppers," he said.

The girls didn't even bother to answer him. As he turned to go down the stairs, the strikers surrounded the dozen scabs.

"It's our jobs you're taking," said Maura.

But none of the scabs would look her in the eye.

"Don't stay here," said Marandino to the scabs. "Come with me, or they may eat you. These ain't girls, they're Zulus."

"It's our jobs you're taking," said Maura more clearly. "There are other jobs, if you look for them. I know it's not easy, but remember, we're on strike, and these are our jobs."

Big Mary took a step closer to one of the scabs. "Hey," she said. "I'm going to make it simple for you. Any girl what takes my job is going to get stuck in the ribs. I swear it here and now. When you least expect it, when you're walking home, somebody's going to come up and stick you good, and that's the truth. You hear what I'm saying, or are you too thick to save your own skin?"

"I said come on," said Marandino. He ran down the stairs with the scabs behind him.

When Marandino came back, there was one police officer with him, club in hand.

"Move away from the door," said the police officer.

"Scab!" said Minnie.

Maura smiled. Behind Marandino there were no longer a dozen girls. Five had gone home.

"Scab! Scab! Scab!" The ugly syllable was taken up by all the girls as they moved away from the police officer. Marandino unlocked the door, but now the remaining seven scabs were separated from him by a gauntlet of twenty chanting workers.

"Scab!" shouted Maura, and she shouted it again, letting the will to keep these girls from taking her job, and the jobs of her friends, overwhelm her. She shouted like a demon, and so did the others. "Scab, scab, scab!" they cried, and the rhythm was strong and the tone was harsh, filled with hate and violence. The seven scabs were stalled under the weight of this terrible sound.

"Come on, damn you!" Marandino shouted at the scabs. But they hardly heard him. Fear had gotten under their skins. Unable to move, they looked at the faces of the strikers and knew that they could not go past them. The foreman had promised them permanent jobs, swearing that the strikers would never be hired again. But looking at the resolve in the strikers' eyes, they wavered. Their own desperation for jobs was not strong enough to fight this. It would be better to work in the laundry than have to walk past these strikers for a month, or a week, or even just a day.

One scab turned and fled.

At once, the strikers ceased their awful litany.

The other scabs looked to Marandino, to the strikers all about the open door, and then they, too, turned around and left, ignoring Marandino's angry words.

"You can't make them scab, buddy," said the police officer. "I wouldn't want to go in there with all these nice girls looking at me like I was dirt. Let me know if you want me to hold your hand again. These girls look pretty tough, see?"

The police officer laughed at his own joke, and, as he turned to go down the stairs, more than one girl smiled her thanks at him.

"They ain't supposed to be on the steps!" shouted Marandino at the departing officer. "The steps is private property, ain't it? Let them stand outside in the gutter where they belong!"

"Hey," said the police officer, "don't shout at me, see? It gives me a headache." To the girls, he added: "Give these bastards hell. You make them lose enough, they'll give you what you want."

Marandino hurriedly locked the door and ran past the hostile strikers, out into the street.

"He's going to get Barker," said Minnie.

It took him two hours to return. And Minnie was right—the foreman had come back with the factory owner, and both men were white-faced with anger. "Tell them," said Baker to Marandino, "that they can either go back to work at once, and work as late as need be until they have caught up with what they have fallen behind on in more than a day's absence, or I will see that they starve. Each and every one of them starve. Tell them. Go ahead and tell them."

"Why don't *you* tell us?" said Maura.

"Who is that girl?" said Barker to Marandino.

"I told you, sir. That's the Irish one. O'Connell, her name is— Maura O'Connell. And if you give them a chance to come back, you better not let her in with them. It's her who's done all this. It's the Irish bitch's fault, this whole thing."

"Mr. Barker," said Maura, "have you looked at our list of demands?"

"What does she want?" said Barker wearily to Marandino.

"Hey!" said Maura, waving her hands in Barker's face while the other girls stared in wonder. "I'm here! Me! I'm talking to you! Sure it's me you're hearing, not Marandino! I'm asking you something! Talk back to *me!*"

Slowly, the factory owner turned to look at the troublemaker. "You have something to tell me?" he asked.

"Have you read our list of demands?"

"No. I haven't seen any list."

"I gave it to him," said Maura, indicating Marandino. "But seeing as how one of our demands was getting rid of him, I can understand why he wouldn't show it to you." From her pocket, she extracted a folded piece of foolscap. "If you'll please read this, sir," she said. "It's all we want to go back to work, all of us."

Barker looked at the list slowly, his face expressionless. When he had finished, he looked from Maura to the other girls. "She speaks for all of you?" he said.

"These are everyone's demands," said Maura, trying to explain that she was not the leader. But big Mary interrupted.

"Whatever Maura says goes, see?" she said.

"Then you can all starve," said Barker, refolding the foolscap and placing it in an inside coat pocket. "I'd sooner see this place burn down than give any of you an extra nickel. Not this way— never. You'd think you'd have some gratitude for a man who's been feeding you all these years. What do you think I am, an idiot? I gave you a pay cut to save your jobs, and you want raises, you want time off! Why don't I just *give* you this factory? Why not let you run everything, and then *you* can hire *me?*"

Angrily waving at Marandino to follow, Barker stomped down the stairs. When they were gone, Mary spoke first. "You got them running scared, Maura! His Highness looked like he was about to crap!"

All the girls crowded about Maura, as if she alone had created this moment, this victory. But Maura knew that little had been accomplished. He hadn't agreed to the demands, nor even asked to negotiate them. She let the girls celebrate nonetheless. They would need the sense of victory to carry them through the rest of the long day, and the uncertain days ahead.

Neither Marandino nor Barker returned the rest of the day, and since it was unlikely that any scabs could be sneaked in late in the afternoon, by three o'clock the girls decided to go home. Jenny, Minnie, and Maura walked from the factory to Houston Street, found a dairy luncheonette with a self-service counter, and bought large bowls of coffee and milk.

"Think of all the work orders that's piling up," said Jenny.

"Barker's gonna lose his shirt if he don't give in to us," said Minnie. "He tries to sweat us out, he's going to go under himself. His customers ain't going to come back if he pulls this much longer."

"He can't pull this much longer," said Jenny. "For him or us. I mean, how is everybody going to live without getting paid?"


Maura had school that night, and though she was tired from the events of the day, she was glad of the chance to forget about the strike for a while. She recited the Pledge of Allegiance with her hand over her heart, enjoying the chorus of foreign accents and the sense of bright anticipation in the room. Soon Mrs. Partridge would speak, her words sharply enunciated, her posture erect, her eyes bright with knowledge. But try as she might, Maura found herself drifting from the comfortable feeling of the class, with its blackboard and sharp pencils and neat stacks of books and papers, to the world of the strike. Barker had said that they could all starve, and she knew that he was right. If not

this week, then next week. Room and board and carfare exacted
its steady toll. What could the girls possibly do if the strike lasted
more than a few days? If it lasted two weeks, they would have
to give in.

"We're frightfully sorry to have to disturb your nap, O'Connell," said Mrs. Partridge, addressing Maura for the third time.
"I'll see you after class," she added with a characteristic smile
that promised little good. Though Maura had indeed become
something of a specially privileged case in the nearly empty
classroom, Mrs. Partridge remained a stickler for discipline.

When class was over, Maura approached the teacher's desk,
fully expecting a reprimand and an additional homework assignment.

"You don't look well, O'Connell. Nothing wrong, I hope?"

"Oh, no, Mrs. Partridge."

"Your job, no doubt, is tiresome."

"I'm sorry I wasn't paying much attention. Sure I didn't
mean—"

"For the love of God," interrupted Mrs. Partridge savagely.
"If I do nothing else in this life but prevent Maura O'Connell
from preceding all her sentences with the word 'sure,' I shall
die a happy woman. You'll only be fit for scrubbing floors and
factory work all your life if you insist on speaking like that!"

"I'm sorry, Mrs. Partridge."

"Don't be sorry, O'Connell. Be correct!" Mrs. Partridge looked
up at the now vacated classroom and motioned for Maura
to sit down. She had never before asked a student to sit in these
after-class sessions. "Look here, girl," she said when Maura was
seated, "you don't want to work in a factory all your life, do
you?"

"No, ma'am."

"A young woman I know—a former student, in fact—has
given notice at her office. She's taken a better-paying job. Where
she's working isn't the best office in the city—far from it.
It only pays four and a half dollars a week. But there's a
wonderful chance for you if you can get it. You could learn
so much, get experience, make the break from the factory.
Even if it's less than you're getting paid now, I'd advise you

without hesitation to talk to this gentleman and see if he might be interested in giving you a job."

"What sort of job?" said Maura, in a daze.

"What sort of job, *ma'am*, if you please. What sort of job, *Mrs. Partridge*, if you please. If forms of polite speech are not second nature to you, they are worthless."

"Yes, ma'am. Thank you, Mrs. Partridge."

"And as to what sort of job—Lord in heaven, O'Connell, this is no time to be particular. It's in an office. It's office work. It's what you went to night school for."

"Is there a type-writing machine there, ma'am?"

"How am I supposed to know? Do you enjoy sewing machines so much that you can't bear the thought of leaving unless there's another machine waiting for you? Look here, the job becomes available in four weeks. But Mr. Curtis shall be interviewing new girls this week and next. Here's his address. You may use my name if you go there. Though he doesn't know me personally, he's been pleased with my former pupil."

Mrs. Partridge handed Maura a white card imprinted with the name of a handkerchief company: Curtis Handkerchiefs, Mr. Luke Curtis, President. The card reminded her of the one left her by Kevin Vane, six months ago. He had never called on her, and she had never called on him, but of course his beautiful white card was still there in her miserable top-floor room. And Curtis Handkerchiefs! How absurd! Why, she worked for a factory making handkerchiefs and underwear. Was that all they made in this famous city? Pretty bits of cloth for the rich to wipe their noses with?

"Maura, are you all right?" Mrs. Partridge said. She had never called her by her Christian name. "You're trembling."

"I'm all right," said Maura. "Thank you for the card, Mrs. Partridge. I do appreciate it, I appreciate it with all my heart." Then Maura kissed her shrewish teacher on the cheek, and fled from the room, clutching the card.

On the streetcar, she began to sob uncontrollably. Imagine working in an office, all quiet and clean, scratching with a pen on beautiful paper, learning how to use the type-writing machine. But she could not see Mr. Luke Curtis tomorrow, or anytime in the near future. How could she? She was on strike, and she was one with the others. They were fighting together, and she could never leave them, not until they had won.


The rest of the week resembled a war.

In some ways, it was the easiest time for Maura and the others. Fighting boredom and indifference while slowly losing all one's money is far more difficult than fighting one's enemy face-to-face. And that week there was a fight every day. Tuesday morning twenty girls waited for Marandino; and when he showed up with ten new scabs, the strikers' fury scared them away. Wednesday was a different story. Only eight girls accompanied Marandino this time, but they were prepared to meet strikers. They kept their eyes to the ground, and the presence of a police officer prevented any of the strikers from physically assaulting the scabs. All eight got inside, and the strikers were infuriated by the humming noises of their machines, run by workers who had crossed their line. Maura insisted that the strikers wait there all day. Their presence intimidated the scabs, no matter what pose of indifference they collectively attempted. Leaving the loft at six o'clock, all were met by cries of "Scab!" and the fact of hatred and loathing.

Thursday, half of these girls were gone too, and replaced by new, desperate girls, eager to brave any humiliation so long as they could make enough to eat. The strikers screamed at them, coming and going, and a few strikers followed terrified scabs into the street after work, causing them to run for their lives.

Friday was the first missed payday, but the girls were gratified by the fact that only five girls showed up with Marandino, and all of them were new. They cursed and threatened them, they called them "scab," they chased them down the stairs after the long day.

On Saturday, Marandino showed up with three girls, and when these non-English-speaking seamstresses, fresh off the boat, saw the mass of twenty angry strikers, they turned around and left Marandino the factory to himself.

"They'll have to give in, won't they?" said Minnie, laughing and slapping Maura delightedly on the back. "They'll have to give us what we want, and pay us extra to catch up on missed work. They'll give in and we'll have it all, because of you."

Because of you, thought Maura, again and again.

That empty Sunday she had a chance to ponder what she had done. She stayed in her cold room, listening to the passing trains. Her mother had written her another letter: Maura's father had passed away, according to the grace of God. It had been a long, lingering illness, and God in His mercy had seen fit to take Bill Dooley away to his final resting place. Maura's mother would mourn him, of course, and not travel to America for six months. She owed her husband that much honor, to wear black, and light candles in the village church, and visit his grave every day. But how she longed to see Maura! And Brendt, too, of course, and Patrick! The months would fly, wrote her mother, and soon she'd be there to keep house for her children, to get a job of her own so as not to be a burden, to cook them their favorite foods and tell them their favorite stories. . . .

All because of you, thought Maura. She had started a strike, and now twenty girls were running out of money. Soon they'd be hungry, they'd be facing the threat of eviction, and no one would have gained anything, except Barker. He could take back whomever he felt like, and on whatever terms he wished.

And all because of herself, her mother still believed that Brendt was alive, that Patrick was well. And now she was coming to America, and what would she find? A filthy room rocked by elevated trains, a daughter without a job, and without a penny.

Waiting for Monday morning, she turned over the two white cards in her possession: that of the handkerchief company whose offices she could not visit, and that of Kevin Vane. If only, she thought, if only there was no strike, and she could take an office job, and save enough money for a bigger place for herself and her mother. As for Kevin Vane's card, it made her wonder how different her life could have been if the handsome young man had truly loved her and respected her. Anything would have been possible then. Her mother could have been met by his carriage at the pier, and whisked away to a life of ease and contentment.

Monday morning the war seemed to be over.

The strikers were there, bleary-eyed with worry, but not a scab appeared to fire their resistance. Marandino never showed up once that day, either, and Barker sat on his money in some distant part of the city.

But no one felt as if the strike were won. Quite the contrary. Everyone had opinions, but most agreed that Barker had simply refused to pay good money for scabs who were afraid to walk past a picket line, and probably were so inexperienced at fine machine work that they got very little done even when they managed to get inside the factory. Barker refused to fight fire with fire. Now he would simply sit. The girls couldn't last without money. If they got new jobs, they'd be gone from the picket line. If they remained on the picket line, they would starve. It might take a week, it might take two weeks, but sooner or later they'd have to come back to work, on his terms.

Tuesday morning was the same. And Wednesday. Thursday morning, the twenty girls had a haunted look about them. They were not fighting—there was no one to fight, it seemed, but themselves. If they could only curb their appetites, live on air instead of food, sleep while standing instead of in a rented bed, then they could survive. But the next day was payday. There were rents to be met, food to be purchased. The first day of November 1898 was at hand, and threatening to be cold and bleak and full of rain and sleet and sorrow.

Maura had not gone to night school since the week before, when Mrs. Partridge had given her the handkerchief company's card. There was no longer a reason for her to go. Her mother was coming, her money was dwindling to nothing, there was no job in sight, and she could not—she would not—desert her fellow workers.

"What's it going to be then, eh?" said big Mary. "Maybe if we knew where Barker lived, we could throw some rocks or stand out in front of his house and hope the newspapers come."

"The newspapers ain't going to come," said Minnie. "We're too damned small for the newspapers to bother with. They won't come till we've all starved to death, and that's the truth, ain't it?"

"Maybe we got to lose," said Angela, the thirteen-year-old. Everyone looked at her hatefully, as if her words were the cause of their misfortune. But then Beryl spoke up, with her quavering, Yiddish-accented voice. "Maybe we got to. If there ain't nothing to do but do it, we got to do it. Face facts. We ain't got no money, and we got to eat."

This broke the ice. Suddenly all the girls were talking at once, and everyone had ideas: Maybe Barker would take them all back, perhaps he'd even give them four dollars, not three-seventy-five. So he wouldn't fire Marandino, and they wouldn't have longer breaks. Maybe someday they'd get these benefits, too. But meanwhile they had to give in, they had to eat. Surely Barker would want them all back, surely Barker would forgive them.

"Screw Barker," said Maura, feeling as if she were playing a part in a play she was just then writing. What would Mrs. Partridge say if she heard her favorite pupil using such language? "Screw the bastard. We're not giving up."

Once again she had halted all argument. All eyes turned to her to see what she would say. In the confused week that had just passed, she had found herself wavering, just as they had wavered. But Maura knew that she had to win this fight for them, because, while she would one day leave this place, most of them would remain workers forever. She drew on her anger. Her inability to properly mourn the father she had found impossible to love; her desperation at the impending arrival of her mother to a penniless daughter; her self-despised tendency to wish that Kevin Vane or Jake Newman would come down and carry her off so that she could live without effort, without struggle—all this fired her fury. She was strong. She was independent. She would succeed, and her success would begin with this struggle with the girls who had redirected the course of her life.

"Ten of us stay here on the picket line," said Maura. "Ten of us work. The ten that work split all their money in half, so we all have enough to eat. And the ten of us on the picket line make damn sure that no scab gets to work in our factory. If there's enough to eat for all of us, we can stay on strike until Barker quits."

"Hey," said Minnie, "that's great, Irish. But where in hell are ten of us going to get jobs in this city? Why do you think it's so easy for Marandino to find scabs to crawl down here?"

"I'm not talking about easy jobs," said Maura. "Just jobs that are always waiting for us. We pick ten of us, and tomorrow morning we go down to work in a laundry."

# ❧ CHAPTER ❧
# TWENTY-ONE

Maura volunteered for the laundry, and immediately nineteen other girls wanted to do the same. Only flattery and cajolery could stem the flow of masochistic self-sacrifice. Mary must stay with the picket line because she was so good at intimidating scabs; Angela and Beryl were too small for laundry work and would probably be rejected. Lucinda had a bad cold; Emmeline had a limp; Jenny's skin broke out from caustic soaps. Even so, they had to draw lots to see who the brave ten would be. Saturday morning it was hard to tell who was more zealous—the girls left behind on the picket line, determined to make their presence doubly felt, or the girls gone off to join the new workers' line at the Hauser Laundry Company.

The Hauser Laundry was located uptown on Second Avenue, in the shadow of the Elevated. It was a block long, half a block wide, and composed of dull red brick. All about it were brightly painted laundry trucks, pulled by ancient horses, driven by young ruffians with whistles round their necks. A metal staircase at the rear of the building led to a bleak gray door marked "Applicants." Here, Maura and Minnie and eight other strikers went on a chill morning, dashed with the filthy drizzle of the city.

Once inside the gray door, the chill air was banished with shocking rapidity. The whole building seemed to be sweating and shaking from the giant engines on the ground floor. About forty girls were on the new-workers' line that morning, and most of them had worked the laundry before. They were back only because there was no alternative. The pay was three dollars for a six-day, ten-hour-a-day workweek. But unlike so many other factories, girls were paid for their hours at the end of each day. So if one only survived a single shift, one could still take home fifty cents. Moreover, overtime was almost always available, at a munificent seven cents an hour. The laundry was a hellish place, but one twelve-hour day could yield sixty-four cents, and those who could stand on their feet for fourteen hours could bring home seventy-eight cents in coin the very day it was earned.

The problem was, few girls lasted longer than a day.

Most of the permanent work force at the laundry was made up of burly black men, as underpaid as the women, and a few alcoholic old women who lived in a fifty-cent-a-week dormitory only a block east. The blacks had the hardest jobs: working the steaming tubs of soapy water, removing hot, water-heavy laundry from one tub and dropping it into steaming rinse water. Hot, clean, wet laundry was passed on to the wringers—usually the burliest and best-paid of the men—and after this, dropped in giant hand trucks for processing.

Maura's group took part in the next, least-skilled process. The still-steaming laundry was laboriously pushed and pulled, in the giant hand trucks, about thirty feet across a wet and steamy floor. Here, the girl hand-truckers had to remove the heavy sheets, towels, napkins, and other laundry from the deep hand trucks and pile them on tables. While they rushed—almost ran— back with their empty trucks for the next load, other girls shook out the piles of laundry into neater piles, in preparation for pressing.

The necessity of rushing was apparent from the first moments in the job. A huge white foreman urged the speedy, powerful black men on with their washing and rinsing and wringing. The steaming laundry had to be dropped into the hand trucks, and the only way for the hand trucks to be ready to receive this bounty was for them to have been emptied on the other side of the room and returned speedily to the region of boiling suds and sweating, bare-chested men. Those who couldn't move fast enough were sent home almost at once, since every worker was a link in a productive chain and could not be slower than anyone else. Maura understood this quickly, and threw herself into the work with a zeal that made the old-timers laugh.

"Give that bitch fifteen minutes and we'll have to scrape her guts off the floor," said one older woman.

"She's still got her shoes on!" said another. "Look at her run, and she's got hot water in her fancy shoes!"

But Maura paid no attention to the old-timers. She kept her eyes on the hand truck at her command as it filled with steaming laundry. The moment it was fully laden, she turned it about on its little wheels and pushed with all her strength, trying to build up some momentum as she hurried across the slippery floor. It felt as hot and humid as an August day, and within five minutes her demure little shirtwaist was soaked through. (Not with *sweat*, she remembered grimly from the teachings of Mrs. Partridge. *Sweat* was for horses, perspiration was for men. Ladies simply *glowed*.)

Once on the other side of the room, the heat let up a bit. But in exchange for the thigh-straining pushing of the hand truck, she had to quickly unload the hot laundry, so painful to the touch, and as she got closer and closer to the bottom of the load, the strain on her back proved terrific. Once unloaded, she raced back with the empty cart, her eyes on the black men, who were sometimes forced to wait for a free hand truck, even with a dozen girls going back and forth without stop.

Minnie and four of the other girls from the handkerchief factory worked at the tables where the hand trucks were unloaded. Some found this easier work than the hand-trucking, but there was not much to be said for either task. The process of shaking out the tangled, hot laundry was at least as physically taxing; neck muscles were attacked in place of back and thigh muscles. Besides, the hand-truckers had a few moments of respite on the rare occasions when they returned to the soapy vats only to find the next batch of hot laundry not yet rinsed out. Those seconds of leaning against the empty cart were pure bliss.

At 8:30, the first new worker quit, knocking over a pile of tangled laundry from her station in disgust. "I ain't a nigger, you bastards! I ain't going to do nigger work!"

The black men, had they been able to hear her over the noise of the hot boilers below them, would not have taken offense. They had only respect for themselves, for a job done well and steadily—a job few white men would be able to bear. As for the girls in this place, they knew what they were for the most part: prostitutes too ugly to attract clients; unemployed, unskilled girls without family; abandoned wives and mistresses; gin-crazed old women—all of them trash, pure and simple.

By nine o'clock, Maura had removed her sodden shoes. By 10:30 the heels of her hands were beginning to blister from pushing the truck. Her arches, unused to stretching, harbored a dull ache. The soles of her feet were as scorched from the hot tile floor as if she had been walking barefoot on desert sands.

"This ain't for human beings," said Minnie as Maura unloaded laundry onto Minnie's table.

"Hurry, Minnie."

"I'm so hot, I feel like my head's got a fever. I ain't eaten so good this week. It's weird to tell you this, Irish, but I don't know if I can make it."

"Hey, Minnie, shut your trap and unload this truck," said Maura. "Think about Barker, when he finds he can't starve us. Think about Marandino, when the son of a bitch is out of a job. Think about making four-twenty-five a week, *sitting down*."

"Barker was right—we had it good," said Minnie.

"That's crap," said Maura. "We had it bad. Here they got it worse is all. I used to live in a place that cost five dollars a week for room and board, and everyone there thought they were poor. They were just clerks, Minnie, making ten and twelve and fifteen dollars, and none of them smarter than you and me."

"Hey, what the hell is this?" said the foreman. "It ain't lunchtime, you two. Move your blooming arses, or get out of here!"

"Yes, sir!" said Maura, throwing herself back into the work.

She grew so tired that the hot tiles beneath her scorched feet no longer bothered her. Her hair, her clothes, her face were all wet with perspiration and steam. Not even in the whorehouse had she felt so completely like a slave, like a draft animal. But now she surrendered herself to the slavery. There was no reason to fight. She looked at this day, at this week, as a bad dream from which she'd awaken to victory. All she had to do was survive it. Fighting was futile, for it would divert her from the straight-line path to the end of the day.

As the black men continued to boil filthy clothes and linens and clean and rinse and wring them, Maura tried to slacken her body to the dictates of her tasks: It was good to be loose, leaning on the empty cart and pushing it lightly, without wasting strength; stretching out her legs, one step after the other, the balls of her feet landing hard on the wet tiles. She waited in a fog of hot steam, looking into the heart of purgatory itself, as black hands lifted steaming masses from huge vats in slow, inexorable motion, placing them in her care, all the while telling herself to be slow, to extend the moment, to draw power from the vast pools of energy around her.

Then she was pushing, feeling herself the next link in a great chain of being, moving the heavy truck across the slick floor, urging bare hands and feet to conquer the thirty feet of space to the sorting tables. It was vital to remain loose. She had to remind herself not to strain her neck muscles, not to twist her back into the forward motion of the cart; for neck and back would be needed in a few moments for entirely different movements. Crashing the cart into a thick plate before the unloading station, Maura would remember to open her eyes and breathe deeply. It was slightly cooler here, she remembered, and the steam hung much less heavily in the air. Bend, she told herself. Quickly. As other carts rushed by, she unloaded, gripping the hot, wet laundry in red, blistering hands and raising it to the table. Faster, she told herself, and then she heard the foreman say what she herself had just thought. "Move it, ladies! This ain't a tea party! Shake it out! Jesus, what's wrong with you girls? You all drunk or something?"

At lunchtime, all the new girls staggered out of the steamy room into the cold and rainy air. The old-timers knew better. It made more sense to hunch in a corner, chew a sausage and drink a bit of gin in the hot and humid environment one's body had spent the last four hours growing used to. Maura and the others stood in shocked silence on the metal stairway clinging to the throbbing brick building. It was cold, but their bodies were too tired to notice. Most didn't bother to eat. The strikers who had never worked in the laundry were still trying to understand how people could allow themselves to be tormented in such fashion. Maura didn't have to waste energy on inspiring the others; all of them understood better than before what their strike was about. The laundry seemed like a logical extension of factory-girl exploitation. Without putting it into words, each of them knew that giving in to men like Barker created places like this laundry.

Late that afternoon, Maura found herself waking from a kind of somnambulism. She'd arrived at the unloading table and had begun to empty her truck when she suddenly realized that she had no memory of how she had gotten there. She didn't know if it was five minutes after the lunch break or five minutes before six.

"What time is it?" she asked Minnie. But Minnie didn't answer. She simply continued to shake out the heavy linen tablecloths before her, and looked up at Maura with dull, feverish eyes. "Minnie? What time is it? Have you any idea what time it is?"

But the hand truck was empty. Maura's machinelike body had already turned round, lusting for the run across the tiles and the blissful, mindless rest in the company of the steamy vats.

"I don't know," said Minnie to Maura's back, but no one heard this, and Minnie continued to shake out the laundry with the precision of an automaton.

As the day wore to a close, Maura grew more awake. She could sense the possibility of victory, and her mind now ran wild with the future opening before her. Next Friday, the girls working at the laundry would distribute half their wages to the girls working the picket line. The pressure would build up on Barker to give in to their demands. Marandino would be fired. The girls would have more money, more rest time, more dignity. And soon she would be lifted out of this steamy hell and placed in a comfortable office job. It was simple to envision herself in a bright blue winter coat, complete with a matching sailor cap, tilted at a jaunty angle, riding the downtown streetcar with all the white-collar nobs.

"It's five o'clock, honey," said the foreman to Maura as she raced across the floor. "Only another hour to blow-out time. You're doing fine."

But as the hour wore on, Maura found herself unwilling to stop. Tomorrow was Sunday, and the laundry would be closed. But she was strong, and the biggest advantage of the laundry was its seven-cents-an-hour overtime. She didn't want to quit. She had gotten it into her head that leaving at six was a kind of failure; that if she couldn't survive into the evening, nothing would ever be a success. Jake came to mind, and she knew that *he* would work into the wee hours of the morning. He would somehow turn the laundry job into the seed for a fortune. If the foreman wouldn't let her continue, everything would fall apart— the strike, the office job, the arrival of her mother from Ireland in the nebulous, terrifying months ahead.

A whistle broke through the din of the downstairs boilers.

The old-timers dropped the work in their hands, not even bothering to straighten out a towel, or a sheet already shaken out of its tangles. Maura didn't stop. Halfway from the tables to the vats, she kept on pushing her empty hand truck to the black men, who, alone among the workers, continued at their tasks without pause.

"Time, honey," said the foreman, putting his hand on Maura's sweat-soaked back.

"No," she said.

"Hey, hot air!" he said. "This ain't a slave camp, even if we do work our niggers pretty hard. You go up to the office and get your four bits, and we'll see you Monday, honey."

"I want to work."

"You've had it."

"They're working," she said, gesturing vaguely toward the black men. "I want overtime."

"I got a new shift coming. And you can't make it no-how, no-way."

"*She's* working," said Maura, spotting one of the older women who had gone back to sorting laundry after a minute's pause.

"You don't get your tail out of here this second, honey, I'm going to light into you, see! I'm doing this for your own good, sugar. I don't want a dead looker on my hands! I could use you

live a heck of a lot better, see?" The foreman slapped Maura's
behind now, and shooed her over to Minnie.

"He won't give me overtime, Minnie," said Maura.

"It's okay, Irish," said Minnie, taking Maura's hand and leading her out through the office, where they each got their fifty
cents for the day. They put on their shoes and flimsy jackets and
went down the metal staircase to the cold and rainy street.

"Let's take the train," said Minnie. But Maura refused. She
insisted that she was not tired, that she wanted not only to save
the five cents but also to savor the chilly air.

Minnie was too weary to argue. She left Maura and climbed
the steps to the train's platform. The other girls from the strikers'
team all went off in different directions—to streetcars, to a saloon
with a sedately marked "ladies' entrance," to a three-mile tramp
downtown. Maura joined two other girls following the spark-
scattering underbelly of the Second Avenue Elevated's tracks,
but her rapid pace and self-absorbed silence soon left them behind.

Where she walked was dark and filthy, lit by an occasional
unbroken gas lamp and the occasional glow of trains passing overhead. Her blistered feet, in their damp low-heeled shoes, walked
with a steady rhythm. That her feet were too swollen for her
shoes, or her body too weak for the walk in the cold air, was
disregarded. She didn't know where she was for the moment,
and she didn't care. The trains shaking overhead startled her, but
not to awareness. She thought of her mother, wondering how
she was bearing up under the strain of her father's death. An
image of the Kerry countryside gave way to a picture of Jake,
in his old clothes and giant peddler's pack, walking through the
hills of upstate New York. Early in the week, Jenny had told her
that Jake had sent "regards" to her, before leaving for a "very
important trip," and wished them the best of luck with the
strike. She remembered how he had kissed her, and how, in his
desire for her, she'd seemed to draw strength from his own
sense of future well-being. That was what she wanted, she reminded herself: to be sure, and proud, and to have a career.

Near Thirty-eighth Street she walked right into a beggar
asking her for change, nearly knocking him over. This brought

her back to her senses, but only for a moment. She felt momentarily frightened at the dark place she found herself in, but a street sign reassured her, and the clatter of a horsecar, and the mighty quaking of a train on the overhead tracks returned her to a sense of calm.

I'm hungry, she thought. All I'm needing is a bit of food in me and a little sleep.

But she was much more exhausted than she realized. When shadowy figures of derelicts began to metamorphose into people she knew, she started with increasing terror. First, a white-haired old beggarwoman approached her with an outstretched palm, and Maura reached out to embrace her, certain that it was Ginny. When the woman recoiled from her, Maura apologized for not calling on her, or writing to her, after all Ginny had done. She tried to explain about the factory, about night school, and Ginny commented in her usual fashion: "You're too stuck-up for your own good, and you don't even know it."

"I'm sorry, Ginny," said Maura, and another beggar under the tracks got out of the way of the delirious girl.

Then she saw Patrick, bearded and ragged, and wet from the sea. He disappeared as another train roared overhead, scattering ashes and sparks. In the approaching light of a gas lamp, she saw the lovely profile of her dead sister Brendt, and she stood rooted in fear, telling herself that she was dreaming, waiting for Brendt to vanish.

"What're youse lookin' at, you young cluck!" said Brendt, twisting her face into a crone's mask.

"I'm sorry," said Maura, realizing finally that the rainy night was filled with phantoms she must ignore. She stepped up her pace, keeping her eyes wide for stumbling men and women, part of the ever-floating derelict population of the great city. What dreams did they have, she wondered, and how far was she from being in their shoes? Wasn't this where one went after the laundry? Weren't these her own people?

But a breath of fresh air from the river wiped away her gloom. The march of tenements and saloons on Second Avenue became more and more familiar, and she was certain that there were to be no more hallucinations that night. The driver of a hansom cab caught sight of her red-gold hair and whistled through his teeth at her from his exalted position above the dismal street.

"Need a ride, sugar? No charge for you if you're going my way."

Maura didn't answer him. She passed Brian's Saloon, and then O'Hurley's Bar and Grill, and then Black's Saloon, and then the little brothel on the corner of Fifteenth Street with its green door and swinging red lantern.

Another block till home. She remembered that there was a bit of cheese left, an apple, some tea. It would be a feast. She would wash every inch of her exhausted body with the cold water in her basin, then lie down to a night and a day of blissful sleep.

But then she saw a carriage, with a top-hatted driver, a whip held defensively in his gloved hands. In its yellow lights she saw another phantom appear, as if from a former life. She recognized him at once. Peering at her through the drizzle, standing tall and straight, was Kevin Vane.

Maura walked right past him, hoping he wasn't real.

"Maura," he said. "It's you, isn't it?"

The phantom followed her to the front door of her tenement. "You're angry with me," he said. "Of course you are, and you have a perfect right to be. But I thought perhaps I could explain best in person. Over dinner. I spoke with your landlady—what a character she is, I thought she'd bite my head off!—and she brought my box up to your room. A little present, from Paris. I'm getting way ahead of myself. I've been waiting a good half-hour, and your landlady said you'd be sure to be home any minute."

He was real, thought Maura.

After six months, he was back, in his carriage, as impossibly clean and fresh-smelling and clear-eyed as ever. The rich and handsome boy whose card she'd kept in her top-floor room without knowing quite why. It was impossible, but, in a night filled with apparitions, this one phantom was Kevin Vane, as ready as ever to ignore the reality of her life and sweep her off her feet.

"I'm tired, Kevin," she said finally. "I have little enough to offer you to eat."

"Offer *me?* Don't be absurd. I've come to take you to dinner. I know it's not very proper of me, but I didn't know what to say

in a note, and you have no telephone, and I'm only back from
Europe all of two days, and I thought surely she'll be brave
enough to dine with me."

Suddenly, Maura was angry. Not so much at Kevin, but at the
state of the world. It was maddening—this rich boy blowing up
out of the past like a mockery of all she was trying to achieve.
She was so tired and weak from a debilitating day in a hellish
job, from walking miles to save a nickel, from the emotional
uncertainty of how the strike would run its course, how her
mother would be able to afford passage to America. And now
this top-hatted phantom had appeared, to put her puny efforts
into perspective.

The truth was, ten girls working for a week in the laundry
would earn thirty dollars to dole out among the twenty strikers;
Kevin must have five times that figure stuck in his pocket. Maura
knew that she could ask him for money—to help her mother,
to help the strikers—but it came to her that she had never looked
so ragged, so tired, so filthy. If only he could have seen her in the
sunlight, dressed in a new suit, her hair washed and shining. It
infuriated her that she was so weak as to think of such inanities.
Wanting to be angry at his wealth, at his blindness, at his never
once calling on her to explain how he felt after Kilgallen's
murderer was set free, all she could do was hope that the
shadows obscured her appearance.

"I can't possibly go out with you," she said, trying to speak
with Mrs. Partridge's clipped accent.

"Of course you can. Haven't you any consideration for my
having waited out here in the cold for half an hour? Look, I know
I was a pig not to call on you back in April, but, frankly, you
didn't make me feel all that welcome. Let me explain over dinner.
I want to hear all about you."

"You have a nerve coming here like this," she said, already
wavering. But what was she thinking? She could barely stand up.
She was sleep-walking not minutes ago, and now was seriously
contemplating going out on the town. As he apologized and
urged her to consider his offer, she interrupted him. "Look.
Maybe you didn't notice. I'm tired. I need a bath. I need some
sleep. If you want to come back for me in an hour and a half,
I'll have dinner with you."

Kevin agreed at once, and she was inside and up the stairs and alone in her room so quickly that for a moment it was the most natural thing in the world to believe that the entire incident had been another figment of her imagination. Maura sat down hard on the edge of her bed and caught her breath from the five flights of stairs. A large blue gift box caught her eye just as a train came screeching to a halt on the platform beneath her window. Imprinted on the box was the name of a shop, Madame Jeanette, and below that, in smaller letters, *Paris*. Inside was a velvet dress, with a cape, hat, and gloves to match. She touched the rich fabric with her red, work-worn hands. Then she slowly took the shoes off her swollen feet, and removed her wet and filthy clothing. Too tired to wash herself, she crawled into bed and fell asleep.

She woke with a shudder, the way she always did from a short nap when still profoundly exhausted. She knew she hadn't slept more than twenty-five minutes, and she tried to will herself not to hurry, but she was quick nonetheless. She ran fresh cold water in the basin from the hallway sink and washed her hair with a bar of soap, shutting her eyes against the shock of the cold. Then, even more quickly, she soaped her body with the cold lather and rinsed it off, toweling herself dry with exaggerated vigor.

She had her own underclothes, but everything else that night was from Kevin. As she tried on the too-large dress, she felt transformed. Smoothing out the lines where the dress had been folded in paper, she admitted to herself that, beyond her anger and resentment, she was somehow glad to see Kevin Vane. It had never been enough for her to explain away her mild attraction to the young man as a desire for riches. She didn't want Kevin, but she was eighteen, and beyond all her troubles she was still vain. It mattered that he had cared enough to pay for her abortion and volunteer his help. But it mattered, too, that he had never seen fit to apologize for not believing her story of white slavery. Looking at her image in the tiny mirror, Maura knew that for six months childish vanity had lurked in her mind. She wanted the rich boy to admit that he had been wrong, and express his love for her. Only then would she feel herself free of him, and his money, and the fact that he had bought her body and felt he could own her soul.

When she was ready, she walked downstairs, wearing her own worn-out shoes. Though her hair was still wet and largely uncombed, the dress too large, and the hat and gloves in her hands, she carried the beauty of her youth and the strength of her dignity. Kevin was waiting in the carriage and he jumped down to open the door for her.

"Please, let's not talk just yet," she said.

There were very simple reasons why Kevin had waited so long to contact Maura again. At first, he had simply wanted to give her the time and space she needed to herself after the abortion. Afterward, he delayed going to see her because he had been bothered by her lack of responsiveness to him; he felt she should have been grateful, and shown it with an affectionate display. By the beginning of May, he was embroiled in a last-ditch attempt to finish his senior-year thesis and prepare for examinations. After he graduated in June, he had only three days to himself before sailing to Europe, and those three days he spent with his fellow graduates, drinking and whoring all over town. It was easy to tell himself then, and afterward in Rome and Florence, Geneva and Paris and London, that his obsession for Maura had been based on the simple fact that she had been the only woman he'd ever made love to. But he had made love to many women— prostitutes of every rank and type—since then. He had thought that this wealth of new experience would shield him from the young girl's strange attractiveness, but in the first moments in the carriage he was already back where he started: a hopelessly silly twenty-one-year-old, infatuated with an uneducated Irish whore.

They drove to a dingy waterfront section of the city, south of Fourteenth Street and unfamiliar to Maura. She thought it strange, so close to her own row of tenements, to see a stunning assembly of coaches lining both sides of a dark, undistinguished street. Only a scarlet-liveried servant coming out of the shadows in front of an unmarked door suggested the luxury behind the bleak facade.

"I just remembered something," said Maura, unable to repress the thought. "When you brought me home from the doctor, I told you about my job. You didn't want me to go back to work. You asked me if you could help me, if you could give me a week's salary. You meant well. But what was funny was what you said. You asked me how much we were paid in the factory. You asked if we got ten dollars a week—you thought it might even have been fifteen!"

"Just a minute!" said Kevin curtly to the doorman, who had begun to open the carriage door. Maura was laughing uncontrollably and tears were welling up in her eyes. He didn't want to embarrass her in front of strangers, and he let her finish her little hysterical moment without comment.

Kevin had no way of knowing how much she was keeping in check, how far she had traveled not just in the last six months but in the last day. It would have been difficult for him to have chosen a worse time than this one to appear out of the night. Undercutting any appreciation of his English suit, his freshly trimmed hair, his brand-new carriage, were visions of the hell she'd lived that day in the laundry. No matter how carefully he treated her, how vigilantly he guarded his tongue, Maura's hands and feet were blistered from the real world he ignored, a world created in part by his father, and one that his generation was eager to rule.

"All right now?" he asked.

"Of course," said Maura, a little snappishly. He didn't understand why she had laughed. "In the sewing factory we were paid four dollars a week, you see. Do you understand what I'm saying? Then they tried to cut us back to three-seventy-five, and so we're on strike. We went on strike, Kevin. You came at a strange time."

Maura made a deliberate attempt to pull herself together. She didn't want Kevin to think she was a fool or a weakling. She reminded herself that she'd slept a bit, and that all she needed was a little food and she'd be fine, perfectly fine.

"It's wonderful how your accent seems to have faded so," said Kevin, trying to be gallant.

"Night school," said Maura. "When you come to Ireland, Mr. Vane, they'll be saying it's you who's got the accent."

"Yes," said Kevin, trying to smile, understanding this as a

joke. He raised a finger to the doorman on the other side of the window glass, and as the carriage door was opened he felt a pang of regret: Perhaps he'd made a mistake in bringing her here. Perhaps it had been a mistake to visit Maura at all.

But as they entered the plush anteroom and he caught sight of Maura's red hair under the candlelight of a huge crystal chandelier, he put aside such worries. She was beautiful. Even with her hair still wet, her scuffed shoes peeking out from under the elegant dress, her naïve eyes wide and full of wonder at the trappings of luxury, no one seemed disposed to laugh. This wasn't Sherry's, nor was it the Waldorf. It was a restaurant used to eccentrics, and to beauties, and Maura seemed to adorn the place with the qualities of both. Kevin knew what he wanted, and he would be gallant, he would be careful, he would take his time with his words and his hands. It would be so simple to get her out of that filthy rooming house, to buy her a wardrobe, to set her up in a bedroom where everything was pink and frilly and smelling of French perfume.

After Kevin had given Maura's cape to an attendant, he took her arm and walked into the adjacent room—a long, high-ceilinged hall glittering with crystal and mirrors and gaslight. Every table was occupied. Men in their fifties and sixties, and young women and girls, some younger than Maura, sat amid a wealth of oversize goblets, gold-plated utensils, and dazzling arrangements of hothouse flowers. But it was not simply a collection of tycoons and their mistresses. Men and women better matched in age and station looked up to examine the newcomers. Actors in silk scarves and narrow suits chattered obliviously among themselves, preening for the audience they knew to be in attendance. A grand matron with a lapdog tipped the trio of gypsy violinists, a wine steward expressed an elaborate apology for the poor quality of a recomended wine, a city official accepted the gift of his dinner with a knowing smile. Everywhere there was motion, riches, corruption. Maura wondered if she should feel insulted at the choice of this restaurant. It was the sort of place to take a gangster, a whore.

But she discarded this notion a moment later when the headwaiter approached, welcoming Kevin by name and taking them at once through the crowded hall and into an adjoining private dining room.

"I hope your father is very well, sir," said the headwaiter.

"Quite," said Kevin.

When the headwaiter had left them, Kevin said: "I hope you'll excuse the vulgarity of what's outside, Maura, but I know of few places in New York where we can eat so well, and be so alone."

They sat at a small round table. A single rose stood tall in a crystal vase; silver candlesticks held two burning tapers; a bottle of champagne cooled in a bucket of crushed ice. Maura found herself gripping the edges of the table. His father was quite well. Hers was dead. The tall rose reminded her of her mother, on her knees in the neat rose garden. There was not much time, and then her poor mother would be here, a widow, and find out about her dead daughter for the first time.

"The last time I was here," Kevin continued, "was just before I went to Europe, actually. The mayor was here, sitting at my father's table. There were about fifteen tables here, I think. Ninety people. But it was only a little crowded, except for the cigar smoke. Not only couldn't you breathe, you couldn't really see too well, either. The waiters must have dropped a hundred trays. It looks like a different place with just our one little table set up. With just the two of us. I can't get over you, Maura. I mean, I tried to remember what you looked like when I was traveling, but there's no substitute for seeing the real thing. You're beautiful. May I pour some champagne?"

"Do you think I could have a piece of bread?"

"Bread? Of course! Whatever you want! Anything!"

Maura heard a little buzz, and wondered what it might mean. Perhaps he had stepped down on a hidden power lever, like the one she used to start her sewing machine. The back room where they sat was about half the size of the main room, but it had none of the other room's furnishings, nothing of its meretricious glamour. She understood what fascinated her about the place, and about Kevin—what attracted her even as it repulsed her: Here was power. It was awesome to sit in the center of such a large space, knowing that the touch of a buzzer would bring the staff of a great restaurant into action, understanding that the whim of a single young man had usurped the space of ninety people to charm one eighteen-year-old girl.

"Would you like some music?" he asked, breaking the champagne bottle's seal.

She shook her head, wondering how he would produce music, whether it would be as simple for him to empty the violinists out of the neighboring room as it was for him to twist the bloated cork out of the bottle's neck, letting a little "pop" of gas escape with a self-congratulatory flourish.

Fresh bread was brought, warm from the oven, and sweet butter on a bed of crushed ice. She took a sip of champagne, she ate three rolls thickly smeared with butter. Kevin watched her closely, not realizing that his words had nothing to do with the rosy glow of pleasure spreading across her lovely face. He explained how sorry he was that she hadn't agreed to go with him to Europe when he'd mentioned it to her last April—how wonderful it would have been to walk through the gardens of Paris with her in June! He knew that he should have called on her before leaving or at least sent her a card from abroad. But, he said, he just didn't know how a letter from him would have been received by Maura.

"May I have some more bread, please?" said Maura.

"Yes."

Once again she heard the muffled buzz. The warden came swiftly. Kevin asked for bread, and ordered their dinner as well. She was smiling now. The bread was so fine! She couldn't remember ever eating such fine bread! She stopped wondering what on earth she was doing in this bizarre place. It was enough for the moment to eat what was brought, to savor it, to understand that it was free, that she need never pay for it in any fashion.

"You're hungry, it seems. It's important to have a good appetite."

Maura looked at him then, trying to understand the purpose of all his small talk. She let herself drift into a fantasy: married to this handsome young man, going to the pier when her mother arrived from Ireland. Well, ma, Patrick is dead, but I am now Mrs. Kevin Vane, and we live in a mansion on Fifth Avenue, and so will you, of course, with your own lady's maid, and a rose garden out back, and every day we'll go to Central Park; we'll stroll along the Mall and feed the fat birds. . . .

"I think perhaps one reason I'm so fond of you," Kevin was saying now, "is how different you are from everyone else I meet. It seems you want nothing from me. You're a difficult person to help. I think, crazy as it seems, that's why we weren't able to stay friends, proper friends."

Maura ate the unfamiliar food on her plate: canvasback duck, asparagus fresh off the train from Florida, wild rice.

"Did I tell you, Kevin," she said, finally initiating some conversation, "that I've been in night school?"

"Yes," he said. "You mentioned it, and I think that's fine. Of course, I hate to see you work so hard and then go off to school at night. Not much time for fun that way, is there? Surely there must be some school you'd be interested in attending during the day? I'd be more than happy to help with the tuition—"

"My father's dead," said Maura suddenly, looking for the reaction in his eyes. But there was no reaction, other than embarrassment. Apparently, such a blunt fact was not polite dinner conversation.

"I'm sorry to hear that."

"My mother wants to come here, to be with me."

"That's only natural."

"I've learned to take dictation very well."

"Ah, yes—shorthand, you mean?"

"No. Just dictation. I plan to learn shorthand."

"That's very industrious of you."

"Today I worked in the Hauser Laundry. I pushed a hand truck through steaming-hot air for ten hours. I thought I'd drop dead. I made fifty cents. This duck is nice. I've never had duck. I hope I'm eating it properly. I wouldn't want to embarrass you. I have a chance for a job in an office. I might not get it if the strike lasts. I can't very well leave the others. Sure it's me who got them into it. We have to keep on, no matter what. No matter what, see?"

Kevin looked at her as she returned to her duck. He felt as if she had just slapped him in the face, and he had no idea why she would have wanted to do that to him. "Maura," he said, "are you angry with me?"

"No," she said. "Thank you for the dress. I didn't thank you before—I'm sorry. I have a lot to thank you for. You've helped me with money when I needed it, and you were my hero. Do you remember when you were my hero, when you came out of nowhere and socked that guy?"

"Of course." Kevin hesitated. If she was grateful, there was hope. Perhaps it was only poverty that made her say such outlandish things. It was natural to be jealous and resentful if one had nothing. "Look, Maura, I don't want to hear about things like you being in a laundry. That's too awful to imagine. I don't know if you're serious when you say something like that, but what I do know is that it must have nothing to do with you. With us. Don't you see? You should always be dressed in velvet and silk and lace. You're too beautiful for anything less. You shouldn't have to even think about factories. I can't stomach the notion of you sitting at a machine. I want to talk to you about Paris. I want to drink champagne with you. I want to make you feel like singing every day of your life."

"What frightens me most is my mother," said Maura, thinking out loud. "I need an apartment for the two of us. If the strike isn't over soon, I don't know what I'm going to do. It would be a miracle if she even had passage money. I don't want to be a disappointment to her."

"May I tell you something?" said Kevin, assuming that her talk was meant for his comment. "I think it's wonderful that a young girl like yourself can be so concerned about her mother. But I wish to God you'd listen to me, to what I have to say, and keep an open mind about it."

"You still haven't mentioned a thing about Kilgallen."

"What?"

"Kilgallen. The son of a bitch who was murdered. You never said a word about the trial. What the trial showed. That I wasn't a whore, Kevin. I was not a whore."

"Of course," said Kevin, fumbling for words, glad that the waiter was nowhere to be seen. "It's just that you've given me so much to think about in one night. I mean the shock of you,

looking so beautiful, more beautiful than ever. Then talking
about a strike—I don't understand who's striking, what you're
striking about, or even if you're serious. For all I know, you're
pulling my leg because you think me a little bit of a stuffed shirt.
And you working in a laundry—for God's sake, the cruelest man
in the world wouldn't sentence someone like you to a place like
that.

"Maura, give me a moment. I mean to understand what you
want, what you're saying. I know what I want. I want to help.
I want to get you out of that filthy rooming house. I want to
bring your mother to America, if it's what you want. She can live
in your house. That would be fine. All I want is to make you
happy. Make you comfortable. It's not my fault if I was born
rich. You needn't hold it against me. Let me just help. Please."

He brought his manicured hand across the table and smiled
at her, waiting for her hand to join his.

"I asked you about Kilgallen," she said.

"For the love of God, woman, why do you want to dwell on
that horrible story? The man was a blackguard, no doubt about
it. I'm as happy as you that he got what he deserved. As for the
Hebrew who shot him, that's another matter. It's a breakdown
of the legal system when a criminal isn't punished, no matter how
well motivated the crime. It was a sham that he was set free.
The man was a murderer, even if he did murder a dog."

"Kevin," said Maura, fixing him with her eyes, "*I asked you.*
What did it feel like? When you read about Kilgallen. When
you heard. When you understood that he was a white slaver, and
that a girl like me had no chance, had no choice. How did you
feel?"

"Look," said Kevin, "let me tell you something about me. I am
not a talker, I am a doer. Can't you understand that? Do you
think if I cared a fig for that whole shameful part of your life I
would be talking to you like this? I think you're adorable.
There's so much I want for you. I want to buy you a house, do
you know that? Not right away, perhaps, but soon, once we see
how we get on. But for the time being, I can find you a lovely
suite of rooms, with a maid, and we'll arrange for passage for
your mother, and she can stay with you. Not in the same room,

of course, but nearby. I'd imagine that we'd both want a little privacy."

"I would like to go home," said Maura, and she stood up abruptly.

"Now what did I say? For God's sake, tell me what I said wrong! Didn't I make it plain enough for you? Do you think if I cared at all about the place I found you in I'd be offering you all this? I said I'm a doer, not a talker, Maura. I want to *show* you that I forgive you everything, not just tell you."

She could not quite believe what she was hearing. Was it impossible for him to look at her as anything but a whore? Did the evidence of a court of law mean nothing to him? Was he not in fact offering her forgiveness for what men like him, in their greed and lust, had created? The world was crazy. The world allowed this rich boy to look down at her from some higher moral plane, even as he proposed that she become his kept woman— even as he suggested, as an added example of his charitable nature, that he would allow her mother a spare room in his one-woman whorehouse. He forgave her, and Maura understood that men saw what they wanted to see, that those who had enslaved her, brutalized her, made her and kept her a whore, operated with near impunity, because they operated in a world where men were blind to the desires of women.

"You have nothing to forgive me for, Kevin," said Maura, fully awake now, and fully aware. "And I'd appreciate it if you'd take me home, at once."

Though Kevin chattered incessantly all the way back to Maura's tenement, going over everything he had said to her in the course of the evening to see where and how he had gone wrong, Maura refused to listen. She let herself down from the carriage, said goodbye curtly and finally, and ran up the stairs to her room. Her anger at his blindness was quickly replaced by a self-satisfied glow. She had dined very well, and the food was nourishing. No longer did she feel guilty at being unable to repay Kevin the fifty dollars he'd spent for her abortion. As for what he had spent for this Parisian gown, that was his problem, not hers. No one had asked him to buy her a dress.

But her self-satisfaction ran deeper than this. As she closed her eyes to the screaming of the Second Avenue Elevated, she felt stronger than ever. She had been offered gold in exchange for her pride, comfort in exchange for her dignity, and she hadn't hesitated. The factory, the strike, the threat of abject poverty hadn't weakened her resolve. She was free of Kevin, rid of any desire for the life he offered. Maura slept, and until her body had its fill of rest, no train could wake her.

# ❧ CHAPTER ❧ TWENTY-TWO

In the first week at Hauser's Laundry, two of the ten girls from the strikers' team became too ill to work—one with influenza, the other with a wrenched back. Still, with the overtime put in by the others, the first week's earnings amounted to twenty-nine dollars, and this sum was shared with the fierce pickets on Franklin Street. The second week brought the girl with influenza back to work, and the one with the wrenched back took someone else's place on the picket line, so that she in turn could work the laundry. The work was so hard, so debilitating, that the only thing that kept the girls going was the knowledge of what they had already suffered. To give up now would mean that they had spent their endless days in the laundry factory for no reason at all. As in the self-enclosed reasoning of inept theologians, the girls insisted on believing in a heavenly reward, simply to explain the miserable earthly existence already endured.

Not until the end of the third week of work in the laundry did the reward seem imminent, and even then it was a reward that the girls could not accept. If only for their newfound sense of righteous indignation, the settlement offered them by Barker had to be laughed at, spat upon, rejected.

Jenny and Mary were waiting at the bottom of the metal staircase outside the Hauser Laundry building at closing time on the third Friday worked by the strikers' team. "What do you look so glum about?" said Minnie. "Jesus, Maura, don't these strikers look piss-poor?"

"Where can we go to talk?" asked Jenny. She hadn't seen

Maura in a week, and in those seven days her friend seemed to have lost as many pounds.

"How's Jake?" said Maura.

"Still not back," said Jenny. "I would have told you."

"Quit looking at me like that," said Maura. "You make me feel like an old hag. Five minutes in the fresh air and I'll look as good as new."

"Five minutes in the fresh air, Irish," said Minnie, "and we're both going to end up in Bellevue with influenza. It must be a hundred degrees in there."

"So let's talk fast," said Maura. "We can walk up to the train platform and talk on the way."

"I saw a coffee shop on the corner," said Mary.

"We can't afford it," said Maura.

They began to walk briskly toward the train station on the avenue. Jenny spoke first.

"There ain't much to talk about, really. I mean, we all said no, see? We even laughed at him, didn't we, Mary?"

"I nearly broke his face," said the big-boned girl.

"Broke whose face?" said Minnie.

"Barker's," said Mary.

"He showed up?" said Maura. "Hey, that's news, all right. That's great news. We got him going. I told you we'd get him to come down. We got him closed more than a month. He's going to have to give in. So? What'd he say?"

"A lot of crap," said Mary.

"Tell me," said Maura.

"About you," said Jenny.

A train roared by overhead, and the girls waited patiently for it to pass. "What did he say?" asked Maura.

"That you can't come back, that you can't never come back, so we all told him to shove it. Ain't that right, Jenny?"

"That's right," said Jenny. "That's what we told him."

"But I don't understand," said Maura. "Why did he mention me? I mean, what else did he say? About the strike, about everything?"

"About everything . . ." said Jenny awkwardly. "About everything else, he said okay, except for Marandino. He ain't going to fire him."

"What?" said Maura, laughing out loud. "You don't mean he said yes to four dollars and twenty-five cents a week?"

"Yeah, he did," said Mary, abashed.

"And the extra lunch time, the extra rest time?"

"Yeah, that too."

"And he said he'd give us four-thirty Saturday," admitted Jenny. "I mean, if you want to hear the whole thing, we got that too, ain't that right? We can get out at half-past four Saturday, and we owe it all to you."

"Take it," said Maura.

"What?" said Minnie. "Hey, Irish, are you crazy? What do you think we are, a bunch of chickenshits?"

"I threw him out," said Mary. "I told him, I says, 'Little man, get your filthy ass out of my sight. Maura Dooley O'Connell is our friend, see? We work together, or we ain't never going to work at all.' "

"Come on," said Maura. "We'll go to the coffee shop."

"You just said it was too expensive!" said Minnie.

"Hey," said Maura, "we can afford it now, right? We just won the strike. You just listen to me and see."

Carefully, doing her best not to incite their resentment, Maura explained to the three girls that she didn't want to go back to work at the sewing factory anyway. There was a chance of a job in an office, and she had to go see about it, and she really thought she might get it.

"I don't believe it, sugar," said Mary.

"Me neither," said Minnie. "You ain't going to sit there and tell me you been on strike for five weeks, three of them in that hellhole, and all along you got a job lined up. That's crap."

"I didn't say it was lined up," said Maura. "Maybe I won't get it. But I want it. It's in an office. If I don't get it, maybe I'll get another."

"She just wants us to get back to work," said Mary. "Hell, I ain't going back to work. It's like I says to Barker, nobody's going to work until our Maura comes back too, and that's it, that's the whole story. You don't want no other job. You just want to help us out and cut your own throat at the same time."

"What's the name of the office?" said Jenny.

"Curtis Handkerchiefs. On Chamber Street. It's the truth,

Jenny. You've got to make them understand that they have to take Barker's offer. Let him think he's won something. I don't care."

Minnie shook her head in disbelief and turned to Jenny. "Nobody would work three weeks in that laundry for nothing. Nobody."

"Yes," said Jenny. "But maybe she's telling the truth. Maybe she didn't do it for nothing, see? She did it for us. I can believe that Maura did it for us."

They all wanted to believe this.

"What's your story?" said Mary after a long silence. "Tell us, Maura. If you didn't want to work no more, what'd you want with a strike?"

"I heard about the job after the strike already started. None of you would have done any different," said Maura. "I couldn't quit once we were all in it together."

"I still can't believe it," said Mary. But she was smiling. The chance of accepting the settlement, the return to work at four dollars and twenty-five cents a week, was beginning to seem possible.

"What if there is no job?" said Minnie. "What if you don't get this office work you want?"

"I will."

"You don't know that," said Jenny. "We can't go back to work if you ain't even got a job."

"I'll get it. I'll go apply tomorrow," said Maura.

But she had one added suggestion: If she did get the job she wanted, they must not tell Barker about it. On the contrary, they must agree to his terms—getting rid of the "troublemaker"—but only in exchange for still another concession on his part. Perhaps another twenty-five cents a week—or, better yet, let him agree to firing Marandino.

"You just get the job," said Minnie. "Then we'll worry about what to do next."


Saturday morning was very bright, the start of one of those rare November days in New York when it is neither as hot as summertime nor as frigid as winter, but breezy and invigorating, the sun taking the bite out of the chilly air. Maura had slept late, till half-past seven, and spent an hour washing and dressing in her only decent shirtwaist. She splurged on a breakfast of bacon and eggs and coffee and toast, and bought the morning *Herald* for the first time in months, so she'd have something to read while waiting for Mr. Luke Curtis in his grand reception room.

Though more than a month had passed since Mrs. Partridge had first given her the man's card, Maura fully expected to get this job. For one thing, four dollars and fifty cents a week was not a handsome wage for an office worker. For another, the previous girl had given a month's notice, so at this point the job must have been open for only a week or two. Most important, Maura was ruled by a feeling of inevitability. Barker had agreed to the strikers' demands, but only if she did not come back. The strikers would agree to Barker's condition, but only if Maura got this job. They had not survived the laundry to be stopped this morning by a job already filled. Though she had long since discarded any religious notions, Maura was overwhelmed by a spirit of optimism that shielded her for the moment from despair. She didn't consider what terrible straits she'd be in if this job didn't materialize. It was too much for her to contemplate that she might be the cause of prolonging the strike, and also her mother's departure from Ireland. It was not till she got off the streetcar on Chambers Street and walked to the tall building where the Curtis Handkerchief Company had offices that she began to be afraid.

But she refused to even name this fear to herself.

She took an elevator to the seventh floor, letting herself be comforted by the elevator operator's approving glance. No one need know she had spent yesterday barefoot and wild-eyed, pushing a hand truck through a steaming hell for five cents an hour.

"Curtis Handkerchiefs, Mr. Luke Curtis, President," was painted in small black letters over a frosted glass pane in a door opposite the elevator. Maura walked to the door and opened it, expecting to find a receptionist.

"Who are you?" said a gruff middle-aged man with a thick shock of black hair. He stood in his shirtsleeves behind a large desk in what was evidently a reception room, but there was no receptionist to be seen. His bad mood seemed to stem from a confused search he was in the process of making: Papers were scattered singly and in piles over the desk, on the floor, in shelves all about the room.

"Mrs. O'Connell, sir," said Maura. "I'm here about the job."

"The job?" said the gruff man, his tone a little more pleasant. "Who sent you?"

"Mrs. Partridge, sir," said Maura.

"I never heard of any Mrs. Partridge," he said. But he straightened up, put down the papers in his hands, and, to add to the formality of the occasion, put on his suit jacket and tightened his old silk tie.

Maura explained that Mrs. Partridge was her night-school teacher and had heard about the job from her former pupil.

"It pays four-fifty a week," said the man.

"Yes, sir."

"You're the first one to apply all morning, and it's past eleven already. Everyone's out of work, but nobody wants a job. It's an old story. My name's Curtis, Mrs. O'Connell. I said it was four-fifty, you heard that?"

"Yes, sir. Do you think you could tell me what the job is about?"

Mr. Curtis smiled. She hadn't balked at the low wages, she had no obvious mental deficiencies, and she was more than pleasant to look at. Quickly he explained that the job was a combination receptionist and clerk. She would have bills to file—he would explain to her how to do this—and she would have correspondence to write for him.

"I can't use the type-writer machine, and I don't know shorthand," she said, but he said that it made no difference.

"Why don't you take your hat off, Mrs. O'Connell," he said. "Make yourself at home."

"Sure it's as easy as that then," she said.

"What's easy?"

"I mean this job. You're saying that I can have it."

"I'm hoping that you'll want it, my dear," he said.

She was in a daze the rest of the day. While Mr. Curtis explained the workings of his little office, she exulted in the fact that she had gotten the job. Anything was possible now. She felt

that Jake would have been proud of her for refusing to entertain
the possibility of failure; but now that she had the job, she felt
a relief so powerful it nearly brought her to tears.

Mr. Curtis owned three small factories in the city: A twelve-
girl handkerchief factory on Charlton Street was the biggest. He
also had an eight-man shop making belts, and a five-man shop
making ladies' hats, but neither of these was flourishing. Only
the handkerchief line was selling briskly, and according to Mr.
Curtis, this was because of his son. "If I had three sons, Mrs.
O'Connell, I'd be a rich man. Only my son knows how to sell.
My other salesmen, they get lost going to Grand Central Station."

That first day was chaotic for Maura. She could do little more
than begin to sort out copies of invoices, copies of orders, copies
of general correspondence. There was an endless jumble of
clients who had disregarded bills for months. A telegram came
from the junior Mr. Curtis in Indiana—he needed a rush order
of handkerchiefs for the biggest men's store in Indianapolis. Mr.
Curtis showed her his office, with its own confused mess of
papers, broken-down filing cabinets, a brand-new telephone, and
a huge type-writer machine. It was the type-writer machine that
attracted her attention most, because for many months she had
hoped to have an opportunity to learn to use one. Type-writers—
or "typists," as they were sometimes called—were in demand for
as much as ten dollars a week in the *Herald*'s employment
columns.

"I'd be much obliged if you could show me something about
how the machine works," said Maura.

"Show you?" he said. "There's nothing to it. It's just a big
expensive waste of money if you ask me. Let me show you Monday. I want us to get out of here before three o'clock today, and
I've got plenty more to show you."

He explained that the four-fifty-a-week salary was for a five-
and-a-half-day week—ordinarily, she would be free after twelve
o'clock Saturday. This seemed such a wonderful bit of news that
Maura couldn't quite believe it.

"You said *three* o'clock today, sir?" she said.

"My dear, I know it's Saturday, but if you can't help me out
with those three extra hours, Monday is going to be a disaster

for me. I'd really appreciate it, and you'll be paid for the extra hours."

"Yes," said Maura, more stunned than before. Free from twelve o'clock Saturday. A chance to learn to be a type-writer. Four and a half dollars a week in an office. No pounding machines, no infernal heat, no foreman. "Yes, sir, I'm very happy to help in any way I can."

Before she knew it, it was three o'clock and Mr. Curtis was tapping her on the shoulder. "You're very fast, it seems," he said, though Maura didn't think she'd done much to clear out the confusion in either inner or outer office. "And I think it was very decent of you to work straight through, not even stopping for lunch. I hope you won't vanish and not come back on Monday. I promise to let you take as long as you need for lunch, and no more extra hours on Saturday."

Maura walked out into the clear light of day. Why, every Saturday she'd see daylight, she'd walk under the sun in the middle of the winter! She hardly knew what to do first: She wanted to write to her mother; she had to buy some clothes for her new job; she had to see the strikers, still on their picket line at the Franklin Street loft. She couldn't remember the last time she'd had three choices, all of them pleasant, all of them leading from such a joyful event.

She took the electric car to see her friends on the picket line, and they could see at once that she had the job. When they all cheered her and embraced her, it was difficult to say what made Maura happier at that moment: the fact that the strike was over and won, or the knowledge that she had not betrayed her friends by leaving them earlier.

Monday morning found Maura at her desk fifteen minutes early. She worked like a demon. When she had made an elementary sorting of the papers on her desk, she went, unbidden, into the inner office and began to do the same for her boss. Mr. Curtis spent much of his time on the telephone, shouting at the foreman in his handkerchief factory, pleading with a man in a bank three blocks away who refused to lend him money, and exploding at his belt salesman in Buffalo for daring to use the expensive long-distance line to call in such a tiny order.

"Mr. Curtis, do you have a moment?" asked Maura toward the end of the afternoon. "Do you think you could show me the machine now?" Her anticipation was palpable.

Mr. Curtis looked at her quizzically. "Say, what is it with you and this type-writer thing, anyway?"

"Well, it's only that you said I could try it today, that you'd show me—"

"All right, all right," said Mr. Curtis. "A promise is a promise. But at this time of day, I may not even have the strength to press down the keys."

He had no clue as to what the machine represented for his earnest new receptionist and clerk; Mr. Curtis could not associate the bulky object with the stuff of dreams. But Maura did. She had no experience, no trade, no valuable skill. Any girl who could read and write and sit up straight in a hard-backed chair could do the office work she was assigned to. But Maura wanted more than this. In an age of machines, the type-writing machine was special: It seemed more an extension of one's own powers than a separate and distinct entity. Maura could join with the machine, and become more than she was: She could be a type-writer. And if she could become this thing, this typist, this type-writer, she would have substance such as she never had before. She would belong to the world as someone of worth, someone with a special knowledge. Wherever she went, this skill would be a part of her. Whatever she did, no matter how others looked at her, she would know that she was capable of something useful, something that could not be taken away from her. Maura wanted to be a typist because if she could become this, she could become anything. The machine had to be mastered, because it was the first step for her into a world that held her in no high regard. She would be a typist, and then she would be a woman of business, and then she would have her place in the world, as good a place as any man.

Mr. Curtis typed with two fingers, and slowly. He used the machine, he said, only when an invoice was ignored for the second time. Then he would type out, under the Curtis Handkerchief Company's majestic letterhead, a plea for the preservation of the capitalist system: If the bill was not paid, how could Curtis Handkerchief meet its own financial obligations? Was not an ignored invoice tantamount to an espousal of anarchy, a vote for the rule of the unruly mob?

"It always works, Mrs. O'Connell," said Mr. Curtis. "This letter always gets them, and they always pay by return mail."

Maura watched as he rolled a sheet of paper into the black machine, squatting on its own little desk. He showed her how he was setting the margins, how he was hitting the space bar to separate the words, how he was shifting to capital letters or small letters by pressing a key. Mr. Curtis used both index fingers, hitting the keys with a fair amount of strength, frequently back-spacing to cross out a word with a string of X's. Slowly—for Mr. Curtis was an exceedingly poor typist—the letter took shape on the page, as prettily as if it had been printed in a book of correspondence.

Maura ventured that his success at getting paid by his delinquent accounts might be due less to the content of the letter than the form in which it arrived. "It's grand to see, Mr. Curtis!" she said. "No wonder a storekeeper getting this wants to pay at once. It's like hearing from the governor, or the church."

She sat down in front of the machine and, at Mr. Curtis's direction, typed out her name in capital letters. "There, it's not so hard. It just takes a bit of time," he said. "Now, if you've had your fun, my dear, we still have a lot of work to accomplish this afternoon."

"Of course, Mr. Curtis," said Maura, smiling beatifically. "Thank you so much. Thank you for showing me the machine."

She went back to work, and Mr. Curtis shook his head. If that was all it took to make his new girl happy, he had himself a real find. In one day the office was shaping up, the piles of neglected correspondence already visibly reduced.

Tuesday morning he found her waiting for him to open the office door at twenty minutes to eight.

"Mrs. O'Connell, I'm beginning to think you don't really exist.

You're much too good to be true. You don't have to be here till eight, and to tell you the truth, if you got here at eight fifteen I wouldn't even notice."

As on the day before, Maura threw herself into her work. Long before twelve o'clock, her hand began to cramp, simply from holding a pen in her hand for such a long and concentrated period. Her back ached, too, from sitting in her uncomfortable chair, and the room was overheated against the cold late-November day. But these discomforts were nothing to a factory girl. She still could not quite believe her good fortune: Everything was so clean and quiet and gentle here. She had stopped by the school the night before to thank Mrs. Partridge, and even as she had told her teacher of the new details of her life, she'd found it hard to believe that she could be so fortunate. "He's fortunate, too," Mrs. Partridge had said. "I want you to remember that, O'Connell. For four-fifty a week, the gentleman is lucky indeed."

Sitting at the reception desk, Maura wrote out, over and over again, the same polite bills for goods sent: Twenty-eight dollars was owed by a store in Milwaukee for an order of ladies' hats; six hundred and ninety dollars from a store in Chicago for an order of handkerchiefs; one hundred and thirty-six dollars was owed by a store in Brooklyn for an order of belts. There was a form to follow, and she followed it. It took ten minutes to write out a letter, with all its figures and compliments and pleasantries. When the ink dried, she'd fold the letter in three, as Mr. Curtis had instructed her, and place it in its envelope and seal it. Once addressed, the envelope looked for all the world like a love letter, with Maura's fair handwriting delicately inviting the reader inside. It was no wonder, thought Maura, that so few bills were paid on time.

"Lunch, Mrs. O'Connell," said Mr. Curtis, coming out of his office. "Come on, get on with you. You look like you're about to wilt."

"Mr. Curtis, sir?" she said. "May I stay?"

"What? Stay where?"

"I'd like to use the machine during lunch, if I may."

"The machine? The type-writing machine? What on earth is wrong with you, Mrs. O'Connell?"

"Nothing, sir. Sure it's just that I want to learn to use it."

"There's nothing to learn, girl. I can use it. You already learned how yesterday. You typed out your name, didn't you?"

"Not like a typist, sir."

"I beg your pardon, my dear," said Mr. Curtis facetiously. "I understand. Mrs. O'Connell has big plans, is that it?"

"Yes," said Maura.

"All right," he said. "It's all yours till twelve-thirty. But at twelve-thirty you get back to your desk, and I don't want to hear that you're too tired or hungry to work a full day."

She was already tired, already hungry. But sitting in front of the great machine lifted her spirits. There was so much to learn that she could barely wait to start. Once again she wrote out her name, all in capitals, then she typed it out with a capital "M" and the rest in small letters. She did it again, and then again, to see if her fingers would remember where to go on the keyboard. Then she wrote out her last name, and on another line she put first and last names together, and typed this over and over again.

"Was that really better than lunch, Mrs. O'Connell?" asked Mr. Curtis when he returned.

"Yes, sir," she said, going back to her desk in the reception room without another word.

A moment later, Mr. Curtis appeared behind her, and placed a big red apple on her desk. "Just on the odd chance that you might be getting a bit hungry at some point in the next six hours, my dear," he said.

And that was not all Mr. Curtis did for Maura.

For all her fine manners and eagerness, it became obvious that the girl was not simply a charming young wife, eager to work for the pleasure of his company. He learned that she was a widow, that she had a mother whom she wished to bring over from Ireland, that the money she made from him was all the money she had in the world. More than a few times he brought her lunch when she stayed at the office to work with the type-writer machine. And when, during the first week in December, she asked if she could stay after closing time, Mr. Curtis presented her with a book: *The Jenner System of Ten-Finger Type-Writing*.

The book became her Bible. In it she learned that every key on the machine was assigned one of her ten fingers, and she resolved to learn all at once what went where, to be able to type-write with her eyes shut. The book had a foldout page that represented the standard keyboard, so that even at home, in her tiny ill-lit room, Maura could memorize the placement of the letters of the alphabet. She never missed a lunch break at the machine, not for three weeks, and she stayed after closing on her first three Saturdays on the job.

One bright day in mid-December, she asked Mr. Curtis if it would be all right to type-write the company's correspondence, instead of writing it by hand.

"Do you have the time for that, Mrs. O'Connell? It would take me five times as long to type-write what I can do by hand."

"I have the time," said Maura.

And suddenly Maura felt that she was coming alive. The type-writing machine was moved from Mr. Curtis's office to her own, and there was no longer a distinction between what she practiced and what she was being paid for. Every bill she wrote out she executed on the type-writing machine; every envelope was addressed with black printed letters; every inquiry was answered in bold typeface; every invoice was backed by the force of the printed page. She learned to clean out the machine, to fix jammed keys, to replace the messy ribbon. When Mr. Curtis wanted something written up on the machine, he no longer dreamed of touching it; this was Maura's province, and he asked her to perform what was required.

Now, at twelve o'clock, she could leave the office and buy herself lunch or a newspaper, or simply take an apple into the park. Saturdays felt almost as good as Sundays. She'd be out at a minute past twelve, and revel in the fact that she had no more duties to return to until the following Monday.

But Maura didn't go completely wild over what she had achieved.

With what she spent on food and carfare, there were only two dollars or so left over each week—and she had to pay half of this for sleeping in her miserable room. She saved what she could, and wrote to her mother frequently, lovingly, always telling her that soon she'd have enough money to send for her; hoping that the love in the letter would somehow make up for a message directing her to come at once. But how could Maura send for her? She needed much more income to support the two of them, to put them in a small apartment, to feed them and clothe them.

In the week before Christmas, Jake Newman blew back into her life. He was waiting for her after work on a dark and cold Tuesday, and when he smiled at her as she came out of her office building, she didn't at first recognize him.

"Say, I would've written you, but I know you've been to night school. I ain't no fool. You got to look good with a girl looks as good as you, so I figure I better not put nothing down on paper. Besides, I was too busy, if you want to know what the hot air's really about. Too busy, and I'm getting rich, and I ain't just talking."

He was wearing a suit, a bit threadbare and certainly second-hand, and it was this outfit and his hat and his muffler that prevented Maura from recognizing him until he'd opened his mouth. She felt that she could understand him even better than before, because she was living with the same sense of forward motion as he. He shocked her by hailing a hansom cab and taking her to a dingy restaurant on the waterfront. It was cheap, but the food was fresh and the room lit by two woodburning fireplaces and a score of candles in earthenware holders.

"I been home, so I know everything about the strike. But all Jenny could tell me about your job is that it pays four-fifty and you're real happy. Oh—and half a day Saturday! Now that ain't bad, even for me! If I could swing a half-day Saturday, I'd be living in paradise."

Maura told him about her job, about her type-writing, about the feeling she was going somewhere at last. She had a career, or the beginnings of one, and there was no telling how far she could go.

"This is great," said Jake. "I'm talking about toothpowder, you're talking about type-writer. Did you think at all about what we talked about?"

"Talked about?" said Maura. She found it difficult to believe that the impulsive young man was trying to re-create the moment when he'd kissed her in October, after they'd walked along the water's edge in Coney Island.

"I'm twenty-one," he said. "My birthday was last week. December seventeenth. Hey, you know what I did on my birthday? I sold toothpowder. It was great—I mean that night out in Coney. It was nice, you know? But what I'm trying to say is, from October to Christmas, things have changed for me. I got the secret, if you know what I'm driving at. I mean, out in Coney I was a little shy. And stupid, too. Shooting off my mouth the way I always did. Saying I can't afford a girl friend, and whatnot. Big man in hurry, that's me in October."

"We don't really have to talk about this," said Maura.

"Say, I don't think you're listening to me. Do you know something? I made a hundred dollars one week out on the road. In one week. Do you know what that means? I got hundreds—I'm going to hit a thousand soon. But that ain't the half of it. I know what the secret is, see? It's *make it yourself*."

He explained about the toothpowder: Tired of getting a fifty-percent profit from a New York pharmacist's own brand of toothpowder, he bought a formula and the use of a doctor's name— Dr. Kalman. Before his extended trip, he had mixed together enough salt and baking soda to fill four hundred small glass bottles. Now, out of the dollar he charged his farmers' wives for the "special formula" toothpowder, his profit was ninety-six cents.

"And toothpowder's only the beginning, see? I mean, why sell some cluck's stove polish? I get the formula, I get my sisters to stay home and make it up for me. I'm going to do that next. Hey, what about soap? You can make soap at home if you got the space for it. Look here, I ain't crazy—I ain't saying I own factories yet. What I'm saying is I got the idea. The idea, see? You look very pretty, Maura. Gee. I never seen a girl so pretty nowhere. So what I told you that night in Coney and everything—that ain't true. I mean, I *can* think about a girl friend."

"I'm trying to get Jenny to go back to night school," said Maura, to change the subject.

"She ought to get married."

"What? Jenny's so young, she doesn't even know what she wants yet."

"*I* know. *I* know what I want. Listen to me. Please, Maura."

"I'll listen to you, Jake," she said.

This sudden attentiveness stalled him. He blushed. He asked her if she'd like some coffee. He told her how much Jenny admired her. Did she know, he asked, that the girls let Marandino come back to the shop? Jenny said it would have never happened if Maura were still with them. When they'd first come back to work without Maura, Barker had agreed to fire his foreman, but just this past week he'd reinstated him. "No one wants to strike again, Jenny says. I mean, they ain't got no principles without you around, she says. You ever think much about your husband? I mean, this time of year?"

"Why this time of year?"

"Christmas. Excuse me if I'm being too nosy. You just tell me."

"It's okay, Jake."

"You might know a little how I feel about you, but there's more you don't know. I mean, I just want to tell you that I was nosy before and I said too much, I asked too much. Like about that girl you knew—Ginny, her name was. She was from a different world, see? And it ain't my business how you come to know her, because when it comes right down to it, she was a damn good girl. A good friend, if you get what I'm saying. What I'm trying to say is if you ever marry again, seeing as how young you are, you think you can love your second husband as much as your first?"

"It's possible."

"Maybe more?"

"Maybe."

"Okay. This is what I've been meaning to ask you. We, all of us—Jenny and my ma and pa and the girls—we all want you to come for Christmas dinner, okay? About one o'clock, if it's okay with you? I'm still in town that day. I mean, next day I'm running off again. I'm breaking in a guy, he's fifteen. I got him selling my line of toothpowder. What I'm doing this for is— Look here. What I want in a wife is somebody I can take care of. She loves me, see, and I love her. She don't work, no way. I work, and take care of her, and she takes care of me and the kids in the way of women. That's what I want. I ain't that fancy, but no wife of mine is going to work—not in a factory, not in an office. I want my wife to have it smooth and easy in life.

"That's what I've been meaning to say, and I hope you'll remember I wasn't born in this country, so if my English ain't that great, it's because I grew up with people who don't speak too good. My folks spoke German. So how about it, Maura?"

"I'm not quite sure what you're asking me, Jake."

"Christmas dinner," he said, blushing. "Will you come?"

Jake didn't ask her to marry him at Christmas dinner, but Jenny and her mother acted not only as if he had, but also as if she had agreed to the proposal. Minnie was there, and, with the sisters, and the dour-faced father, and the two boarders, it was a reunion, a family affair. Jake spoke about the trip he was beginning the next day, spreading out his plans and his dreams like a feast for all of them to share. When he took Maura home, he kissed her, and then held her at arm's length and told her that he would miss her. "You're going to live real good, Maura. You were meant to have the best, and I want you to know what I'm thinking. With those little hot-dog stands in Coney, and this toothpowder, and I'm getting more and more ideas, and salesmen on the road, and— See, I'm just twenty-one. Things look good. I mean, you've got to admit things look good, and what I want is only the best. You shouldn't have to work so hard."

And when he was gone, Maura missed him.

His assertiveness was so mixed with shyness, his experience with naïveté, that, unlike all the other men who had tried to control her life, his efforts were leavened with sweetness, with affection. But each time he returned to New York from his up-state sales trips, she found herself pulling away from him. Without realizing it, he belittled her own little triumphs. When Mr. Curtis raised her weekly wages to five dollars the first week in February, Jake could only respond with a sad shaking of his head: "How I hate to see you working like that, so hard, and all you get for it is living in that joint."

In a sense, Jake was the spur in her side that kept reminding her of the time her mother would come from Ireland, and how little she'd saved in the ten weeks she'd been with Mr. Curtis. He bludgeoned her with his love words, beating her down with the stark reality of how little she'd achieved, and how much he would like to offer her.

She turned nineteen that month, and on the first day of March she received a letter from her mother. There was to be no more waiting, her mother wrote. Her children treated her badly, and she missed Maura and Brendt and was coming to join them. She was taking the steamship *Liberty*, and she had her passage money. The *Liberty* would sail from Cork on the tenth of March and arrive in New York eight days later. She promised not to be a burden to them, and she sent them her love and a mother's blessing.

# ❧ CHAPTER ❧
# TWENTY-THREE

Maura was not prepared for her mother's letter. She had anticipated the feelings of love and regret, fear and uncertainty that would come with her mother's approach, and its threat of responsibility; she understood that she would be faced with the awful confusion of a child coming to care for a parent. But she was not ready for any of it. All her understanding and anticipation were for some future event. There was not enough time. It was out of control. She had not gotten herself ready. There was no home for her mother, and not enough money.

The next morning, a Wednesday, she walked into Mr. Curtis's office with the letter crushed in her hand. "Have you a minute, sir?" she asked, her green eyes determined. "I wanted to ask you if you're pleased with my work."

"*Pleased*," he said, laughing. "Of course I'm pleased. You don't think I'd have given you a fifty-cent raise just because I like the color of your hair."

"I would like another raise, sir, if it's possible."

"Another raise?" Mr. Curtis frowned and leaned back in his creaky leather chair. "My dear, with all due consideration, it's unusual enough to get a raise after working two months, but it's positively unheard of to get a raise *every* month."

"I would like a raise of four dollars, sir."

"What did you say?" said Mr. Curtis. "I didn't quite catch that."

Maura repeated her request.

"You're making five dollars now. You're asking me to practically double your salary."

"If it's possible, and I think it is," she said. "If it's not, or you don't want to, then I'm afraid that this shall be my last week here, as I can't afford to keep the job under any other circumstances."

"Slow down, hold your horses," he said, and went on to explain that she was not being logical, that she was not acting like herself. He'd never paid any girl nearly so much money. If she needed a few dollars for a new dress, he'd be happy to lend it to her. But it would be better for her to learn economy, to cut her expenses.

"I need the money," she insisted.

"Nine dollars is not what anyone pays an office girl! You're talking about a man's wages! You show me a girl who earns so much money! Nine dollars is what a salesman makes to feed his wife and child!"

Maura opened the day's *Herald* to the employment section. She had underlined four job offers with a thick red crayon.

"Sure it looks like they're paying women ten dollars, Mr. Curtis. That's what it says for type-writers, and that's where I'm going if you don't pay me nine."

Mr. Curtis sat down, the *Herald* in his lap. He seemed unable to take his eyes from the incredible figures. Maura continued in a softer tone: "It's not that I'm ungrateful, sir. I'm very grateful for what you've given me. I'm not forgetting that you gave me my type-writing book, that you offered me the use of the machine when I was learning. Without you, I couldn't have afforded to learn to type-write, and that's why I want to stay here."

"I can't afford to pay my girl nine dollars," he said.

But the impossible was happening. Before her eyes, she could see him wavering. She would not say anything about her mother, she would not plead, and she would not cry. "You can, sir," she said. "It's a fact the accounts are being paid faster than before. The bill I sent to Milwaukee came back paid in one week, and it's never come back faster than two months before. I've checked in the files, Mr. Curtis."

"My belt salesman is getting nine dollars a week himself."

"I'm worth just as much as the belt salesman."

"You're worth a heck of a lot more than any belt salesman, Maura," said Mr. Curtis. "But just what in blazes am I supposed to do if he ever finds out he's getting the same wages as my office girl?"

"Tell him I'm not an office girl. Tell him I'm a trained typist, sir. Tell him it's what you have to pay to keep her working."

Mr. Curtis came up to seven-fifty, and when Maura shook her head, he stood up and turned round, and sat down, and then agreed to nine dollars a week. It was then that she burst into tears. Only after he had sat her down and given her a glass of water could she bring herself to tell him the news of her mother's impending arrival.

"Why don't we make the raise start from last week, my dear?" he said calmly. "Simply as a gesture of my regard."

The rest of that week was a blur. Mr. Curtis insisted that Maura leave an hour early each day so she could look at apartments for rent. The crowded Elevated trains took her into the open spaces of Harlem and Washington Heights; to the new buildings going up on the west side of Central Park; to dark little flats in the East Seventies built out of shoddy new materials; and to tiny four-room apartments, the leftover servants' suites in former Greenwich Village mansions. Everything was expensive. Even with her huge new salary, Maura didn't think it wise to spend more than nine dollars a month for rent, and for that figure she could find nothing but the sort of tenement lived in by Jake's family.

Saturday was the fifth of March, and Maura decided to take a risk: She paid the first month's rent on a third-floor walk-up on West Fifteenth Street, only a few blocks from her old room at Mrs. Saunders's boardinghouse. The rent was twelve dollars and fifty cents a month for three furnished rooms with bath and kitchen, towels and linens included. Even with the previous day's paycheck, Maura had only eleven dollars left in the world after she'd paid the rent. And all the rest of the day, as she moved her things out of her miserable Fourteenth Street rooming house, her stomach rumbled in fear.

Sunday, Jake swooped back down upon New York, and

heard Maura's news and her new address from Jenny. He was knocking on her new door before noon.

"These are swell digs, honey. Let me guess . . . they're eleven-seventy-five a month, but you're just a heck of a daughter."

She told him they were twelve-fifty, and he whistled between his front teeth and sat himself down in her front room and began to tell her *his* latest accomplishments: A pharmacist in Albany and two grocers in Buffalo were stocking his toothpowder, while his new salesman was eating up territory with the enthusiasm of a convert. It was only six weeks before he'd open up his board-walk stalls, and eight weeks before he'd have his own brand of stove polish.

"There are things I got to do first, see? I mean, it's like how I admire you for what you've done for your ma, and I think it's real crazy that you got the guy up to nine bucks for the week, but what I got to do first is, like you, get the folks out of that slum they're in and put them up in Brooklyn. Near the beach, see? I can talk them into it, tell them it's for me, not them, so my pa can hang on to his pride and all, even when he's working his kid's stalls on Coney Island. Pride's important. . . . Why do you make me nervous? You're the only one, see? Do you know what I'm driving at?"

"Maybe," said Maura. "And I can't think about it now."

"You can't think about it? Think about how *I* can't think about it! I mean, all the money's tied up. I got to move the family, and I'm pouring my bucks into toothpowder and stove polish and soap. Also, I'm looking at stores right here in town. Small, but that's where you start. You got to start somewhere. And that's what I'm saying. I like you, you know that."

"Yes."

"And I knew about your ma, and I always thought that was fine, but I didn't know she was coming so fast. I figured maybe we'd start a little easier than that—like a two-room place. The big stuff comes later. But I say if she's coming, great. I ain't going to change my mind. Even if this joint's twelve-fifty."

"Jake," she said, wanting what he was about to offer, but wanting more than that to temper it, to change it, to make it as right for her as it was for him. "Listen to me, please. I like you too."

"Well, I don't like you. I love you, see?"

"Maybe I love you too," she said.

"Then it's settled. It's all settled," he said, but she stood up and put her hands on his shoulders so that he couldn't get out of his chair.

"No, Jake," she said. "We're not ready. We're too young."

"Hey, you're nineteen, for crying out loud. I'm twenty-one. You know how many people our age have got five kids already? And what're you saying? You've already been married, and you're younger than me."

"That's not what I mean."

"Then what *do* you mean?"

"I don't want to stop working, for one thing," she said, though this was just the tip of an iceberg whose hidden bulk she could not discern.

"I appreciate that," said Jake. "I know what a fighter you are. Why do you think I love you? I mean, nine bucks a week ain't hay. You've got something. But that's going to change. I don't want you to have to work. You should be home. With your mother. With your children. With *our* children."

"You don't understand," said Maura.

She told him that she had a plan, less grand than his, perhaps, but a plan. Type-writing was going to be more and more important in the world of business. She had learned to be a type-writer all by herself, and in a short time had doubled her salary. More important, she had *earned* the increase, because her company had benefited from her skill. She wanted to save money, she explained, and start a school for type-writers. She could rent a machine first, for use only at night. Start with a few students, charge them very little. Let them learn, get better-paying jobs. They'd send friends. She'd buy a type-writing machine. She'd start renting space for day and night courses. Didn't he see the possibilities? A whole school for type-writers! Perhaps she could expand this in years to come: teach general office skills; hire teachers; open offices in other cities. Anything was possible. Just look what he'd begun to do with a little toothpowder.

Jake looked at her strangely for nearly a minute in silence. "You don't want to marry me, right?"

"Not now, Jake. I'm not ready."

"I don't understand. I'm sorry, I'd like to. But—I don't."

"I'm not ready," she said again. "There are things I want to do. Not just to make money. Things I want to do."

"Type-writing?"

"Not just that."

"I just thought—" he began, but the twenty-one-year-old boy was feeling the weight of the rebuff, and his voice caught. He nearly started to cry, but he steeled himself. "The school sounds like it might work."

"Not for a long time. I need to save up plenty."

"Sure."

"Do you understand what I said before? Maybe I love you too?"

"No," he said. "I don't. I want to work, and make something, not for me but my family, and I want you to be my family. That's what I'm saying, so I don't understand too good all the rest of it. I mean, I think this is going to be hard for you when your mother comes, and I wanted us to be married by then, see? I want everything the best for you, because I love you."

Maura kissed him then. There was nothing else she could say. He had offered her marriage, she had turned him down. He'd told her his vision of married life, and she'd tried to explain that she couldn't yet imagine herself a part of that life. First she had to learn to live a life on her own. Before she could come together with Jake, she had to fully create herself; and he, in turn, must learn to take notice of that creation.

"I'm leaving tomorrow," he said. "Back upstate. I'll be back in April, first week, see? Want to come out to Coney then, see what the place looks like in the rain?"

"I'd love to," she said.

"Okay," said Jake. This time he took her in his arms, resolved not to think. She had not refused to go to Coney Island with him, and she had not refused to return his embrace. For the moment, that would be enough for him.

The next day was March 7, and Maura found herself looking through the sailing schedules in the back of the *Herald* to se if there was any mention of the *Liberty*. There wasn't, and she

took out the crumpled letter from her mother to check the date
of departure from Cork—March 10. But suddenly, her eyes
caught hold of a tiny story on the page of sailing schedules:
"Girl, Age Four, Survives Crossing, While Mother and Father
Perish." Beneath the double line of type was a single paragraph,
giving the name of the child, the names of her dead parents,
and noting that various infectious diseases were still quite com-
monly contracted in the steerage, sometimes with results as
frightening as the "coffin ships" of fifty years before.

Maura broke out in a cold sweat, and a red wall of terror
blew up behind her shut eyes. Stupidly, she read her mother's
letter again, then folded it up and clutched it to her mouth. She
had not once considered what she should have known all along.
Whatever money her mother had saved, it could not be enough
to sail second-class. Her mother would be sailing steerage.

Like a silly child, she had always envisioned her mother
coming to New York in the silky wrappings of a dream; coming
to the golden city in just the way Maura had wanted for herself.

If only there were a way to stop her, she thought. If only
one of the magical New York City telephones could reach all
the way to Kerry, if only the miserable village from which she'd
come had a string of telegraph poles, if only a letter could fly
across the ocean with a ferocious warning: *Don't go down into
the steerage.*

But Maura knew that it was too late. In a day or two, her
mother would be en route to Cork, waiting for the ship to leave.
In five days she'd be belowdecks, listening to the turning of
the ship's screws, the weak moaning of half-dead passengers,
the terrible cries of an emigrant who'd just lost a spouse, or
a child. In a week she might be dead, tossed into the sea like
Patrick. Even if she survived, she'd have to live through hunger
and thirst, stench and humiliation and disease. Maura tried to
imagine her gentle mother, half mad in the eyes of the world,
trying to make her way past the insulting officials at Ellis Island,
but the image wouldn't come. Her mother's red hair, her fine
features and fragile frame, her deep-set gray-green eyes lost in
a reverie of beauty that others didn't see—these would be judged
the absolute lineaments of insanity. Even the kindest immigra-

tion officer would chalk the letter "M"—for madness—on her mother's cloak, and put her on the next boat back to Ireland.

"What is it, Maura?" said Mr. Curtis, coming up to where she sat at her desk.

"Nothing, sir," she said.

But he pulled up a chair and sat down next to her. "You're crying," he said. "Why don't you tell me what's wrong?"

When she started to talk, it came out in a torrent: Her mother was weak and frail, and if she died on the boat, it would be Maura's fault for not sending her money. If one were desperate enough, there were ways to make enough to send to an old mother. Kevin Vane would have given her money, he would have given her whatever she needed. Even Jake would have helped her, if only she'd had the foresight to ask. Didn't Mr. Curtis understand? Her mother was coming to New York, and she was going to be shoved into a stinking hole and fed garbage, and then be shipped back to Ellis Island because of the look in her eyes. What did it matter that she'd given all her money to poor Patrick to take Maura with him to America? What did it matter that her mother was kind, and full of fables and rhymes and legends? So what if her family was nothing but priests and nuns and teachers, and she had taught her daughters to read and write and pray to God? She'd come off that ship and they'd turn her around and send her back. If the way to New York didn't kill her, the way back to Ireland surely would.

"Maura," said Mr. Curtis, holding her shoulders even while she continued to talk. "My dear girl. All you have to do is meet your mother's boat."

"Meet the boat?" said Maura, not understanding what her employer might mean. For a moment she had forgotten that she wasn't helpless, that life wasn't simply a series of accidents outside her control. "But I don't know what class she's in—not for sure. If she goes second-class, they let her off in Manhattan. But if it's steerage she's in, they don't. She goes to Ellis Island."

Suddenly she broke away from Mr. Curtis and got to her feet. She smiled. "Of course. You're right. I meet the boat. I find out where it docks, and meet it in Manhattan. If she doesn't get off there, I'll get a cab to the Battery and a ferry to Ellis Island, and if anyone tries to send her home, I'll kill him."

The *Liberty*'s arrival date was changed three times in the next ten days, but finally, on the seventeenth of March, the shipping company announced a following-day arrival. Her mother's ship would dock at Pier 11, just south of the Washington Market, at six o'clock in the morning.

Alone in her bed the night before the docking, Maura tried to ignore the fear coming alive again in her belly. She tried to think of other things: She imagined her mother cooking their meals, and pictured the two of them before the fireplace in the new flat. Gradually, her mother would understand that, although Brendt and Patrick were gone, their lives could be full. She would make her realize how much she had missed her, how she had longed for her face, for her touch, for the soft rhythm of her speech.

But Maura couldn't keep the fear from growing. The images came back to her relentlessly: the black-bearded steward doling out water, Fiona's keening for her dead husband, Patrick's pale face in the dim lamplight the night before he died. She tried to hold on to the possibility that her mother would arrive at Pier 11, leaving the ship with the first- and second-class passengers. Mr. Curtis himself was taking her there the next morning in his carriage, hopeful that Mrs. Dooley would be able to disembark no matter what class she was traveling.

Afraid of the morning, Maura's night dragged on endlessly. If only she had written to her mother about the steerage, she thought. If only she'd told her the truth about Patrick, about how he had died like a dog, eating rotten food, lying sleeplessly, surrounded by the ill and defeated. If only she herself had been able to return to Ireland and bring her mother back to America, caring for her all the way.

Unable to sleep, Maura dressed for the cold day, and at five o'clock in the morning she let herself out of the apartment house and waited at the curb for Mr. Curtis's modest little carriage. Curtis was on time, arriving at half-past five, but by then Maura was chilled to the bone.

"My dear girl, you're behaving absurdly," he said as he helped her in and the driver turned the carriage about on the dark, deserted street. "You don't want to greet your mother shivering like a ninny, do you? Have a sip of this—go on." As Mr. Curtis settled her beneath a great tartan lap robe, Maura took a bit of brandy, unable to speak through her frozen lips. In what seemed like moments, they arrived at the West Side pier, still a good hour before the sun would rise over Manhattan.

"That's the ship," said Mr. Curtis, pointing to the string of lamps hovering alongside the dock in the darkness. He had to restrain her from going to it at once. He pointed out that no one was disembarking, and no one would be until at least half-past six, when the customs authorities arrived. There would be no one to talk to until then.

"You don't have to wait for me, sir," said Maura. "I can attend to this myself."

"Maura, my dear child, please take a nap," said Mr. Curtis.

"I can't sleep."

"Well then, don't. But don't tell me not to help you, if that's what I'm aiming to do, all right?"

"Yes, sir."

She took another sip of the brandy, closed her eyes against the dark, and settled down under the lap robe, trying to remain alert for the coming dawn. But fatigue won out. She slept for forty minutes, and when she woke she cried out at the sight of light, and customs men, and porters, and hansom cabs, and a gangplank reaching from the steamship *Liberty* to the pier. She threw off the lap robe and opened the carriage door.

"Where are you going, Maura?" said Mr. Curtis. "No one's come down from the ship."

"No one, sir? You're sure? I'll just go and talk to the officer."

She was out of the carriage before he could stop her; and by the time he caught up to her, she had cornered a straight-backed young man wearing a heavy blue coat and carrying a clipboard.

"Pardon me, sir, I'm looking for a Mrs. Dooley," said Maura, out of breath, her eyes bright with hope.

"Are you then, miss?" said the ship's officer, smiling at the pretty young face. "Well, if I can help you in any way, I'm only too happy. Off the *Liberty*, is she?"

"Yes, sir."

"Dooley, you said, is that right?" He had already begun to look at the first of several sheets in his hands. "Is that first or second class, miss?"

"I don't know," said Maura. "Couldn't I just look at it?"

Mr. Curtis had come over to them, and explained to the young officer: "We're not sure what class Mrs. Dooley chose. It's possible she went third-class."

"Steerage?" said the young man, obviously astonished. Steerage passengers were not met at the pier by beautiful young women, or gentlemen with their own carriages. Maura had come round to the young man's side, and quickly read the names on the first-class sheet: four names under the heading "Gentlemen," one name under the heading "Ladies." At her urging, the officer turned to the second-class sheet. Here there were seven gentlemen and four ladies, none of them bearing her mother's name.

"Please, sir," said Maura as she tried to turn to the next page.

He became suddenly reluctant. "You can't possibly look at the steerage list, miss," he said, with a trace of authority in his voice. "It's a very long list, and it's not accurate, as some of the names there are no longer with us, and some of the names shouldn't have been there to begin with."

"Please," said Maura, and not heeding him, she turned the second-class sheet over and found the first of many third-class sheets. Here the names were grouped in two columns—"Males" and "Females"—and the columns ran to the bottom of the page.

"I can't allow this, miss," said the officer, taking his clipboard from her hands and covering the steerage sheets with those of first and second class. "If Mrs. Dooley is traveling third-class, she will disembark at Ellis Island in about four hours from now, and you may certainly meet her there, at your convenience."

"Perhaps we should do that, my dear," said Mr. Curtis.

"*What?*" said Maura, suddenly furious.

"Go to Ellis Island, I mean. There we can do the best for your mother, I should imagine."

"When do they get off the boat?" she said to the young officer, who seemed to be trying to back away from them.

"I'm really very busy, miss. Any moment. I have to be at the customs shed."

"Wait," said Maura, and she took his arm and pulled him close to her. "You don't understand. I want my mother off that boat right now."

"I can't help you."

"If she's alive and she's in the filthy stinking steerage, I want her off that boat right now, even if I have to go up there and drag her off myself."

The officer laughed self-consciously, as if good-naturedly trying to turn aside the young girls threat. "Maura," said Mr. Curtis. "Please, there really is nothing we can do here."

"I have nineteen dollars," she said to the young officer. "That's all I've got, but it's yours if you get her off the boat with first and second class."

"Don't be ridiculous," said the young man, but Maura had taken the bills from her purse and she held them in a wad two inches from the officer's face.

"I want my mother off that boat," said Maura.

"I'm very sorry, truly I am," he said, his eyes lingering on the cash. "But I'm not even sure she's in there. A lot of passengers didn't get to Cork on time—the weather was frightful. We had a terrible trip of it, too. Mortality rate was very high in steerage. I don't know any of the passengers there. I was never down there once this crossing. I really have to go, they're coming down."

Suddenly there was laughter and shouting, as the first of the upper-deck passengers walked down the gangplank. A friend on the pier stood with a bouquet of hothouse flowers and an open bottle of champagne. Elegant women in costly furs moved languidly in the cold dawn air, raising their muffs to the arriving passengers, who were shunted at once to the little customs shed a few yards away. Maura thought of only two things at that moment: that her mother was listed with the "females," and not the "ladies"; and that if she was still alive, she must be spared Ellis Island, just like the "ladies" and "gentlemen" of first and second class.

Mr. Curtis had taken a few bills out of his wallet and was talking earnestly to the young officer, his voice low and full of fellowship.

"I don't know, sir," said the young man. "It's trouble you're

asking for. For me and for you. I don't even know my way
around down there."

But he couldn't seem to take his eyes off Mr. Curtis's greater
bribe. As he hesitated, Maura took hold of his arm again. "I'll
go with you," she said. "I know the steerage, and I know my own
mother."

"I don't know," he said again, but Curtis put the bills into
his hand, and the officer pocketed the bribe, looking from the
ship to the customs shed and back.

"Stay here, sir," said Maura to Curtis, and her tone left no
room for dispute. She grabbed the ship's officer and pulled him
along toward the gangplank, not letting go of his arm till they
were on board.

An officer stopped them almost at once, but Maura was too
swept up in a rush of memory and longing and fear to take
notice. "Terrible mistake here," the young officer was saying.
"Lady supposed to come first-class went steerage. A bit daft,
you know. All hell going to break loose. Company's orders to get
her off here. This is her daughter. Mistake, terrible mistake."

He caught up with Maura as she pushed past the departing
passengers and found the steep staircase leading below. "Couldn't
I send someone for her, miss? The place is not fit . . ."

If only she is alive, thought Maura. God, please let her be
alive.

A sailor said something to the officer behind her as she reached
the last staircase, and the stench began to hit her. She wondered
whether Fiona had made it back to Ireland, or whether she was
dead too. She wondered whether the black-bearded steward
had found another slaver like Kilgallen, so that any pretty
girls who lasted the voyage wouldn't be wasted on the three-
dollar-a-week factories. Let her be alive, she thought, and then
she entered the steerage.

It was just the same as she had left it—even though this was
another ship, and another time and place. This was her steerage,
these were her people, and as she looked around at the
wretched bodies lying together in the half-dark, she could see
Patrick's face, glowing with love and the certainty of death,
she could see Brendt stepping back into space, leaving behind

the misery of living on earth. She would have stayed there an hour, finding all the dead she'd left behind, but for a woman who found her almost at once.

"Maura," said her mother's voice, and she stepped back, away from the ghost, away from the stench of the bodies; she stepped back up the first few steps of the stairway leading toward light and air.

"Maura," said her mother again, and she was no ghost, but a white-faced woman with gray-green eyes, her hair redder than her daughter's, though shot through with gray and so matted and filthy that it seemed to be sticking to her skull. Maura looked at her a moment longer before deciding that it was true, and then, without even kissing her, without saying a word, she took her mother's hand and pulled her up the staircase, out of the steerage, into the full early-morning light.

Mrs. Dooley followed Maura to the railing, and stopped to look at the confusion of stevedores, porters, and officials on the pier below. "Thank you for getting me here," she said to Maura. Then they finally embraced, and Maura remembered the crossing to America in her mother's frail, exhausted frame, in the sense of final victory coming through the stench and the tears.

Mr. Curtis met them at the gangplank, and all three went into the customs shed, on line with the first- and second-class passengers. Mrs. Dooley held herself very erect and answered the perfunctory questions of the bored official with the soft, rhythmic accent of the south of Ireland. No one asked her to undress, to submit to a medical examination, to testify to the fact of potential employment: Mrs. Dooley was a respectable widow come to New York to live with her daughter, and no one shouted at her, no one put her in a quarantine cage, no one threatened to ship her home.

"It's cold in America," said Mrs. Dooley as they left the customs shed, with Maura still rejoicing at having been able to save her mother from the nightmare of Ellis Island. When Mr. Curtis left them to find his driver and carriage in the growing crush of vehicles along the pier, Mrs. Dooley turned away. "Brendt is dead," she said, not asking, simply stating an old, sad certainty.

"Yes, mother," said Maura.

"I knew. She never wrote."

"I'm sorry. I couldn't write you."

"And Patrick—he's dead, too, is he not?"

"Yes, mother."

"Did Brendt die on the boat?" asked Mrs. Dooley, her voice no longer soft, the words rising in an expectation of sorrow.

"No," said Maura.

"Thanks be to God for that, then," said Mrs. Dooley. "Thanks be to God that she didn't die on the boat."

Mother looked at daughter now, and Maura watched her mother's eyes twist away from a vision of Brendt. In the space of a moment, Mrs. Dooley was finding something beautiful to contemplate, some image of peace and solace to block out everything that was ugly in the world. "Thanks be to God I have you," said Mrs. Dooley, "and you're so healthy and good and fine."

They held each other there, waiting for Mr. Curtis to take them into the city. Maura didn't know whether her mother realized that she had arrived in New York exactly one month after her birthday. They would celebrate in any case. She was only just nineteen, with still almost an entire year to go before the century would draw to a close.

No matter what Maura had suffered, it was past. She was young, ready to greet the new century. Perhaps one day she'd marry Jake, and they'd bring children into the world. For now, it was enough to know that she was free, and strong, her own protector. What she had dreamed in Ireland would never take place, but what she dreamed now in New York was possible. With work, with luck, with zeal, she would find love and fulfillment. She would find happiness in this new land.